H. P. Lovecr—— ——ost of his life
in Providenc—— ——n twentieth-
century supe—— ——nany classic
horror storie—— ——which were
published in —— ——937, are *The
Shadow over Innsmouth* (1936), *The Case of Charles Dexter Ward*
(1951), *At the Mountain of Madness and Other Novels of Terror*
(1964), *Dagon and Other Macabre Tales* (1965) and *The Horror
in the Museum and Other Revisions* (1970).

'Go thou to H. P. Lovecraft and shudder'
The Sun

'These tales of horror are in the true gothic tradition . . . full
of hinted terrors and unholy stenches. They are something
very much out of the ordinary, a real collector's piece for
connoisseurs of the unusual! Lovers of the macabre, the
sinister, and the uncanny, take note'
The Guardian

'For those who like the thoroughly ghastly, the loudly
macabre, with all the stenches and moans of ravished
churchyards, this is the book'
Ruper Croft-Cooke

By the same author

H. P. LOVECRAFT

H. P. Lovecraft Omnibus 1:

At the Mountains of Madness and other
novels of terror

Introduction by August Derleth

PANTHER
Granada Publishing

Panther Books
Granada Publishing Ltd
8 Grafton Street, London W1X 3LA

This one-volume edition published by Panther Books 1985

First published in Great Britain in one volume by
Victor Gollancz Ltd 1966

ISBN 0-586-06322-6

Printed and bound in Great Britain by
Collins, Glasgow

Set in Baskerville

H. P. Lovecraft's Novels

by August Derleth

H. P. Lovecraft wrote only three novels among his many short stories and novelettes, and each of them is properly viewed as a short novel – that is, longer than the novella form, but not yet a full-length novel. The most ambitious of these is undoubtedly *The Case of Charles Dexter Ward*, originally written in 1927–1928, but not published until 1941, when an abridged version appeared in *Weird Tales*. The first full-length version was published in 1943 in *Beyond the Wall of Sleep*, since which time it has been separately published in England, and in America has been turned into a typical horror movie with Vincent Price in the leading role – titled, hilariously enough, with typical Hollywood vagary, *Edgar Allan Poe's Haunted Palace*! Second in length is *At the Mountains of Madness* written in 1931, and preceding the longer novel in date of publication, in *Astounding Stories*, where it, too, was somewhat abridged.

The third, *The Dream-Quest of Unknown Kadath*, was very probably conceived and written well in advance of the other novels, sometime in the early or mid-1920's, but, unlike those novels, it was evidently never extensively revised and remains the least satisfactory of them. It is properly not a part of the Cthulhu Mythos – to which both *The Case of Charles Dexter Ward* and *At the Mountains of Madness* belong – but, despite certain facets borrowed from the Mythos, it belongs rather to an earlier period of Lovecraft's work when he was more obviously under the influence of Lord Dunsany's fantastic tales. It is one of four stories written about Randolph Carter, who came into existence as representing Lovecraft himself in a dream story of Lovecraft's titled *The*

Statement of Randolph Carter, written in 1919, when such work as Lovecraft was then producing was making occasional appearances in the amateur press publications of that day. It is very probable that *The Dream-Quest of Unknown Kadath* was begun not long after, and evidence suggests that it was worked at at intervals over several years, for its general looseness suggests that Lovecraft initially at least had no very clear plan for it.

The *Dream-Quest of Unknown Kadath* was put aside for future revision but the Cthulhu Mythos enlisted most of his creative interest from the mid-1920's onward. Nevertheless, Lovecraft twice returned to Randolph Carter after completing *The Dream-Quest of Unknown Kadath*, carrying on Carter's story. In 1926, he wrote *The Silver Key*, and in 1932, at the urging of his friend and correspondent, E. Hoffman Price, he was persuaded – after Price himself had written his version of a sequel to *The Silver Key* – to expand and revise Price's story, which was ultimately published as a collaboration under the title of *Through the Gates of the Silver Key*. All four of the related stories are published here in their proper sequence.

The Carter tales are essentially Dunsanian in mood and style, for all their increasing drawing upon the Cthulhu Mythos, and they are secondary to the two remaining works in this collection. *At the Mountains of Madness* represents a radical departure in setting, at least for it is Lovecraft's only tale set in the Antarctic wastes, and its convincing atmosphere of horror may be attributed in part to Lovecraft's own horror of and allergy to any temperature lower than 20° and frequently, later in life, 30°.

However unsatisfactory *The Dream-Quest of Unknown Kadath* may be on analysis, *The Case of Charles Dexter Ward* and *At the Mountains of Madness* are two of Lovecraft's most successful macabre tales. Each is carefully wrought, though, with Lovecraft's customary uncertainty about his work, *The Case of Charles Dexter Ward* was never submitted to an editor during his lifetime, and *At the Mountains of Madness*, rejected by *Weird Tales*, was withdrawn from submission – '*At the Mountains of Madness*,' wrote Lovecraft later, 'represents the most serious work I have attempted, and its rejection was a very discouraging influence.' – and was accepted by *Astounding Stories* only through the offices of an agent, Julius Schwartz, the sole occasion of the instrumentation of an agent in the placing of Lovecraft's stories, though Donald Wandrei and others of Lovecraft's friends and correspondents sold stories for him in the face of Lovecraft's reluctance to submit after one rejection.

Unlike *The Dream-Quest of Unknown Kadath*, which was interrupted constantly by Lovecraft's revisionary tasks and by his interests in amateur pressdom, *The Case of Charles Dexter Ward* and *At the Mountains of Madness* were brought into being without any significant hiatus, and without interruption other than correspondence. Lovecraft was comparatively reticent about *The Case of Charles Dexter Ward* in his correspondence, other than to refer to its length and to his reluctance to prepare a typescript from the manuscript written and revised in his spidery script, but not *At the Mountains of Madness*, about which he was beset by doubts which rejection of the manuscript by the editor of *Weird Tales* only strengthened. '*At the Mountains of Madness* has a certain kind of cumulative horror,' he wrote in April 1931, shortly after beginning his revision of the manuscript, 'but is altogether too slow for the cheap artificial markets. . . Half of the pages are corrected, transposed, and interlined beyond all human legibility!' Lovecraft was so dubious about the merit of the story or its effectiveness that he infected some of his correspondents sufficiently with his own doubts to leave them, too, uncertain about the story at first reading, but, like most of his longer works, *At the*

Mountains of Madness grows in power and effectiveness at each successive reading. So, too, *The Case of Charles Dexter Ward*. For sheer cumulative horror, these two novels must stand among the best fiction of H. P. Lovecraft.

At the Mountains of Madness

I am forced into speech because men of science have refused to follow my advice without knowing why. It is altogether against my will that I tell my reasons for opposing this contemplated invasion of the antarctic – with its vast fossil hunt and its wholesale boring and melting of the ancient ice caps. And I am the more reluctant because my warning may be in vain.

Doubt of the real facts, as I must reveal them, is inevitable; yet, if I suppressed what will seem extravagant and incredible, there would be nothing left. The hitherto withheld photographs, both ordinary and aerial, will count in my favor, for they are damnably vivid and graphic. Still, they will be doubted because of the great lengths to which clever fakery can be carried. The ink drawings of course, will be jeered at as obvious impostures, notwithstanding a strangeness of technique which art experts ought to remark and puzzle over.

In the end I must rely on the judgment and standing of the few scientific leaders who have, on the one hand, sufficient independence of thought to weigh my data on its own hideously convincing merits or in the light of certain primordial and highly baffling myth cycles; and on the other hand, sufficient influence to deter the exploring world in general from any rash and over ambitious program in the region of those mountains of madness. It is an unfortunate fact that relatively obscure men like myself and my associates, connected only with a small university, have little chance of making an impression where matters of a wildly bizarre or highly controversial nature are concerned.

It is further against us that we are not, in the strictest sense, specialists in the fields which came primarily to be concerned. As a geologist, my object in leading the Miskatonic University Expedition was wholly that of securing deep-level specimens of rock and soil from various parts of the antarctic continent aided by the remarkable drill devised by Professor Frank H. Pabodie of our engineering department. I had no wish to be a pioneer in any other field than this, but I did hope that the use of this new mechanical appliance at different points along previously explored paths would bring to light materials of a sort hitherto unreached by the ordinary methods of collection.

Pabodie's drilling apparatus, as the public already knows from our reports, was unique and radical in its lightness, portability, and capacity to combine the ordinary artesian drill principle with the principle of the small circular rock drill in such a way as to cope quickly with strata of varying hardness. Steel head, jointed rods, gasoline motor, collapsible wooden derrick, dynamiting paraphernalia, cording, rubbish-removal auger, and sectional piping for bores five inches wide and up to one thousand feet deep all formed, with needed accessories, no greater load than three seven-dog sledges could carry. This was made possible by the clever aluminum alloy of which most of the metal objects were fashioned. Four large Dornier aeroplanes, designed especially for the tremendous altitude flying necessary on the antarctic plateau and with added fuel-warming and quick-starting devices worked out by Pabodie, could transport our entire expedition from a base at the edge of the great ice barrier to various suitable inland points, and from these points a sufficient quota of dogs would serve us.

We planned to cover as great an area as one antarctic season – or longer, if absolutely necessary – would permit, operating mostly in the mountain ranges and on the plateau south of Ross Sea; regions explored in varying degree by

Shackleton, Amundsen, Scott, and Byrd. With frequent changes of camp, made by aeroplane and involving distances great enough to be of geological significance, we expected to unearth a quite unprecedented amount of material – especially in the pre-Cambrian strata of which so narrow a range of antarctic specimens had previously been secured. We wished also to obtain as great as possible a variety of the upper fossiliferous rocks, since the primal life history of this bleak realm of ice and death is of the highest importance to our knowledge of the earth's past. That the antarctic continent was once temperate and even tropical, with a teeming vegetable and animal life of which the lichens, marine fauna, arachnida, and penguins of the northern edge are the only survivals, is a matter of common information; and we hoped to expand that information in variety, accuracy, and detail. When a simple boring revealed fossiliferous signs, we would enlarge the aperture by blasting, in order to get specimens of suitable size and condition.

Our borings, of varying depth according to the promise held out by the upper soil or rock, were to be confined to exposed, or nearly exposed, land surfaces – these inevitably being slopes and ridges because of the mile or two-mile thickness of solid ice overlying the lower levels. We could not afford to waste drilling the depth of any considerable amount of mere glaciation, though Pabodie had worked out a plan for sinking copper electrodes in thick clusters of borings and melting off limited areas of ice with current from a gasoline-driven dynamo. It is this plan – which we could not put into effect except experimentally on an expedition such as ours – that the coming Starkweather-Moore Expedition proposes to follow, despite the warnings I have issued since our return from the antarctic.

The public knows of the Miskatonic Expedition through our frequent wireless reports to the *Arkham Advertiser* and

Associated Press, and through the later articles of Pabodie and myself. We consisted of four men from the University – Pabodie, Lake of the biology department, Atwood of the physics department – also a meteorologist – and myself, representing geology and having nominal command – besides sixteen assistants: seven graduate students from Miskatonic and nine skilled mechanics. Of these sixteen, twelve were qualified aeroplane pilots, all but two of whom were competent wireless operators. Eight of them understood navigation with compass and sextant, as did Pabodie, Atwood and I. In addition, of course, our two ships – wooden ex-whalers, reinforced for ice conditions and having auxiliary steam – were fully manned.

The Nathaniel Derby Pickman Foundation, aided by a few special contributions, financed the expedition; hence our preparations were extremely thorough, despite the absence of great publicity. The dogs, sledges, machines, camp materials, and unassembled parts of our five planes were delivered in Boston, and there our ships were loaded. We were marvelously well-equipped for our specific purposes, and in all matters pertaining to supplies, regimen, transportation, and camp construction we profited by the excellent example of our many recent and exceptionally brilliant predecessors. It was the unusual number and fame of these predecessors which made our own expedition – ample though it was – so little noticed by the world at large.

As the newspapers told, we sailed from Boston Harbor on 2nd September 1930, taking a leisurely course down the coast and through the Panama Canal, and stopping at Samoa and Hobart, Tasmania, at which latter place we took on final supplies. None of our exploring party had ever been in the polar regions before, hence we all relied greatly on our ship captains – J. B. Douglas, commanding the brig *Arkham*, and serving as commander of the sea party and Georg Thorfinnssen, commanding the barque *Miskatonic* – both veteran whalers in antarctic waters.

As we left the inhabited world behind the sun sank lower and lower in the north, and stayed longer and longer above the horizon each day. At about 62° South Latitude we sighted our first icebergs – tablelike objects with vertical sides – and just before reaching the antarctic circle, which we crossed on 20th October with appropriately quaint ceremonies, we were considerably troubled with field ice. The falling temperature bothered me considerably after our long voyage through the tropics, but I tried to brace up for the worse rigors to come. On many occasions the curious atmospheric effects enchanted me vastly; these including a strikingly vivid mirage – the first I had ever seen – in which distant bergs became the battlements of unimaginable cosmic castles.

Pushing through the ice, which was fortunately neither extensive nor thickly packed, we regained open water at South Latitude 67°, East Longitude 175°. On the morning of 26th October a strong land blink appeared on the south, and before noon we all felt a thrill of excitement at beholding a vast, lofty, and snow-clad mountain chain which opened out and covered the whole vista ahead. At last we had encountered an outpost of the great unknown continent and its cryptic world of frozen death. These peaks were obviously the Admiralty Range discovered by Ross, and it would now be our task to round Cape Adare and sail down the east coast of Victoria Land to our contemplated base on the shore of McMurdo Sound, at the foot of the volcano Erebus in South Latitude 77° 9'.

The last lap of the voyage was vivid and fancy-stirring. Great barren peaks of mystery loomed up constantly against the west as the low northern sun of noon or the still lower horizon-grazing southern sun of midnight poured its hazy reddish rays over the white snow, bluish ice and water lanes, and black bits of exposed granite slope. Through the desolate summits swept raging, intermittent gusts of the terrible antarctic wind; whose cadences sometimes held vague suggestions of a wild and half-sentient musical piping, with notes extending over a wide range, and which for some subconscious mnemonic reason seemed to me disquieting and even dimly terrible. Something about the scene reminded me of the strange and disturbing Asian paintings of Nicholas Roerich, and of the still stranger and more disturbing descriptions of the evilly fabled plateau of Lerg which occur in the dreaded *Necronomicon* of the mad Arab Abdul Alhazred. I was rather sorry, later on, that I had ever looked into that monstrous book at the college library.

On the 7th of November, sight of the westward range having been temporarily lost, we passed Franklin Island; and the next day descried the cones of Mts. Erebus and Terror on Ross Island ahead, with the long line of the Parry Mountains beyond. There now stretched off to the east the low, white line of the great ice barrier, rising perpendicularly to a height of two hundred feet like the rocky cliffs of Quebec, and marking the end of southward navigation. In the afternoon we entered McMurdo Sound and stood off the coast in the lee of smoking Mt. Erebus. The scoriac peak towered up some twelve thousand, seven hundred feet against the eastern sky, like a Japanese print of the sacred Fujiyama, while beyond it rose the white, ghostlike height of Mt. Terror, ten thousand, nine hundred feet in altitude, and now extinct as a volcano.

Puffs of smoke from Erebus came intermittently, and one of the graduate assistants – a brilliant young fellow named Danforth – pointed out what looked like lava on the snowy slope, remarking that this mountain, discovered in 1840, had undoubtedly been the source of Poe's image when he wrote seven years later:

16

> – the lavas that restlessly roll
> Their sulphurous currents down Yaanek
> In the ultimate climes of the pole—
> That groan as they roll down Mount Yaanek
> In the realms of the boreal pole

Danforth was a great reader of bizarre material, and had talked a good deal of Poe. I was interested myself because of the antarctic scene of Poe's only long story – the disturbing and enigmatical *Arthur Gordon Pym*. On the barren shore, and on the lofty ice barrier in the background, myriads of grotesque penguins squawked and flapped their fins, while many fat seals were visible on the water, swimming or sprawling across large cakes of slowly drifting ice.

Using small boats, we effected a difficult landing on Ross Island shortly after midnight on the morning of the 9th, carrying a line of cable from each of the ships and preparing to unload supplies by means of a breeches-buoy arrangement. Our sensations on first treading antarctic soil were poignant and complex, even though at this particular point the Scott and Shackleton expeditions had preceded us. Our camp on the frozen shore below the volcano's slope was only a provisional one, headquarters being kept aboard the *Arkham*. We landed all our drilling apparatus, dogs, sledges, tents, provisions, gasoline tanks, experimental ice-melting outfit, cameras, both ordinary and aerial, aeroplane parts, and other accessories, including three small portable wireless outfits – besides those in the planes – capable of communicating with the *Arkham's* large outfit from any part of the antarctic continent that we would be likely to visit. The ship's outfit, communicating with the outside world, was to convey press reports to the *Arkham Advertiser's* powerful wireless station on Kingsport Head, Massachusetts. We hoped to complete our work during a single antarctic summer; but if this proved impossible we would winter on the *Arkham*, sending the *Miskatonic* north before the freezing of the ice for another summer's supplies.

I need not repeat what the newspapers have already published about our early work: of our ascent of Mt. Erebus; our successful mineral borings at several points on Ross Island and the singular speed with which Pabodie's apparatus accomplished them, even through solid rock layers; our provisional test of the small ice-melting equipment; our perilous ascent of the great barrier with sledges and supplies; and our final assembling of five huge aeroplanes at the camp atop the barrier. The health of our land party – twenty men and fifty-five Alaskan sledge dogs – was remarkable, though of course we had so far encountered no really destructive temperatures or windstorms. For the most part, the thermometer varied between zero and 20° or 25° above, and our experience with New England winters had accustomed us to rigors of this sort. The barrier camp was semi-permanent, and destined to be a storage cache for gasoline, provisions, dynamite, and other supplies.

Only four of our planes were needed to carry the actual exploring material, the fifth being left with a pilot and two men from the ships at the storage cache to form a means of reaching us from the *Arkham* in case all our exploring planes were lost. Later, when not using all the other planes for moving apparatus, we would employ one or two in a shuttle transportation service between this cache and another permanent base on the great plateau from six hundred to seven hundred miles southward, beyond Beardmore Glacier. Despite the almost unanimous accounts of appalling winds and tempests that pour down from the plateau, we determined to dispense with intermediate bases, taking our chances in the interest of economy and probable efficiency.

Wireless reports have spoken of the breathtaking, four-hour non-shop flight of our squadron on 21st November over the lofty shelf ice, with vast peaks rising on the west, and the unfathomed silences echoing to the sound of our engines. Wind troubled us only moderately, and our radio compasses helped us through the one opaque fog we encountered. When the vast rise looomed ahead, between Latitudes 83° and 84°, we knew we had reached Beardmore Glacier, the largest valley glacier in the world, and that the frozen sea was now giving place to a frowning and mountainous coast line. At last we were truly entering the white, aeon-dead world of the ultimate south. Even as we realized it we saw the peak of Mt Nansen in the eastern distance, towering up to its height of almost fifteen thousand feet.

The successful establishment of the southern base above the glacier in Latitude 86° 7', East Longitude 174° 23', and the phenomenally rapid and effective borings and blastings made at various points reached by our sledge trips and short aeroplane flights, are matters of history; as is the arduous and triumphant ascent of Mt Nansen by Pabodie and two of the graduate students – Gedney and Carroll – on 13th to 15th December. We were some eight thousand, five hundred feet above sea-level, and when experimental drillings revealed solid ground only twelve feet down through the snow and ice at certain points, we made considerable use of the small melting apparatus and sunk bores and performed dynamiting at many places where no previous explorer had ever thought of securing mineral specimens. The pre-Cambrian granites and beacon sandstones thus obtained confirmed our belief that this plateau was homogeneous with the great bulk of the continent to the west, but somewhat different from the parts lying eastward below South America – which we then thought to form a separate and smaller continent divided from the larger one by a frozen junction of Ross and Weddell Seas, though Byrd has since disproved the hypothesis.

In certain of the sandstones, dynamited and chiseled after boring revealed their nature, we found some highly interesting fossil markings and fragments; notably ferns, seaweeds, trilobites, crinoids, and such mollusks as linguellae and gastropods – all of which seemed of real significance in connection with the region's primordial history. There was also a queer triangular, striated marking, about a foot in greatest diameter, which Lake pieced together with three fragments of slate brought up from a deep-blasted aperture. These fragments came from a point to the westward, near the Queen Alexandra Range; and Lake, as a biologist, seemed to find their curious marking unusually puzzling and provocative, though to my geological eye it looked not unlike some of the ripple effects reasonably common in the sedimentary rocks. Since slate is no more than a metamorphic formation into which a sedimentary stratum is pressed, and since the pressure itself produces odd distorting effects on any markings which may exist, I saw no reason for extreme wonder over the striated depression.

On 6th January, 1931, Lake, Pabodie, Danforth and the other six students, four mechanics, and myself flew directly over the south pole in two of the great planes, being forced down once by a sudden high wind, which fortunately, did not develop into a typical storm. This was, as the papers have stated, one of several observation flights, during others of which we tried to discern new topographical features in areas unreached by previous explorers. Our early flights were disappointing in this latter respect, though they afforded us some magnificent examples of the richly fantastic and deceptive mirages of the polar regions, of which our sea voyage had given us some brief foretastes. Distant mountains floated in the sky as enchanted cities, and often the whole white world would dissolve into a gold, silver, and scarlet land of Dunsanian dreams and adventurous expectancy under the magic of the low midnight sun. On cloudy days we had considerable trouble in flying owing to the tendency of snowy earth and sky to merge into one

20

mystical opalescent void with no visible horizon to mark the junction of the two.

At length we resolved to carry out our original plan of flying five hundred miles eastward with all four exploring planes and establishing a fresh sub-base at a point which would probably be on the smaller continental division, as we mistakenly conceived it. Geological specimens obtained there would be desirable for purposes of comparison. Our health so far had remained excellent – lime juice well offsetting the steady diet of tinned and salted food, and temperatures generally above zero enabling us to do without our thickest furs. It was now midsummer, and with haste and care we might be able to conclude work by March and avoid a tedious wintering through the long antarctic night. Several savage windstorms had burst upon us from the west, but we had escaped damage through the skill of Atwood in devising rudimentary aeroplane shelters and windbreaks of heavy snow blocks, and reinforcing the principal camp buildings with snow. Our good luck and efficiency had indeed been almost uncanny.

The outside world knew, of course, of our program, and was told also of Lake's strange and dogged insistence on a westward – or rather, northwestward – prospecting trip before our radical shift to the new base. It seems that he had pondered a great deal, and with alarmingly radical daring, over that triangular striated marking in the slate; reading into it certain contradictions in nature and geological period which whetted his curiosity to the utmost, and made him avid to sink more borings and blastings in the west-stretching formation to which the exhumed fragments evidently belonged. He was strangely convinced that the marking was the print of some bulky, unknown, and radically unclassifiable organism of considerably advanced evolution, notwithstanding that the rock which bore it was of so vastly ancient a date – Cambrian if not actually pre-

Cambrian – as to preclude the probable existence not only of all highly evolved life, but of any life at all above the unicellular or at most the trilobite stage. These fragments, with their odd marking, must have been five hundred million to a thousand million years old.

II

Popular imagination, I judge, responded actively to our wireless bulletins of Lake's start northwestward into regions never trodden by human foot or penetrated by human imagination, though we did not mention his wild hopes of revolutionizing the entire sciences of biology and geology. His preliminary sledging and boring journey of 11th to 18th January with Pabodie and five others – marred by the loss of two dogs in an upset when crossing one of the great pressure ridges in the ice – had brought up more and more of the Archaean slate; and even I was interested by the singular profusion of evident fossil markings in that unbelievably ancient stratum. These markings, however, were of very primitive life forms involving no great paradox except that any life forms should occur in rock as definitely pre-Cambrian as this seemed to be; hence I still failed to see the good sense of Lake's demand for an interlude in our time-saving program – an interlude requiring the use of all four planes, many men, and the whole of the expedition's mechanical apparatus. I did not, in the end, veto the plan, though I decided not to accompany the northwestward party despite Lake's plea for my geological advice. While they were gone, I would remain at the base with Pabodie and five men and work out final plans for the eastward shift. In preparation for this transfer, one of the planes had begun to move up a good gasoline supply from McMurdo Sound;

but this could wait temporarily. I kept with me one sledge and nine dogs, since it is unwise to be at any time without possible transportation in an utterly tenantless world of aeon-long death.

Lake's subexpedition into the unknown, as everyone will recall, sent out its own reports from the shortwave transmitters on the planes; these being simultaneously picked up by our apparatus at the southern base and by the *Arkham* at McMurdo Sound, whence they were relayed to the outside world on wave lengths up to fifty meters. The start was made 22nd January at 4 A.M.; and the first wireless message we received came only two hours later, when Lake spoke of descending and starting a small-scale ice-melting and bore at a point some three hundred miles away from us. Six hours after that a second and very excited message told of the frantic, beaver-like work whereby a shallow shaft had been sunk and blasted, culminating in the discovery of slate fragments with several markings approximately like the one which had caused the original puzzlement.

Three hours later a brief bulletin announced the resumption of the flight in the teeth of a raw and piercing gale; and when I dispatched a message of protest against further hazards, Lake replied curtly that his new specimens made any hazard worth taking. I saw that his excitement had reached the point of mutiny, and that I could do nothing to check this headlong risk of the whole expedition's success; but it was appalling to think of his plunging deeper and deeper into that treacherous and sinister white immensity of tempests and unfathomed mysteries which stretched off for some fifteen hundred miles to the half-known, half-suspected coast line of Queen Mary and Knox Lands.

Then, in about an hour and a half more, came that doubly excited message from Lake's moving plane, which almost reversed my sentiments and made me wish I had accompanied the party:

23

'10:05 P.M. On the wing. After snowstorm, have spied mountain range ahead higher than any hitherto seen. May equal Himalayas, allowing for height of plateau. Probable Latitude 76° 15', Longitude 113° 10' E. Reaches far as can see to right and left. Suspicion of two smoking cones. All peaks black and bare of snow. Gale blowing off them impedes navigation.'

After that Pabodie, the men, and I hung breathlessly over the receiver. Thought of this titanic mountain rampart seven hundred miles away inflamed our deepest sense of adventure; and we rejoiced that our expedition, if not ourselves personally, had been its discoverers. In half an hour Lake called us again:

'Moulton's plane forced down on plateau in foothills, but nobody hurt and perhaps can repair. Shall transfer essentials to other three for return or further moves if necessary, but no more heavy plane travel needed just now. Mountains surpass anything in imagination. Am going up scouting in Carroll's plane, with all weight out.

'You can't imagine anything like this. Highest peaks must go over thirty-five thousand feet. Everest out of the running. Atwood to work out height with theodolite while Carroll and I go up. Probably wrong about cones, for formations look stratified. Possibly pre-Cambrian slate with other strata mixed in. Queer sky line effects – regular sections of cubes clinging to highest peaks. Whole thing marvelous in red-gold light of low sun. Like land of mystery in a dream or gateway to forbidden world of untrodden wonder. Wish you were here to study.'

Though it was technically sleeping time, not one of us listeners thought for a moment of retiring. It must have been a good deal the same at McMurdo Sound, where the supply cache and the *Arkham* were also getting the messages; for Captain Douglas gave out a call congratulating everybody on the important find, and Sherman, the cache operator, seconded his sentiments. We were sorry, of course, about the damaged aeroplane, but hoped it could be easily mended. Then, at 11 P.M., came another call from Lake:

'Up with Carroll over highest foothills. Don't dare try really tall peaks in present weather, but shall later. Frightful work climbing, and hard going at this altitude, but worth it. Great range fairly solid, hence can't get any glimpses beyond. Main summits exceed Himalayas, and very queer. Range looks like pre-Cambrian slate, with plain signs of many other upheaved strata. Was wrong about volcanism. Goes farther in either direction than we can see. Swept clear of snow above about twenty-one thousand feet.

'Odd formations on slopes of highest mountains. Great low square blocks with exactly vertical sides, and rectangular lines of low, vertical ramparts, like the old Asian castles clinging to steep mountains in Roerich's paintings. Impressive from distance. Flew close to some, and Carroll thought they were formed of smaller separate pieces, but that is probably weathering. Most edges crumbled and rounded off as if exposed to storms and climate changes for millions of years.

'Parts, especially upper parts, seem to be of lighter-colored rock than any visible strata on slopes proper, hence of evidently crystalline origin. Close flying shows many cave mouths, some unusually regular in outline, square or semicircular. You must come and investigate. Think I saw rampant squarely on top of one peak. Height seems about thirty thousand to thirty-five thousand feet. Am up twenty-one thousand, five hundred myself, in devilish, gnawing cold. Wind whistles and pipes through passes and in and out of caves, but no flying danger so far.'

From then on for another half hour Lake kept up a running fire of comment, and expressed his intention of climbing some of the peaks on foot. I replied that I would join him as soon as he could send a plane, and that Pabodie and I would work out the best gasoline plan – just where and how to concentrate our supply in view of the expedition's altered character. Obviously, Lake's boring operations, as well as his aeroplane activities, would require a great deal for the new base which he planned to establish at the foot of the mountains; and it was possible that the eastward flight might not be made, after all, this season. In connection with this business I called Captain Douglas and asked him to get as much as possible out of the ships and up the barrier with the single dog team we had left there. A direct route across the unknown region between Lake and McMurdo Sound was what we really ought to establish.

Lake called me later to say that he had decided to let the camp stay where Moulton's plane had been forced down, and where repairs had already progressed somewhat. The ice sheet was very thin, with dark ground here and there visible, and he would sink some borings and blasts at that very point before making any sledge trips or climbing expeditions. He spoke of the ineffable majesty of the whole scene, and the queer state of his sensations at being in the lee of vast, silent pinnacles whose ranks shot up like a wall reaching the sky at the world's rim. Atwood's theodolite observations had placed the height of the five tallest peaks at from thirty thousand to thirty-four thousand feet. The windswept nature of the terrain clearly disturbed Lake, for it argued the occasional existence of prodigious gales, violent beyond anything we had so far encountered. His camp lay a little more than five miles from where the higher foothills rose abruptly. I could almost trace a note of subconscious alarm in his words – flashed across a glacial void of seven hundred miles – as he urged that we all hasten with the matter and get the strange, new region disposed of as soon as possible. He was about to rest now, after a continuous day's work of almost unparalleled speed, strenuousness and results.

In the morning I had a three-cornered wireless talk with Lake and Captain Douglas at their widely separated bases. It was agreed that one of Lake's planes would come to my base for Pabodie, the five men, and myself, as well as for all the fuel it could carry. The rest of the fuel question, depending on our decision about an easterly trip, could wait for a few days, since Lake had enough for immediate camp heat and borings. Eventually the old southern base ought to be restocked but if we postponed the easterly trip we would not use it till the next summer, and meanwhile, Lake must send a plane to explore a direct route between his new mountains and McMurdo Sound.

Pabodie and I prepared to close our base for a short or long period, as the case might be. If we wintered in the antarctic we would probably fly straight from Lake's base to the *Arkham* without returning to this spot. Some of our conical tents had already been reinforced by blocks of hard snow, and now we decided to complete the job of making a permanent village. Owing to a very liberal tent supply, Lake had with him all that his base would need, even after our arrival. I wirelessed that Pabodie and I would be ready for the northwestward move after one day's work and one night's rest.

Our labors, however, were not very steady after 4 P.M., for about that time Lake began sending in the most extraordinary and excited messages. His working day had started unpropitiously, since an aeroplane survey of the nearly-exposed rock surfaces showed an entire absence of

27

those Archaean and primordial strata for which he was looking, and which formed so great a part of the colossal peaks that loomed up at a tantalizing distance from the camp. Most of the rocks glimpsed were apparently Jurassic and Comanchian sandstones and Permian and Triassic schists, with now and then a glassy black outcropping suggesting a hard and slaty coal. This rather discouraged Lake, whose plans all hinged on unearthing specimens more than five hundred million years older. It was clear to him that in order to recover the Archaean slate vein in which he had found the odd markings, he would have to make a long sledge trip from these foothills to the steep slopes of the gigantic mountains themselves.

He had resolved, nevertheless, to do some local boring as part of the expedition's general program; hence he set up the drill and put five men to work with it while the rest finished settling the camp and repairing the damaged aeroplane. The softest visible rock – a sandstone about a quarter of a mile from the camp – had been chosen for the first sampling; and the drill had made excellent progress without much supplementary blasting. It was about three hours afterward, following the first really heavy blast of the operation, that the shouting of the drill crew was heard; and that young Gedney – the acting foreman – rushed into the camp with the startling news.

They had struck a cave. Early in the boring the sandstone had given place to a vein of Comanchian limestone, full of minute fossil cephalopods, corals, echini, and spirifera, and with occasional suggestions of siliceous sponges and marine vertebrate bones – the latter probably of teleosts, sharks, and ganoids. This, in itself, was important enough, as affording the first vertebrate fossils the expedition had yet secured; but when shortly afterward the drill head dropped through the stratum into apparent vacancy, a wholly new and doubly intense wave of excitement spread among the

28

excavators. A good-sized blast had laid open the subterrene secret; and now, through a jagged aperture perhaps five feet across and three feet thick, there yawned before the avid searchers a section of shallow limestone hollowing worn more than fifty million years ago by the trickling ground waters of a bygone tropic world.

The hollowed layer was not more than seven or eight feet deep but extended off indefinitely in all directions and had a fresh, slightly moving air which suggested its membership in an extensive subterranean system. Its roof and floor were abundantly equipped with large stalactites and stalagmites, some of which met in columnar form; but important above all else was the vast deposit of shells and bones, which in places nearly choked the passage. Washed down from unknown jungles of Mesozoic tree ferns and fungi, and forests of Tertiary cycads, fan palms, and primitive angiosperms, this osseous medley contained representatives of more Cretaceous, Eocene, and other animal species than the greatest paleontologist could have counted or classified in a year. Mollusks, crustacean armor, fishes, amphibians, reptiles, birds, and early mammals – great and small, known and unknown. No wonder Gedney ran back to the camp shouting and no wonder every one else dropped work and rushed headlong through the biting cold to where the tall derrick marked a new found gateway to secrets of inner earth and vanished aeons.

When Lake had satisfied the first keen edge of his curiosity he scribbled a message in his notebook and had young Moulton run back to the camp to dispatch it by wireless. This was my first word of the discovery, and it told of the identification of early shells, bones of ganoids and placoderms, remnants of labyrinthodonts and thecodonts, great mosasaur skull fragments, dinosaur vertabrae and armor plates, pterodactyl teeth and wing bones, Archaeopteryx debris Miocene sharks' teeth, primitive bird skulls,

29

and other bones of archaic mammals such as palaeotheres, Xiphodons, Eohippi, Oreodons, and titanotheres. There was nothing as recent as a mastodon, elephant, true camel, deer, or bovine animal; hence Lake concluded that the last deposits had occurred during the Oligocene Age, and that the hallowed stratum had lain in its present dried, dead, and inaccessible state for at least thirty million years.

On the other hand, the prevalence of very early life forms was singular in the highest degree. Though the limestone formation was, on the evidence of such typical imbedded fossils as ventriculites, positively and unmistakably Comanchian and not a particle earlier, the free fragments in the hollow space included a surprising proportion from organisms hitherto considered as peculiar to far older periods – even rudimentary fishes, mollusks, and corals as remote as the Silurian or Ordovician. The inevitable inference was that in this part of the world there had been a remarkable and unique degree of continuity between the life of over three hundred million years ago and that of only thirty million years ago. How far this continuity had extended beyond the Oligocene Age when the cavern was closed was of course past all speculation. In any event, the coming of the frightful ice in the Pleistocene some five hundred thousand years ago – a mere yesterday as compared with the age of this cavity – must have put an end to any of the primal forms which had locally managed to outlive their common terms.

Lake was not content to let his first message stand, but had another bulletin written and dispatched across the snow to the camp before Moulton could get back. After that Moulton stayed at the wireless in one of the planes, transmitting to me – and to the *Arkham* for relaying to the outside world – the frequent postscripts which Lake sent him by a succession of messengers. Those who followed the newspapers will remember the excitement created among men of science by that afternoon's reports – reports which have finally led, after all these years, to the organization of that very Starkweather-Moore Expedition which I am so anxious to dissuade from its purposes. I had better give the messages literally as Lake sent them, and as our base operator McTighe translated them from the pencil shorthand:

'Fowler makes discovery of highest importance in sandstone and limestone fragments from blasts. Several distinct triangular striated prints like those in Archaean slate, proving that source survived from over six hundred million years ago to Comanchian times without more than moderate morphological changes and decreases in average size, Comanchian prints apparently more primitive or decadent, if anything, than older ones. Emphasize importance of discovery in press. Will mean to biology what Einstein has meant to mathematics and physics. Joins up with my previous work and amplifies conclusions.

'Appears to indicate, as I suspected, that earth has seen whole cycle or cycles of organic life before known one that begins with Archaeozoic cells. Was evolved and specialized not later than a thousand million years ago, when planet was young and recently uninhabitable for any life forms or normal protoplasmic structure. Question arises when, where, and how development took place.'

'Later. Examining certain skeletal fragments of large land and marine saurians and primitive mammals, find singular local wounds or injuries to bony structure not attributable to any known predatory or carnivorous animal of any period. Of two sorts – straight, penetrant bores, and apparently hacking incisions. One or two cases of cleanly severed bones. Not many specimens affected. Am sending

31

to camp for electric torches. Will extend search area underground by hacking away stalactites.'

'Still later. Have found peculiar soapstone fragment about six inches across and an inch and a half thick, wholly unlike any visible local formation – greenish, but no evidences to place its period. Has curious smoothness and regularity. Shaped like five-pointed star with tips broken off and signs of other cleavage at inward angles and in center of surface. Small, smooth depression in center of unbroken surface. Arouses much curiosity as to source and weathering. Probably some freak of water action. Carroll, with magnifier, thinks he can make out additional markings of geologic significance. Groups of tiny dots in regular patterns. Dogs growing uneasy as we work, and seem to hate this soapstone. Must see if it has any peculiar odor. Will report again when Mills gets back with light and we start on underground area.'

'10:15 P.M. Important discovery. Orrendorf and Watkins, working underground at 9:45 with light, found monstrous barrel-shaped fossil of wholly unknown nature; probably vegetable unless overgrown specimen of unknown marine radiata. Tissue evidently preserved by mineral salts. Tough as leather, but astonishing flexibility retained in places. Marks of broken-off parts at ends and around sides. Six feet end to end, three and five-tenths feet central diameter, tapering to one foot at each end. Like a barrel with five bulging ridges in place of staves. Lateral breakages, as of thinnish stalks, are at equator in middle of these ridges. In furrows between ridges are curious growths – combs or wings that fold up and spread out like fans. All greatly damaged but one, which gives almost seven-foot wing spread. Arrangement reminds one of certain monsters of primal myth, especially fabled Elder Things in *Necronomicon*.

'These wings seem to be membranous, stretched on frame work of glandular tubing. Apparent minute orifices in frame tubing at wing tips. Ends of body shriveled, giving no clue to interior or to what has been broken off there. Must dissect when we get back to camp. Can't decide whether vegetable or animal. Many features obviously of almost incredible primitiveness. Have set all hands cutting stalactites and looking for further specimens. Additional scarred bones found, but these must wait. Having trouble with dogs. They can't endure the new specimen, and would probably tear it to pieces if we didn't keep it at a distance from them.'

'11:30 P.M. Attention, Dyer, Pabodie, Douglas. Matter of highest – I might say transcendent – importance. *Arkham* must relay to Kingsport Head Station at once. Strange barrel growth is the Archaean thing that left prints in rocks. Mills, Boudreau, and Fowler discover cluster of thirteen more at underground point forty feet from aperture. Mixed with curiously rounded and configured soapstone fragments smaller than one previously found – star-shaped, but no marks of breakage except at some of the points.

'Of organic specimens, eight apparently perfect, with all appendages. Have brought all to surface, leading off dogs to distance. They cannot stand the things. Give close attention to description and repeat back for accuracy. Papers must get this right.

'Objects are eight feet long all over. Six-foot, five-ridged barrel torso three and five tenths feet central diameter, one foot end diameters. Dark gray, flexible, and infinitely tough. Seven-foot membranous wings of same color, found folded, spread out of furrows between ridges. Wing framework tubular or glandular, of lighter gray, with orifices at wing tips. Spread wings have serrated edge. Around equator, one at central apex of each of five vertical, stave-like ridges are five systems of light gray flexible arms or tentacles found tightly folded to torso but expansible to maximum length of over three feet. Like arms of primitive crinoid. Single stalks three inches diameter branch after six inches into five substalks, each of which branches after eight inches into small, tapering tentacles or tendrils, giving each stalk a total of twenty-five tentacles.

'At top of torso blunt, bulbous neck of lighter gray, with gill-like suggestions, holds yellowish five-pointed starfish-shaped apparent head covered with three-inch wiry cilia of various prismatic colors.

'Head thick and puffy, about two feet point to point, with three-inch flexible yellowish tubes projecting from each point. Set in exact center of top probably breathing aperture. At end of each tube is spherical expansion where yellowish membrane rolls back on handling to reveal glassy, red-irised globe, evidently an eye.

'Five slightly longer reddish tubes start from inner angles of starfish-shaped head and end in saclike swellings of same color which, upon pressure, open to bell-shaped orifices two inches maximum diameter and lined with sharp, white tooth-like projections – probably mouths. All these tubes, cilia, and points of starfish head, found folded tightly down; tubes and points clinging to bulbous neck and torso. Flexibility surprising despite vast toughness.

'At bottom of torso, rough but dissimilarly functioning counterparts of head arrangements exist. Bulbous light-gray pseudoneck, without gill suggestions, holds greenish five-pointed starfish arrangement.

'Tough, muscular arms four feet long and tapering from seven inches diameter at base to about two and five-tenths at point. To each point is attached small end of a greenish five-veined membranous triangle eight inches long and six wide at farther end. This is the paddle, fin, or pseudofoot

34

which has made prints in rocks from a thousand million to fifty or sixty million years old.

'From inner angles of starfish arrangement project two-foot reddish tubes tapering from three inches diameter at base to one at tip. Orifices at tips. All these parts infinitely tough and leathery, but extremely flexible. Four-foot arms with paddles undoubtedly used for locomotion of some sort, marine or otherwise. When moved, display suggestions of exaggerated muscularity. As found, all these projections tightly folded over pseudoneck and end of torso, corresponding to projections at other end.

'Cannot yet assign positively to animal or vegetable kingdom, but odds now favor animal. Probably represents incredibly advanced evolution of radiata without loss of certain primitive features. Echinoderm resemblances unmistakable despite local contradictory evidences.

'Wing structure puzzles in view of probable marine habitat, but may have use in water navigation. Symmetry is curiously vegetablelike, suggesting vegetable's essential up-and-down structure rather than animal's fore-and-aft structure. Fabulously early date of evolution, preceding even simplest Archaean protozoa hitherto known, baffles all conjecture as to origin.

'Complete specimens have such uncanny resemblance to certain creatures of primal myth that suggestion of ancient existence outside antarctic becomes inevitable. Dyer and Pabodie have read *Necronomicon* and seen Clark Ashton Smith's nightmare paintings based on text, and will understand when I speak of Elder Things supposed to have created all earth life as jest or mistake. Students have always thought conception formed from morbid imaginative treatment of very ancient tropical radiata. Also like prehistoric folklore things Wilmarth has spoken of – Cthulhu cult appendages, etc.

'Vast field of study opened. Deposits probably of late

Cretaceous or early Eocene period, judging from associated specimens. Massive stalactites deposited above them. Hard work hewing out, but toughness prevented damage. State of preservation miraculous, evidently owing to limestone action. No more found so far, but will resume search later. Job now to get fourteen huge specimens to camp without dogs, which bark furiously and can't be trusted near them.

'With nine men – three left to guard the dogs – we ought to manage the three sledges fairly well, though wind is bad. Must establish plane communication with McMurdo Sound and begin shipping material. But I've got to dissect one of these things before we take any rest. Wish I had a real laboratory here. Dyer better kick himself for having tried to stop my westward trip. First the world's greatest mountains, and then this. If this last isn't the high spot of the expedition, I don't know what is. We're made scientifically. Congrats, Pabodie, on the drill that opened up the cave. Now will *Arkham* please repeat description?'

The sensations of Pabodie and myself at receipt of this report were almost beyond description, nor were our companions much behind us in enthusiasm. McTighe, who had hastily translated a few high spots as they came from the droning receiving set, wrote out the entire message from his shorthand version as soon as Lake's operator signed off. All appreciated the epoch-making significance of the discovery, and I sent Lake congratulations as soon as the *Arkham's* operator had repeated back the descriptive parts as requested; and my example was followed by Sherman from his station at the McMurdo Sound supply cache, as well as by Captain Douglas of the *Arkham*. Later, as head of the expedition, I added some remarks to be relayed through the *Arkham* to the outside world. Of course, rest was an absurd thought amidst this excitement; and my only wish was to get to Lake's camp as quickly as I could. It disappointed me

36

when he sent word that a rising mountain gale made early aerial travel impossible.

But within an hour and a half interest again rose to banish disappointment. Lake, sending more messages, told of the completely successful transportation of the fourteen great specimens to the camp. It had been a hard pull, for the things were surprisingly heavy; but nine men had accomplished it very neatly. Now some of the party were hurriedly building a snow corral at a safe distance from the camp, to which the dogs could be brought for greater convenience in feeding. The specimens were laid out on the hard snow near the camp, save for one on which Lake was making crude attempts at dissection.

This dissection seemed to be a greater task than had been expected, for, despite the heat of a gasoline stove in the newly raised laboratory tent, the deceptively flexible tissues of the chosen specimen – a powerful and intact one – lost nothing of their more than leathery toughness. Lake was puzzled as to how he might make the requisite incisions without violence destructive enough to upset all the structural niceties he was looking for. He had, it is true, seven more perfect specimens; but these were too few to use up recklessly unless the cave might later yield an unlimited supply. Accordingly he removed the specimen and dragged in one which, though having remnants of the starfish arrangements at both ends, was badly crushed and partly disrupted along one of the great torso furrows.

Results, quickly reported over the wireless, were baffling and provocative indeed. Nothing like delicacy or accuracy was possible with instruments hardly able to cut the anomalous tissue, but the little that was achieved left us all awed and bewildered. Existing biology would have to be wholly revised, for this thing was no product of any cell growth science knows about. There had been scarcely any mineral replacement, and despite an age of perhaps forty

37

million years the internal organs were wholly intact. The leathery, undeteriorative, and almost indestructible quality was an inherent attribute of the thing's form of organization, and pertained to some paleogean cycle of invertebrate evolution utterly beyond our powers of speculation. At first all that Lake found was dry, but as the heated tent producted its thawing effect, organic moisture of pungent and offensive odor was encountered toward the thing's uninjured side. It was not blood, but a thick, dark-green fluid apparently answering the same purpose. By the time Lake reached this stage all thirty-seven dogs had been brought to the still uncompleted corral near the camp, and even at that distance set up a savage barking and show of restlessness at the acrid, diffusive smell.

Far from helping to place the strange entity, this provisional dissection merely deepened its mystery. All guesses about its external members had been correct, and on the evidence of these one could hardly hesitate to call the thing animal; but internal inspection brought up so many vegetable evidences that Lake was left hopelessly at sea. It had digestion and circulation, and eliminated waste matter through the reddish tubes of its starfish-shaped base. Cursorily, one would say that its respiratory apparatus handled oxygen rather than carbon dioxide; and there were odd evidences of air-storage chambers and methods of shifting respiration from the external orifice to at least two other fully developed breathing systems – gills and pores. Clearly, it was amphibian and probably adapted to long airless hibernation periods as well. Vocal organs seemed present in connection with the main respiratory system, but they presented anomalies beyond immediate solution. Articulate speech, in the sense of syllable utterance, seemed barely conceivable, but musical piping notes covering a wide range were highly probable. The muscular system was almost prematurely developed.

The nervous system was so complex and highly developed as to leave Lake aghast. Though excessively primitive and archaic in some respects, the thing had a set of ganglial centers and connectives arguing the very extremes of specialized development. Its five-lobed brain was surprisingly advanced, and there were signs of a sensory equipment, served in part through the wiry cilia of the head, involving factors alien to any other terrestrial organism. Probably it had more than five senses, so that its habits could not be predicted from any existing analogy. It must, Lake thought, have been a creature of keen sensitiveness and delicately differentiated functions in its primal world – much like the ants and bees of today. It reproduced like the vegetable crytogams, especially the Pteridophyta, having spore cases at the tips of the wings and evidently developing from a thallus or prothallus.

But to give it a name at this stage was mere folly. It looked like a radiate, but was clearly something more. It was partly vegetable, but had three-fourths of the essentials of animal structure. That it was marine in origin, its symmetrical contour and certain other attributes clearly indicated; yet one could not be exact as to the limit of its later adaptations. The wings, after all, held a persistent suggestion of the aerial. How it could have undergone its tremendously complex evolution on a new-born earth in time to leave prints in Archaean rocks was so far beyond conception as to make Lake whimsically recall the primal myths about Great Old Ones who filtered down from the stars and concocted earth life as a joke or mistake; and the wild tales of cosmic hill things from outside told by a folklorist colleague in Miskatonic's English department.

Naturally, he considered the possibility of the pre-Cambrian prints having been made by a less evolved ancestor of the present specimens, but quickly rejected this too-facile theory upon considering the advanced structural qualities of the older fossils. If anything, the later contours showed decadence rather than higher evolution. The size of the pseudofeet had decreased, and the whole morphology seemed coarsened and simplified. Moreover, the nerves and organs just examined held singular suggestions of retrogression from forms still more complex. Atrophied and vestigial parts were surprisingly prevalent. Altogether, little could be said to have been solved; and Lake fell back on mythology for a provisional name – jocosely dubbing his finds 'The Elder Ones'.

At about 2:30 A.M., having decided to postpone further work and get a little rest, he covered the dissected organism with a tarpaulin, emerged from the laboratory tent, and studied the intact specimens with renewed interest. The ceaseless antarctic sun had begun to limber up their tissues a trifle, so that the head points and tubes of two or three showed signs of unfolding; but Lake did not believe there was any danger of immediate decomposition in the almost sub-zero air. He did, however, move all the undissected specimens close together and throw a spare tent over them in order to keep off the direct solar rays. That would also help to keep their possible scent away from the dogs, whose hostile unrest was really becoming a problem, even at their substantial distance and behind the higher and higher snow walls which an increased quota of the men were hastening to raise around their quarters. He had to weigh down the corners of the tent cloth with heavy blocks of snow to hold it in place amidst the rising gale, for the titan mountains seemed about to deliver some gravely severe blasts. Early apprehensions about sudden antarctic winds were revived, and under Atwood's supervision precautions were taken to bank the tents, new dog corral, and crude aeroplane shelters with snow on the mountainward side. These latter shelters, begun with hard snow blocks during odd moments, were by no means as high as they should have been; and Lake finally detached all hands from other tasks to work on them.

It was after four when Lake at last prepared to sign off and advised us all to share the rest period his outfit would take when the shelter walls were a little higher. He held some friendly chat with Pabodie over the ether, and repeated his praise of the really marvelous drills that had helped him make his discovery. Atwood also sent greetings and praises. I gave Lake a warm word of congratulation, owning up that he was right about the western trip, and we all agreed to get in touch by wireless at ten in the morning. If the gale was then over, Lake would send a plane for the party at my base. Just before retiring I dispatched a final message to the *Arkham* with instructions about toning down the day's news for the outside world, since the full details seemed radical enough to rouse a wave of incredulity until further substantiated.

III

None of us, I imagine, slept very heavily or continuously that morning. Both the excitement of Lake's discovery and the mounting fury of the wind were against such a thing. So savage was the blast, even where we were, that we could not help wondering how much worse it was at Lake's camp, directly under the vast unknown peaks that bred and delivered it. McTighe was awake at ten o'clock and tried to get Lake on the wireless, as agreed, but some electrical condition in the disturbed air to the westward seemed to prevent communication. We did, however, get the *Arkham*, and Douglas told me that he had likewise been vainly trying to reach Lake. He had not known about the wind, for very little was blowing at McMurdo Sound, despite its persistent rage where we were.

Throughout the day we all listened anxiously and tried to get Lake at intervals, but invariably without results. About noon a positive frenzy of wind stampeded out of the west, causing us to fear for the safety of our camp; but it eventually died down, with only a moderate relapse at 2 P.M. After three o'clock it was very quiet, and we redoubled our efforts to get Lake. Reflecting that he had four planes, each provided with an excellent short-wave outfit, we could not imagine any ordinary accident capable of crippling all his wireless equipment at once. Nevertheless the stony silence continued, and when we thought of the delirious force the wind must have had in his locality we could not help making the most direful conjectures.

By six o'clock our fears had become intense and definite, and after a wireless consultation with Douglas and Thorfinnssen I resolved to take steps toward investigation. The fifth aeroplane, which we had left at the McMurdo Sound supply cache with Sherman and two sailors, was in good shape and ready for instant use, and it seemed that the very emergency for which it had been saved was now upon us. I got Sherman by wireless and ordered him to join me with the plane and the two sailors at the southern base as quickly as possible, the air conditions being apparently highly favorable. We then talked over the personnel of the coming investigation party, and decided that we would include all hands, together with the sledge and dogs which I had kept with me. Even so great a load would not be too much for one of the huge planes built to our special orders for heavy machinery transportation. At intervals I still tried to reach Lake with the wireless, but all to no purpose.

Sherman, with the sailors Gunnarsson and Larsen, took off at seven-thirty; and reported a quiet flight from several points on the wing. They arrived at our base at midnight, and all hands at once discussed the next move. It was risky business sailing over the antarctic in a single aeroplane

42

without any line of bases, but no one drew back from what seemed like the plainest necessity. We turned in at two o'clock for a brief rest after some preliminary loading of the plane, but were up again in four hours to finish the loading and packing.

At 7:15 A.M., 25th January, we started flying northwestward under McTighe's pilotage with ten men, seven dogs, a sledge, a fuel and food supply, and other items including the plane's wireless outfit. The atmosphere was clear, fairly quiet, and relatively mild in temperature, and we anticipated very little trouble in reaching the latitude and longitude designated by Lake as the site of his camp. Our apprehensions were over what we might find, or fail to find, at the end of our journey, for silence continued to answer all calls dispatched to the camp.

Every incident of that four-and-a-half-hour flight is burned into my recollection because of its crucial position in my life. It marked my loss, at the age of fifty-four, of all that peace and balance which the normal mind possesses through its accustomed conception of external nature and nature's laws. Thenceforward the ten of us – but the student Danforth and myself above all others – were to face a hideously amplified world of lurking horrors which nothing can erase from our emotions, and which we would refrain from sharing with mankind in general if we could. The newspapers have printed the bulletins we sent from the moving plane, telling of our non-stop course, our two battles with treacherous upper-air gales, our glimpse of the broken surface where Lake had sunk his mid-journey shaft three days before, and our sight of a group of those strange fluffy snow cylinders noted by Amundsen and Byrd as rolling in the wind across the endless leagues of frozen plateau. There came a point, though, when our sensations could not be conveyed in any words the press would understand, and a latter point when we had to adopt an actual rule of strict censorship.

The sailor Larsen was first to spy the jagged line of witch-like cones and pinnacles ahead, and his shouts sent everyone to the windows of the great cabined plane. Despite our speed, they were very slow in gaining prominence; hence we knew that they must be infinitely far off, and visible only because of their abnormal height. Little by little, however, they rose grimly into the western sky; allowing us to distinguish various bare, bleak, blackish summits, and to catch the curious sense of fantasy which they inspired as seen in the reddish antarctic light against the provocative background of iridescent ice-dust clouds. In the whole spectacle there was a persistent, pervasive hint of stupendous secrecy and potential revelation. It was as if these stark, nightmare spires marked the pylons of a frightful gateway into forbidden spheres of dream, and complex gulfs of remote time, space, and ultradimensionality. I could not help feeling that they were evil things – mountains of madness whose farther slopes looked out over some accursed ultimate abyss. That seething, half-luminous cloud background held ineffable suggestions of a vague, ethereal beyondness far more than terrestrially spatial, and gave appalling reminders of the utter remoteness, separateness, desolation, and aeon-long death of this untrodden and unfathomed austral world.

It was young Danforth who drew our notice to the curious regularities of the higher mountain sky line – regularities like clinging fragments of perfect cubes, which Lake had mentioned in his messages, and which indeed justified his comparison with the dreamlike suggestions of primordial temple ruins, on cloudy Asian mountaintops so subtly and strangely painted by Roerich. There was indeed something hauntingly Roerich-like about this whole unearthly continent of mountainous mystery. I had felt it in October when we first caught sight of Victoria Land, and I felt it afresh now. I felt, too, another wave of uneasy consciousness of Archaean mythical resemblance; of how disturbingly this lethal realm corresponded to the evilly famed plateau of Leng in the primal writings. Mythologists have placed Leng in Central Asia; but the racial memory of man – or of his predecessors – is long, and it may well be that certain tales have come down from lands and mountains and temples of horror earlier than Asia and earlier than any human world we know. A few daring mystics have hinted at a pre-Pleistocene origin for the fragmentary Pnakotic Manuscripts, and have suggested that the devotees of Tsathoggua were as alien to mankind as Tsathoggua itself. Leng, wherever in space or time it might brood, was not a region I would care to be in or near, nor did I relish the proximity of a world that had ever bred such ambiguous and Archaean monstrosities as those Lake had just mentioned. At the moment I felt sorry that I had ever read the abhorred *Necronomicon*, or talked so much with that unpleasantly erudite folklorist Wilmarth at the university.

This mood undoubtedly served to aggravate my reaction to the bizarre mirage which burst upon us from the increasingly opalescent zenith as we drew near the mountains and began to make out the cumulative undulations of the foothills. I had seen dozens of polar mirages during the preceding weeks, some of them quite as uncanny and fantastically vivid as the present sample; but this one had a wholly novel and obscure quality of menacing symbolism, and I shuddered as the seething labyrinth of fabulous walls and towers and minarets loomed out of the troubled ice vapors above our heads.

The effect was that of a Cyclopean city of no architecture known to man or to human imagination, with vast aggregations of night-black masonry embodying monstrous perversions of geometrical laws. There were truncated cones, sometimes terraced or fluted, surmounted by tall cylindrical shafts here and there bulbously enlarged and often capped

45

with tiers of thinnish scalloped disks; and strange beetling, table-like constructions suggesting piles of multitudinous rectangular slabs or circular plates of five-pointed stars with each one overlapping the one beneath. There were composite cones and pyramids either alone or surmounting cylinders or cubes or flatter truncated cones and pyramids, and occasional needle-like spires in curious clusters of five. All of these febrile structures seemed knit together by tubular bridges crossing from one to the other at various dizzy heights, and the implied scale of the whole was terrifying and oppressive in its sheer gigantism. The general type of mirage was not unlike some of the wilder forms observed and drawn by the arctic whaler Scoresby in 1820, but at this time and place, with those dark, unknown mountain peaks soaring stupendously ahead, that anomalous elder-world discovery in our minds, and the pall of probable disaster enveloping the greater part of our expedition, we all seemed to find in it a taint of latent malignity and infinitely evil portent.

I was glad when the mirage began to break up, though in the process the various nightmare turrets and cones assumed distorted, temporary forms of even vaster hideousness. As the whole illusion dissolved to churning opalescence we began to look earthward again, and saw that our journey's end was not far off. The unknown mountains ahead rose dizzily up like a fearsome rampart of giants, their curious regularities showing with startling clearness even without a field glass. We were over the lowest foothills now, and could see amidst the snow, ice, and bare patches of their main plateau a couple of darkish spots which we took to be Lake's camp and boring. The higher foothills shot up between five and six miles away, forming a range almost distinct from the terrifying line of more than Himalayan peaks beyond them. At length Ropes – the student who had relieved McTighe at the controls – began to head

46

downward toward the left-hand dark spot whose size marked it as the camp. As he did so, McTighe sent out the last uncensored wireless message the world was to receive from our expedition.

Everyone, of course, has read the brief and unsatisfying bulletins of the rest of our antarctic sojourn. Some hours after our landing we sent a guarded report of the tragedy we found, and reluctantly announced the wiping out of the whole Lake party by the frightful wind of the preceding day, or of the night before that. Eleven known dead, young Gedney missing. People pardoned our hazy lack of details through realization of the shock the sad event must have caused us, and believed us when we explained that the mangling action of the wind had rendered all eleven bodies unsuitable for transportation outside. Indeed, I flatter myself that even in the midst of our distress, utter bewilderment, and soul-clutching horror, we scarcely went beyond the truth in any specific instance. The tremendous significance lies in what we dared not tell; what I would not tell now but for the need of warning others off from nameless terrors.

It is a fact that the wind had brought dreadful havoc. Whether all could have lived through it, even without the other thing, is gravely open to doubt. The storm, with its fury of madly driven ice particles, must have been beyond anything our expedition had encountered before. One aeroplane shelter – all, it seems, had been left in a far too flimsy and inadequate state – was nearly pulverized – and the derrick at the distant boring was entirely shaken to pieces. The exposed metal of the grounded planes and drilling machinery was bruised into a high polish, and two of the small tents were flattened despite their snow banking. Wooden surfaces left out in the blaster were pitted and denuded of paint, and all signs of tracks in the snow were completely obliterated. It is also true that we found none of

47

the Archaean biological objects in a condition to take outside as a whole. We did gather some minerals from a vast, tumbled pile, including several of the greenish soapstone fragments whose odd five-pointed rounding and faint patterns of grouped dots caused so many doubtful comparisons; and some fossil bones, among which were the most typical of the curiously injured specimens.

None of the dogs survived, their hurriedly built snow inclosure near the camp being almost wholly destroyed. The wind may have done that, though the greater breakage on the side next the camp, which was not the windward one, suggests an outward leap or break of the frantic beasts themselves. All three sledges were gone, and we have tried to explain that the wind may have blown them off into the unknown. The drill and ice-melting machinery at the boring were too badly damaged to warrant salvage, so we used them to choke up that subtly disturbing gateway to the past which Lake had blasted. We likewise left at the camp the two most shaken up of the planes; since our surviving party had only four real pilots – Sherman, Danforth, McTighe, and Ropes – in all, with Danforth in a poor nervous shape to navigate. We brought back all the books, scientific equipment, and other incidentals we could find, though much was rather unaccountably blown away. Spare tents and furs were either missing or badly out of condition.

It was approximately 4 P.M., after wide plane cruising had forced us to give Gedney up for lost, that we sent our guarded message to the *Arkham* for relaying; and I think we did well to keep it as calm and noncommittal as we succeeded in doing. The most we said about agitation concerned our dogs, whose frantic uneasiness near the biological specimens was to be expected from poor Lake's accounts. We did not mention, I think, their display of the same uneasiness when sniffing around the queer greenish soapstones and certain other objects in the disordered

48

region — objects including scientific instruments, aeroplanes, and machinery, both at the camp and at the boring, whose parts had been loosened, moved, or otherwise tampered with by winds that must have harbored singular curiosity and investigativeness.

About the fourteen biological specimens we were pardonably indefinite. We said that the only ones we discovered were damaged, but that enough was left of them to prove Lake's description wholly and impressively accurate. It was hard work keeping our personal emotions out of this matter — and we did not mention numbers or say exactly how we had found those which we did find. We had by that time agreed not to transmit anything suggesting madness on the part of Lake's men, and it surely looked like madness to find six imperfect monstrosities carefully buried upright in nine-foot snow graves under five-pointed mounds punched over with groups of dots in patterns exactly like those on the queer greenish soapstones dug up from Mesozoic or Tertiary times. The eight perfect specimens mentioned by Lake seemed to have been completely blown away.

We were careful, too, about the public's general peace of mind; hence Danforth and I said little about that frightful trip over the mountains the next day. It was the fact that only a radically lightened plane could possibly cross a range of such height which mercifully limited that scouting tour to the two of us. On our return at 1 A.M., Danforth was close to hysterics, but kept an admirably stiff upper lip. It took no persuasion to make him promise not to show our sketches and the other things we brought away in our pockets, not to say anything more to the others than what we had agreed to relay outside, and to hide our camera films for private development later on; so that part of my present story will be as new to Pabodie, McTighe, Ropes, Sherman, and the rest as it will be to the world in general. Indeed, Danforth is closer mouthed than I: for he saw, or thinks he saw, one thing he will not tell even me.

As all know, our report included a tale of a hard ascent – a confirmation of Lake's opinion that the great peaks are of Archaean slate and other very primal crumpled strata unchanged since at least middle Comanchian times; a conventional comment on the regularity of the clinging cube and rampart formations; a decision that the cave mouths indicate dissolved calcareous veins; a conjecture that certain slopes and passes would permit of the scaling and crossing of the entire range by seasoned mountaineers; and remark that the mysterious other side holds a lofty and immense superplateau as ancient and unchanging as the mountains themselves – twenty thousand feet in elevation, with grotesque rock formations protruding through a thin glacial layer and with low gradual foothills between the general plateau surface and the sheer precipices of ths highest peaks.

This body of data is in every respect true so far as it goes, and it completely satisfied the men at the camp. We laid our absence of sixteen hours – a longer time than our announced flying, landing, reconnoitering, and rock-collecting program called for – to a long mythical spell of adverse wind conditions, and told truly of our landing on the farther foothills. Fortunately our tale sounded realistic and prosaic enough not to tempt any of the others into emulating our flight. Had any tried to do that, I would have used every ounce of my persuasion to stop them – and I do not know what Danforth would have done. While we were gone, Pabodie, Sherman, Ropes, McTighe, and Williamson had worked like beavers over Lake's two best planes, fitting them again for use despite the altogether unaccountable juggling of their operative mechanism.

We decided to load all the planes the next morning and start back for our old base as soon as possible. Even though indirect, that was the safest way to work toward McMurdo Sound; for a straightline flight across the most utterly unknown stretches of the aeon-dead continent would involve many additional hazards. Further exploration was hardly feasible in view of our tragic decimation and the ruin of our drilling machinery. The doubts and horrors around us – which we did not reveal – made us wish only to escape from this austral world of desolation and brooding madness as swiftly as we could.

As the public knows, our return to the world was accomplished without further disasters. All planes reached the old base on the evening of the next day – 27th January – after a swift nonstop flight; and on the 28th we made McMurdo Sound in two laps, the one pause being very brief, and occasioned by a faulty rudder in the furious wind over the ice shelf after we had cleared the great plateau. In five days more, the *Arkham* and *Miskatonic*, with all hands and equipment on board, were shaking clear of the thickening field ice and working up Ross Sea with the mocking mountains of Victoria Land looming westward against a troubled antarctic sky and twisting the wind's wails into a wide-ranged musical piping which chilled my soul to the quick. Less than a fortnight later we left the last hint of polar land behind us and thanked heaven that we were clear of a haunted, accursed realm where life and death, space and time, have made black and blasphemous alliances in the unknown epochs since matter first writhed and swam on the planet's scarce-cooled crust.

Since our return we have all constantly worked to discourage antarctic exploration, and have kept certain doubts and guesses to ourselves with splendid unity and faithfulness. Even young Danforth, with his nervous breakdown, has not flinched or babbled to his doctors – indeed, as I have said, there is one thing he thinks he alone saw which he will not tell even me, though I think it would help

51

his psychological state if he would consent to do so. It might explain and relieve much, though perhaps the thing was no more than the delusive aftermath of an earlier shock. That is the impression I gather after those rare, irresponsible moments when he whispers disjointed things to me – things which he repudiates vehemently as soon as he gets a grip on himself again.

It will be hard work deterring others from the great white south, and some of our efforts may directly harm our cause by drawing inquiring notice. We might have known from the first that human curiosity is undying, and that the results we announced would be enough to spur others ahead on the same age-long pursuit of the unknown. Lake's reports of those biological monstrosities had aroused naturalists and palaeontologists to the highest pitch, though we were sensible enough not to show the detached parts we had taken from the actual buried specimens, or our photographs of those specimens as they were found. We also refrained from showing the more puzzling of the scarred bones and greenish soapstones; while Danforth and I have closely guarded the pictures we took or drew on the superplateau across the range, and the crumpled things we smoothed, studied in terror, and brought away in our pockets.

But now that Starkweather-Moore party is organizing, and with a thoroughness far beyond anything our outfit attempted. If not dissuaded, they will get to the innermost nucleus of the antarctic and melt and bore till they bring up that which we know may end the world. So I must break through all reticences at last – even about that ultimate, nameless thing beyond the mountains of madness.

IV

It is only with vast hesitancy and repugnance that I let my mind go back to Lake's camp and what we really found there – and to that other thing beyond the mountains of madness. I am constantly tempted to shirk the details, and to let hints stand for actual facts and ineluctable deductions. I hope I have said enough already to let me glide briefly over the rest; the rest, that is, of the horror at the camp. I have told of the wind ravaged terrain, the damaged shelters, the disarranged machinery, the varied uneasinesses of our dogs, the missing sledges and other items, the deaths of men and dogs, the absence of Gedney, and the six insanely buried biological specimens, strangely sound in texture for all their structural injuries, from a world forty million years dead. I do not recall whether I mentioned that upon checking up the canine bodies we found one dog missing. We did not think much about that till later – indeed, only Danforth and I have thought of it at all.

The principal things I have been keeping back relate to the bodies, and to certain subtle points which may or may not lend a hideous and incredible kind of rationale to the apparent chaos. At the time, I tried to keep the men's minds off those points; for it was so much simpler – so much more normal – to lay everything to an outbreak of madness on the part of some of Lake's party. From the look of things, that demon mountain wind must have been enough to drive any man mad in the midst of this center of all earthly mystery and desolation.

The crowning abnormality, of course, was the condition of the bodies – men and dogs alike. They had all been in some terrible kind of conflict, and were torn and mangled in fiendish and altogether inexplicable ways. Death, so far as we could judge, had in each case come from strangulation or laceration. The dogs had evidently started the trouble, for the state of their ill-built corral bore witness to its forcible breakage from within. It had been set some distance from the camp because of the hatred of the animals for those hellish Archaean organisms, but the precaution seemed to have been taken in vain. When left alone in that monstrous wind, behind flimsy walls of insufficient height, they must have stampeded – whether from the wind itself, or from some subtle, increasing odor emitted by the nightmare specimens, one could not say.

But whatever had happened, it was hideous and revolting enough. Perhaps I had better put squeamishness aside and tell the worst at last – though with a categorical statement of opinion, based on the first-hand observations and most rigid deductions of both Danforth and myself, that the then missing Gedney was in no way responsible for the loathsome horrors we found. I have said that the bodies were frightfully mangled. Now I must add that some were incised and subtracted from in the most curious, cold-blooded, and inhuman fashion. It was the same with dogs and men. All the healthier, fatter bodies, quadrupedal or bipedal, had had their most solid masses of tissue cut out and removed, as by a careful butcher; and around them was a strange sprinkling of salt – taken from the ravaged provision chests on the planes – which conjured up the most horrible associations. The thing had occurred in one of the crude aeroplane shelters from which the plane had been dragged out, and subsequent winds had effaced all tracks which could have supplied any plausible theory. Scattered bits of clothing, roughly slashed from the human incision subjects, hinted no clues. It is useless to bring up the half impression of certain faint snow prints on one shielded corner of the ruined inclosure – because that impression did not concern

54

human prints at all, but was clearly mixed up with all the talk of fossil prints which poor Lake had been giving throughout the preceding weeks. One had to be careful of one's imagination in the lee of those overshadowing mountains of madness.

As I have indicated, Gedney and one dog turned out to be missing in the end. When we came on that terrible shelter we had missed two dogs and two men; but the fairly unharmed dissecting tent, which we entered after investigating the monstrous graves, had something to reveal. It was not as Lake had left it, for the covered parts of the primal monstrosity had been removed from the improvised table. Indeed, we had already realized that one of the six imperfect and insanely buried things we had found – the one with the trace of a peculiarly hateful odor – must represent the collected sections of the entity which Lake had tried to analyze. On and around that laboratory table were strewn other things, and it did not take long for us to guess that those things were the carefully though oddly and inexpertly dissected parts of one man and one dog. I shall spare the feelings of survivors by omitting mention of the man's identity. Lake's anatomical instruments were missing, but there were evidences of their careful cleansing. The gasoline stove was also gone, though around it we found a curious litter of matches. We buried the human parts beside the other ten men, and the canine parts with the other thirty-five dogs. Concerning the bizarre smudges on the laboratory table, and on the jumble of roughly handled illustrated books scattered near it, we were much too bewildered to speculate.

This formed the worst of the camp horror, but other things were equally perplexing. The disappearance of Gedney, the one dog, the eight uninjured biological specimens, the three sledges, and certain instruments, illustrated technical and scientific books, writing materials, electric

55

torches and batteries, food and fuel, heating apparatus, spare tents, fur suits, and the like, was utterly beyond sane conjecture; as were likewise the spatterfringed ink blots on certain pieces of paper, and the evidences of curious alien fumbling and experimentation around the planes and all other mechanical devices both at the camp and at the boring. The dogs seemed to abhor this oddly disordered machinery. Then, too, there was the upsetting of the larder, the disappearance of certain staples, and the jarringly comical heap of tin cans pried open in the most unlikely ways and at the most unlikely places. The profusion of scattered matches, intact, broken, or spent, formed another minor enigma – as did the two or three tent cloths and fur suits which we found lying about with peculiar and unorthodox slashings conceivably due to clumsy efforts at unimaginable adaptations. The maltreatment of the human and canine bodies, and the crazy burial of the damaged Archaean specimens, were all of a piece with this apparent disintegrative madness. In view of just such an eventuality as the present one, we carefully photographed all the main evidences of insane disorder at the camp; and shall use the prints to buttress our pleas against the departure of the proposed Starkweather-Moore Expedition.

Our first act after finding the bodies in the shelter was to photograph and open the row of insane graves with the five-pointed snow mounds. We could not help noticing the resemblance of these monstrous mounds, with their clusters of grouped dots, to poor Lake's descriptions of the strange greenish soapstones; and when we came on some of the soapstones themselves in the great mineral pile we found the likeness very close indeed. The whole general formation, it must be made clear, seemed abominably suggestive of the starfish head of the Archaean entities; and we agreed that the suggestion must have worked potently upon the sensitized minds of Lake's overwrought party.

For madness – centering in Gedney as the only possible surviving agent – was the explanation spontaneously adopted by everybody so far as spoken utterance was concerned; though I will not be so naive as to deny that each of us may have harbored wild guesses which sanity forbade him to formulate completely. Sherman, Pabodie, and McTighe made an exhaustive aeroplane cruise over all the surrounding territory in the afternoon, sweeping the horizon with field glasses in quest of Gedney and of the various missing things; but nothing came to light. The party reported that the titan barrier range extended endlessly to right and left alike, without any diminution in height or essential structure. On some of the peaks, though, the regular cube and rampart formations were bolder and plainer, having doubly fantastic similitudes to Roerich-painted Asian hill ruins. The distribution of cryptical cave mouths on the black snow-denuded summits seemed roughly even as far as the range could be traced.

In spite of all the prevailing horrors we were left with enough sheer scientific zeal and adventurousness to wonder about the unknown realm beyond those mysterious mountains. As our guarded messages stated, we rested at midnight after our day of terror and bafflement – but not without a tentative plan for one or more range-crossing altitude flights in a lightened plane with aerial camera and geologist's outfit, beginning the following morning. It was decided that Danforth and I try it first, and we awaked at 7 A.M. intending an early flight; however, heavy winds – mentioned in our brief bulletin to the outside world – delayed our start till nearly nine o'clock.

I have already repeated the noncommittal story we told the men at camp – and relayed outside – after our return sixteen hours later. It is now my terrible duty to amplify this account by filling in the merciful blanks with hints of what we really saw in the hidden transmontane world –

hints of the revelations which have finally driven Danforth to nervous collapse. I wish he would add a really frank word about the thing which he thinks he alone saw – even though it was probably a nervous delusion – and which was perhaps the last straw that put him where he is; but he is firm against that. All I can do is to repeat his later disjointed whispers about what set him shrieking as the plane soared back through the wind-tortured mountain pass after that real and tangible shock which I shared. This will form my last word. If the plain signs of surviving elder horrors in what I disclose be not enough to keep others from meddling with the inner antarctic – or at least from prying too deeply beneath the surface of that ultimate waste of forbidden secrets and inhuman, aeon-cursed desolation – the responsibility for unnamable and perhaps immeasurable evils will not be mine.

Danforth and I, studying the notes made by Pabodie in his afternoon flight and checking up with a sextant, had calculated that the lowest available pass in the range lay somewhat to the right of us, within sight of camp, and about twenty-three thousand or twenty-four thousand feet above sea level. For this point, then, we first headed in the lightened plane as we embarked on our flight of discovery. The camp itself, on foothills which sprang from a high continental plateau, was some twelve thousand feet in altitude; hence the actual height increase necessary was not so vast as it might seem. Nevertheless we were acutely conscious of the rarefied air and intense cold as we rose; for, on account of visibility conditions, we had to leave the cabin windows open. We were dressed, of course, in our heaviest furs.

As we drew near the forbidding peaks, dark and sinister above the line of crevasse-riven snow and interstitial glaciers, we noticed more and more the curiously regular formations clinging to the slopes; and thought again of the strange Asian paintings of Nicholas Roerich. The ancient and wind-weathered rock strata fully verified all of Lake's bulletins, and proved that these pinnacles had been towering up in exactly the same way since a surprisingly early time in earth's history – perhaps over fifty million years. How much higher they had once been, it was futile to guess; but everything about this strange region pointed to obscure atmospheric influences unfavorable to change, and calculated to retard the usual climatic processes of rock disintegration.

But it was the mountainside tangle of regular cubes, ramparts, and cave mouths which fascinated and disturbed us most. I studied them with a field glass and took aerial photographs while Danforth drove; and at times I relieved him at the controls – though my aviation knowledge was purely an amateur's – in order to let him use the binoculars. We could easily see that much of the material of the things was a lightish Archaean quartzite, unlike any formation visible over broad areas of the general surface; and that their regularity was extreme and uncanny to an extent which poor Lake had scarcely hinted.

As he had said, their edges were crumbled and rounded from untold aeons of savage weathering; but their preternatural solidity and tough material had saved them from obliteration. Many parts, especially those closest to the slopes, seemed identical in substance with the surrounding rock surface. The whole arrangement looked like the ruins of Macchu Picchu in the Andes, or the primal foundation walls of Kish as dug up by the Oxford Field Museum Expedition in 1929; and both Danforth and I obtained that occasional impression of separate Cyclopean blocks which Lake had attributed to his flight-companion Carroll. How to account for such things in this place was frankly beyond me, and I felt queerly humbled as a geologist. Igneous formations often have strange regularities – like the famous

Giants' Causeway in Ireland – but this stupendous range, despite Lake's original suspicion of smoking cones, was above all else non-volcanic in evident structure.

The curious cave mouths, near which the odd formations seemed most abundant, presented another albeit a lesser puzzle because of their regularity of outline. They were, as Lake's bulletin had said, often approximately square or semicircular; as if the natural orifices had been shaped to greater symmetry by some magic hand. Their numerousness and wide distribution were remarkable, and suggested that the whole region was honeycombed with tunnels dissolved out of limestone strata. Such glimpses as we secured did not extend far within the caverns, but we saw that they were apparently clear of stalactites and stalagmites. Outside, those parts of the mountain slopes adjoining the apertures seemed invariably smooth and regular; and Danforth thought that the slight cracks and pittings of the weathering tended toward unusual patterns. Filled as he was with the horrors and strangenesses discovered at the camp, he hinted that the pittings vaguely resembled those baffling groups of dots sprinkled over the primeval greenish soapstones, so hideously duplicated on the madly conceived snow mounds above those six buried monstrosities.

We had risen gradually in flying over the higher foothills and along toward the relatively low pass we had selected. As we advanced we occasionally looked down at the snow and ice of the land route, wondering whether we could have attempted the trip with the simpler equipment of earlier days. Somewhat to our surprise we saw that the terrain was far from difficult as such things go; and that despite the crevasses and other bad spots it would not have been likely to deter the sledges of a Scott, a Shackleton, or an Amundsen. Some of the glaciers appeared to lead up to wind-bared passes with unusual continuity, and upon reaching our chosen pass we found that its case formed no exception.

Our sensations of tense expectancy as we prepared to round the crest and peer out over an untrodden world can hardly be described on paper; even though we had no cause to think the regions beyond the range essentially different from those already seen and traversed. The touch of evil mystery in these barrier mountains, and in the beckoning sea of opalescent sky glimpsed betwixt their summits, was a highly subtle and attenuated matter not to be explained in literal words. Rather was it an affair of vague psychological symbolism and aesthetic association – a thing mixed up with exotic poetry and paintings, and with archaic myths lurking in shunned and forbidden volumes. Even the wind's burden held a peculiar strain of conscious malignity; and for a second it seemed that the composite sound included a bizarre musical whistling or piping over a wide range as the blast swept in and out of the omnipresent and resonant cave mouths. There was a cloudy note of reminiscent repulsion in this sound, as complex and unplaceable as any of the other dark impressions.

We were now, after a slow ascent, at a height of twenty-three thousand, five hundred and seventy feet according to the aneroid; and had left the region of clinging snow definitely below us. Up here were only dark, bare slopes and the start of rough-ribbed glaciers – but with those provocative cubes, ramparts, and echoing cave mouths to add a portent of the unnatural, the fantastic, and the dreamlike. Looking along the line of high peaks, I thought I could see the one mentioned by poor Lake, with a rampart exactly on top. It seemed to be half lost in a queer antarctic haze – such a haze, perhaps, as had been responsible for Lake's early notion of volcanism. The pass loomed directly before us, smooth and windswept between its jagged and malignly frowning pylons. Beyond it was a sky fretted with

swirling vapors and lighted by the low polar sun – the sky of
that mysterious farther realm upon which we felt no human
eye had ever gazed.

A few more feet of altitude and we would behold that
realm. Danforth and I, unable to speak except in shouts
amidst the howling, piping wind that raced through the
pass and added to the noise of the unmuffled engines,
exchanged eloquent glances. And then, having gained those
last few feet, we did indeed stare across the momentous
divide and over the unsampled secrets of an elder and
utterly alien earth.

V

I think that both of us simultaneously cried out in mixed
awe, wonder, terror, and disbelief in our own senses as we
finally cleared the pass and saw what lay beyond. Of
course, we must have had some natural theory in the back
of our heads to steady our faculties for the moment.
Probably we thought of such things as the grotesquely
weathered stones of the Garden of the Gods in Colorado, or
the fantastically symmetrical wind-carved rocks of the
Arizona desert. Perhaps we even half thought the sight a
mirage like that we had seen the morning before on first
approaching those mountains of madness. We must have
had some such normal notions to fall back upon as our eyes
swept that limitless, tempest-scarred plateau and grasped
the almost endless labyrinth of colossal, regular, and
geometrically eurythmic stone masses which reared their
crumbled and pitted crests above a glacial sheet not more
than forty or fifty feet deep at its thickest, and in places
obviously thinner.

The effect of the monstrous sight was indescribable, for

some fiendish violation of known natural law seemed certain at the outset. Here, on a hellishly ancient table-land fully twenty thousand feet high, and in a climate deadly to habitation since a prehuman age not less than five hundred thousand years ago, there stretched nearly to the vision's limit a tangle of orderly stone which only the desperation of mental self-defense could possibly attribute to any but a conscious and artificial cause. We had previously dismissed, so far as serious thought was concerned, any theory that the cubes and ramparts of the mountainsides were other than natural in origin. How could they be otherwise, when man himself could scarcely have been differentiated from the great apes at the time when this region succumbed to the present unbroken reign of glacial death?

Yet now the sway of reason seemed irrefutably shaken, for this Cyclopean maze of squared, curved, and angled blocks had features which cut off all comfortable refuge. It was, very clearly, the blasphemous city of the mirage in stark, objective, and ineluctable reality. That damnable portent had had a material basis after all – there had been some horizontal stratum of ice dust in the upper air, and this shocking stone survival had projected its image across the mountains according to the simple laws of reflection. Of course, the phantom had been twisted and exaggerated, and had contained things which the real source did not contain; yet now, as we saw that real source, we thought it even more hideous and menacing than its distant image.

Only the incredible, unhuman massiveness of these vast stone towers and ramparts had saved the frightful thing from utter annihilation in the hundreds of thousands – perhaps millions – of years it had brooded there amidst the blasts of a bleak upland. 'Corona Mundi – Roof of the World—' All sorts of fantastic phrases sprang to our lips as we looked dizzily down at the unbelievable spectacle. I thought again of the eldritch primal myths that had so persistently haunted me since my first sight of this dead antarctic world – of the demoniac plateau of Leng, of the Mi-Go, or abominable Snow Men of the Himalayas, of the Pnakotic Manuscripts with their prehuman implications, of the Cthulhu cult, of the *Necronomicon*, and of the Hyperborean legends of formless Tsathoggua and the worse than formless star spawn associated with that sementity.

For boundless miles in every direction the thing stretched off with very little thinning; indeed, as our eyes followed it to the right and left along the base of the low, gradual foothills which separated it from the actual mountain rim, we decided that we could see no thinning at all except for an interruption at the left of the pass through which we had come. We had merely struck, at random, a limited part of something of incalculable extent. The foothills were more sparsely sprinkled with grotesque stone structures, linking the terrible city to the already familiar cubes and ramparts which evidently formed its mountain outposts. These latter, as well as the queer cave mouths, were as thick on the inner as on the outer sides of the mountains.

The nameless stone labyrinth consisted, for the most part, of walls from ten to one hundred and fifty feet in ice-clear height, and of a thickness varying from five to ten feet. It was composed mostly of prodigious blocks of dark primordial slate, schist, and sandstone – blocks in many cases as large as $4 \times 6 \times 8$ feet – though in several places it seemed to be carved out of a solid, uneven bed rock of pre-Cambrian slate. The buildings were far from equal in size, there being innumerable honeycomb arrangements of enormous extent as well as smaller separate structures. The general shape of these things tended to be conical, pyramidal, or terraced; though there were many perfect cylinders, perfect cubes, clusters of cubes, and other rectangular forms, and a peculiar sprinkling of angled edifices whose five-pointed ground plan roughly suggested modern fortifications. The builders had made constant and expert use of the principle of the arch, and domes had probably existed in the city's heyday.

The whole tangle was monstrously weathered, and the glacial surface from which the towers projected was strewn with fallen blocks and immemorial debris. Where the glaciation was transparent we could see the lower parts of the gigantic piles, and we noticed the ice-preserved stone bridges which connected the different towers at varying distances above the ground. On the exposed walls we could detect the scarred places where other and higher bridges of the same sort had existed. Closer inspection revealed countless largish windows; some of which were closed with shutters of a petrified material originally wood, though most gaped open in a sinister and menacing fashion. Many of the ruins, of course, were roofless, and with uneven though wind-rounded upper edges; whilst others, of a more sharply conical or pyramidal model or else protected by higher surrounding structures, preserved intact outlines despite the omnipresent crumbling and pitting. With the field glass we could barely make out what seemed to be sculptural decorations in horizontal bands – decorations including those curious groups of dots whose presence on the ancient soapstones now assumed a vastly larger significance.

In many places the buildings were totally ruined and the ice sheet deeply riven from various geologic causes. In other places the stonework was worn down to the very level of the glaciation. One broad swath, extending from the plateau's interior to a cleft in the foothills about a mile to the left of the pass we had traversed, was wholly free from buildings. It probably represented, we concluded, the course of some great river which in Tertiary times – millions of years ago – had poured through the city and into some prodigious subterranean abyss of the great barrier range. Certainly, this was above all a region of caves, gulfs, and underground secrets beyond human penetration.

Looking back to our sensations, and recalling our dazedness at viewing this monstrous survival from aeons we had thought prehuman, I can only wonder that we preserved the semblance of equilibrium, which we did. Of course, we knew that something – chronology, scientific theory, or our own consciousness – was woefully awry; yet we kept enough poise to guide the plane, observe many things quite minutely, and take a careful series of photographs which may yet serve both us and the world in good stead. In my case, ingrained scientific habit may have helped; for above all my bewilderment and sense of menace there burned a dominant curiosity to fathom more of this age-old secret – to know what sort of beings had built and lived in this incalculably gigantic place, and what relation to the general world of its time or of others times so unique a concentration of life could have had.

For this place could be no ordinary city. It must have formed the primary nucleus and center of some archaic and unbelievable chapter of earth's history whose outward ramifications, recalled only dimly in the most obscure and distorted myths, had vanished utterly amidst the chaos of terrene convulsions long before any human race we know had shambled out of apedom. Here sprawled a Palaeogaean megalopolis compared with which the fabled Atlantis and Lemuria, Commoriom and Uzuldaroum, and Olathoë in the land of Lomar are recent things of today – not even of yesterday; a megalopolis ranking with such whispered prehuman blasphemies as Valusia, R'lyeh, Ib in the land of Mnar, and the Nameless City of Arabia Deserta. As we flew above that tangle of stark titan towers my imagination sometimes escaped all bounds and roved aimlessly in realms of fantastic associations – even weaving links betwixt this lost world and some of my own wildest dreams concerning the mad horror at the camp.

The plane's fuel tank, in the interest of greater lightness, had been only partly filled; hence we now had to exert caution in our explorations. Even so, however, we covered an enormous extent of ground – or rather, air – after swooping down to a level where the wind became virtually negligible. There seemed to be no limit to the mountain range, or to the length of the frightful stone city which bordered its inner foothills. Fifty miles of flight in each direction showed no major change in the labyrinth of rock and masonry that clawed up corpselike through the eternal ice. There were, though, some highly absorbing diversifications; such as the carvings on the canyon where that broad river had once pierced the foothills and approached its sinking place in the great range. The headlands at the stream's entrance had been boldly carved into Cyclopean pylons; and something about the ridgy, barrel-shaped designs stirred up oddly vague, hateful, and confusing semi-remembrances in both Danforth and me.

We also came upon several star-shaped open spaces, evidently public squares, and noted various undulations in the terrain. Where a sharp hill rose, it was generally hollowed out into some sort of rambling stone edifice; but there were at least two exceptions. Of these latter, one was too badly weathered to disclose what had been on the jutting eminence, while the other still bore a fantastic conical monument carved out of the solid rock and roughly resembling such things as the well-known Snake Tomb in the ancient valley of Petra.

Flying inland from the mountains, we discovered that the city was not of infinite width, even though its length along the foothills seemed endless. After about thirty miles the grotesque stone buildings began to thin out, and in ten more miles we came to an unbroken waste virtually without signs of sentient artifice. The course of the river beyond the city seemed marked by a broad, depressed line, while the land assumed a somewhat greater ruggedness, seeming to slope slightly upward as it receded in the mist-hazed west.

So far we had made no landing, yet to leave the plateau without an attempt at entering some of the monstrous structures would have been inconceivable. Accordingly, we decided to find a smooth place on the foothills near our navigable pass, there grounding the plane and preparing to do some exploration on foot. Though these gradual slopes were partly covered with a scattering of ruins, low flying soon disclosed an ample number of possible landing places. Selecting that nearest to the pass, since our flight would be across the great range and back to camp, we succeeded about 12:30 P.M. in effecting a landing on a smooth, hard snow field wholly devoid of obstacles and well adapted to a swift and favorable take-off later on.

It did not seem necessary to protect the plane with a snow banking for so brief a time and in so comfortable an absence of high winds at this level; hence we merely saw that the landing skis were safely lodged, and that the vital parts of the mechanism were guarded against the cold. For our foot journey we discarded the heaviest of our flying furs, and took with us a small outfit consisting of pocket compass, hand camera, light provisions, voluminous notebooks and paper, geologist's hammer and chisel, specimen bags, coil of climbing rope, and powerful electric torches with extra batteries; this equipment having been carried in the plane on the chance that we might be able to effect a landing, take ground pictures, make drawings and topographical sketches, and obtain rock specimens from some bare slope, outcropping, or mountain cave. Fortunately we had a supply of extra paper to tear up, place in a spare specimen bag, and use on the ancient principle of hare and hounds for marking our course in any interior mazes we might be able to penetrate. This had been brought in case we found some cave system with air quiet enough to allow such a rapid and easy method in place of the usual rock-chipping method of trail blazing.

Walking cautiously downhill over the crusted snow toward the stupendous stone labyrinth that loomed against the opalescent west, we felt almost as keen a sense of imminent marvels as we had felt on approaching the unfathomed mountain pass four hours previously. True, we had become visually familiar with the incredible secret concealed by the barrier peaks; yet the prospect of actually entering primordial walls reared by conscious beings perhaps millions of years ago – before any known race of men could have existed – was none the less awesome and potentially terrible in its implications of cosmic abnormality. Though the thinness of the air at this prodigious altitude made exertion somewhat more difficult than usual, both Danforth and I found ourselves bearing up very well, and felt equal to almost any task which might fall to our lot. It took only a few steps to bring us to a shapeless ruin worn level with the snow, while ten or fifteen rods farther on there was a huge, roofless rampart still complete in its gigantic five-pointed outline and rising to an irregular height of ten or eleven feet. For this latter we headed; and when at last we were actually able to touch its weathered Cyclopean blocks, we felt that we had established an unprecedented and almost blasphemous link with forgotten aeons normally closed to our species.

This rampart, shaped like a star and perhaps three hundred feet from point to point, was built of Jurassic sandstone blocks of irregular size, averaging 6×8 feet in surface. There was a row of arched loopholes or windows about four feet wide and five feet high, spaced quite symmetrically along the points of the star and at its inner angles, and with the bottoms about four feet from the glaciated surface. Looking through these, we could see that the masonry was fully five feet thick, that there were no partitions remaining within, and that there were traces of banded carvings or bas-reliefs on the interior walls – facts we had indeed guessed before, when flying low over this rampart and others like it. Though lower parts must have originally existed, all traces of such things were now wholly obscured by the deep layer of ice and snow at this point.

We crawled through one of the windows and vainly tried to decipher the nearly effaced mural designs, but did not attempt to disturb the glaciated floor. Our orientation flights had indicated that many buildings in the city proper were less ice-choked, and that we might perhaps find wholly clear interiors leading down to the true ground level if we entered those structures still roofed at the top. Before we left the rampart we photographed it carefully, and studied its mortarless Cyclopean masonry with complete bewilderment. We wished that Pabodie were present, for his engineering knowledge might have helped us guess how such titanic blocks could have been handled in that unbelievably remote age when the city and its outskirts were built up.

The half-mile walk down hill to the actual city, with the upper wind shrieking vainly and savagely through the skyward peaks in the background, was something of which the smallest details will always remain engraved on my mind. Only in fantastic nightmares could any human beings but Danforth and me conceive such optical effects. Between us and the churning vapors of the west lay that monstrous tangle of dark stone towers, its outré and incredible forms impressing us afresh at every new angle of vision. It was a mirage in solid stone, and were it not for the photographs I would still doubt that such a thing could be. The general type of masonry was identical with that of the rampart we had examined; but the extravagant shapes which this masonry took in its urban manifestations were past all description.

Even the pictures illustrate only one or two phases of its

endless variety, preternatural massiveness, and utterly alien exoticism. There were geometrical forms for which an Euclid would scarcely find a name – cones of all degrees of irregularity and truncation, terraces of every sort of provocative disproportion, shafts with odd bulbous enlargements, broken columns in curious groups, and five-pointed or five-ridged arrangements of mad grotesqueness. As we drew nearer we could see beneath certain transparent parts of the ice sheet, and detect some of the tubular stone bridges that connected the crazily sprinkled structures at various heights. Of orderly streets there seemed to be none, the only broad open swath being a mile to the left, where the ancient river had doubtless flowed through the town into the mountains.

Our field glasses showed the external, horizontal bands of nearly effaced sculptures and dot groups to be very prevalent, and we could half imagine what the city must once have looked like – even though most of the roofs and tower tops had necessarily perished. As a whole, it had been a complex tangle of twisted lanes and alleys, all of them deep canyons, and some little better than tunnels because of the overhanging masonry or overarching bridges. Now, outspread below us, it loomed like a dream fantasy against a westward mist through whose northern end the low, reddish antarctic sun of early afternoon was struggling to shine; and when, for a moment, that sun encountered a denser obstruction and plunged the scene into temporary shadow, the effect was subtly menacing in a way I can never hope to depict. Even the faint howling and piping of the unfelt wind in the great mountain passes behind us took on a wilder note of purposeful malignity. The last stage of our descent to the town was unusually steep and abrupt, and a rock outcropping at the edge where the grade changed led us to think that an artificial terrace had once existed there. Under the glaciation, we believed, there must be a flight of steps or its equivalent.

When at last we plunged into the town itself, clambering over fallen masonry and shrinking from the oppressive nearness and dwarfing height of omnipresent crumbling and pitted walls, our sensations again became such that I marvel at the amount of self-control we retained. Danforth was frankly jumpy, and began making some offensively irrelevant speculations about the horror at the camp – which I resented all the more because I could not help sharing certain conclusions forced upon us by many features of this morbid survival from nightmare antiquity.

The speculations worked on his imagination, too; for in one place – where a debris littered alley turned a sharp corner – he insisted that he saw faint traces of ground markings which he did not like; whilst elsewhere he stopped to listen to a subtle, imaginary sound from some undefined point – a muffled musical piping, he said, not unlike that of the wind in the mountain caves, yet somehow disturbingly different. The ceaseless five-pointedness of the surrounding architecture and of the few distinguishable mural arabesques had a dimly sinister suggestiveness we could not escape, and gave us a touch of terrible subconscious certainty concerning the primal entities which had reared and dwelt in this unhallowed place.

Nevertheless, our scientific and adventurous souls were not wholly dead, and we mechanically carried out our program of chipping specimens from all the different rock types represented in the masonry. We wished for a rather full set in order to draw better conclusions regarding the age of the place. Nothing in the great outer walls seemed to date from later than the Jurassic and Comanchian periods, nor was any piece of stone in the entire place of a greater recency than the Pliocene Age. In stark certainty, we were wandering amidst a death which had reigned at least five hundred thousand years, and in all probability even longer.

As we proceeded through this maze of stone-shadowed

twilight we stopped at all available apertures to study interiors and investigate entrance possibilities. Some were above our reach, whilst others led only into ice-choked ruins as unroofed and barren as the rampart on the hill. One, though spacious and inviting, opened on a seemingly bottomless abyss without visible means of descent. Now and then we had a chance to study the petrified wood of a surviving shutter, and were impressed by the fabulous antiquity implied in the still discernible grain. These things had come from Mesozoic gymnosperms and conifers – especially Cretaceous cycads – and from fan palms and early angiosperms of plainly Tertiary date. Nothing definitely later than the Pliocene could be discovered. In the placing of these shutters – whose edges showed the former presence of queer and long-vanished hinges – usage seemed to be varied – some being on the outer and some on the inner side of the deep embrasures. They seemed to have become wedged in place, thus surviving the rustings of their former and probably metallic fixtures and fastenings.

After a time we came across a row of windows – in the bulges of a colossal five-edged cone of undamaged apex – which led into a vast, well-preserved room with stone flooring; but these were too high in the room to permit descent without a rope. We had a rope with us, but did not wish to bother with this twenty-foot drop unless obliged to – especially in this thin plateau air where great demands were made upon the heart action. This enormous room was probably a hall or concourse of some sort, and our electric torches showed bold, distinct, and potentially startling sculptures arranged round the walls in broad, horizontal bands separated by equally broad strips of conventional arabesques. We took careful note of this spot, planning to enter here unless a more easily gained interior were encountered.

Finally, though, we did encounter exactly the opening we

wished, an archway about six feet wide and ten feet high, marking the former end of an aerial bridge which had spanned an alley about five feet above the present level of glaciation. These archways, of course, were flush with upper-story floors, and in this case one of the floors still existed. The building thus accessible was a series of rectangular terraces on our left facing westward. That across the alley, where the other archway yawned, was a decrepit cylinder with no windows and with a curious bulge about ten feet above the aperture. It was totally dark inside, and the archway seemed to open on a well of illimitable emptiness.

Heaped debris made the entrance to the vast left-hand building doubly easy, yet for a moment we hesitated before taking advantage of the long-wished chance. For though we had penetrated into this tangle of archaic mystery, it required fresh resolution to carry us actually inside a complete and surviving building of a fabulous elder world whose nature was becoming more and more hideously plain to us. In the end, however, we made the plunge, and scrambled up over the rubble into the gaping embrasure. The floor beyond was of great slate slabs, and seemed to form the outlet of a long, high corridor with sculptured walls.

Observing the many inner archways which led off from it, and realizing the probable complexity of the nest of apartments within, we decided that we must begin our system of hare-and-hound trail blazing. Hitherto our compasses, together with frequent glimpses of the vast mountain range between the towers in our rear, had been enough to prevent our losing our way; but from now on, the artificial substitute would be necessary. Accordingly we reduced our extra paper to shreds of suitable size, placed these in a bag to be carried by Danforth, and prepared to use them as economically as safety would allow. This method would probably gain us immunity from straying, since there did not appear to be any strong air currents inside the primordial masonry. If such should develop, or if our paper supply should give out, we could of course fall back on the more secure though more tedious and retarding method of rock chipping.

Just how extensive a territory we had opened up, it was impossible to guess without a trial. The close and frequent connection of the different buildings made it likely that we might cross from one to another on bridges underneath the ice, except where impeded by local collapses and geologic rifts, for very little glaciation seemed to have entered the massive constructions. Almost all the areas of transparent ice had revealed the submerged windows as tightly shuttered, as if the town had been left in that uniform state until the glacial sheet came to crystallize the lower part for all succeeding time. Indeed, one gained a curious impression that this place had been deliberately closed and deserted in some dim, bygone aeon, rather than overwhelmed by any sudden calamity or even gradual decay. Had the coming of the ice been foreseen, and had a nameless population left *en masse* to seek a less doomed abode? The precise physiographic conditions attending the formation of the ice sheet at this point would have to wait for later solution. It had not, very plainly, been a grinding drive. Perhaps the pressure of accumulated snows had been responsible, and perhaps some flood from the river, or from the bursting of some ancient glacial dam in the great range, had helped to create the special state now observable. Imagination could conceive almost anything in connection with this place.

VI

It would be cumbrous to give a detailed, consecutive account of our wanderings inside that cavernous, aeon-dead honeycomb of primal masonry – that monstrous lair of elder secrets which now echoed for the first time, after uncounted epochs, to the tread of human feet. This is especially true because so much of the horrible drama and revelation came from a mere study of the omnipresent mural carvings. Our flashlight photographs of those carvings will do much toward proving the truth of what we are now disclosing, and it is lamentable that we had not a larger film supply with us. As it was, we made crude notebook sketches of certain salient features after all our films were used up.

The building which we had entered was one of great size and elaborateness, and gave us an impressive notion of the architecture of that nameless geologic past. The inner partitions were less massive than the outer walls, but on the lower levels were excellently preserved. Labyrinthine complexity, involving curiously irregular difference in floor levels, characterized the entire arrangement; and we should certainly have been lost at the very outset but for the trail of torn paper left behind us. We decided to explore the more decrepit upper parts first of all, hence climbed aloft in the maze for a distance of some one hundred feet, to where the topmost tier of chambers yawned snowily and ruinously open to the polar sky. Ascent was effected over the steep, transversely ribbed stone ramps or inclined planes which everywhere served in lieu of stairs. The rooms we encountered were of all imaginable shapes and proportions, ranging from five-pointed stars to triangles and perfect cubes. It might be safe to say that their general average was about

30×30 feet in floor area, and 20 feet in height, though many larger apartments existed. After thoroughly examining the upper regions and the glacial level we descended, story by story, into the submerged part, where indeed we soon saw we were in a continuous maze of connected chambers and passages probably leading over unlimited areas outside this particular building. The Cyclopean massiveness and gigantism of everything about us became curiously oppressive; and there was something vaguely but deeply inhuman in all the contours, dimensions, proportions, decorations, and constructional nuances of the blasphemously archaic stonework. We soon realized, from what the carvings revealed, that this monstrous city was many million years old.

We cannot yet explain the engineering principles used in the anomalous balancing and adjustment of the vast rock masses, though the function of the arch was clearly much relied on. The rooms we visited were wholly bare of all portable contents, a circumstance which sustained our belief in the city's deliberate desertion. The prime decorative feature was the almost universal system of mural sculpture, which tended to run in continuous horizontal bands three feet wide and arranged from floor to ceiling in alternation with bands of equal width given over to geometrical arabesques. There were exceptions to this rule of arrangement, but its preponderance was overwhelming. Often, however, a series of smooth cartouches containing oddly patterned groups of dots would be sunk along one of the arabesque bands.

The technique, we soon saw, was mature, accomplished, and aesthetically evolved to the highest degree of civilized mastery, though utterly alien in every detail to any known art tradition of the human race. In delicacy of execution no sculpture I have ever seen could approach it. The minutest details of elaborate vegetation, or of animal life, were rendered with astonishing vividness despite the bold scale of the carvings; whilst the conventional designs were marvels of skillful intricacy. The arabesques displayed a profound use of mathematical principles, and were made up of obscurely symmetrical curves and angles based on the quantity of five. The pictorial bands followed a highly formalized tradition, and involved a peculiar treatment of perspective, but had an artistic force that moved us profoundly notwithstanding the intervening gulf of vast geologic periods. Their method of design hinged on a singular juxtaposition of the cross section with the two-dimensional silhouette, and embodied an analytical psychology beyond that of any known race of antiquity. It is useless to try to compare this art with any represented in our museums. Those who see our photographs will probably find its closest analogue in certain grotesque conceptions of the most daring futurists.

The arabesque tracery consisted altogether of depressed lines, whose depth on unweathered walls varied from one to two inches. When cartouches with dot groups appeared – evidently as inscriptions in some unknown and primordial language and alphabet – the depression of the smooth surface was perhaps an inch and a half, and of the dots perhaps a half inch more. The pictorial bands were in countersunk low relief, their background being depressed about two inches from the original wall surface. In some specimens marks of a former coloration could be detected, though for the most part the untold aeons had disintegrated and banished any pigments which may have been applied. The more one studied the marvelous technique the more one admired the things. Beneath their strict conventionalization one could grasp the minute and accurate observation and graphic skill of the artists; and indeed, the very conventions themselves served to symbolize and accentuate the real essence or vital differentiation of every object delineated. We felt, too, that besides these recognizable excellences there were others lurking beyond the reach of our perceptions. Certain touches here and there gave vague hints of latent symbols and stimuli which another mental and emotional background, and a fuller or different sensory equipment, might have made of profound and poignant significance to us.

The subject matter of the sculptures obviously came from the life of the vanished epoch of their creation, and contained a large proportion of evident history. It is this abnormal historic-mindedness of the primal race – a chance circumstance operating, through coincidence, miraculously in our favor – which made the carvings so awesomely informative to us, and which caused us to place their photography and transcription above all other considerations. In certain rooms the dominant arrangement was varied by the presence of maps, astronomical charts, and other scientific designs of an enlarged scale – these things giving a naïve and terrible corroboration to what we gathered from the pictorial friezes and dadoes. In hinting at what the whole revealed, I can only hope that my account will not arouse a curiosity greater than sane caution on the part of those who believe me at all. It would be tragic if any were to be allured to that realm of death and horror by the very warning meant to discourage them.

Interrupting these sculptured walls were high windows and massive twelve-foot doorways; both now and then retaining the petrified wooden planks – elaborately carved and polished – of the actual shutters and doors. All metal fixtures had long ago vanished, but some of the doors remained in place and had to be forced aside as we progressed from room to room. Window frames with odd transparent panes – mostly elliptical – survived here and there, though in no considerable quantity. There were also frequent niches of great magnitude, generally empty, but once in a while containing some bizarre object carved from green soapstone which was either broken or perhaps held too inferior to warrant removal. Other apertures were undoubtedly connected with bygone mechanical facilities – heating, lighting, and the like – of a sort suggested in many of the carvings. Ceilings tended to be plain, but had sometimes been inlaid with green soapstone or other tiles, mostly fallen now. Floors were also paved with such tiles, though plain stonework predominated.

As I have said, all furniture and other movables were absent; but the sculptures gave a clear idea of the strange devices which had once filled these tomblike, echoing rooms. Above the glacial sheet the floors were generally thick with detritus, litter, and debris, but farther down this condition decreased. In some of the lower chambers and corridors there was little more than gritty dust or ancient incrustations. while occasional areas had an uncanny air of newly swept immaculateness. Of course, where rifts or collapses had occurred, the lower levels were as littered as the upper ones. A central court – as in other structures we had seen from the air – saved the inner regions from total darkness; so that we seldom had to use our electric torches in the upper rooms except when studying sculptured details. Below the ice cap, however, the twilight deepened; and in many parts of the tangled ground level there was an approach to absolute blackness.

To form even a rudimentary idea of our thoughts and feelings as we penetrated this aeon-silent maze of unhuman masonry one must correlate a hopelessly bewildering chaos of fugitive moods, memories, and impressions. The sheer appalling antiquity and lethal desolation of the place were enough to overwhelm almost any sensitive person, but added to these elements were the recent unexplained horror at the camp, and the revelations all too soon effected by the terrible mural sculptures around us. The moment we came upon a perfect section of carving, where no ambiguity of interpretation could exist, it took only a brief study to give us the hideous truth – a truth which it would be naïve to claim Danforth and I had not independently suspected before, though we had carefully refrained from even hinting it to each other. There could now be no further merciful doubt about the nature of the beings which had built and inhabited this monstrous dead city millions of years ago, when man's ancestors were primitive archaic mammals, and vast dinosaurs roamed the tropical steppes of Europe and Asia.

We had previously clung to a desperate alternative and insisted – each to himself – that the omnipresence of the five-pointed motif meant only some cultural or religious exaltation of the Archaean natural object which had so patently embodied the quality of five-pointedness; as the decorative motifs of Minoan Crete exalted the sacred bull, those of Egypt the scarabaeus, those of Rome the wolf and the eagle, and those of various savage tribes some chosen totem animal. But this lone refuge was now stripped from us, and we were forced to face definitely the reason-shaking realization which the reader of these pages had doubtless long ago anticipated. I can scarcely bear to write it down in black and white even now, but perhaps that will not be necessary.

The things once rearing and dwelling in this frightful masonry in the age of dinosaurs were not indeed dinosaurs, but far worse. Mere dinosaurs were new and almost brainless objects – but the builders of the city were wise and old, and had left certain traces in rocks even then laid down well nigh a thousand million years – rocks laid down before the true life of earth had advanced beyond plastic groups of cells – rocks laid down before the true life of earth had existed at all. They were the makers and enslavers of that life, and above all doubt the originals of the fiendish elder myths which things like the Pnakotic Manuscripts and the *Necronomicon* affrightedly hint about. They were the great 'Old Ones' that had filtered down from the stars when the earth was young – the beings whose substance an alien evolution had shaped, and whose powers were such as this planet had never bred. And to think that only the day before Danforth and I had actually looked upon fragments of their millennially fossilized substance – and that poor Lake and his party had seen their complete outlines—

It is of course impossible for me to relate in proper order the stages by which we picked up what we know of that monstrous chapter of pre-human life. After the first shock of the certain revelation we had to pause a while to recuperate, and it was full three o'clock before we got started on our actual tour of systematic research. The sculptures in the building we entered were of relatively late date – perhaps two million years ago – as checked up by geological, biological, and astronomical features – and embodied an art which would be called decadent in comparison with that of specimens we found in older buildings after crossing bridges under the glacial sheet. One edifice hewn from the solid rock seemed to go back forty or possibly fifty million years – to the lower Eocene or upper Cretaceous – and contained bas-reliefs of an artistry surpassing anything else, with one tremendous exception, that we encountered. That was, we have since agreed, the oldest domestic structure we traversed.

Were it not for the support of those flashlights soon to be made public, I would refrain from telling what I found and inferred, lest I be confined as a madman. Of course, the infinitely early parts of the patchwork tale – representing the preterrestrial life of the star-headed beings on other planets, in other galaxies, and in other universes – can readily be interpreted as the fantastic mythology of those beings themselves; yet such parts sometimes involved designs and diagrams so uncannily close to the latest findings of mathematics and astrophysics that I scarcely know what to think. Let others judge when they see the photographs I shall publish.

Naturally, no one set of carvings which we encountered told more than a fraction of any connected story, nor did we even begin to come upon the various stages of that story in their proper order. Some of the vast rooms were independent units as far as their designs were concerned, whilst in other cases a continuous chronicle would be carried through a series of rooms and corridors. The best of the maps and diagrams were on the walls of a frightful abyss below even the ancient ground level – a cavern perhaps two hundred feet square and sixty feet high, which had almost undoubtedly been an educational center of some sort. There were many provoking repetitions of the same material in different rooms and buildings, since certain chapters of experience, and certain summaries or phases of racial history, had evidently been favorites with different decorators or dwellers. Sometimes, though, variant versions of the same theme proved useful in settling debatable points and filling up gaps.

I still wonder that we deduced so much in the short time at our disposal. Of course, we even now have only the barest outline – and much of that was obtained later on from a study of the photographs and sketches we made. It may be the effect of this later study – the revived memories and vague impressions acting in conjunction with his general sensitiveness and with that final supposed horror-glimpse whose essence he will not reveal even to me – which has been the immediate source of Danforth's present breakdown. But it had to be; for we could not issue our warning intelligently without the fullest possible information, and the issuance of that warning is a prime necessity. Certain lingering influences in that unknown antarctic world of disordered time and alien natural law make it imperative that further exploration be discouraged.

VII

The full story, so far as deciphered, will eventually appear in an official bulletin of Miskatonic University. Here I shall sketch only the salient highlights in a formless, rambling way. Myth or otherwise, the sculptures told of the coming of those star-headed things to the nascent, lifeless earth out of cosmic space – their coming, and the coming of many other alien entities such as at certain times embark upon spatial pioneering. They seemed able to traverse the interstellar ether on their vast membranous wings – thus oddly confirming some curious hill folklore long ago told me by an antiquarian colleague. They had lived under the sea a good deal, building fantastic cities and fighting terrific battles with nameless adversaries by means of intricate devices employing unknown principles of energy. Evidently their scientific and mechanical knowledge far surpassed man's today, though they made use of its more widespread and elaborate forms only when obliged to. Some of the sculptures suggested that they had passed through a stage of mechanized life on other planets, but had receded upon finding its effects emotionally unsatisfying. Their preternatural toughness of organization and simplicity of natural wants made them peculiarly able to live on a high plane without the more specialized fruits of artificial manufacture, and even without garments, except for occasional protection against the elements.

It was under the sea, at first for food and later for other purposes, that they first created earth life – using available substances according to long-known methods. The more

84

elaborate experiments came after the annihilation of various cosmic enemies. They had done the same thing on other planets, having manufactured not only necessary foods, but certain multicellular protoplasmic masses capable of molding their tissues into all sorts of temporary organs under hypnotic influence and thereby forming ideal slaves to perform the heavy work of the community. These viscous masses were without doubt what Abdul Alhazred whispered about as the 'Shoggoths' in his frightful *Necronomicon*, though even that mad Arab had not hinted that any existed on earth except in the dreams of those who had chewed a certain alkaloidal herb. When the star-headed Old Ones on this planet had synthesized their simple food forms and bred a good supply of Shoggoths, they allowed other cell groups to develop into other forms of animal and vegetable life for sundry purposes, extirpating any whose presence became troublesome.

With the aid of the Shoggoths, whose expansions could be made to lift prodigious weights, the small, low cities under the sea grew to vast and imposing labyrinths of stone not unlike those which later rose on land. Indeed, the highly adaptable Old Ones had lived much on land in other parts of the universe, and probably retained many traditions of land construction. As we studied the architecture of all these sculptured palaeogean cities, including that whose aeon-dead corridors we were even then traversing, we were impressed by a curious coincidence which we have not yet tried to explain, even to ourselves. The tops of the buildings, which in the actual city around us had, of course, been weathered into shapeless ruins ages ago, were clearly displayed in the bas-reliefs, and showed vast clusters of needle-like spires, delicate finials on certain cone and pyramid apexes, and tiers of thin, horizontal scalloped disks capping cylindrical shafts. This was exactly what we had seen in that monstrous and portentous mirage, cast by a dead city where such sky-line features had been absent for thousands and tens of thousands of years, which loomed on our ignorant eyes across the unfathomed mountains of madness as we first approached poor Lake's ill-fated camp.

Of the life of the Old Ones, both under the sea and after part of them migrated to land, volumes could be written. Those in shallow water had continued the fullest use of the eyes at the ends of their five main head tentacles, and had practiced the arts of sculpture and writing in quite the usual way – the writing accomplished with a stylus on water-proof waxen surfaces. Those lower down in the ocean depths, though they used a curious phosphorescent organism to furnish light, pieced out their vision with obscure special senses operating through the prismatic cilia on their heads – senses which rendered all the Old Ones partly independent of light in emergencies. Their forms of sculpture and writing had changed curiously during the descent, embodying certain apparently chemical coating processes – probably to secure phosphorescence – which the bas-reliefs could not make clear to us. The beings moved in the sea partly by swimming – using the lateral crinoid arms – and partly by wriggling with the lower tier of tentacles containing the pseudofeet. Occasionally they accomplished long swoops with the auxiliary use of two or more sets of their fanlike folding wings. On land they locally used the pseudofeet, but now and then flew to great heights or over long distances with their wings. The many slender tentacles into which the crinoid arms branched were infinitely deli-cate, flexible, strong, and accurate in muscular-nervous coordination – ensuring the utmost skill and dexterity in all artistic and other manual operations.

The toughness of the things was almost incredible. Even the terrific pressure of the deepest sea bottoms appeared powerless to harm them. Very few seemed to die at all except by violence, and their burial places were very limited. The fact that they covered their vertically inhumed dead with five-pointed inscribed mounds set up thoughts in Danforth and me which made a fresh pause and recuperation necessary after the sculptures revealed it. The beings multiplied by means of spores – like vegetable pteridophytes, as Lake had suspected – but, owing to their prodigious toughness and longevity, and consequent lack of replacement needs, they did not encourage the large-scale development of new prothallia except when they had new regions to colonize. The young matured swiftly, and received an education evidently beyond any standard we can imagine. The prevailing intellectual and aesthetic life was highly evolved, and produced a tenaciously enduring set of customs and institutions which I shall describe more fully in my coming monograph. These varied slightly according to sea or land residence, but had the same foundations and essentials.

Though able, like vegetables, to derive nourishment from inorganic substances, they vastly preferred organic and especially animal food. They ate uncooked marine life under the sea, but cooked their viands on land. They hunted game and raised meat herds – slaughtering with sharp weapons whose odd marks on certain fossil bones our expedition had noted. They resisted all ordinary temperatures marvelously, and in their natural state could live in water down to freezing. When the great chill of the Pleistocene drew on, however – nearly a million years ago – the land dwellers had to resort to special measures, including artificial heating – until at last the deadly cold appears to have driven them back into the sea. For their prehistoric flights through cosmic space, legend said, they absorbed certain chemicals and became almost independent of eating, breathing, or heat conditions – but by the time of the great cold they had lost track of the method. In any case they could not have prolonged the artifical state indefinitely without harm.

Being nonpairing and semivegetable in structure, the Old

Ones had no biological basis for the family phase of mammal life, but seemed to organize large households on the principles of comfortable space-utility and – as we deduced from the pictured occupations and diversions of co-dwellers – congenial mental association. In furnishing their homes they kept everything in the center of the huge rooms, leaving all the wall spaces free for decorative treatment. Lighting, in the case of the land inhabitants, was accomplished by a device probably electro-chemical in nature. Both on land and under water they used curious tables, chairs and couches like cylindrical frames – for they rested and slept upright with folded-down tentacles – and racks for the hinged sets of dotted surfaces forming their books.

Government was evidently complex and probably socialistic, though no certainties in this regard could be deduced from the sculptures we saw. There was extensive commerce, both local and between different cities – certain small, flat counters, five-pointed and inscribed, serving as money. Probably the smaller of the various greenish soapstones found by our expedition were pieces of such currency. Though the culture was mainly urban, some agriculture and much stock raising existed. Mining and a limited amount of manufacturing were also practiced. Travel was very frequent, but permanent migration seemed relatively rare except for the vast colonizing movements by which the race expanded. For personal locomotion no external aid was used, since in land, air, and water movement alike the Old Ones seemed to possess excessively vast capacities for speed. Loads, however, were drawn by beasts of burden – Shoggoths under the sea, and a curious variety of primitive vertebrates in the later years of land existence.

These vertebrates, as well as an infinity of other life forms – animal and vegetable, marine, terrestrial, and aerial – were the products of unguided evolution acting on life cells made by the Old Ones, but escaping beyond their radius of attention. They had been suffered to develop unchecked because they had not come in conflict with the dominant beings. Bothersome forms, of course, were mechanically exterminated. It interested us to see in some of the very last and most decadent sculptures a shambling, primitive mammal, used sometimes for food and sometimes as an amusing buffoon by the land dwellers, whose vaguely simian and human foreshadowings were unmistakable. In the building of land cities the huge stone blocks of the high towers were generally lifted by vast-winged pterodactyls of a species heretofore unknown to paleontology.

The persistence with which the Old Ones survived various geologic changes and convulsions of the earth's crust was little short of miraculous. Though few of none of their first cities seem to have remained beyond the Archaean Age, there was no interruption in their civilization or in the transmission of their records. Their original place of advent to the planet was the Antarctic Ocean, and it is likely that they came not long after the matter forming the moon was wrenched from the neighbouring South Pacific. According to one of the sculptured maps the whole globe was then under water, with stone cities scattered farther and farther from the antarctic as aeons passed. Another map shows a vast bulk of dry land around the South Pole, where it is evident that some of the beings made experimental settlements, though their main centers were transferred to the nearest sea bottom. Later maps, which display the land mass as cracking and drifting, and sending certain detached parts northward, uphold in a striking way the theories of continental drift lately advanced by Taylor, Wegener, and Joly.

With the upheaval of new land in the South Pacific tremendous events began. Some of the marine cities were hopelessly shattered, yet that was not the worst misfortune.

Another race – a land race of beings shaped like octopi and probably corresponding to fabulous pre-human spawn of Cthulhu – soon began filtering down from cosmic infinity and precipitated a monstrous war which for a time drove the Old Ones wholly back to the sea – a colossal blow in view of the increasing land settlements. Later peace was made, and the new lands were given to the Cthulhu spawn whilst the Old Ones held the sea and the older lands. New land cities were founded – the greatest of them in the antarctic, for this region of first arrival was sacred. From then on, as before, the antarctic remained the center of the Old Ones' civilization, and all the cities built there by the Cthulhu spawn were blotted out. Then suddenly the lands of the Pacific sank again, taking with them the frightful stone city of R'lyeh and all the cosmic octopi, so that the Old Ones were again supreme on the planet except for one shadowy fear about which they did not like to speak. At a rather later age their cities dotted all the land and water areas of the globe – hence the recommendation in my coming monograph that some archaeologist make systematic borings with Pabodie's type of apparatus in certain widely spread regions.

The steady trend down the ages was from water to land – a movement encouraged by the rise of new land masses, though the ocean was never wholly deserted. Another cause of the landward movement was the new difficulty in breeding and managing the Shoggoths upon which successful sea life depended. With the march of time, as the sculptures sadly confessed, the art of creating new life from inorganic matter had been lost, so that the Old Ones had to depend on the molding of forms already in existence. On land the great reptiles proved highly tractable; but the Shoggoths of the sea, reproducing by fission and acquiring a dangerous degree of accidental intelligence, presented for a time a formidable problem.

They had always been controlled through the hypnotic suggestions of the Old Ones, and had modeled their tough plasticity into various useful temporary limbs and organs; but now their self-modeling powers were sometimes exercised independently, and in various imitative forms implanted by past suggestion. They had, it seems, developed a semistable brain whose separate and occasionally stubborn volition echoed the will of the Old Ones without always obeying it. Sculptured images of these Shoggoths filled Danforth and me with horror and loathing. They were normally shapeless entities composed of a viscous jelly which looked like an agglutination of bubbles, and each averaged about fifteen feet in diameter when a sphere. They had, however, a constantly shifting shape and volume – throwing out temporary developments or forming apparent organs of sight, hearing, and speech in imitation of their masters, either spontaneously or according to suggestion.

They seem to have become peculiarly intractable toward the middle of the Permian Age, perhaps one hundred and fifty million years ago, when a veritable war of resubjugation was waged upon them by the marine Old Ones. Pictures of this war, and of the headless, slime-coated fashion in which the Shoggoths typically left their slain victims, held a marvelously fearsome quality despite the intervening abyss of untold ages. The Old Ones had used curious weapons of molecular and atomic disturbance against the rebel entities, and in the end had achieved a complete victory. Thereafter the sculptures showed a period in which Shoggoths were tamed and broken by armed Old Ones as the wild horses of the American west were tamed by cowboys. Though during the rebellion the Shoggoths had shown an ability to live out of water, this transition was not encouraged – since their usefulness on land would hardly have been commensurate with the trouble of their management.

During the Jurassic Age the Old Ones met fresh adversity in the form of a new invasion from outer space – this time by half-fungous, half-crustacean creatures – creatures undoubtedly the same as those figuring in certain whispered hill legends of the north, and remembered in the Himalayas as the Mi-Go, or Abominable Snow Men. To fight these beings the Old Ones attempted, for the first time since their terrene advent, to sally forth again into the planetary ether; but, despite all traditional preparations, found it no longer possible to leave the earth's atmosphere. Whatever the old secret of interstellar travel had been, it was now definitely lost to the race. In the end the Mi-Go drove the Old Ones out of all the northern lands, though they were powerless to disturb those in the sea. Little by little the slow retreat of the elder race to their original antarctic habitat was beginning.

It was curious to note from the pictured battles that both the Cthulhu spawn and the Mi-Go seem to have been composed of matter more widely different from that which we know than was the substance of the Old Ones. They were able to undergo transformations and reintegrations impossible for their adversaries, and seem therefore to have originally come from even remoter gulfs of cosmic space. The Old Ones, but for their abnormal toughness and peculiar vital properties, were strictly material, and must have had their absolute origin within the known space-time continuum – whereas the first sources of the other beings can only be guessed at with bated breath. All this, of course, assuming that the nonterrestrial linkages and the anomalies ascribed to the invading foes are not pure mythology. Conceivably, the Old Ones might have invented a cosmic framework to account for their occasional defeats, since historical interest and pride obviously formed their chief psychological element. It is significant that their annals failed to mention many advanced and potent races of beings whose mighty cultures and towering cities figure persistently in certain obscure legends.

The changing state of the world through long geologic ages appeared with startling vividness in many of the sculptured maps and scenes. In certain cases existing science will require revision, while in other cases its bold deductions are magnificently confirmed. As I have said, the hypothesis of Taylor, Wegener, and Joly that all the continents are fragments of an original antarctic land mass which cracked from centrifugal force and drifted apart over a technically viscous lower surface – an hypothesis suggested by such things as the complementary outlines of Africa and South America, and the way the great mountain chains are rolled and shoved up – receives striking support from this uncanny source.

Maps evidently showing the Carboniferous world of a hundred million or more years ago displayed significant rifts and chasms destined later to separate Africa from the once continuous realms of Europe (then the Valusia of primal legend), Asia, the Americas, and the antarctic continent. Other charts – and most significantly one in connection with the founding fifty million years ago of the vast dead city around us – showed all the present continents well differentiated. And in the latest discoverable specimen – dating perhaps from the Pliocene Age – the approximate world of today appeared quite clearly despite the linkage of Alaska with Siberia, of North America with Europe through Greenland, and of South America with the antarctic continent through Graham Land. In the Carboniferous map the whole globe – ocean floor and rifted land mass alike – bore symbols of the Old Ones' vast stone cities, but in the later charts the gradual recession toward the antarctic became very plain. The final Pliocene specimen showed no land cities except on the antarctic continent and the tip of South America, nor any ocean cities north of the fiftieth parallel of

South Latitude. Knowledge and interest in the northern world, save for a study of coast lines probably made during long exploration flights on those fanlike membranous wings, had evidently declined to zero among the Old Ones.

Destruction of cities through the upthrust of mountains, the centrifugal rending of continents, the seismic convulsions of land or sea bottom, and other natural causes was a matter of common record; and it was curious to observe how fewer and fewer replacements were made as the ages wore on. The vast dead megalopolis that yawned around us seemed to be the last general center of the race – built early in the Cretaceous Age after a titanic earth buckling had obliterated a still vaster predecessor not far distant. It appeared that this general region was the most sacred spot of all, where reputedly the first Old Ones had settled on a primal sea bottom. In the new city – many of whose features we could recognize in the sculptures, but which stretched fully a hundred miles along the mountain range in each direction beyond the farthest limits of our aerial survey – there were reputed to be preserved certain sacred stones forming part of the first sea-bottom city, which thrust up to light after long epochs in the course of the general crumbling of strata.

VIII

Naturally, Danforth and I studied with especial interest and a peculiarly personal sense of awe everything pertaining to the immediate district in which we were. Of this local material there was naturally a vast abundance; and on the tangled ground level of the city we were lucky enough to find a house of very late date whose walls, though somewhat damaged by a neighbouring rift, contained sculptures of decadent workmanship carrying the story of the region much beyond the period of Pliocene map whence we derived our last general glimpse of the prehuman world. This was the last place we examined in detail, since what we found there gave us a fresh immediate objective.

Certainly, we were in one of the strangest, weirdest, and most terrible of all the corners of earth's globe. Of all existing lands it was infinitely the most ancient. The conviction grew upon us that this hideous upland must indeed be the fabled nightmare plateau of Leng which even the mad author of the *Necronomicon* was reluctant to discuss. The great mountain chain was tremendously long – starting as a low range at Luitpold Land on the coast of Weddell Sea and virtually crossing the entire continent. The really high part stretched in a mighty arc from about Latitude 82°, E. Longitude 60° to Latitude 70°, E. Longitude 115°, with its concave side toward our camp and its seaward end in the region of that long, ice-locked coast whose hills were glimpsed by Wilkes and Mawson at the antarctic circle.

Yet even more monstrous exaggerations of nature seemed disturbingly close at hand. I have said that these peaks are higher than the Himalayas, but the sculptures forbid me to say that they are earth's highest. That grim honor is beyond doubt reserved for something which half the scriptures hesitated to record at all, whilst others approached it with obvious repugnance and trepidation. It seems that there was one part of the ancient land – the first part that ever rose from the waters after the earth had flung off the moon and the Old Ones had seeped down from the stars – which had come to be shunned as vaguely and namelessly evil. Cities built there had crumbled before their time, and had been found suddenly deserted. Then when the first great earth buckling had convulsed the region in the Comanchian Age, a frightful line of peaks had shot suddenly up amidst the most appalling din and chaos – and earth had received the loftiest and most terrible mountains.

If the scale of the carvings was correct, these abhorred things must have been much over forty thousand feet high – radically vaster than even the shocking mountains of madness we had crossed. They extended it appeared from about Latitude 77°, E. Longitude 70° to Latitude 70°, E. Longitude 100° – less than three hundred miles away from the dead city, so that we would have spied their dreaded summits in the dim western distance had it not been for that vague, opalescent haze. Their northern end must likewise be visible from the long antarctic circle coast line at Queen Mary Land.

Some of the Old Ones, in the decadent days, had made strange prayers to those mountains – but none ever went near them or dared to guess what lay beyond. No human eye had ever seen them, and as I studied the emotions conveyed in the carvings I prayed that none ever might. There are protecting hills along the coast beyond them – Queen Mary and Kaiser Wilhelm Lands – and I thank Heaven no one has been able to land and climb those hills. I am not as sceptical about old tales and fears as I used to be, and I do not laugh now at the prehuman sculptor's notion that lightning paused meaningfully now and then at each of the brooding crests, and that an unexplained glow shone from one of those terrible pinnacles all through the long polar night. There may be a very real and very monstrous meaning in the old Pnakotic whispers about Kadath in the Cold Waste.

But the terrain close at hand was hardly less strange, even if less namelessly accursed. Soon after the founding of the city the great mountain range became the seat of the principal temples, and many carvings showed what grotesque and fantastic towers had pierced the sky where now we saw only the curiously clinging cubes and ramparts. In the course of ages the caves had appeared, and had been shaped into adjuncts of the temples. With the advance of still later epochs all the limestone veins of the region were hollowed out by ground waters, so that the mountains, the foothills, and the plains below them were a veritable network of connected caverns and galleries. Many graphic sculptures told of explorations deep underground, and of the final discovery of the Stygian sunless sea that lurked at earth's bowels.

This vast nighted gulf had undoubtedly been worn by the great river which flowed down from the nameless and horrible westward mountains, and which had formerly turned at the base of the Old Ones' range and flowed beside that chain into the Indian Ocean between Budd and Totten Lands on Wilkes's coast line. Little by little it had eaten away the limestone hill base at its turning, till at last its sapping currents reached the caverns of the ground waters and joined with them in digging a deeper abyss. Finally its whole bulk emptied into the hollow hills and left the old bed toward the ocean dry. Much of the later city as we now found it had been built over that former bed. The Old Ones, understanding what had happened, and exercising their always keen artistic sense, had carved into ornate pylons those headlands of the foothills where the great stream began its descent into eternal darkness.

This river, once crossed by scores of noble stone bridges, was plainly the one whose extinct course we had seen in our aeroplane survey. Its position in different carvings of the city helped us to orient ourselves to the scene as it had been at various stages of the region's age-long, aeon-dead history, so that we were able to sketch a hasty but careful map of the salient features – squares, important buildings, and the like – for guidance in further explorations. We could soon reconstruct in fancy the whole stupendous thing as it was a million or ten million or fifty million years ago, for the sculptures told us exactly what the buildings and mountains and squares and suburbs and landscape setting and luxuriant Tertiary vegetation had looked like. It must have had a marvelous and mystic beauty, and as I thought of it I almost forgot the clammy sense of sinister oppression with which the city's inhuman age and massiveness and deadness and remoteness and glacial twilight had choked and weighed on my spirit. Yet according to certain carvings the denizens of that city had themselves known the clutch of oppressive terror; for there was a somber and recurrent type of scene in which the Old Ones were shown in the act of recoiling affrightedly from some object – never allowed to appear in the design – found in the great river and indicated as having been washed down through waving, vine-draped cycad forests from those horrible westward mountains.

It was only in the one late-built house with the decadent carvings that we obtained any foreshadowing of the final calamity leading to the city's desertion. Undoubtedly there must have been many sculptures of the same age elsewhere, even allowing for the slackened energies and aspirations of a stressful and uncertain period; indeed, very certain evidence of the existence of others came to us shortly afterward. But this was the first and only set we directly encountered. We meant to look farther later on; but as I have said, immediate conditions dictated another present objective. There would, though, have been a limit – for after all hope of a long future occupancy of the place had perished among the Old Ones, there could not but have been a complete cessation of mural decoration. The ultimate blow, of course, was the coming of the great cold which once held most of the earth in thrall, and which has never departed from the ill-fated poles – the great cold that, at the world's other extremity, put an end to the fabled lands of Lomar and Hyperborea.

Just when this tendency began in the antarctic it would be hard to say in terms of exact years. Nowadays we set the beginning of the general glacial periods at a distance of about five hundred thousand years from the present, but at the poles the terrible scourge must have commenced much earlier. All quantitative estimates are partly guesswork, but it is quite likely that the decadent sculptures were made considerably less than a million years ago, and that the actual desertion of the city was complete long before the conventional opening of the Pleistocene – five hundred thousand years ago – as reckoned in terms of the earth's whole surface.

In the decadent sculptures there were signs of thinner vegetation everywhere, and of a decreased country life on the part of the Old Ones. Heating devices where shown in the house, and winter travelers were represented as muffled in protective fabrics. Then we saw a series of cartouches – the continuous band arrangement being frequently inter- rupted in these late carvings – depicting a constantly growing migration to the nearest refuges of greater warmth – some fleeing to cities under the sea off the far-away coast, and some clambering down through networks of limestone caverns in the hollow hills to the neighboring black abyss of subterrene waters.

In the end it seems to have been the neighboring abyss which received the greatest colonization. This was partly due, no doubt, to the traditional sacredness of this special region, but may have been more conclusively determined by the opportunities it gave for continuing the use of the great temples on the honeycombed mountains, and for retaining the vast land city as a place of summer residence and base of communication with various mines. The link- age of old and new abodes was made more effective by means of several gradings and improvements along the connecting routes, including the chiseling of numerous direct tunnels from the ancient metropolis to the black abyss – sharply down-pointing tunnels whose mouths we carefully drew, according to our most thoughtful estimates, on the guide map we were compiling. It was obvious that at least two of these tunnels lay within a reasonable exploring distance of where we were – both being on the mountainward edge of the city, one less than a quarter of a mile toward the ancient river course, and the other perhaps twice that distance in the opposite direction.

The abyss, it seems had shelving shores of dry land at certain places, but the Old Ones built their new city under water – no doubt because of its greater certainty of uniform warmth. The depth of the hidden sea appears to have been very great, so that the earth's internal heat could ensure its habitability for an indefinite period. The beings seem to have had no trouble in adapting themselves to part-time – and eventually, of course, whole-time – residence under water, since they had never allowed their gill systems to atrophy. There were many sculptures which showed how they had always frequently visited their submarine kinsfolk elsewhere, and how they had habitually bathed on the deep bottom of their great river. The darkness of inner earth could likewise have been no deterrent to a race accustomed to long antarctic nights.

Decadent though their style undoubtedly was, these latest carvings had a truly epic quality where they told of the building of the new city in the cavern sea. The Old Ones had gone about it scientifically – quarrying insoluble rocks from the hearth of the honeycombed mountains, and employing expert workers from the nearest submarine city to perform the construction according to the best methods. These workers brought with them all that was necessary to establish the new venture – Shoggoth tissue from which to breed stone lifters and subsequent beasts of burden for the cavern city, and other protoplasmic matter to mold into phosphorescent organisms for lighting purposes.

At last a mighty metropolis rose on the bottom of that Stygian sea, its architecture much like that of the city above, and its workmanship displaying relatively little decadence because of the precise mathematical element inherent in building operations. The newly bred Shoggoths grew to enormous size and singular intelligence, and were represented as taking and executing orders with marvelous quickness. They seemed to converse with the Old Ones by mimicking their voices – a sort of musical piping over a wide range, if poor Lake's dissection had indicated aright – and to work more from spoken commands than from hypnotic suggestions as in earlier times. They were, however, kept in admirable control. The phosphorescent organisms supplied light with vast effectiveness, and doubtless atoned for the loss of the familiar auroras of the outerworld night.

Art and decoration were pursued, though of course with a certain decadence. The Old Ones seemed to realize this falling off themselves, and in many cases anticipated the policy of Constantine the Great by transplanting especially fine blocks of ancient carving from their land city, just as the emperor, in a similar age of decline, stripped Greece and Asia of their finest art to give his new Byzantine capital greater splendors than its own people could create. That the transfer of sculptured blocks had not been more extensive was doubtless owing to the fact that the land city was not at first wholly abandoned. By the time total abandonment did occur – and it surely must have occurred before the polar Pleistocene was far advanced – the Old Ones had perhaps become satisfied with their decadent art – or had ceased to recognize the superior merit of the older carvings. At any rate, the aeon-silent ruins around us had certainly undergone no wholesale sculptural denudation, though all the best separate statues, like other movables, had been taken away.

The decadent cartouches and dadoes telling this story were, as I have said, the latest we could find in our limited search. They left us with a picture of the Old Ones shuttling back and forth betwixt the land city in summer and the sea-cavern city in winter, and sometimes trading with the sea-bottom cities off the antarctic coast. By this time the ultimate doom of the land city must have been recognized, for the sculptures showed many signs of the cold's malign encroachments. Vegetation was declining, and the terrible snows of the winter no longer melted completely even in midsummer. The saurian live stock were nearly all dead, and the mammals were standing it none too well. To keep on with the work of the upper world it had become necessary to adapt some of the amorphous and curiously cold-resistant Shoggoths to land life – a thing the Old Ones had formerly been reluctant to do. The great river was now lifeless, and the upper sea had lost most of its denizens except the seals and whales. All the birds had flown away, save only the great, grotesque penguins.

What had happened afterward we could only guess. How long had the new sea-cavern city survived? Was it still down there, a stony corpse in eternal blackness? Had the subterranean waters frozen at last? To what fate had the ocean-bottom cities of the outer world been delivered? Had any of the Old Ones shifted north ahead of the creeping ice cap? Existing geology shows no trace of their presence. Had the frightful Mi-Go been still a menace in the outer land world of the north? Could one be sure of what might or might not linger, even to this day, in the lightless and unplumbed abyss of earth's deepest waters? Those things had seemingly been able to withstand any amount of pressure – and men of the sea have fished up curious objects at times. And has the killer-whale theory really explained the savage and mysterious scars on antarctic seals noticed a generation ago by Borchgrevingk?

The specimens found by poor Lake did not enter into these guesses, for their geologic setting proved them to have lived at what must have been a very early date in the land city's history. They were, according to their location, certainly not less than thirty million years old, and we reflected that in their day the sea-cavern city, and indeed the cavern itself, had had no existence. They would have remembered an older scene, with lush Tertiary vegetation everywhere, a younger land city of flourishing arts around them, and a great river sweeping northward along the base of the mighty mountains toward a faraway tropic ocean.

And yet we could not help thinking about these specimens – expecially about the eight perfect ones that were missing from Lake's hideously ravaged camp. There was something abnormal about that whole business – the strange things we had tried so hard to lay to somebody's madness – those frightful graves – the amount and nature of the missing material – Gedney – the unearthly toughness of those archaic monstrosities, and the queer vital freaks the sculptures now showed the race to have – Danforth and I had seen a good deal in the last few hours, and were prepared to believe and keep silent about many appalling and incredible secrets of primal nature.

IX

I have said that our study of the decadent sculptures brought about a change in our immediate objective. This, of course, had to do with the chiseled avenues to the black inner world, of whose existence we had not known before, but which we were now eager to find and traverse. From the evident scale of the carvings we deduced that a steeply descending walk of about a mile through either of the neighboring tunnels would bring us to the brink of the dizzy, sunless cliffs about the great abyss; down whose sides paths, improved by the Old Ones, led to the rocky shore of the hidden and nighted ocean. To behold this fabulous gulf in stark reality was a lure which seemed impossible of resistance once we knew of the thing – yet we realized we must begin the quest at once if we expected to include it in our present trip.

It was now 8 P.M., and we did not have enough battery replacements to let our torches burn on forever. We had done so much studying and copying below the glacial level that our battery supply had had at least five hours of nearly continuous use, and despite the special dry cell formula would obviously be good for only about four more – though by keeping one torch unused, except for especially interesting or difficult places, we might manage to eke out a safe margin beyond that. It would not do to be without a light in these Cyclopean catacombs, hence in order to make the abyss trip we must give up all further mural deciphering. Of course we intended to revisit the place for days and perhaps weeks of intensive study and photography – curiosity having long ago got the better of horror – but just now we must hasten.

Our supply of trail-blazing paper was far from unlimited, and we were reluctant to sacrifice spare notebooks or sketching paper to augment it, but we did let one large notebook go. If worse came to worst we could resort to rock chipping – and of course it would be possible, even in case of really lost direction, to work up to full daylight by one channel or another if granted sufficient time for plentiful trial and error. So at last we set off eagerly in the indicated direction of the nearest tunnel.

According to the carvings from which we had made our

map, the desired tunnel mouth could not be much more than a quarter of a mile from where we stood; the intervening space showing solid-looking buildings quite likely to be penetratable still at a sub-glacial level. The opening itself would be in the basement – on the angle nearest the foothills – of a vast five-pointed structure of evidently public and perhaps ceremonial nature, which we tried to identify from our aerial survey of the ruins.

No such structure came to our minds as we recalled our flight, hence we concluded that its upper parts had been greatly damaged, or that it had been totally shattered in an ice rift we had noticed. In the latter case the tunnel would probably turn out to be choked, so that we would have to try the next nearest one – the one less than a mile to the north. The intervening river course prevented our trying any of the more southern tunnels on this trip; and indeed, if both of the neighboring ones were choked it was doubtful whether our batteries would warrant an attempt on the next northerly one – about a mile beyond our second choice.

As we threaded our dim way through the labyrinth with the aid of map and compass – traversing rooms and corridors in every stage of ruin or preservation, clambering up ramps, crossing upper floors and bridges and clambering down again, encountering choked doorways and piles of debris, hastening now and then along finely preserved and uncannily immaculate stretches, taking false leads and retracing our way(in such cases removing the blind paper trail we had left), and once in a while striking the bottom of an open shaft through which daylight poured or trickled down – we were repeatedly tantalized by the sculptured walls along our route. Many must have told tales of immense historical importance, and only the prospect of later visits reconciled us to the need of passing them by. As it was, we slowed down once in a while and turned on our second torch. If we had had more films we would certainly have paused briefly to photograph certain bas-reliefs, but time-consuming hand-copying was clearly out of the question.

I come now once more to a place where the temptation to hesitate, or to hint rather than state, is very strong. It is necessary, however, to reveal the rest in order to justify my course in discouraging further exploration. We had wormed our way very close to the computed site of the tunnel's mouth – having crossed a second-story bridge to what seemed plainly the tip of a pointed wall, and descended to a ruinous corridor especially rich in decadently elaborate and apparently ritualistic sculptures of late workmanship – when, shortly before 8.30 P.M., Danforth's keen young nostrils gave us the first hint of something unusual. If we had had a dog with us, I suppose we would have been warned before. At first we could not precisely say what was wrong with the formerly crystal-pure air, but after a few seconds our memories reacted only too definitely. Let me try to state the thing without flinching. There was an odor – and that odor was vaguely, subtly, and unmistakably akin to what had nauseated us upon opening the insane grave of the horror poor Lake had dissected.

Of course the revelation was not as clearly cut at the time as it sounds now. There were several conceivable explanations, and we did a good deal of indecisive whispering. Most important of all, we did not retreat without further investigation; for having come this far we were loath to be balked by anything short of certain disaster. Anyway, what we must have suspected was altogether too wild to believe. Such things did not happen in any normal world. It was probably sheer irrational instinct which made us dim our single torch – tempted no longer by the decadent and sinister sculptures that leered menacingly from the oppressive walls – and which softened our progress to a cautious tiptoeing and crawling over the increasingly littered floor and heaps of debris.

Danforth's eyes as well as nose proved better than mine, for it was likewise he who first noticed the queer aspect of the debris after we had passed many half-choked arches leading to chambers and corridors on the ground level. It did not look quite as it ought after countless thousands of years of desertion, and when we cautiously turned on more light we saw that a kind of swath seemed to have been lately tracked through it. The irregular nature of the litter precluded any definite marks, but in the smoother places there were suggestions of the dragging of heavy objects. Once we thought there was a hint of parallel tracks as if of runners. This was what made us pause again.

It was during that pause that we caught – simultaneously this time – the other odor ahead. Paradoxically, it was both a less frightful and a more frightful odor – less frightful intrinsically, but infinitely appalling in this place under the known circumstances – unless, of course, Gedney – for the odor was the plain and familiar one of common petrol – every-day gasoline.

Our motivation after that is something I will leave to psychologists. We knew now that some terrible extension of the camp horrors must have crawled into this nighted burial place of the aeons, hence could not doubt any longer the existence of nameless conditions – present or at least recent – just ahead. Yet in the end we did let sheer burning curiosity – or anxiety – or autohypnotism – or vague thoughts of responsibility toward Gedney – or what not – drive us on. Danforth whispered again of the print he thought he had seen at the alley turning in the ruins above; and of the faint musical piping – potentially of tremendous significance in the light of Lake's dissection report, despite its close resemblance to the cave-mouth echoes of the windy peaks – which he thought he had shortly afterward half heard from unknown depths below. I, in my turn, whispered of how the camp was left – of what had disappeared, and of how the madness of a lone survivor might have conceived the inconceivable – a wild trip across the monstrous mountains and descent into the unknown, primal masonry –

But we could not convince each other, or even ourselves, of anything definite. We had turned off all light as we stood still, and vaguely noticed that a trace of deeply filtered upper day kept the blackness from being absolute. Having automatically begun to move ahead, we guided ourselves by occasional flashes from our torch. The disturbed debris formed an impression we could not shake off, and the smell of gasoline grew stronger. More and more ruin met our eyes and hampered our feet, until very soon we saw that the forward way was about to cease. We had been all too correct in our pessimistic guess about that rift glimpsed from the air. Our tunnel quest was a blind one, and we were not even going to be able to reach the basement out of which the abyssward aperture opened.

The torch, flashing over the grotesquely carved walls of the blocked corridor in which we stood, showed several doorways in various states of obstruction; and from one of them the gasoline odor – quite submerging that other hint of odor – came with especial distinctness. As we looked more steadily, we saw that beyond a doubt there had been a slight and recent clearing away of debris from that particular opening. Whatever the lurking horror might be, we believed the direct avenue toward it was now plainly manifest. I do not think anyone will wonder that we waited an appreciable time before making any further motion.

And yet, when we did venture inside that black arch, our first impression was one of anticlimax. For amidst the littered expanse of that sculptured crypt – a perfect cube with sides of about twenty feet – there remained no recent

108

object of instantly discernible size; so that we looked instinctively, though in vain, for a farther doorway. In another moment, however, Danforth's sharp vision had descried a place where the floor debris had been disturbed; and we turned on both torches full strength. Though what we saw in that light was actually simple and trifling, I am none the less reluctant to tell of it because of what it implied. It was a rough leveling of the debris, upon which several small objects lay carelessly scattered, and at one corner of which a considerable amount of gasoline must have been spilled lately enough to leave a strong odor even at this extreme super-plateau altitude. In other words, it could not be other than a sort of camp – a camp made by questing beings who, like us, had been turned back by the unexpectedly choked way to the abyss.

Let me be plain. The scattered objects were, so far as substance was concerned, all from Lake's camp; and consisted of tin cans as queerly opened as those we had seen at that ravaged place, many spent matches, three illustrated books more or less curiously smudged, an empty ink bottle with its pictorial and instructional carton, a broken fountain pen, some oddly snipped fragments of fur and tent cloth, a used electric battery with circular of directions, a folder that came with our type of tent heater, and a sprinkling of crumpled papers. It was all bad enough but when we smoothed out the papers and looked at what was on them we felt we had come to the worst. We had found certain inexplicably blotted papers at the camp which might have prepared us, yet the effect of the sight down there in the prehuman vaults of a nightmare city was almost too much to bear.

A mad Gedney might have made the groups of dots in imitation of those found on the greenish soapstones, just as the dots on those insane five-pointed grave mounds might have been made; and he might conceivably have prepared rough, hasty sketches – varying in their accuracy or lack of it – which outlined the neighboring parts of the city and traced the way from a circularly represented place outside our previous route – a place we identified as a great cylindrical tower in the carvings and as a vast circular gulf glimpsed in our aerial survey – to the present five-pointed structure and the tunnel mouth therein.

He might, I repeat, have prepared such sketches; for those before us were quite obviously compiled, as our own had been, from late sculptures somewhere in the glacial labyrinth, though not from the ones which we had seen and used. But what that art-blind bungler could never have done was to execute those sketches in a strange and assured technique perhaps superior, despite haste and carelessness, to any of the decadent carvings from which they were taken – the characteristic and unmistakable technique of the Old Ones themselves in the dead city's heyday.

There are those who will say Danforth and I were utterly mad not to flee for our lives after that; since our conclusions were now – notwithstanding their wildness – completely fixed, and of a nature I need not even mention to those who have read my account as far as this. Perhaps we were mad – for have I not said those horrible peaks were mountains of madness? But I think I can detect something of the same spirit – albeit in a less extreme form – in the men who stalk deadly beasts through African jungles to photograph them or study their habits. Half paralysed with terror though we were, there was nevertheless fanned within us a blazing flame of awe and curiosity which triumphed in the end.

Of course we did not mean to face that – or those – which we knew had been there, but we felt that they must be gone by now. They would by this time have found the other neighboring entrance to the abyss, and have passed within, to whatever night-black fragments of the past might await them in the ultimate gulf – the ultimate gulf they had never seen. Or if that entrance, too, was blocked, they would have gone on to the north seeking another. They were, we remembered, partly independent of light.

Looking back to that moment, I can scarcely recall just what precise form our new emotions took – just what change of immediate objective it was that so sharpened our sense of expectancy. We certainly did not mean to face what we feared – yet I will not deny that we may have had a lurking, unconscious wish to spy certain things from some hidden vantage point. Probably we had not given up our zeal to glimpse the abyss itself, though there was interposed a new goal in the form of that great circular place shown on the crumpled sketches we had found. We had at once recognized it as a monstrous cylindrical tower figuring in the very earliest carvings, but appearing only as a prodigious round aperture from above. Something about the impressiveness of its renderings, even in these hasty diagrams, made us think that its subglacial levels must still form a feature of peculiar importance. Perhaps it embodied architectural marvels as yet unencountered by us. It was certainly of incredible age according to the sculptures in which it figured – being indeed among the first things built in the city. Its carvings, if preserved, could not but be highly significant. Morever, it might form a good present link with the upper world – a shorter route than the one we were so carefully blazing, and probably that by which those others had descended.

At any rate, the thing we did was to study the terrible sketches – which quite perfectly confirmed our own – and start back over the indicated course to the circular place; the course which our nameless predecessors must have traversed twice before us. The other neighboring gate to the abyss would lie beyond that. I need not speak of our journey – during which we continued to leave an economical trail of paper – for it was precisely the same in kind as that by which we had reached the cul-de-sac; except that it tended to adhere more closely to the ground level and even descend to basement corridors. Every now and then we could trace certain disturbing marks in the debris or litter underfoot; and after we had passed outside the radius of the gasoline scent we were again faintly conscious – spasmodically – of that more hideous and more persistent scent. After the way had branched from our former course we sometimes gave the rays of our single torch a furtive sweep along the walls; noting in almost every case the well-nigh omnipresent sculptures, which indeed seem to have formed a main aesthetic outlet for the Old Ones.

About 9:30 P.M., while traversing a long, vaulted corridor whose increasingly glaciated floor seemed somewhat below the ground level and whose roof grew lower as we advanced, we began to see strong daylight ahead and were able to turn off our torch. It appeared that we were coming to the vast circular place, and that our distance from the upper air could not be very great. The corridor ended in an arch surprisingly low for these megalithtic ruins, but we could see much through it even before we emerged. Beyond there stretched a prodigious round space – fully two hundred feet in diameter – strewn with debris and containing many choked archways corresponding to the one we were about to cross. The walls were – in available spaces – boldly sculptured into a spiral band of heroic proportions; and displayed, despite the destructive weathering caused by the openness of the spot, an artistic splendor far beyond anything we had encountered before. The littered floor was quite heavily glaciated, and we fancied that the true bottom lay at a considerably lower depth.

But the salient object of the place was the titanic stone ramp which, eluding the archways by a sharp turn outward into the open floor, wound spirally up the stupendous cylindrical wall like an inside counterpart of those once

112

climbing outside the monstrous towers or ziggurats of antique Babylon. Only the rapidity of our flight, and the perspective which confounded the descent with the tower's inner wall, had prevented our noticing this feature from the air, and thus caused us to seek another avenue to the subglacial level. Pabodie might have been able to tell what sort of engineering held it in place, but Danforth and I could merely admire and marvel. We could see mighty stone corbels and pillars here and there, but what we saw seemed inadequate to the function performed. The thing was excellently preserved up to the present top of the tower – a highly remarkable circumstance in view of its exposure – and its shelter had done much to protect the bizarre and disturbing cosmic sculptures on the walls.

As we stepped out into the awesome half daylight of this monstrous cylinder bottom – fifty million years old, and without doubt the most primally ancient structure ever to meet our eyes – we saw that the ramp-traversed sides stretched dizzily up to a height of fully sixty feet. This, we recall from our aerial survey, meant an outside glaciation of some forty feet; since the yawning gulf we had seen from the plane had been at the top of an approximately twenty-foot mound of crumbled masonry, somewhat sheltered for three-fourths of its circumference by the massive curving walls of a line of higher ruins. According to the sculptures the original tower had stood in the center of an immense circular plaza, and had been perhaps five hundred or six hundred feet high, with tiers of horizontal disks near the top, and a row of needlelike spires along the upper rim. Most of the masonry had obviously toppled outward rather than inward – a fortunate happening, since otherwise the ramp might have been shattered and the whole interior choked. As it was, the ramp showed sad battering; whilst the choking was such that all the archways at the bottom seemed to have been recently cleared.

It took us only a moment to conclude that this was indeed the route by which those others had descended, and that this would be the logical route for our own ascent despite the long trail of paper we had left elsewhere. The tower's mouth was no farther from the foothills and our waiting plane than was the great terraced building we had entered, and any further subglacial exploration we might make on this trip would lie in this general region. Oddly, we were still thinking about possible later trips – even after all we had seen and guessed. Then, as we picked our way cautiously over the debris of the great floor, there came a sight which for the time excluded all other matters.

It was the neatly huddled array of three sledges in that farther angle of the ramp's lower and outward-projecting course which had hitherto been screened from our view. There they were – the three sledges missing from Lake's camp – shaken by a hard usage which must have included forcible dragging along great reaches of snowless masonry and debris, as well as much hand portage over utterly unnavigable places. They were carefully and intelligently packed and strapped, and contained things memorably familiar enough: the gasoline stove, fuel cans, instrument cases, provision tins, tarpaulins obviously bulging with books, and some bulging with less obvious contents – everything derived from Lake's equipment.

After what we had found in that other room, we were in a measure prepared for this encounter. The really great shock came when we stepped over and undid one tarpaulin whose outlines had peculiarly disquieted us. It seems that others as well as Lake had been interested in collecting typical specimens; for there were two here, both stiffly frozen, perfectly preserved, patched with adhesive plaster where some wounds around the neck had occurred, and wrapped with care to prevent further damage. They were the bodies of young Gedney and the mission dog.

114

X

Many people will probably judge us callous as well as mad for thinking about the northward tunnel and the abyss so soon after our somber discovery, and I am not prepared to say that we would have immediately revived such thoughts but for a specific circumstance which broke in upon us and set up a whole new train of speculations. We had replaced the tarpaulin over poor Gedney and were standing in a kind of mute bewilderment when the sounds finally reached our consciousness – the first sounds we had heard since descending out of the open where the mountain wind whined faintly from its unearthly heights. Well-known and mundane though they were, their presence in this remote world of death was more unexpected and unnerving than any grotesque or fabulous tones could possibly have been – since they gave a fresh upsetting to all our notions of cosmic harmony.

Had it been some trace of that bizarre musical piping over a wide range which Lake's dissection report had led us to expect in those others – and which, indeed, our overwrought fancies had been reading into every wind howl we had heard since coming on the camp horror – it would have had a kind of hellish congruity with the aeon-dead region around us. A voice from other epochs belongs in a graveyard of other epochs. As it was, however, the noise shattered all our profoundly seated adjustments – all our tacit acceptance of the inner antarctic as a waste utterly and irrevocably void of every vestige of normal life. What we heard was not the fabulous note of any buried blasphemy of elder earth from whose supernal toughness an age-denied polar sun had evoked a monstrous response. Instead, it was a thing so mockingly normal and so unerringly familiarized by our sea days of Victoria Lane and our camp days at McMurdo Sound that we shuddered to think of it here, where such things ought not to be. To be brief – it was simply the raucous squawking of a penguin.

The muffled sound floated from subglacial recesses nearly opposite to the corridor whence we had come – regions manifestly in the direction of that other tunnel to the vast abyss. The presence of a living water bird in such a direction – in a world whose surface was one of age-long and uniform lifelessness – could lead to only one conclusion; hence our first thought was to verify the objective reality of the sound. It was, indeed, repeated, and seemed at times to come from more than one throat. Seeking its source, we entered an archway from which much debris had been cleared; resuming our trail blazing – with an added paper supply taken with curious repugnance from one of the tarpaulin bundles on the sledges – when we left daylight behind.

As the glaciated floor gave place to a litter of detritus, we plainly discerned some curious, dragging tracks; and once Danforth found a distinct print of a sort whose description would be only too superfluous. The course indicated by the penguin cries was precisely what our map and compass prescribed as an approach to the more northerly tunnel mouth, and we were glad to find that a bridgeless thorough-fare on the ground and basement levels seemed open. The tunnel, according to the chart, ought to start from the basement of a large pyramidal structure which we seemed vaguely to recall from our aerial survey as remarkably well-preserved. Along our path the single torch showed a customary profusion of carvings, but we did not pause to examine any of these.

Suddenly a bulky white shape loomed up ahead of us, and we flashed on the second torch. It is odd how wholly this new quest had turned our minds from earlier fears of what might lurk near. Those other ones, having left their supplies in the great circular place, must have planned to return after their scouting trip toward or into the abyss; yet we had now discarded all caution concerning them as completely as if they had never existed. This white, waddling thing was fully six feet high, yet we seemed to realize at once that it was not one of those others. They were larger and dark, and according to the sculptures, their motion over land surfaces was a swift, assured matter despite the queerness of their sea-born tentacle equipment. But to say that the white thing did not profoundly frighten us would be vain. We were indeed clutched for an instant by primitive dread almost sharper than the worst of our reasoned fears regarding those others. Then came a flash of anticlimax as the white shape sidled into a lateral archway to our left to join two others of its kind which had summoned it in raucous tones. For it was only a penguin – albeit of a huge, unknown species larger than the greatest of the known king penguins, and monstrous in its combined albinism and virtual eyelessness.

When we had followed the thing into the archway and turned both our torches on the indifferent and unheeding group of three we saw that they were all eyeless albinos of the same unknown and gigantic species. Their size reminded us of some of the archaic penguins depicted in the Old Ones' sculptures, and it did not take us long to conclude that they were descended from the same stock – undoubtedly surviving through a retreat to some warmer inner region whose perpetual blackness had destroyed their pigmentation and atrophied their eyes to mere useless slits. That their present habitat was the vast abyss we sought, was not for a moment to be doubted; and this evidence of the gulf's continued warmth and habitability filled us with the most curious and subtly perturbing fancies.

We wondered, too, what had caused these three birds to venture out of their usual domain. The state and silence of the great dead city made it clear that it had at no time been an habitual seasonal rookery, whilst the manifest indifference of the trio to our presence made it seem odd that any passing party of those others should have startled them. Was it possible that those others had taken some aggressive action or tried to increase their meat supply? We doubted whether that pungent odor which the dogs had hated could cause an equal antipathy in these penguins, since their ancestors had obviously lived on excellent terms with the Old Ones – an amicable relationship which must have survived in the abyss below as long as any of the Old Ones remained. Regretting – in a flare-up of the old spirit of pure science – that we could not photograph these anomalous creatures, we shortly left them to their squawking and pushed on toward the abyss whose openness was now so positively proved to us, and whose exact direction occasional penguin tracts made clear.

Not long afterward a steep descent in a long, low, doorless, and peculiarly sculptureless corridor led us to believe that we were approaching the tunnel mouth at last. We had passed two more penguins, and heard others immediately ahead. Then the corridor ended in a prodigious open space which made us gasp involuntarily – a perfect inverted hemisphere, obviously deep underground; fully a hundred feet in diameter and fifty feet high, with low archways opening around all parts of the circumference but one, and that one yawning cavernously with a black, arched aperture which broke the symmetry of the vault to a height of nearly fifteen feet. It was the entrance to the great abyss.

In this vast hemisphere, whose concave roof was impressively though decadently carved to a likeness of the primordial celestial dome, a few albino penguins waddled – aliens there, but indifferent and unseeing. The black tunnel yawned indefinitely off at a steep, descending grade, its aperture adorned with grotesquely chiseled jambs and lintel. From that cryptical mouth we fancied a current of slightly warmer air and perhaps even a suspicion of vapor proceeded; and we wondered what living entities other than penguins the limitless void below, and the contiguous honeycombings of the land and the titan mountains, might conceal. We wondered, too, whether the trace of mountain-top smoke at first suspected by poor Lake, as well as the odd haze we had ourselves perceived around the rampart-crowned peak, might not be caused by the tortuous-channeled rising of some such vapor from the unfathomed regions of earth's core.

Entering the tunnel, we saw that its outline was – at least at the start – about fifteen feet each way – sides, floor, and arched roof composed of the usual megalithic masonry. The sides were sparsely decorated with cartouches of conventional designs in a late, decadent style; and all the construction and carving were marvelously well-preserved. The floor was quite clear, except for a slight detritus bearing outgoing penguin tracks and the inward tracks of these others. The farther one advanced, the warmer it became; so that we were soon unbuttoning our heavy garments. We wondered whether there were any actually igneous manifestations below, and whether the waters of that sunless sea were hot. After a short distance the masonry gave place to solid rock, though the tunnel kept the same proportions and presented the same aspect of carved regularity. Occasionally its varying grade became so steep that grooves were cut in the floor. Several times we noted the mouths of small lateral galleries not recorded in our diagrams; none of them such as to complicate the problem of our return, and all of them welcome as possible refuges in case we met unwelcome entities on their way back from the abyss. The nameless scent of such things was very distinct. Doubtless it was

119

suicidally foolish to venture into that tunnel under the known conditions, but the lure of the unplumbed is stronger in certain persons than most suspect – indeed, it was just such a lure which had brought us to this unearthly polar waste in the first place. We saw several penguins as we passed along, and speculated on the distance we would have to traverse. The carvings had led us to expect a steep downhill walk of about a mile to the abyss, but our previous wanderings had shown us that matters of scale were not wholly to be depended on.

After about a quarter of a mile that nameless scent became greatly accentuated, and we kept very careful track of the various lateral openings we passed. There was no visible vapor as at the mouth, but this was doubtless due to the lack of contrasting cooler air. The temperature was rapidly ascending, and we were not surprised to come upon a careless heap of material shudderingly familiar to us. It was composed of furs and tent cloth taken from Lake's camp, and we did not pause to study the bizarre forms into which the fabrics had been slashed. Slightly beyond this point we noticed a decided increase in the size and number of the side galleries, and concluded that the densely honeycombed region beneath the higher foothills must now have been reached. The nameless scent was now curiously mixed with another and scarcely less offensive odor – of what nature we could not guess, though we thought of decaying organisms and perhaps unknown subterranean fungi. Then came a startling expansion of the tunnel for which the carvings had not prepared us – a broadening and rising into a lofty, natural-looking elliptical cavern with a level floor, some seventy-five feet long and fifty broad, and with many immense side passages leading away into cryptical darkness.

Though this cavern was natural in appearance, an inspection with both torches suggested that it had been formed by the artificial destruction of several walls between adjacent honeycombings. The walls were rough, and the high, vaulted roof was thick with stalactites; but the solid rock floor had been smoothed off, and was free from all debris, detritus, or even dust to a positively abnormal extent. Except for the avenue through which we had come, this was true of the floors of all the great galleries opening off from it; and the singularity of the condition was such as to set us vainly puzzling. The curious new fetor which had supplemented the nameless scent was excessively pungent here; so much so that it destroyed all trace of the other. Something about this whole place, with its polished and almost glistening floor, struck us as more vaguely baffling and horrible than any of the monstrous things we had previously encountered.

The regularity of the passage immediately ahead, as well as the larger proportion of penguin-droppings there, prevented all confusion as to the right course amidst this plethora of equally great cave mouths. Nevertheless we resolved to resume our paper trailblazing if any further complexity should develop; for dust tracks, of course, could no longer be expected. Upon resuming our direct progress we cast a beam of torchlight over the tunnel walls – and stopped short in amazement at the supremely radical change which had come over the carvings in this part of the passage. We realized, of course, the great decadence of the Old Ones' sculpture at the time of the tunneling, and had indeed noticed the inferior workmanship of the arabesques in the stretches behind us. But now, in this deeper section beyond the cavern, there was a sudden difference wholly transcending explanation – a difference in basic nature as well as in mere quality, and involving so profound and calamitous a degradation of skill that nothing in the hitherto observed rate of decline could have led one to expect it.

This new and degenerate work was coarse, bold, and wholly lacking in delicacy of detail. It was countersunk with exaggerated depth in bands following the same general line as the sparse cartouches of the earlier sections, but the height of the reliefs did not reach the level of the general surface. Danforth had the idea that it was a second carving – a sort of palimpsest formed after the obliteration of a previous design. In nature it was wholly decorative and conventional, and consisted of crude spirals and angles roughly following the quintile mathematical tradition of the Old Ones, yet seemingly more like a parody than a perpetuation of that tradition. We could not get it out of our minds that some subtly but profoundly alien element had been added to the aesthetic feeling behind the technique – an alien element, Danforth guessed, that was responsible for the laborious substitution. It was like, yet disturbingly unlike, what we had come to recognize as the Old Ones' art; and I was persistently reminded of such hybrid things as the ungainly Palmyrene sculptures fashioned in the Roman manner. That others had recently noticed this belt of carving was hinted by the presence of a used flashlight battery on the floor in front of one of the most characteristic cartouches.

Since we could not afford to spend any considerable time in study, we resumed our advance after a cursory look; though frequently casting beams over the walls to see if any further decorative changes developed. Nothing of the sort was perceived, though the carvings were in places rather sparse because of the numerous mouths of smooth-floored lateral tunnels. We saw and heard fewer penguins, but thought we caught a vague suspicion of an infinitely distant chorus of them somewhere deep within the earth. The new and inexplicable odor was abominably strong, and we could detect scarcely a sign of that other nameless scent. Puffs of visible vapor ahead bespoke increasing contrasts in temperature, and the relative nearness of the sunless sea cliffs of the great abyss. Then, quite unexpectedly, we saw certain obstructions on the polished floor ahead – obstructions which were quite definitely not penguins – and turned on our second torch after making sure that the objects were quite stationary.

XI

Still another time have I come to a place where it is very difficult to proceed. I ought to be hardened by this stage; but there are some experiences and intimations which scar too deeply to permit of healing, and leave only such an added sensitiveness that memory reinspires all the original horror. We saw, as I have said, certain obstructions on the polished floor ahead; and I may add that our nostrils were assailed almost simultaneously by a very curious intensification of the strange prevailing fetor, now quite plainly mixed with the nameless stench of those others which had gone before. The light of the second torch left no doubt of what the obstructions were, and we dared approach them only because we could see, even from a distance, that they were quite as past all harming power as had been the six similar specimens unearthed from the monstrous star-mounded graves at poor Lake's camp.

They were, indeed, as lacking in completeness as most of those we had unearthed – though it grew plain from the thick, dark green pool gathering around them that their incompleteness was of infinitely greater recency. There seemed to be only four of them, whereas Lake's bulletins would have suggested no less than eight as forming the group which had preceded us. To find them in this state was wholly unexpected, and we wondered what sort of monstrous struggle had occurred down here in the dark.

Penguins, attacked in a body, retaliate savagely with their beaks and our ears now made certain the existence of a rookery far beyond. Had those others disturbed such a place and aroused murderous pursuit? The obstructions did not suggest it, for penguins' beaks against the tough tissues Lake had dissected could hardly account for the terrible damage our approaching glance was beginning to make out. Besides, the huge blind birds we had seen appeared to be singularly peaceful.

Had there, then, been a struggle among those others, and were the absent four responsible? If so, where were they? Were they close at hand and likely to form an immediate menace to us? We glanced anxiously at some of the smooth-floored lateral passages as we continued our slow and frankly reluctant approach. Whatever the conflict was, it had clearly been that which had frightened the penguins into their unaccustomed wandering. It must, then, have arisen near that faintly heard rookery in the incalculable gulf beyond, since there were no signs that any birds had normally dwelt here. Perhaps, we reflected, there had been a hideous running fight, with the weaker party seeking to get back to the cached sledges when their pursuers finished them. One could picture the demoniac fray between namelessly monstrous entities as it surged out of the black abyss with great clouds of frantic penguins squawking and scurrying ahead.

I say that we approached those sprawling and incomplete obstructions slowly and reluctantly. Would to Heaven we had never approached them at all, but had run back at top speed out of that blasphemous tunnel with the greasily smooth floors and the degenerate murals aping and mocking the things they had superseded – run back, before we had seen what we did see, and before our minds were burned with something which will never let us breathe easily again!

Both of our torches were turned on the prostrate objects, so that we soon realized the dominant factor in their incompleteness. Mauled, compressed, twisted, and ruptured as they were, their chief common injury was total decapitation. From each one the tentacled starfish head had been removed; and as we drew near we saw that the manner of removal looked more like some hellish tearing or suction than like any ordinary form of cleavage. Their noisome dark-green ichor formed a large, spreading pool; but its stench was half overshadowed by the newer and stranger stench, here more pungent than at any other point along our route. Only when we had come very close to the sprawling obstructions could we trace that second, unexplainable fetor to any immediate source – and the instant we did so Danforth, remembering certain very vivid sculptures of the Old Ones' history in the Permian Age one hundred and fifty million years ago, gave vent to a nerve-tortured cry which echoed hysterically through that vaulted and archaic passage with the evil, palimpsest carvings.

I came only just short of echoing his cry myself; for I had seen those primal sculptures, too, and had shudderingly admired the way the nameless artist had suggested that hideous slime coating found on certain incomplete and prostrate Old Ones – those whom the frightful Shoggoths had characteristically slain and sucked to a ghastly headlessness in the great war of resubjugation. They were infamous, nightmare sculptures even when telling of age-old, bygone things; for Shoggoths and their work ought not to be seen by human beings or portrayed by any beings. The mad author of the *Necronomicon* had nervously tried to swear that none had been bred on this planet, and that only drugged dreamers had even conceived them. Formless protoplasm able to mock and reflect all forms and organs

125

and processes – viscous agglutinations of bubbling cells – rubbery fifteen-foot spheroids infinitely plastic and ductile – slaves of suggestion, builders of cities – more and more sullen, more and more intelligent, more and more amphibious, more and more imitative! Great God! What madness made even those blasphemous Old Ones willing to use and carve such things?

And now, when Danforth and I saw the freshly glistening and reflectively iridescent black slime which clung thickly to those headless bodies and stank obscenely with that new, unknown odor whose cause only a diseased fancy could envisage – clung to those bodies and sparkled less voluminously on a smooth part of the accursedly resculptured wall in a series of grouped dots – we understood the quality of cosmic fear to its uttermost depths. It was not fear of those four missing others – for all too well did we suspect they would do no harm again. Poor devils! After all, they were not evil things of their kind. They were the men of another age and another order of being. Nature had played a hellish jest on them – as it will on any others that human madness, callousness, or cruelty may hereafter dig up in that hideously dead or sleeping polar waste – and this was their tragic homecoming. They had not been even savages – for what indeed had they done? That awful awakening in the cold of an unknown epoch – perhaps an attack by the furry, frantically barking quadrupeds, and a dazed defense against them and the equally frantic white simians with the queer wrappings and paraphernalia ... poor Lake, poor Gedney ... and poor Old Ones! Scientists to the last – what had they done that we would not have done in their place? God, what intelligence and persistence! What a facing of the incredible, just as those carven kinsmen and forebears had faced things only a little less incredible! Radiates, vegetables, monstrosities, star spawn – whatever they had been, they were men!

They had crossed the icy peaks on whose templed slopes they had once worshipped and roamed among the tree ferns. They had found their dead city brooding under its curse, and had read its carven latter days as we had done. They had tried to reach their living fellows in fabled depths of blackness they had never seen – and what had they found? All this flashed in unison through the thoughts of Danforth and me as we looked from those headless, slime-coated shapes to the loathsome palimpsest sculptures and the diabolical dot groups of fresh slime on the wall beside them – looked and understood what must have triumphed and survived down there in the Cyclopean water city of that nighted, penguin-fringed abyss, whence even now a sinister curling mist had begun to belch pallidly as if in answer to Danforth's hysterical scream.

The shock of recognizing that monstrous slime and headlessness had frozen us into mute, motionless statues, and it is only through later conversations that we have learned of the complete identity of our thoughts at that moment. It seemed aeons that we stood there, but actually it could not have been more than ten or fifteen seconds. That hateful, pallid mist curled forward as if veritably driven by some remoter advancing bulk – and then came a sound which upset much of what we had just decided, and in so doing broke the spell and enabled us to run like mad past squawking, confused penguins over our former trail back to the city, along ice-sunken megalithic corridors to the great open circle, and up that archaic spiral ramp in a frenzied, automatic plunge for the sane outer air and light of day.

The new sound, as I have intimated, upset much that we had decided; because it was what poor Lake's dissection had led us to attribute to those we had judged dead. It was, Danforth later told me, precisely what he had caught in infinitely muffled form when at that spot beyond the alley corner above the glacial level; and it certainly had a shocking resemblance to the wind pipings we had both heard around the lofty mountain caves. At the risk of seeming puerile I will add another thing, too, if only because of the surprising way Danforth's impressions chimed with mine. Of course common reading is what prepared us both to make the interpretation, though Danforth has hinted at queer notions about unsuspected and forbidden sources to which Poe may have had access when writing his *Arthur Gordon Pym* a century ago. It will be remembered that in that fantastic tale there is a word of unknown but terrible and prodigious significance connected with the antarctic and screamed eternally by the gigantic spectrally snowy birds of that malign region's core. '*Tekeli-li! Tekeli-li!*' That, I may admit, is exactly what we thought we heard conveyed by that sudden sound behind the advancing white mist – that insidious musical piping over a singularly wide range.

We were in full flight before three notes or syllables had been uttered, though we knew that the swiftness of the Old Ones would enable any scream-roused and pursuing survivor of the slaughter to overtake us in a moment if it really wished to do so. We had a vague hope, however, that nonaggressive conduct and a display of kindred reason might cause such a being to spare us in case of capture, if only from scientific curiosity. After all, if such a one had nothing to fear for itself it would have no motive in harming us. Concealment being futile at this juncture, we used our torch for a running glance behind, and perceived that the mist was thinning. Would we see at last, a complete and living specimen of those others? Again came that insidious musical piping – '*Tekeli-li! Tekeli-li!*'

Then, noting that we were actually gaining on our pursuer, it occurred to us that the entity might be wounded. We could take no chances, however, since it was very obviously approaching in answer to Danforth's scream, rather than in flight from any other entity. The timing was too close to admit of doubt. Of the whereabouts of that less conceivable and less mentionable nightmare – that fetid, unglimpsed mountain of slime-spewing protoplasm whose race had conquered the abyss and sent land pioneers to recarve and squirm through the burrows of the hills – we could form no guess; and it cost us a genuine pang to leave this probably crippled Old One – perhaps a lone survivor – to the peril of recapture and a nameless fate.

Thank Heaven we did not slacken our run. The curling mist had thickened again, and was driving ahead with increased speed; whilst the straying penguins in our rear were squawking and screaming and displaying signs of a panic really surprising in view of their relatively minor confusion when we had passed them. Once more came that sinister, wide-ranged piping – '*Tekeli-li! Tekeli-li!*' We had been wrong. The thing was not wounded, but had merely paused on encountering the bodies of its fallen kindred and the hellish slime inscription above them. We could never know what that demon message was – but those burials at Lake's camp had shown how much importance the beings attached to their dead. Our recklessly used torch now revealed ahead of us the large open cavern where various ways converged, and we were glad to be leaving those morbid palimpsest sculptures – almost felt even when scarcely seen – behind.

Another thought which the advent of the cave inspired was the possibility of losing our pursuer at this bewildering focus of large galleries. There were several of the blind albino penguins in the open space, and it seemed clear that their fear of the oncoming entity was extreme to the point of unaccountability. It at that point we dimmed our torch to the very lowest limit of traveling need, keeping it strictly in front of us, the frightened squawking motions of the huge birds in the mist might muffle our footfalls, screen our true course, and somehow set up a false lead. Amidst the churning, spiraling fog the littered and unglistening floor of the main tunnel beyond this point, as differing from the other morbidly polished burrows, could hardly form a highly distinguishing feature; even, so far as we could conjecture, for those indicated special senses which made the Old Ones partly, though imperfectly, independent of light in emergencies. In fact, we were somewhat apprehensive lest we go astray ourselves in our haste. For we had, of course, decided to keep straight on toward the dead city; since the consequences of loss in those unknown foothill honeycombings would be unthinkable.

The fact that we survived and emerged is sufficient proof that the thing did take a wrong gallery whilst we providentially hit on the right one. The penguins alone could not have saved us, but in conjunction with the mist they seem to have done so. Only a benign fate kept the curling vapors thick enough at the right moment, for they were constantly shifting and threatening to vanish. Indeed, they did lift for a second just before we emerged from the nauseously resculptured tunnel into the cave; so that we actually caught our first and only half glimpse of the oncoming entity as we cast a final, desperately fearful glance backward before dimming the torch and mixing with the penguins in the hope of dodging pursuit. If the fate which screened us was benign, that which gave us the half glimpse was infinitely the opposite; for to that flash of semivision can be traced a full half of the horror which has ever since haunted us.

Our exact motive in looking back again was perhaps no more than the immemorial instinct of the pursued to gauge the nature and course of its pursuer; or perhaps it was an automatic attempt to answer a subconscious question raised by one of our senses. In the midst of our flight, with all our faculties centered on the problem of escape, we were in no condition to observe and analyze details; yet even so our latent brain cells must have wondered at the message brought them by our nostrils. Afterward we realized what it was – that our retreat from the fetid slime coating on those headless obstructions, and the coincident approach of the pursuing entity had not brought us the exchange of stenches which logic called for. In the neighborhood of the prostrate things that new and lately unexplainable fetor had been wholly dominant; but by this time it ought to have largely given place to the nameless stench associated with those others. This it had not done – for instead, the newer and less bearable smell was now virtually undiluted, and growing more and more poisonously insistent each second.

So we glanced back simultaneously, it would appear; though no doubt the incipient motion of one prompted the imitation of the other. As we did so we flashed both torches full strength at the momentarily thinned mist; either from sheer primitive anxiety to see all we could, or in a less primitive but equally unconscious effort to dazzle the entity before we dimmed our light and dodged among the penguins of the labyrinth center ahead. Unhappy act! Not Orpheus himself, or Lot's wife, paid much more dearly for a backward glance. And again came that shocking, wide-ranged piping – '*Tekeli-li! Tekeli-li!*'

I might as well be frank – even if I cannot bear to be quite direct – in stating what we saw; though at the time we felt that it was not to be admitted even to each other. The words reaching the reader can never even suggest the awfulness of the sight itself. It crippled our consciousness so completely that I wonder we had the residual sense to dim our torches as planned, and to strike the right tunnel toward the dead city. Instinct alone must have carried us through – perhaps better than reason could have done; though if that was what saved us, we paid a high price. Of reason we certainly had little enough left.

Danforth was totally unstrung, and the first thing I remember of the rest of the journey was hearing him light-headedly chant an hysterical formula in which I alone of mankind could have found anything but insane irrelevance. It reverberated in falsetto echoes among the squawks of the penguins; reverberated through the vaultings ahead, and – thank God – through the now empty vaultings behind. He could not have begun it at once – else we would not have been alive and blindly racing. I shudder to think of what a shade of difference in his nervous reactions might have brought.

'South Station Under – Washington Under – Park Street Under – Kendall – Central – Harvard—' The poor fellow was chanting the familiar stations of the Boston-Cambridge tunnel that burrowed through our peaceful native soil thousands of miles away in New England, yet to me the ritual had neither irrelevance nor home feeling. It had only horror, because I knew unerringly the monstrous, nefandous analogy that had suggested it. We had expected, upon looking back, to see a terrible and incredible moving entity if the mists were thin enough; but of that entity we had formed a clear idea. What we did see – for the mists were indeed all too malignly thinned – was something altogether different, and immeasurably more hideous and detestable. It was the utter, objective embodiment of the fantastic novelist's 'thing that should not be'; and its nearest comprehensible analogue is a vast onrushing subway train as one sees it from a station platform – the great black front looming colossally out of infinite subterranean distance, constellated with strangely colored lights and filling the prodigious burrow as a piston fills a cylinder.

But we were not on a station platform. We were on the track ahead as the nightmare, plastic column of fetid black iridescence oozed tightly onward through its fifteen-foot sinus, gathering unholy speed and driving before it a spiral,

132

rethickening cloud of the pallid abyss vapor. It was a terrible, indescribable thing vaster than any subway train – a shapeless congeries of protoplasmic bubbles, faintly self-luminous, and with myriads of temporary eyes forming and unforming as pustules of greenish light all over the tunnel-filling front that bore down upon us, crushing the frantic penguins and slithering over the glistening floor that it and its kind had swept so evilly free of all litter. Still came that eldritch, mocking cry – *'Tekeli-li! Tekeli-li!'* and at last we remembered that the demoniac Shoggoths – given life, thought, and plastic organ patterns solely by the Old Ones, and having no language save that which the dot groups expressed – had likewise no voice save the imitated accents of their bygone masters.

XII

Danforth and I have recollections of emerging into the great sculptured hemisphere and of threading our back trail through the Cyclopean rooms and corridors of the dead city; yet these are purely dream fragments involving no memory of volition, details or physical exertion. It was as if we floated in a nebulous world or dimension without time, causation, or orientation. The gray half-daylight of the vast circular space sobered us somewhat; but we did not go near those cached sledges or look again at poor Gedney and the dog. They have a strange and titanic mausoleum, and I hope the end of this planet will find them still undisturbed.

It was while struggling up the colossal spiral incline that we first felt the terrible fatigue and short breath which our race through the thin plateau air had produced; but not even fear of collapse could make us pause before reaching the normal outer realm of sun and sky. There was something vaguely appropriate about our departure from those buried epochs; for as we wound our panting way up the sixty-foot cylinder of primal masonry we glimpsed beside us a continuous procession of heroic sculptures in the dead race's early and undecayed technique – a farewell from the Old Ones, written fifty million years ago.

Finally scrambling out at the top, we found ourselves on a great mound of tumbled blocks, with the curved walls of higher stonework rising westward, and the brooding peaks of the great mountains showing beyond the more crumbled structures toward the east. The low antarctic sun of midnight peered redly from the southern horizon through rifts in the jagged ruins, and the terrible age and deadness of the nightmare city seemed all the starker by contrast with such relatively known and accustomed things as the features of the polar landscape. The sky above was a churning and opalescent mass of tenuous ice-vapors, and the cold clutched at our vitals. Wearily resting the outfit-bags to which we had instinctively clung throughout our desperate flight, we rebuttoned our heavy garments for the stumbling climb down the mound and the walk through the aeon-old stone maze to the foothills where our aeroplane waited. Of what had set us fleeing from that darkness of earth's secret and archaic gulfs we said nothing at all.

In less than a quarter of an hour we had found the steep grade to the foothills – the probable ancient terrace – by which we had descended, and could see the dark bulk of our great plane amidst the sparse ruins on the rising slope ahead. Halfway uphill toward our goal we paused for a momentary breathing spell, and turned to look again at the fantastic tangle of incredible stone shapes below us – once more outlined mystically against an unknown west. As we did so we saw that the sky beyond had lost its morning haziness; the restless ice-vapors having moved up to the zenith, where their mocking outlines seemed on the point of

134

settling into some bizarre pattern which they feared to make quite definite or conclusive.

There now lay revealed on the ultimate white horizon behind the grotesque city a dim, elfin line of pinnacled violet whose needle-pointed heights loomed dreamlike against the beckoning rose color of the western sky. Up toward this shimmering rim sloped the ancient tableland, the depressed course of the bygone river traversing it as an irregular ribbon of shadow. For a second we gasped in admiration of the scene's unearthly cosmic beauty, and then vague horror began to creep into our souls. For this far violet line could be nothing else than the terrible mountains of the forbidden land – highest of earth's peaks and focus of earth's evil; harborers of nameless horrors and Archaean secrets; shunned and prayed to by those who feared to carve their meaning; untrodden by any living thing on earth, but visited by the sinister lightnings and sending strange beams across the plains in the polar night – beyond doubt the unknown archetype of that dreaded Kadath in the Cold Waste beyond abhorrent Leng, whereof primal legends hint evasively.

If the sculptured maps and pictures in that prehuman city had told truly, these cryptic violet mountains could not be much less than three hundred miles away; yet none the less sharply did their dim elfin essence appear above that remote and snowy rim, like the serrated edge of a monstrous alien planet about to rise into unaccustomed heavens. Their height, then, must have been tremendous beyond all comparison – carrying them up into tenuous atmospheric strata peopled only by such gaseous wraiths as rash flyers have barely lived to whisper of after unexplainable falls. Looking at them, I thought nervously of certain sculptured hints of what the great bygone river had washed down into the city from their accursed slopes – and wondered how much sense and how much folly had lain in the fears of those Old Ones

135

who carved them so reticently. I recalled how their northerly end must come near the coast at Queen Mary Land, where even at that moment Sir Douglas Mawson's expedition was doubtless working less than a thousand miles away; and hoped that no evil fate would give Sir Douglas and his men a glimpse of what might lie beyond the protecting coastal range. Such thoughts formed a measure of my overwrought condition at the time – and Danforth seemed to be even worse.

Yet long before we had passed the great star-shaped ruin and reached our plane our fears had become transferred to the lesser but vast-enough range whose recrossing lay ahead of us. From these foothills the black, ruin-crusted slopes reared up starkly and hideously against the east, again reminding us of those strange Asian paintings of Nicholas Roerich; and when we thought of the frightful amorphous entities that might have pushed their fetidly squirming way even to the topmost hollow pinnacles, we could not face without panic the prospect of again sailing by those suggestive skyward cave mouths where the wind made sounds like an evil musical piping over a wide range. To make matters worse, we saw distinct traces of local mist around several of the summits – as poor Lake must have done when he made that early mistake about volcanism – and thought shiveringly of that kindred mist from which we had just escaped; of that, and of the blasphemous, horror-fostering abyss whence all such vapors came.

All was well with the plane, and we clumsily hauled on our heavy flying furs, Danforth got the engine started without trouble, and we made a very smooth take-off over the nightmare city. Below us the primal Cyclopean masonry spread out as it had done when first we saw it, and we began rising and turning to test the wind for our crossing through the pass. At a very high level there must have been great disturbance, since the ice-dust clouds of the zenith were doing all sorts of fantastic things; but at twenty-four thousand feet, the height we needed for the pass, we found navigation quite practicable. As we drew close to the jutting peaks the wind's strange piping again became manifest, and I could see Danforth's hands trembling at the controls. Rank amateur that I was, I thought at that moment that I might be a better navigator than he in effecting the dangerous crossing between pinnacles; and when I made motions to change seats and take over duties he did not protest. I tried to keep all my skill and self-possession about me and stared at the sector of reddish farther sky betwixt the walls of the pass – resolutely refusing to pay attention to the puffs of mountain-top vapor, and wishing that I had wax-stopped ears like Ulysses' men off the Siren's coast to keep that disturbing wind-piping from my consciousness.

But Danforth, released from his piloting and keyed up to a dangerous nervous pitch, could not keep quiet. I felt him turning and wriggling about as he looked back at the terrible receding city, ahead at the cave-riddled, cube-barnacled peaks, sidewise at the bleak sea of snowy, rampart-strewn foothills, and upward at the seething, grotesquely clouded sky. It was then, just as I was trying to steer safely through the pass, that his mad shrieking brought us so close to disaster by shattering my tight hold on myself and causing me to fumble helplessly with the controls for a moment. A second afterward my resolution triumphed and we made the crossing safely – yet I am afraid that Danforth will never be the same again.

I have said that Danforth refused to tell me what final horror made him scream out so insanely – a horror which, I feel sadly sure, is mainly responsible for his present break-down. We had snatches of shouted conversation above the wind's piping and the engine's buzzing as we reached the safe side of the range and swooped slowly down toward the camp, but that had mostly to do with the pledges of secrecy we had made as we prepared to leave the nightmare city. Certain things, we had agreed, were not for people to know and discuss lightly – and I would not speak of them now but for the need of heading off that Starkweather-Moore expedition, and others, at any cost. It is absolutely necessary, for the peace and safety of mankind, that some of earth's dark, dead corners and unplumbed depths be let alone; lest sleeping abnormalities wake to resurgent life, and blasphemously surviving nightmares squirm and splash out of their black lairs to newer and wider conquests.

All that Danforth has ever hinted is that the final horror was a mirage. It was not, he declares, anything connected with the cubes and caves of those echoing, vaporous, wormily-honeycombed mountains of madness which we crossed; but a single fantastic, demoniac glimpse, among the churning zenith clouds, of what lay back of those other violet westward mountains which the Old Ones had shunned and feared. It is very probable that the thing was a sheer delusion born of the previous stresses we had passed through, and of the actual though unrecognized mirage of the dead transmontane city experienced near Lake's camp the day before; but it was so real to Danforth that he suffers from it still.

He has on rare occasions whispered disjointed and irresponsible things about 'The black pit', 'the carven rim', 'the proto-Shoggoths', 'the windowless solids with five dimensions', 'the nameless cylinder', 'the elder Pharos', 'Yog-Sothoth', 'the primal white jelly', 'the color out of space', 'the wings', 'the eyes in darkness', 'the moon-ladder', 'the original, the eternal, the undying', and other bizarre conceptions; but when he is fully himself he repudiates all this and attributes it to his curious and macabre reading of earlier years. Danforth, indeed, is known to be among the few who have ever dared go completely through that worm-riddled copy of the *Necronomicon* kept under lock and key in the college library.

The higher sky, as we crossed the range, was surely vaporous and disturbed enough; and although I did not see the zenith I can well imagine that its swirls of ice dust may have taken strange forms. Imagination, knowing how vividly distant scenes can sometimes be reflected, refracted, and magnified by such layers of restless cloud, might easily have supplied the rest – and, of course, Danforth did not hint any of these specific horrors till after his memory had had a chance to draw on his bygone reading. He could never have seen so much in one instantaneous glance.

At the time, his shrieks were confined to the repetition of a single, mad word of all too obvious source: '*Tekeli-li! Tekeli-li!*'

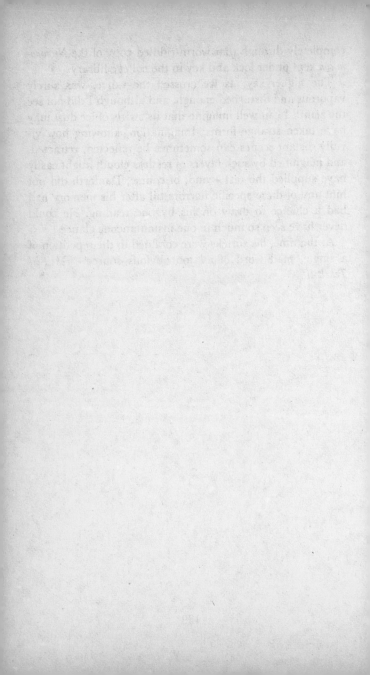

The Case of
Charles Dexter
Ward

'The essential Saltes of Animals may be so prepared and preserved, that an ingenious Man may have the whole Ark of Noah in his owne Studie and raise the fine shape of an Animal out of its Ashes at his Pleasure; and by the lyke method from the essential Saltes of humane Dust, a Philosopher may, without any criminal Necromancy, call up the Shape of any dead Ancestour from the Dust whereinto his Bodie has been incinerated.'
Borellus

CHAPTER ONE

A Result and a Prologue

1

From a private hospital for the insane near Providence, Rhode Island, there recently disappeared an exceedingly singular person. He bore the name of Charles Dexter Ward, and was placed under restraint most reluctantly by the grieving father who had watched his aberration grow from a mere eccentricity to a dark mania involving both a possibility of murderous tendencies and a peculiar change in the apparent contents of his mind. Doctors confess themselves quite baffled by his case, since it presented oddities of a general physiological as well as psychological character.

In the first place, the patient seemed oddly older than his twenty-six years would warrant. Mental disturbance, it is true, will age one rapidly; but the face of this young man had taken on a subtle cast which only the very aged normally acquire. In the second place, his organic processes showed a certain queerness of proportion, which nothing in medical experience can parallel. Respiration and heart action had a baffling lack of symmetry, the voice was lost, so that no sounds above a whisper were possible, digestion was incredibly prolonged and minimized, and neural reactions to standard stimuli bore no relation to anything heretofore recorded, either normal or pathological. The skin had a morbid chill and dryness, and the cellular structure of the tissue seemed exaggeratedly coarse and loosely knit. Even a large olive birthmark on his right hip had disappeared, while there had formed on his chest a very peculiar mole or blackish spot of which no trace existed before. In general,

143

all physicians agree that in Ward the processes of metabolism had become retarded to a degree beyond precedent.

Psychologically, too, Charles Ward was unique. His
madness held no affinity to any sort recorded in even the
latest and most exhaustive of treatises, and was enjoined to
be a mental force which would have made him a genius or a
leader had it not been twisted into strange and grotesque
forms. Dr Willett, who was Ward's family physician affirms
that the patient's gross mental capacity, as gauged by his
response to matters outside the sphere of his insanity, had
actually increased since the seizure. Ward, it is true, was
always a scholar and an antiquarian; but even his most
brilliant early work did not show the prodigious grasp and
insight displayed during his examinations by the alienists.
It was, indeed, a difficult matter to obtain a legal commit-
ment to the hospital, so powerful and lucid did the youth's
mind seem; and only on the evidence of others, and on the
strength of many abnormal gaps in his stock of information
as distinguished from his intelligence was he finally placed
in confinement. To the very moment of his vanishment he
was an omnivorous reader and as great a conversationalist
as his poor voice permitted; and shrewd observers, failing to
foresee his escape, freely predicted that he would not be
long in gaining his discharge from custody.

2

Only Dr Willett, who had brought Charles Ward into the
world and watched his growth of body and mind ever since,
seemed frightened at the thought of this future freedom. He
had had a terrible experience and had made a terrible
discovery which he dared not reveal to his skeptical colleagues. Willett, indeed, presents a minor mystery all his

own in his connection with the case. He was the last to see the patient before his flight, and emerged from that final conversation in a state of mixed horror and relief which several recalled when Ward's escape became known three hours later. That escape itself is one of the unsolved wonders of Dr Waite's hospital. A window open above a sheer drop of sixty feet would hardly explain it, yet after that talk with Willett the youth was undeniably gone. Willett himself has no public explanations to offer, though he seems strangely easier in mind than before the escape. Many, indeed, feel that he would like to say more if he thought any considerable number would believe him. He had found Ward in his room, but shortly after his departure the attendants knocked in vain. When they opened the door the patient was not there, and all they found was the open window with a chill April breeze blowing in a cloud of fine bluish-gray dust that almost choked them. True, the dogs howled some time before, but that was while Willett was still present, and they had caught nothing and shown no disturbance later on. Ward's father was told at once over the telephone, but he seemed more saddened than surprised. By the time Dr Waite called in person, Dr Willett had been talking with him, and both disavowed any knowledge or complicity in the escape. Only from certain closely confidential friends of Willett and the senior Ward have any clues been gained, and even these are too wildly fantastic for general credence. The one fact which remains is that up to the present time no trace of the missing madman has been unearthed.

Charles Ward was an antiquarian from infancy, no doubt gaining his taste from the venerable town around him, and from the relics of the past which filled every corner of his parents' old mansion in Prospect Street on the crest of the hill. With the years his devotion to ancient things increased; so that history, genealogy, and the study of Colonial architecture, furniture, and craftsmanship at length crowded everything else from his sphere of interests. These tastes are important to remember in considering his madness; for although they do not form its absolute nucleus, they play a prominent part in its superficial form. The gaps of information which the alienists noticed were all related to modern matters and were invariably offset by a correspondingly excessive though outwardly concealed knowledge of bygone matters as brought out by adroit questioning: so that one would have fancied the patient literally transferred to a former age through some obscure sort of autohypnosis. The odd thing was that Ward seemed no longer interested in the antiquaries he knew so well. He had, it appears, lost his regard for them through sheer familiarity; and all his final efforts were obviously bent toward mastering those common facts of the modern world which had been so totally and unmistakably expunged from his brain. That this wholesale deletion had occurred, he did his best to hide; but it was clear to all who watched him that his whole program of reading and conversation was determined by a frantic wish to imbibe such knowledge of his own life and of the ordinary practical and cultural background of the twentieth century as ought to have been his by virtue of his birth in 1902 and his education in the schools of our own time. Alienists are now wondering how, in view of his wholly impaired stock of data, the escaped patient manages to cope with the complicated world of today; the dominant opinion being that he is "lying low" in some humble and unexacting position till his stock of modern information can be brought up to the normal.

The beginning of Ward's madness is a matter of dispute among alienists. Dr Lyman, the eminent Boston authority, places it in 1919 or 1920, during the boy's last year at the Moses Brown School, where he suddenly turned from the study of the past to the study of the occult, and refused to qualify for college on the ground that he had individual researches of much greater importance to make. This is certainly brought out by Ward's altered habits at the time, especially by his continual search through town records and among old burying grounds for a certain grave dug in 1771; the grave of an ancestor named Joseph Curwen, some of whose papers he professed to have found behind the panelling of a very old house in Olney Court, on Stampers Hill, which Curwen was known to have occupied.

It is, broadly speaking, undeniable that the winter of 1919–20 saw a great change in Ward; whereby he abruptly stopped his general antiquarian pursuits and embarked on a desperate delving into occult subjects both at home and abroad, varied only by this strangely persistent search for his forefather's grave.

From this opinion, however, Dr. Willett substantially dissents, basing his verdict on his close and continuous knowledge of the patient, and on certain frightful investigations and discoveries which he made toward the last. Those investigations and discoveries have left their mark upon him; so that his voice trembles when he tells them, and his hand trembles when he tries to write of them. Willett admits that the change of 1919–20 would ordinarily appear to mark the beginning of a progressive decadence which culminated in the horrible sad uncanny alienation of 1928, but believes from personal observation that a finer distinction must be made. Granting freely that the boy was always ill-balanced temperamentally, and prone to be unduly susceptible and enthusiastic in his responses to phenomena around him, he refuses to concede that the early alteration marked the actual passage from sanity to madness; crediting instead Ward's own statement that he had discovered or rediscovered something whose effect on human thought was likely to be marvelous and profound.

The true madness, he is certain, came with a later change; after the Curwen portrait and the ancient papers had been unearthed; after a trip to strange foreign places had been made, and some terrible invocations chanted under strange and secret circumstances; after certain *answers* to these invocations had been plainly indicated, and a frantic letter penned under agonizing and inexplicable conditions; after the wave of vampirism and the ominous Pawtuxet gossip; and after the patient's memory commenced to exclude contemporary images whilst his voice failed and his physical aspect underwent the subtle modification so many subsequently noticed.

It was only about this time, Willett points out with much acuteness, that the nightmare qualities became indubitably linked with Ward, and the doctor feels shudderingly sure that enough solid evidence exists to sustain the youth's claim regarding his crucial discovery. In the first place, two workmen of high intelligence saw Joseph Curwen's ancient papers found. Secondly, the boy once showed him those papers and a page of the Curwen diary, and each of the documents had every appearance of genuineness. The hole where Ward claimed to have found them is a visible reality, and Willett had a very convincing final glimpse of them in surroundings which can scarcely be believed and can never perhaps be proved. Then there were the mysteries and coincidences of the Orne and Hutchinson letters, and the problem of the Curwen penmanship and of what the detectives brought to light about Dr Allen; these things, and the terrible message in mediaeval minuscules found in Willett's pocket when he gained consciousness after his shocking experience.

And most conclusive of all, there are the two hideous *results* which the doctor obtained from a certain pair of formulae during his final investigations; results which virtually proved the authenticity of the papers and of their monstrous implications at the same time that those papers were borne for ever from human knowledge.

3

One must look back at Charles Ward's earlier life as at something belonging as much to the past as the antiquities he loved so keenly. In the autumn of 1918, and with a considerable show of zest in the military training of the period, he had begun his Junior year at the Moses Brown School, which lies very near his home. The old main building, erected in 1819, had always charmed his youthful antiquarian sense; and the spacious park in which the Academy is set appealed to his eye for landscape. His social activities were few; and his hours were spent mainly at home, in rambling walks, in his classes and drills, and in pursuit of antiquarian and genealogical data at the City Hall, the State House, the Public Library, the Athenaeum, the Historical Society, the John Carter Brown and John Hay Libraries of Brown University, and the newly opened Shepley Library in Benefit Street. One may picture him yet as he was in those days; tall, slim, and blond, with studious eyes and a slight stoop, dressed somewhat carelessly, and giving a dominant impression of harmless awkwardness rather than attractiveness.

His walks were always adventures in antiquity, during which he managed to recapture from the myriad relics of a glamorous old city a vivid and connected picture of the centuries before. His home was a great Georgian mansion atop the well-nigh precipitous hill that rises just east of the river, and from the rear windows of its rambling wings he could look dizzily out over all the clustered spires, domes, roofs and sky-scraper summits of the lower town to the purple hills of the countryside beyond. Here he was born, and from the lovely classic porch of the double-bayed brick façade his nurse had first wheeled him in his carriage; past the little white farmhouse of two hundred years before that the town had long overtaken, and on toward the stately colleges along the stately, sumptuous street, whose old square brick mansions and smaller wooden houses with narrow, heavy-columned Doric porches dreamed solid and exclusive amidst their generous yards and gardens.

He had been wheeled, too, along sleepy Congdon Street, one tier lower down on the steep hill, and with all its eastern houses on high terraces. The small wooden houses averaged a greater age here, for it was up this hill that the growing town had climbed; and in these rides he had imbibed something of the colour of a quaint Colonial village. The nurse used to stop and sit on the benches of Prospect Terrace to chat with policemen; and one of the child's first memories was of the great westward sea of hazy roofs and domes and steeples and far hills which he saw one winter afternoon from that great railed embankment, all violet and mystic against a fevered apocalyptic sunset of reds and golds and purples and curious greens. The vast marble dome of the State House stood out in massive silhouette, its crowning statue haloed fantastically by a break in one of the tinted stratus clouds that barred the flaming sky.

When he was larger his famous walks began; first with his impatiently dragged nurse and then alone in dreamy meditation. Farther and farther down that almost perpendicular hill he would venture, each time reaching older and quainter levels of the ancient city. He would hesitate gingerly down vertical Jenckes Street with its back walls and Colonial gables to the shady Benefit Street corner, where before him was a wooden antique with an Ionic-pilastered pair of doorways, and beside him a prehistoric gambrel-roofer with a bit of primal farmyard remaining, and the

150

great Judge Durfee house with its fallen vestiges of Georgian grandeur. It was getting to be slum here; but the titan elms cast a restoring shadow over the place, and the boy used to stroll south past the long lines of pre-Revolutionary homes with their great central chimneys and classic portals. On the eastern side they were set high over basements with railed double flights of stone steps, and the young Charles could picture them as they were when the street was new, and red heels and periwigs set off the painted pediments whose signs of wear were now becoming so visible.

Westward the hill dropped almost as steeply as above, down to the old Town Street that the founders had laid out at the river's edge in 1636. Here ran innumerable little lanes with leaning, huddled houses of immense antiquity; and, fascinated though he was, it was long before he dared to thread their archaic verticality for fear they would turn out to be a dream or a gateway to unknown terrors. He found it much less formidable to continue along Benefit Street past the iron fence of St John's hidden churchyard and the rear of the 1761 Colony House and the moldering bulk of the Golden Ball Inn where Washington stopped. At Meeting Street—the successive Gaol Lane and King Street of other periods—he would look upward to the east and see the arched flight of steps to which the highway had to resort in climbing the slope, and downward to the west, glimpsing the old brick Colonial schoolhouse that smiles across the road at the ancient sign of Shakespear's Head where the *Providence Gazette and Country-Journal* was printed before the Revolution. Then came the exquisite First Baptist Church of 1775, luxurious with its matchless Gibbs steeple, and the Georgian roofs and cupolas hovering by. Here and to the southward the neighborhood became better, flowering at last into a marvelous group of early mansions; but still the little ancient lanes led off down the precipice to the west; spectral in their many-peaked archaism, and dipping to a

151

riot of iridescent decay where the wicked old waterfront recalls its proud East India days amidst polyglot vice and squalor, rotting wharves and blear-eyed ship-chandleries and such surviving alley names as Packet, Bullion, Gold, Silver, Coin, Doubloon, Sovereign, Guilder, Dollar, Dime, and Cent.

Sometimes, as he grew taller and more adventurous, young Ward would venture down into this maelstrom of tottering houses, broken transoms, bubbling steps, twisted balustrades, swarthy faces, and nameless odors; winding from South Main to South Water, searching out the docks where the bay and sound steamers still touched, and returning northward at this lower level past the steep-roofed 1816 warehouses and the broad square at the Great Bridge, here the 1773 Market House still stands firm on its ancient arches. In that square he would pause to drink in the bewildering beauty of the old town as it rises on the eastward bluff, decked with its Georgian spires and crowned by the vast new Christian Science dome as London is crowned by St Paul's. He liked mostly to reach this point in the late afternoon, when the slanting sunlight touches the Market House and the ancient hill roofs and belfries with gold, and throws magic around the dreaming wharves where Providence Indiamen used to ride at anchor. After a long look he would grow almost dizzy with a poet's love for the sight, and then he would scale the slope homeward in the dusk past the old white church and up the narrow precipitous ways where yellow gleams would begin to peep out in small-paned windows and through fanlights set high over double flights of steps with curious wrought-iron railings.

At other times, and in later years, he would seek for vivid contrasts; spending half a walk in the crumbling colonial regions northwest of his home, where the hill drops to the lower eminence of Stampers Hill with its ghetto and Negro quarter clustering round the place where the Boston stagecoach used to start before the Revolution, and the other half in the gracious southernly realm about George, Benevolent, Power, and Williams Streets, where the old slope holds unchanged the fine estates and bits of walled garden and steep green lane in which so many fragrant memories linger. These rambles, together with the diligent studies which accompanied them, certainly account for a large amount of the antiquarian lore which at last crowded the modern world from Charles Ward's mind; and illustrates the mental soil upon which fell, in that fateful winter of 1919–20, the seeds that came to such strange and terrible fruition.

Dr Willett is certain that, up to this ill-omened winter of first change, Charles Ward's antiquarianism was free from every trace of the morbid. Graveyards held for him no particular attraction beyond their quaintness and historic value, and of anything like violence or savage instinct he was utterly devoid. Then, by insidious degrees, there appeared to develop a curious sequel to one of his genealogical triumphs of the year before; when he had discovered among his maternal ancestors a certain very long-lived man named Joseph Curwen, who had come from Salem in March of 1692, and about whom a whispered series of highly peculiar and disquieting stories clustered.

Ward's great-great-grandfather Welcome Potter had in 1785 married a certain 'Ann Tillinghast, daughter to Mrs Eliza, daughter to Captain James Tillinghast,' of whose paternity the family had preserved no trace. Late in 1918, whilst examining a volume of original town records in manuscript, the young genealogist encountered an entry describing a legal change of name, by which in 1772 a Mrs Eliza Curwen, widow of Joseph Curwen, resumed, along with her seven-year-old daughter Ann, her maiden name of Tillinghast; on the ground 'that her Husband's name was become a publick Reproach by Reason of what was knowne after his Decease; the which confirming an antient common Rumour, tho' not to be credited by a loyall Wife till so proven as to be wholely past Doubting.' This entry came to light upon the accidental separation of two leaves which had been carefully pasted together and treated as one by a laboured revision of the page numbers.

It was at once clear to Charles Ward that he had indeed discovered a hitherto unknown great-great-great-grandfather. The discovery doubly excited him because he had already heard vague reports and seen scattered allusions relating to this person about whom there remained so few publicly available records, aside from those becoming public only in modern times, that it almost seemed as if a conspiracy had existed to blot him from memory. What did appear, moreover, was of such singular and provocative nature that one could not fail to imagine curiously what it was the colonial recorders were so anxious to conceal and forget, or to suspect that the deletion had reasons all too valid.

Before this, Ward had been content to let his romancing about old Joseph Curwen remain in the idle stage; but having discovered his own relationship to this apparently 'hushed-up' character, he proceeded to hunt out as systematically as possible whatever he might find concerning him. In this excited quest he eventually succeeded beyond his highest expectations, for old letters, diaries and sheaves of unpublished memoirs in cobwebbed Providence garrets and elsewhere yielded many illuminating passages which their writers had not thought it worthwhile to destroy. One important sidelight came from a point as remote as New York, where some Rhode Island colonial correspondence was stored in the Museum at Frances' Tavern. The really crucial thing, though, and what in Dr Willett's opinion formed the definite source of Ward's undoing, was the matter found in August 1919 behind the paneling of the crumbling house in Olney Court. It was that, beyond a doubt, which opened up those black vistas whose end was deeper than the pit.

CHAPTER TWO

An Antecedent and a Horror

1

Joseph Curwen, as revealed by the rambling legends embodied in what Ward heard and unearthed, was a very astonishing, enigmatic, obscurely horrible individual. He had fled from Salem to Providence—that universal haven of the odd, the free, and the dissenting—at the beginning of the great witchcraft panic, being in fear of accusation because of his solitary ways and queer chemical or alchemical experiments. He was a colorless-looking man of about thirty, and was soon found qualified to become a freeman of Providence, thereafter buying a home lot just north of Gregory Dexter's at about the foot of Olney Street. His house was built on Stampers Hill west of the Town Street, in what later became Olney Court; and in 1761 he replaced this with a larger one, on the same site, which is still standing.

Now the first odd thing about Joseph Curwen was that he did not seem to grow much older than he had been on his arrival. He engaged in shipping enterprises, purchased wharfage near Mile-End Cove, helped rebuild the Great Bridge in 1713, and the Congregational Church on the hill; but always did he retain the nondescript aspect of a man not greatly over thirty or thirty-five. As decades mounted up, this singular quality began to excite wide notice; but Curwen always explained it by saying that he came of hardy forefathers, and practiced a simplicity of living which did not wear him out. How such simplicity could be reconciled with the inexplicable comings and goings of the secretive merchant, and with the queer gleamings of his windows at all hours of night, was not very clear to the townsfolk; and they were prone to assign other reasons for his continued youth and longevity. It was held, for the most part, that Curwen's incessant mixings and boilings of chemicals had much to do with his condition. Gossip spoke of the strange substances he brought from London and the Indies on his ships or purchased in Newport, Boston and New York; and when old Dr Jabez Bowen came from Rehoboth and opened his apothecary shop across the Great Bridge at the Sign of the Unicorn and Mortar, there was ceaseless talk of the drugs, acids, and metals that the taciturn recluse incessantly bought or ordered from him. Acting on the assumption that Curwen possessed a wondrous and secret medical skill, many suffers of various sorts applied to him for aid; but though he appeared to encourage their belief in a non-committal way, and always gave them odd-coloured potions in response to their requests, it was observed that his ministrations to others seldom proved of benefit. At length, when over fifty years had passed since the stranger's advent, and without producing more than five years' apparent change in his face and physique, the people began to whisper more darkly; and to meet more than half-way that desire for isolation which he had always shown.

Private letters and diaries of the period reveal, too, a multitude of other reasons why Joseph Curwen was marveled at, feared, and finally shunned like a plague. His passion for graveyards, in which he was glimpsed at all hours and under all conditions, was notorious; though no one had witnessed any deed on his part which could actually be termed ghoulish. On the Pawtuxet Road he had a farm, at which he generally lived during the summer, and to which he would frequently be seen riding at various odd times of the day or night. Here his only visible servants, farmers, and caretakers were a sullen pair of Narragansett Indians; the husband dumb and curiously scarred, and the wife of a very repulsive cast of countenance, probably due to a mixture of Negro blood. In the lean-to of this house was the laboratory where most of the chemical experiments were conducted. Curious porters and teamers who delivered bottles, bags or boxes at the small rear doors would exchange accounts of the fantastic flasks, crucibles, alembics and furnaces they saw in the low, shelved room; and prophesied in whispers that the close-mouthed 'chymist' – by which they meant *alchemist*–would not be long in finding the Philosopher's Stone. The nearest neighbors to this farm – the Fenners, a quarter of a mile away–had still queerer things to tell of certain sounds which they insisted came from the Curwen place in the night. There were cries, they said, and sustained howlings; and they did not like the large number of livestock which thronged the pastures, for no such amount was needed to keep a lone old man and a very few servants in meat, milk, and wool. The identity of the stock seemed to change from week to week as new droves were purchased from the Kingstown farmers. Then, too, there was something very obnoxious about a certain great stone outbuilding with only high narrow slits for windows.

Great Bridge idlers had much to say of Curwen's town house in Olney Court; not so much the fine new one built in 1761, when the man must have been nearly a century old but the first low gambrel-roofed one with the windowless attic and shingled sides whose timbers he took the peculiar precaution of burning after its demolition. Here there was less mystery, it is true; but the hours at which lights were seen, the secretiveness of the two swarthy foreigners who comprised the only menservants, the hideous indistinct mumbling of the incredibly aged French housekeeper, the large amounts of food seen to enter a door within which only four persons lived, and the *quality* of certain voices often heard in muffled conversation at highly unseasonable times, all combined with what was known of the Pawtuxet farm to give the place a bad name.

In choicer circles, too, the Curwen home was by no means undiscussed; for, as the newcomer had gradually worked into the church and trading life of the town, he had naturally made acquaintances of the better sort, whose company and conversation he was well fitted to enjoy. His birth was known to be good, since the Curwens or Carwens of Salem needed no introduction in New England. It developed that Joseph Curwen had traveled much in very early life, living for a time in England and making at least two voyages to the Orient; and his speech, when he deigned to use it, was that of a learned and cultivated Englishman. But for some reason or other Curwen did not care for society. Whilst never actually rebuffing a visitor, he always reared such a wall of reserve that few could think of anything to say to him which would not sound inane.

There seemed a lurk in his bearing some cryptic, sardonic arrogance, as if he had come to find all human beings dull through having moved among stranger and more potent entities. When Dr Checkley, the famous wit, came from Boston in 1738 to be rector of King's Church, he did not neglect calling on one of whom he had heard so much; but left in a very short while because of some sinister undercurrent he detected in his host's discourse. Charles Ward told his father, when they discussed Curwen one winter evening, that he would give much to learn what the mysterious old man had said to the sprightly cleric, but that all diarists agree concerning Dr Checkley's reluctance to repeat anything he had heard. The good man had been hideously shocked, and could never recall Joseph Curwen without a visible loss of the gay urbanity for which he was famed.

More definite, however, was the reason why another man

of taste and breeding avoided the haughty hermit. In 1746 Mr John Merritt, an elderly English gentleman of literary and scientific leanings, came from Newport to the town which was so rapidly overtaking it in standing, and built a fine country seat on the Neck in what is now the heart of the best residence section. He lived in considerable style and comfort, keeping the first coach and liveried servants in town, and taking great pride in his telescope, his microscope, and his well-chosen library of English and Latin books. Hearing of Curwen as the owner of the best library in Providence, Mr Merritt early paid him a call, and was more cordially received than most other callers at the house had been. His admiration for his host's ample shelves, which besides the Greek, Latin, and English classics were equipped with a remarkable battery of philosophical, mathematical and scientific works including Paracelsus, Agricola, Van Helmont, Sylvius, Glauber, Boyle, Boerhaave, Becher, and Stahl, led Curwen to suggest a visit to the farmhouse and laboratory whither he had never invited anyone before; and the two drove out at once in Mr Merritt's coach.

Mr Merritt always confessed to seeing nothing really horrible at the farmhouse, but maintained that the titles of the books in the special library of thaumaturgical, alchemical, and theological subjects which Curwen kept in a front room were alone sufficient to inspire him with a lasting loathing. Perhaps, however, the facial expression of the owner in exhibiting them contributed much of the prejudice. This bizarre collection, besides a host of standard works which Mr Merritt was not too alarmed to envy, embraced nearly all the cabalists, demonologists, and magicians known to man; and was a treasure-house of lore in the doubtful realms of alchemy anf astrology. Hermes Trismegistus in Mesnard's edition, the *Turba Philosopharum*, Geber's *Liber Investigationis*; and Artephous' *Key of Wisdom*;

all were there; with the cabalistic *Zohar*, Peter Jamm's set of *Albertus Magnus*, Raymond Lully's *Ars Magna et Ultima* in Zetzner's edition, Roger Bacon's *Thesaurus Chemicus*, Fludd's *Clavis Alchimiae*, Trithemius' *De Lapide Philosophico* crowding them close. Mediaeval Jews and Arabs were represented in profusion, and Mr Merritt turned pale when upon taking down a fine volume conspicuously labelled as the *Qanoon-e'-Islam*, he found it was in truth the forbidden *Necronomicon* of the mad Arab Abdul Alhazred, of which he had heard such monstrous things whispered some years previously after the exposure of nameless rites at the strange little fishing village of Kingsport, in the Province of the Massachusetts-Bay.

But oddly enough, the worthy gentleman owned himself most impalpably disquieted by a mere minor detail. On the huge mahogany table there lay face downward a badly worn copy of Borellus, bearing many cryptical marginalia and interlineations in Curwen's hand. The book was open to about its middle, and one paragraph displayed such thick and tremulous pen-strokes beneath the lines of mystic black-letters that the visitor could not resist scanning it through. Whether it was the nature of the passage under-scored, or the feverish heaviness of the strokes which formed the underscoring, he could not tell; but something in that combination affected him very badly and very peculiarly. He recalled it to the end of his days, writing it down from memory in his diary and once trying to recite it to his close friend Dr Checkley till he saw how greatly it disturbed the urbane rector. It read:

'The essential Saltes of Animals may be so prepared and preserved, that an ingenious Man may have the whole Ark of Noah in his owne Studie, and raise the fine Shape of an Animal out of its Ashes at his Pleasure, and by the lyke Method from the essential Saltes of humane Dust, a Philosopher may, without any criminal Necromancy, call up the Shape of any dead Ancestour from the Dust whereinto his Bodie has been incinerated.'

It was near the docks along the southerly part of the Town Street, however, that the worst things were muttered about Joseph Curwen. Sailors are superstitious folk; and the seasoned salts who manned the infinite rum, slaves and molasses sloops, the rakish privateers and the great brigs of the Browns, Crawfords, and Tillinghasts, all made strange furtive signs of protection when they saw the slim, deceptively young-looking figure with its yellow hair and slight stoop, entering the Curwen warehouse in Doubloon Street or talking with captains and supercargoes on the long quay where the Curwen ships rode restlessly. Curwen's own clerks and captains hated and feared him, and all his sailors were mongrel riff-raff from Martinique, St Eustatius, Havana, or Port Royal. It was, in a way, the frequency with which these sailors were replaced, which inspired the acutest and most tangible part of the fear in which the old man was held. A crew would be turned loose in the town on shore leave, some of its members perhaps charged with this errand or that; and when reassembled it would be almost sure to lack one or more men. That many of the errands had concerned the farm on the Pawtuxet Road, and that few of the sailors had ever been seen to return from that place, was not forgotten; so that in time it became exceedingly difficult for Curwen to keep his oddly assorted hands. Almost invariably several would desert soon after hearing the gossip of the Providence wharves, and their replacement in the West Indies became an increasingly great problem to the merchant.

By 1760 Joseph Curwen was virtually an outcast, suspected of vague horrors and demoniac alliances which seemed all the more menacing because they could not be named, understood, or even proved to exist. The last straw

But of course the effect of all this belated mending was necessarily slight. Curwen continued to be avoided and distrusted, as indeed the one fact of his continued air of youth at a great age would have been enough to warrant; and he could see that in the end his fortunes would be likely to suffer. His elaborate studies and experiments, whatever they may have been, apparently required a heavy income for their maintenance; and since a change of environment would deprive him of the trading advantages he had gained, it would not have profited him to begin anew in a different region just then. Judgment demanded that he patch up his relations with the townfolk of Providence, so that his presence might no longer be a signal for hushed conversation, transparent excuses of errands elsewhere, and a general atmosphere of restraint and uneasiness. His clerks, being now reduced to the shiftless and impecunious residue whom no one else would employ, were giving him much worry; and he held to his sea-captains and mates only by shrewdness in gaining some kind of ascendancy over them–a mortgage, a promissory note, or a bit of information very pertinent to their welfare. In many cases, diarists have recorded with some awe, Curwen showed almost the power of a wizard in unearthing family secrets for questionable use. During the final five years of his life it seemed as though only direct talks with the long-dead could possibly have furnished some of the data which he had so glibly at his tongue's end.

About this time the crafty scholar hit upon a last desperate expedient to regain his footing in the community. Hitherto a complete hermit, he now determined to contract an advantageous marriage, securing as a bridge some lady whose mentioned position would make all ostracism of his home impossible. It may be that he also had deeper reasons for wishing an alliance; reasons so far outside the known cosmic sphere that only papers found a century and a half

165

after his death caused anyone to suspect them; but of this nothing certain can ever be learned. Naturally he was aware of the horror and indignation with which any ordinary courtship of his would be received, hence he looked about for some likely candidate upon whose parents he might exert a suitable pressure. Such candidates, he found, were not at all easy to discover, since he had very particular requirements in the way of beauty, accomplishments, and social security. At length his survey narrowed down to the household of one of his best and oldest shipcaptains, a widower of high birth and unblemished standing named Dutie Tillinghast, whose only daughter Eliza seemed dowered with every conceivable advantage save prospects as an heiress. Captain Tillinghast was completely under the domination of Curwen; and consented, after a terrible interview in his cupolaed house on Power's Lane hill, to sanction the blasphemous alliance.

Eliza Tillinghast was at that time eighteen years of age, and had been reared as gently as the reduced circumstances of her father permitted. She had attended Stephen Jackson's school opposite the Court House Parade and had been diligently instructed by her mother, before the latter's death of small-pox in 1757, in all the arts and refinements of domestic life. A sampler of hers, worked in 1753 at the age of nine, may still be found in the rooms of the Rhode Island Historical Society. After her mother's death she had kept the house, aided only by one old black woman. Her arguments with her father concerning the proposed Curwen marriage must have been painful indeed; but of these we have no record. Certain it is that her engagement to young Ezra Weeden, second mate of the Crawford packet *Enterprise*, was dutifully broken off, and that her union with Joseph Curwen took place on the seventh of March, 1763, in the Baptist church, in the presence of one of the most distinguished assemblages which the town could boast; the ceremony being performed by the younger Samuel Winson. The *Gazette* mentioned the event very briefly, and in most surviving copies the item in question seems to be cut or torn out. Ward found a single intact copy after much search in the archives of a private collector of note, observing with amusement the meaningless urbanity of the language;

'Monday evening last, Mr Joseph Curwen, of this Town, Merchant, was married to Miss Eliza Tillinghast, Daughter of Captain Dutie Tillinghast, a young lady who has real Merit, added to a beautiful Person, to grace the connubial State and perpetuate its Felicity.'

The collection of Durfee-Arnold letters, discovered by Charles Ward shortly before his first reputed madness in the private collection of Melville F. Peters of George Street, and covering this and a somewhat antecedent period, throws vivid light on the outrage done to public sentiment by this ill-assorted match. The social influence of the Tillinghasts, however, was not to be denied; and once more Joseph Curwen found his house frequented by persons whom he could never otherwise have induced to cross his threshold. His acceptance was by no means complete, and his bride was socially the sufferer through her forced venture; but at all events the fall of utter ostracism was somewhat worn down. In his treatment of his wife the strange bridegroom astonished both her and the community by displaying an extreme graciousness and consideration. The new house in Olney Court was now wholly free from disturbing manifestations, and although Curwen was much absent at the Pawtuxet farm which his wife never visited, he seemed more like a normal citizen than at any other time in his long years of residence. Only one person remained in open enmity with him, this being the youthful ship's officer whose engagement to Eliza Tillinghast had been so abruptly broken. Ezra Weeden had frankly vowed vengeance and, though of a quiet and ordinarily mild disposition, was now gaining a hatred-dogged purpose which boded no good to the usurping husband.

On the seventh of May, 1765, Curwen's only child Ann was born; and was christened by the Reverend John Graves of King's Church, of which both husband and wife had become communicants shortly after their marriage in order to compromise between their respective Congregational and Baptist affiliations. The record of this birth, as well as that of the marriage two years before, was stricken from most copies of the church and town annals where it ought to appear; and Charles Ward located both with the greatest difficulty after his discovery of the widow's change of name had apprised him of his own relationship, and engendered the feverish interest which culminated in his madness. The birth entry, indeed, was found very curiously through correspondence with the heirs of the loyalist Dr Graves, who had taken with him a duplicate set of records when he left his pastorate at the outbreak of the Revolution. Ward had tried this source because he knew that his great-great-grandmother, Ann Tillinghast Potter, had been an Episcopalian.

Shortly after the birth of his daughter, an event he seemed to welcome with a fervor greatly out of keeping with his usual coldness, Curwen resolved to sit for a portrait. This he had painted by a very gifted Scotsman named Cosmo Alexander, then a resident of Newport, and since famous as the early teacher of Gilbert Stuart. The likeness was said to have been executed on a wall-panel of the library of the house in Olney Court, but neither of the two old diaries mentioning it gave any hint of its ultimate disposition. At this period the erratic scholar showed signs of unusual abstraction, and spent as much time as he possibly could at his farm on the Pawtuxet Road. He seemed, it was stated, in a condition of suppressed excitement or suspense; as if expecting some phenomenal thing or on the brink of some strange discovery. Chemistry or alchemy would appear to have played a great part, for he took from his house to the farm the greater number of his volumes on that subject.

His affectation of civic interest did not diminish, and he lost no opportunities for helping such leaders as Stephen Hopkins, Joseph Brown, and Benjamin West in their efforts to raise the cultural tone of the town, which was then much below the level of Newport in its patronage of the liberal arts. He had helped Daniel Jenckes found his bookshop in 1763, and was thereafter his best customer, extending aid likewise to the struggling *Gazette* that appeared each Wednesday at the Sign of Shakespear's Head. In politics he ardently supported Governor Hopkins against the Ward party whose prime strength was in Newport, and his really eloquent speech at Hacher's Hall in 1765 against the setting off of North Providence as a separate town with a pre-ward vote in the General Assembly did more than any other one thing to wear down the prejudice against him. But Ezra Weeden, who watched him closely, sneered cynically at all this outward activity; and freely swore it was no more than a mask for some nameless traffic with the blackest gulfs of Tartarus. The revengeful youth began a systematic study of the man and his doings whenever he was in port; spending hours at night by the wharves with a dory in readiness when he saw lights in the Curwen warehouses, and following the small boat which would sometimes steal quietly off and down the bay. He also kept as close a watch as possible on the Pawtuxet farm, and was once severely bitten by the dogs the old Indian couple loosed upon him.

By the autumn of 1770 Weeden decided that the time was
very sudden, and gained a wide notice amongst the curious townsfolk; for the air of suspense and expectancy
dropped like an old cloak, giving instant place to an ill-
concealed exaltation of perfect triumph. Curwen seemed to
have difficulty in restraining himself from public haran-
gues on what he had found or learned or made; but
apparently the need of secrecy was greater than the longing to share his rejoicing, for no explanation was ever
offered by him. It was after this transition, which appears
to have come early in July, that the sinister scholar began
to astonish people by his possession of information which
only their long-dead ancestors would seem to be able to
impart.

But Curwen's feverish secret activities by no means
ceased with this change. On the contrary, they tended
rather to increase; so that more and more of his shipping
business was handled by the captains whom he now bound
to him by ties of fear as potent as those of bankruptcy had
been. He altogether abandoned the slave trade, alleging
that its profits were constantly decreasing. Every possible
moment was spent at the Pawtuxet farm; though there
were rumors now and then of his presence in places
which, though not actually near graveyards, were yet so
situated in relation to graveyards that thoughtful people
wondered just how thorough the old merchant's change of
habits really was. Ezra Weeden, though his periods of
espionage were necessarily brief and intermittent on account of his sea voyaging, had a vindictive persistence
which the bulk of the practical townsfolk and farmers

lacked; and subjected Curwen's affairs to a scrutiny such as they had never had before.

Many of the odd maneuvers of the strange merchant's vessels had been taken for granted on account of the unrest of the times, when every colonist seemed determined to resist the provisions of the Sugar Act which hampered a prominent traffic. Smuggling and evasion were the rule in Narragansett Bay, and nocturnal landings of illicit cargoes were continuous commonplaces. But Weeden, night after night, following the lighters or small sloops which he saw steal off from the Curwen warehouses at the Town Street docks, soon felt assured that it was not merely His Majesty's armed ships which the sinister skulker was anxious to avoid. Prior to the change in 1766 these boats had for the most part contained chained Negroes, who were carried down and across the bay and landed at an obscure point on the shore just north of Pawtuxet; being afterward driven up the bluff and across country to the Curwen farm, where they were locked in that enormous stone outbuilding which had only high narrow slits for windows. After that change, however, the whole program was altered. Importation of slaves ceased at once, and for a time Curwen abandoned his midnight sailings. Then, about the spring of 1767, a new policy appeared. Once more the lighters grew wont to put out from the black silent docks, and this time they would go down the bay some distance, perhaps as far as Nanquit Point, where they would meet and receive cargo from strange ships of considerable size and widely varied appearance. Curwen's sailors would then deposit this cargo at the usual point on the shore, and transport it overland to the farm; locking it in the same cryptical stone building which had formerly received the Negroes. The cargo consisted almost wholly of boxes and cases, of which a large proportion were oblong and heavy and disturbingly suggestive of coffins.

Weeden always watched the farm with unremitting assiduity, visiting it each night for long periods, and seldom letting a week go by without a sight except when the ground bore a footprint-revealing snow. Even then he would often walk as close as possible in the traveled road or on the ice of the neighboring river, to see what tracks others might have left. Finding his own vigils interrupted by nautical duties, he hired a tavern companion named Eleazar Smith to continue the survey during his absences; and between them the two could have set in motion some extraordinary rumors. That they did not do so was only because they knew the effect of publicity would be to warn their quarry and make further progress impossible. Instead, they wished to learn something definite before taking any action. What they did learn must have been startling indeed, and Charles Ward spoke many times to his parents of his regret at Weeden's later burning of his notebooks. All that can be told of their discoveries is what Eleazar Smith jotted down in a none too coherent diary, and what other diarists and letter writers have timidly repeated from the statements which they finally made—and according to which the farm was only the outer shell of some vast and revolting menace, of a scope and depth too profound and intangible for more than shadowy comprehension.

It is gathered that Weeden and Smith became early convinced that a great series of tunnels and catacombs, inhabited by a very sizeable staff of persons besides the old Indian and his wife, underlay the farm. The house was an old peaked relic of the middle seventeenth century with enormous stack chimney and diamond-paned lattice windows, the laboratory being in a lean-to toward the north, where the roof came nearly to the ground. This building stood clear of any other; yet, judging by the different voices heard at odd times within, it must have been accessible through secret passages beneath. These voices, before 1766,

172

were mere mumblings and Negro whisperings and frenzied screams, coupled with curious chants or invocations. After that date, however, they assumed a very singular and terrible cast as they ran the gamut betwixt dronings of dull acquiescence and explosions of frantic fury, rumblings of conversation and whines of entreaty, pantings of eagerness and shouts of protest. They appeared to be in different languages, all known to Curwen, whose rasping accents were frequently distinguishable in reply, reproof, or threatening.

Sometimes it seemed that several persons must be in the house; Curwen, certain captives, and the guards of those captives. There were voices of a sort that neither Weeden nor Smith had ever heard before despite their wide knowledge of foreign ports, and many that they did seem to place as belonging to this or that nationality. The nature of the conversations seemed always a kind of catechism, as if Curwen were extorting some sort of information from terrified or rebellious prisoners.

Weeden had many verbatim reports of overheard scraps in his notebook, for English, French, and Spanish, which he knew, were frequently used; but of these nothing has survived. He did, however, say that besides a few ghoulish dialogues in which the past affairs of Providence families were concerned, most of the questions and answers he could understand were historical or scientific; occasionally pertaining to very remote places and ages. Once, for example, an alternately raging and sullen figure was questioned in French about the Black Prince's massacre at Limoges in 1370, as if there were some hidden reason which he ought to know. Curwen asked the prisoner—if prisoner it were—whether the order to slay was given because of the Sign of the Goat found on the altar in the ancient Roman crypt beneath the cathedral, or whether the Dark Man of the Haute Vienne Coven had spoke the Three Words. Failing to obtain replies, the inquisitor had seemingly resorted to extreme means; for there was a terrific shriek followed by silence and muttering and a bumping sound.

None of these colloquies was ever ocularly witnessed, since the windows were always heavily draped. Once, though, during a discourse in an unknown tongue, a shadow was seen on the curtain which startled Weeden exceedingly; reminding him of one of the puppets in a show he had seen in the autumn of 1764 in Hacher's Hall, when a man from Germantown, Pennsylvania, had given a clever mechanical spectacle advertised as a 'View of the Famous City of Jerusalem, in which are represented Jerusalem, the Temple of Solomon, his Royal Throne, the noted Towers, and Hills, likewise the Sufferings of Our Saviour from the Garden of Gethsemane to the Cross on the Hill of Golgotha; an artful piece of Statuary, Worthy to be seen by the Curious.' It was on this occasion that the listener, who had crept close to the window of the front room whence the speaking proceeded, gave a start which roused the old Indian pair and caused them to loose the dogs on him. After that no more conversations were ever heard in the house, and Weeden and Smith concluded that Curwen had transferred his field of action to regions below.

That such regions in truth existed, seemed amply clear from many things. Faint cries and groans unmistakably came up now and then from what appeared to be the solid earth in places far from any structure; whilst hidden in the bushes along the river-bank in the rear, where the high ground sloped steeply down to the valley of the Pawtuxet, there was found an arched oaken door in a frame of heavy masonry, which was obviously an entrance to caverns within the hill. When or how these catacombs could have been constructed, Weeden was unable to say; but he frequently pointed out how easily the place might have been reached by bands of unseen workmen from the river. Joseph

Curwen put his mongrel seamen to diverse uses indeed! During the heavy spring rains of 1769 the two watchers kept a sharp eye on the steep river-bank to see if any subterrene secrets mights be washed to light, and were rewarded by the sight of a profusion of both human and animal bones in places where deep gullies had been worn in the banks. Naturally, there might be many explanations of such things in the rear of a stock farm, and in a locality where old Indian burying-grounds were common, but Weeden and Smith drew their own inferences.

It was in January 1770, whilst Weeden and Smith were still debating vainly on what, if anything, to think or do about the whole bewildering business, that the incident of the *Fortaleza* occurred. Exasperated by the burning of the revenue sloop *Liberty* at Newport during the previous summer, the custom fleet under Admiral Wallace had adopted an increased vigilance concerning strange vessels; and on this occasion His Majesty's armed schooner *Cygnet*, under Captain Harry Leshe, captured, after a short pursuit one early morning, the scow *Fortaleza* of Barcelona, Spain, under Captain Manuel Arruda, bound according to its log from Grand Cairo, Egypt, to Providence. When searched for contraband material, this ship revealed the astonishing fact that its cargo consisted exclusively of Egyptian mummies, consigned to 'Sailor A.B.C.', who would come to remove his goods in a lighter just off Nanquit Point and whose identity Captain Arruda felt himself in honor bound not to reveal. The Vice-Admiralty Court at Newport, at a loss what to do in view of the non-contraband nature of the cargo on the one hand and of the unlawful secrecy of the entry on the other hand, compromised on Collector Robinson's recommendation by freeing the ship but forbidding it a port in Rhode Island waters. There were later rumors of its having been seen in Boston Harbor, though it never openly entered the Port of Boston.

This extraordinary incident did not fail of wide remark in Providence and there were not many who doubted the existence of some connection between the cargo of mummies and the sinister Joseph Curwen. His exotic studies and his curious chemical importations being common knowledge, and his fondness for graveyards being common suspicion; it did not take much imagination to link him with a freakish importation which could not conceivably have been destined for anyone else in the town. As if conscious of this natural belief, Curwen took care to speak casually on several occasions of the chemical value of the balsams found in mummies; thinking perhaps that he might make the affair seem less unnatural, yet stopping just short of admitting his participation. Weeden and Smith, of course, felt no doubt whatsoever of the significance of the thing; and indulged in the wildest theories concerning Curwen and his monstrous labors.

The following spring, like that of the year before, had heavy rains; and the watchers kept careful track of the river-bank behind the Curwen farm. Large sections were washed away, and a certain number of bones discovered; but no glimpse was afforded of any actual subterranean chambers or burrows. Something was rumored, however, at the village of Pawtuxet about a mile below, where the river flows in falls over a rocky terrace to join the placid landlocked cover. There, where quaint old cottages climbed the hill from the rustic bridge, and fishing-smacks lay anchored at their sleepy docks, a vague report went round of things that were floating down the river and flashing into sight for a minute as they went over the falls. Of course the Pawtuxet is a long river which winds through many settled regions abounding in graveyards, and of course the spring rains had been very heavy; but the fisherfolk about the bridge did not like the wild way that one of the things stared as it shot down to the still water below, or the way that another half cried out, although its condition had greatly departed from that of objects which normally cry out. That rumor sent Smith – for Weeden was just then at sea–in haste to the river-bank behind the farm; where surely enough there remained the evidences of an extensiver cave-in. There was, however, no trace of a passage into the steep bank; for the miniature avalanche had left behind a solid wall of mixed earth and shrubbery from aloft. Smith went to the extent of some experimental digging, but was deterred by lack of success–or perhaps by fear of possible success. It is interesting to speculate on what the persistent and revengeful Weeden would have done had he been ashore at the time.

3

By the autumn of 1770 Weeden decided that the time was ripe to tell others of his discoveries; for he had a large number of facts to link together, and a second eye-witness to refute the possible charge that jealousy and vindictiveness had spurred his fancy. As his first confidant he selected Captain James Mathewson of the *Enterprise*, who on the one hand knew him well enough not to doubt his veracity, and on the other hand was sufficiently influential in the town to be heard in turn with respect. The colloquy took place in an upper room of Sabin's Tavern near the docks, with Smith present to corroborate virtually every statement; and it could be seen that Captain Mathewson was tremendously impressed. Like nearly everyone else in the town he had had black suspicions of his own anent Joseph Curwen; hence it needed only this confirmation and enlargement of data to convince him absolutely. At the end of the conference he was very grave, and enjoined strict silence upon the two younger men. He would, he said, transmit the information separately to some ten or so of the most learned and prominent citizens of Providence; ascertaining their views and following whatever advice they might have to offer. Secrecy would probably be essential in any case, for this was no matter that the town constables or militia could cope with; and above all else the excitable crowd must be kept in ignorance, lest there be enacted in these already troublous times a repetition of that frightful Salem panic of less than a century before which had first brought Curwen hither.

The right persons to tell, he believed, would be Dr Benjamin West, whose pamphlet on the late transit of Venus proved him a scholar and keen thinker; Reverend James Manning, President of the College which had just moved up from Warren and was temporarily housed in the new King Street school-house awaiting the completion of its building on the hill above Presbyterian Lane; ex-Governor Stephen Hopkins, who had been a member of the Philosophical Society at Newport, and was a man of very broad perceptions; John Carter, publisher of the *Gazette*; all four of the Brown brothers, John, Joseph, Nicholas and Moses, who formed the recognized local magnates, and of whom Joseph was an amateur scientist of parts; old Dr Jabez Bowen, whose erudition was considerable, and who had much first-hand knowledge of Curwen's odd purchases, and Captain Abraham Whipple, a privateersman of phenomenal boldness and energy who could be counted on to lead in any active measures needed. These men, if favorable, might eventually be brought together for collective deliberation; and with them would rest the responsibility of deciding whether or not to inform the Governor of the Colony, Joseph Wanton of Newport, before taking action.

The mission of Captain Mathewson prospered beyond his highest expectations; for whilst he found one or two of the chosen confidants somewhat skeptical of the possible ghostly side of Weeden's tale, there was not one who did not think it necessary to take some sort of secret and co-ordinated action. Curwen, it was clear, formed a vague potential menace to the welfare of the town and Colony; and must be eliminated at any cost. Late in December 1770, a group of eminent townsmen met at the home of Stephen Hopkins and debated tentative measures. Weeden's notes, which he had given to Captain Mathewson, were carefully read; and he and Smith were summoned to give testimony anent details. Something very like fear seized the whole assemblage before the meeting was over, though there ran through that fear a grim determination which Captain Whipple's bluff and resonant profanity best expressed. They would not notify the Governor, because a more than legal course seemed necessary. With hidden powers of uncertain extent apparently at his disposal, Curwen was not a man who could safely be warned to leave town. Nameless reprisals might ensue, and, even if the sinister creature complied, the removal would be no more than the shifting of an unclean burden to another place. The times were lawless, and the men who had flouted the King's revenue forces for years were not the ones to balk at sterner things when duty impelled. Curwen must be surprised at his Pawtuxet farm by a large raiding-party of seasoned privateersmen and given one decisive chance to explain himself. If he proved a madman, amusing himself with shrieked and imaginary conversations in different voices, he would be properly confined. If something graver appeared and if the underground horrors indeed turned out to be real, he and all with him must die. It could be done quietly, and even the widow and her father need not be told how it came about.

While these serious steps were under discussion there occurred in the town an incident so terrible and inexplicable that for a time little else was mentioned for miles around. In the middle of a moonlight January night with heavy snow underfoot there resounded over the river and up the hill a shocking series of cries which brought sleepy heads to every window; and people around Weybosset Point saw a great white thing plunging frantically along the badly cleared space in front of the Turk's Head. There was a baying of dogs in the distance, but this subsided as soon as the clamor of the awakened town became audible. Parties of men with lanterns and muskets hurried out to see what was happening, but nothing rewarded their search. The next morning, however, a giant, muscular body, stark naked, was found on the jams of ice around the southern piers of the Great Bridge, where the Long Dock stretched out beside Abbott's distil-house, and the identity of this object became a theme for endless speculation and whispering. It was not so much the younger as the older folk who whispered, for only in the patriarchs did that rigid face with horror-bulging eyes strike any chord of memory. They, shaking as they did so, exchanged furtive murmurs of wonder and fear; for in those stiff, hideous features lay a resemblance so marvellous as to be almost an identity – and that identity was with a man who had died full fifty years before.

Ezra Weeden was present at the finding; and remembering the baying of the night before, set out along Weybosset Street and across Muddy Dock Bridge whence the sound had come. He had a curious expectancy, and was not surprised when, reaching the edge of the settled district where the street merged into the Pawtuxet Road, he came upon some very curious tracks in the snow. The naked giant had been pursued by dogs and many booted men, and the returning tracks of the hounds and their masters could be easily traced. They had given up the chase upon coming too near the town. Weeden smiled grimly, and as a perfunctory detail traced the footprints back to their source. It was the Pawtuxet farm of Joseph Curwen, as he well knew it would be; and he would have given much had the yard been less confusingly trampled. As it was, he dared not seem too interested in full daylight. Dr Bowen, to whom Weeden went at once with his report, performed an autopsy on the strange corpse, and discovered peculiarities which baffled him utterly. The digestive tracts of the huge man seemed never to have been in use, whilst the whole skin had a coarse, loosely-knit texture impossible to account for. Impressed by what the old men whispered of this body's likeness to the long-dead blacksmith Daniel Green, whose great-grandson Aaron Hoppin was a supercargo in Curwen's employ, Weeden asked casual questions till he found where Green was buried. That night a party of ten visited the old North Burying Ground opposite Herrenden's Lane and opened a grave. They found it vacant, precisely as they had expected.

Meanwhile arrangements had been made with the post riders to intercept Joseph Curwen's mail, and shortly before the incident of the naked body there was found a letter from one Jedediah Orne of Salem which made the cooperating citizens think deeply. Parts of it, copied and preserved in the private archives of the family where Charles Ward found it, ran as follows:

'I delight that you continue in ye getting at Olde Matters in your Way, and doe not think better was done at Mr Hutchinson's in Salem-Village. Certainly, there was Noth'g butt ye liveliest Awfulness in that which H. rais'd up from what we cou'd gather onlie a part of. What you sente did not Worke, whether because Any Thing miss'g, or because ye Wordes were not Righte from my Speak'g or yr copy'g. Alone am at a Loss. I have not ye Chymicall art to followe Borellus, and owne my Self confounded by ye VII. Booke of ye *Necronomicon* that you recommende. But I wou'd have you Observe what was told to us aboute tak'g Care whom to calle up, for you are Sensible what Mr Mather writ in ye Marginalia

181

of——, and can judge how truly that Horrendous thing is reported. I say to you againe, doe not call upp Any that you can not put downe; by the Which I meane, Any that can in Turne call up somewhat against you, whereby your Powerfullest Devices may not be of use. Ask of the Lesser, lest the greater shall not wish to Answer, and shall commande more than you. I was frighted when I read of your know'g what Ben Zaristnatmik hadde in his Ebony Boxe, for I was conscious who must have tolde you. And againe I ask that you shalle write me as Jedediah and not Simon. In this Community a Man may not live too long, and you knowe my Plan by which I came back as my Son. I am desirous you will Acquaint me with what ye Blacke Man learnt from Sylvanus Cocidius in ye Vault, under ye Roman wall, and will be oblig'd for ye Lend'g of ye MS you speak of.'

Another and unsigned letter from Philadelphia provoked equal thought, especially for the following passage:

'I will observe what you say respecting the sending of Accounts only by yr Vessels, but can not always be certain when to expect them. In the Matter spoke of, I require only one more thing; but wish to be sure I apprehend you exactly. You inform me, that no Part must be missing if the finest Effects are to be had, but you can not but know how hard it is to be sure. It seems a great Hazard and Burthen to take away the whole Box, and in Town (i.e., St Peter's, St Paul's, St Mary's, or Christ Church) it can scarce be done at all. But I know what Imperfections were in the one rais'd up October last, and how many live Specimens you were forc'd to imploy before you hit upon the right Mode in the year 1766; so will be guided by you in all Matters. I am impatient for yr Brig, and inquire daily at Mr Biddle's Wharf.'

A third suspicious letter was in an unknown tongue and even an unknown alphabet. In the Smith diary found by Charles Ward a single oft-repeated combination of characters is clumsily copied; and authorities at Brown University have pronounced the alphabet Amharic or Abyssinian, although they do not recognize the word. None of these epistles was ever delivered to Curwen, though the disappearance of Jedediah Orne from Salem as recorded shortly afterward showed that the Providence men took certain quiet steps. The Pennsylvania Historical Society also has some curious letter received by Dr Shippen regarding the presence of an unwholesome character in Philadelphia. But more decisive steps were in the air, and it is in the secret assemblages of sworn and tested sailors and faithful old privateersmen in the Brown warehouses by night that we must look for the main fruits of Weeden's disclosures. Slowly and surely a plan of campaign was under development which would leave no trace of Joseph Curwen's noxious mysteries.

Curwen, despite all precautions, apparently felt that something was in the wind; for he was now remarked to wear an unusually worried look. His coach was seen at all hours in the town and on the Pawtuxet Road, and he dropped little by little the air of forced geniality with which he had latterly sought to combat the town's prejudice. The nearest neighbors to his farm, the Fenners, one night remarked a great shaft of light shooting into the sky from some aperture in the roof of that cryptical stone building with the high, excessively narrow windows; an event which they quickly communicated to John Brown in Providence. Mr Brown had become the executive leader of the select group bent on Curwen's extirpation, and had informed the Fenners that some action was about to be taken. This he deemed needful because of the impossibility of their not witnessing the final raid; and he explained his course by saying that Curwen was known to be a spy of the customs officers at Newport, against whom the hand of every Providence shipper, merchant, and farmer was openly or clandestinely raised. Whether the ruse was wholly believed by neighbours who had seen so many queer things is not certain, but at any rate the Fenners were willing to connect any evil with a man of such queer ways. To them Mr Brown had entrusted the duty of watching the Curwen farmhouse, and of regularly reporting every incident which took place there.

4

The probability that Curwen was on guard and attempting unusual things, as suggested by the odd shaft of light, precipitated at last the action so carefully devised by the band of serious citizens. According the the Smith diary a company of about one hundred men met at ten P.M. on Friday, April twelfth, 1771, in the great room of Thurston's Tavern at the Sign of the Golden Lion on Weybosset Point across the bridge. Of the guiding group of prominent men in addition to the leader, John Brown, there were present Dr Bowen, with his case of surgical instruments, President Manning without the great periwig (the largest in the Colonies) for which he was noted, Governor Hopkins, wrapped in his dark cloak and accompanied by his seafaring brother Eseh, whom he had initiated at the last moment with the permission of the rest, John Carter, Captain Mathewson, and Captain Whipple, who was to lead the actual raiding party. These chiefs conferred apart in a rear chamber, after which Captain Whipple emerged to the great room and gave the gathered seamen their last oaths and instructions. Eleazer Smith was with the leaders as they sat in the rear apartment awaiting the arrival of Ezra Weeden, whose duty was to keep track of Curwen and report the departure of his coach for the farm.

About ten-thirty a heavy rumble was heard on the Great Bridge, followed by the sound of a coach in the street outside; and at that hour there was no need of waiting for Weeden in order to know that the doomed man had set out for his last night of unhallowed wizardry. A moment later,

184

as the receding coach clattered faintly over the Muddy Dock Bridge, Weeden appeared; and the raiders fell silently into military order in the street, shouldering the firelocks, fowling-pieces, or whaling harpoons which they had with them. Weeden and Smith were with the party, and of the deliberating citizens there were present for active service Captain Whipple, the leader, Captain Eseh Hopkins, John Carter, President Manning, Captain Mathewson, and Dr Bowen; together with Moses Brown, who had come up at the eleventh hour though absent from the preliminary session in the tavern. All these freemen and their hundred sailors began the long march without delay, grim and a trifle apprehensive as they left the Muddy Dock behind and mounted the gentle rise of Broad Street toward the Pawtuxet Road. Just beyond Elder Snow's church some of the men turned back to take a parting look at Providence lying outspread under the early spring stars. Steeples and gables rose dark and shapely, and salt breezes swept up gently from the cove north of the Bridge. Vega was climbing above the great hill across the water, whose crest of trees was broken by the roof-line of the unfinished College edifice. At the foot of that hill and along the narrow mounting lanes of its side the old town dreamed; Old Providence, for whose safety and sanity so monstrous and colossal a blasphemy was about to be wiped out.

An hour and a quarter later the raiders arrived, as previously agreed, at the Fenner farmhouse, where they heard a final report on their intended victim. He had reached his farm over half an hour before, and the strange light had soon afterward shot once into the sky but there were no lights in any visible windows. This was always the case of late. Even as this news was given another great glare arose toward the south, and the party realized that they had indeed come close to the scene of awesome and unnatural wonders. Captain Whipple now ordered his

185

force to separate into three divisions; one of twenty men under Eleazer Smith to strike across to the shore and guard the landing place against possible reinforcements for Curwen, until summoned by a messenger for desperate service; a second of twenty men under Captain Eseh Hopkins to steal down into the river valley behind the Curwen farm and demolish with axes or gunpowder the oaken door in the high, steep bank; and the third to close in on the house and adjacent buildings themselves. Of this division one third was to be led by Captain Mathewson to the cryptical stone edifice with high narrow windows, another third to follow Captain Whipple himself to the main farmhouse, and the remaining third to preserve a circle around the whole group of buildings until summoned by a final emergency signal.

The river party would break down the hillside door at the sound of a single whistle-blast, waiting and capturing anything which might issue from the regions within. At the sound of two whistle blasts it would advance through the aperture to oppose the enemy or join the rest of the raiding contingent. The party at the stone building would accept these respective signals in an analogous manner; forcing an entrance at the first, and at the second descending whatever passage into the ground might be discovered, and joining the general or focal warfare expected to take place within the caverns. A third or emergency signal of three blasts would summon the immediate reserve from its general guard duty; its twenty men dividing equally and entering the unknown depths through both farmhouse and stone building. Captain Whipple's belief in the existence of catacombs was absolute, and he took no alternative into consideration when making his plans. He had with him a whistle of great power and shrillness and did not fear any upsetting or misunderstanding of signals. The final reserve at the landing, of course, was nearly out of the whistle's range, hence would require a special messenger if needed for help. Moses Brown and John Carter went with Captain Hopkins to the river-bank, while President Manning was detailed with Captain Mathewson to the stone building. Dr Bowen, with Ezra Weeden, remained in Captain Whipple's party which was to storm the farmhouse itself. The attack was to begin as soon as a messenger from Captain Hopkins had joined Captain Whipple to notify him of the river party's readiness. The leader would then deliver the loud single blast, and the various advance parties would commence their simultaneous attack on three points. Shortly before one A.M. the three divisions left the Fenner farmhouse; one to guard the landing, another to seek the river valley and the hillside door, and the third to subdivide and attend to the actual buildings of the Curwen farm.

Eleazer Smith, who accompanied the shore-guarding party, records in his diary an uneventful march and a long wait on the bluff by the bay; broken once by what seemed to be the distant sound of the signal whistle and again by a peculiar muffled blend of roaring and crying and a powder blast which seemed to come from the same direction. Later on one man thought he caught some distant gunshots, and still later Smith himself felt the throb of titanic thunderous words resounding in upper air. It was just before dawn that a single haggard messenger with wild eyes and a hideous unknown odor about his clothing appeared and told the detachment to disperse quietly to their homes and never again think or speak of the night's doings or of him who had been Joseph Curwen. Something about the bearing of the messenger carried a conviction which his mere words could never have conveyed; for though he was a seaman known to many of them, there was something obscurely lost or gained in his soul which set him forevermore apart. It was the same later on when they met other old companions who had gone into that zone of horror. Most of them had lost or gained something imponderable and indescribable. They had seen or heard or felt something which was not for human creatures, and could not forget it. From them there was never any gossip, for to even the commonest of mortal instincts there are terrible boundaries. And from that single messenger the party at the shore caught a nameless awe which almost sealed their own lips. Very few are the rumors which ever came from any of them, and Eleazer Smith's diary is the only written record which has survived from that whole expedition which set forth from the Sign of the Golden Lion under the Stars.

Charles Ward, however, discovered another vague sidelight in some Fenner correspondence which he found in New London, where he knew another branch of the family had lived. It seems that the Fenners, from whose house the doomed farm was distantly visible, had watched the departing columns of raiders; and had heard very clearly the angry barking of the Curwen dogs, followed by the first shrill blast which precipitated the attack. The first blast had been followed by a repetition of the great shaft of light from the stone building, and in another moment, after a quick sounding of the second signal ordering a general invasion, there had come a subdued prattle of musketry followed by a horrible roaring cry which the correspondent, Luke Fenner had represented in his epistle by the characters 'Waaaah-rrrr—R'waaahrrr'. This cry, however, had possessed a quality which no mere writing could convey, and the correspondent mentions that his mother fainted completely at the sound. It was later repeated less loudly, and further but more muffled evidences of gunfire ensued; together with a loud explosion of powder from the direction of the river. About an hour afterward all the dogs began to bark frightfully, and there were vague ground rumblings so marked that the candlesticks tottered on the mantelpiece. A strong smell of sulphur was noted; and Luke Fenner's father declared that he heard the third or emergency whistle signal, though the others failed to detect it. Muffled musketry sounded again, followed by a deep scream less piercing but even more horrible than those which had preceded it; a kind of throaty, nastily plastic cough or gurgle whose quality as a scream must have come more from its continuity and psychological import than from its actual acoustic value.

Then the flaming thing burst into sight at a point where the Curwen farm ought to lie, and the human cries of desperate and frightened men were heard. Muskets flashed and cracked, and the flaming thing fell to the ground. A second flaming thing appeared, and a shriek of human crying was plainly distinguished. Fenner wrote that he could even gather a few words belched in frenzy: 'Almighty, protect thy lamb!' Then there were more shots, and the second flaming thing fell. After that came silence for about three-quarters of an hour; at the end of which time little Arthur Fenner, Luke's brother, exclaimed that he saw 'a red fog' going up to the stars from the accursed farm in the distance. No one but the child can testify to this, but Luke admits the significant coincidence implied by the panic of almost convulsive fright which at the same moment arched the backs and stiffened the fur of the three cats then within the room.

Five minutes later a chill wind blew up, and the air became suffused with such an intolerable stench that only the strong freshness of the sea could have prevented its being noticed by the shore party or by any wakeful souls in Pawtuxet village. This stench was nothing which any of the Fenners had ever encountered before, and produced a kind of clutching, amorphous fear beyond that of the tomb or the charnel-house. Close upon it came the awful voice which no hapless hearer will ever be able to forget. It thundered out of the sky like a doom, and windows rattled as its echoes died away. It was deep and musical; powerful as a brass organ, but evil as the forbidden books of the Arabs. What it said no man can tell, for it spoke in an unknown tongue, but this is the writing Luke Fenner set down to portray the demoniac intonations: 'DEESMEES – JESHET – BONEDOSEFEDUVEMA – ENTTEMOSS.' Not till the year 1919 did any soul link this crude transcript with anything else in mortal knowledge, but Charles Ward paled as he recognized what Mirandola had denounced in shudders as the ultimate horror among black magic's incantations.

An unmistakably human shout or deep chorused scream seemed to answer this malign wonder from the Curwen farm after which the unknown stench grew complex with an added odor equally intolerable. A wailing distinctly different from the scream now burst out, and was protracted ululantly in rising and falling paroxysms. At times it became almost articulate, though no auditor could trace any definite words; and at one point it seemed to verge toward the confines of diabolic and hysterical laughter. Then a yell of utter, ultimate fright and stark madness wrenched from scores of human throats; a yell which came strong and clear despite the depth from which it must have burst; after which darkness and silence ruled all things. Spirals of acrid smoke ascended to blot out the stars, though no flames appeared, and no buildings were observed to be gone or injured on the following day.

Toward dawn two frightened messengers with monstrous and unplaceable odors saturating their clothing knocked at the Fenner door and requested a keg of rum for which they paid very well indeed. One of them told the family that the affair of Joseph Curwen was over, and that the events of the night were not to be mentioned again. Arrogant as the order seemed, the aspect of him who gave it took away all resentment and lent it a fearsome authority; so that only these furtive letters of Luke Fenner, which he urged his Connecticut relative to destroy, remain to tell what was seen and heard. The non-compliance of that relative, whereby the letters were saved after all, has alone kept the matter from a merciful oblivion. Charles Ward had one detail to add as a result of a long canvass of Pawtuxet residents for ancestral traditions. Old Charles Slocum of that village said that there was known to his grandfather a queer rumor concerning a charred, distorted body found in the fields a week after the death of Joseph Curwen was announced. What kept the talk alive was the notion that this body, so far as could be seen in its burnt and twisted condition, was neither thoroughly human nor wholly allied to any animal which Pawtuxet folk had ever seen or read about.

5

Not one man who participated in that terrible raid could ever be induced to say a word concerning it, and every fragment of the vague data which survives comes from those outside the final fighting party. There is something frightful in the care with which these actual raiders destroyed such scraps which bore the least allusion to the matter.

Eight sailors had been killed, but although their bodies were not produced their families were satisfied with the statement that a clash with customs officers had occurred. The same statement also covered the numerous cases of wounds, all of which were extensively bandaged and treated only by Dr Jabez Bowen, who had accompanied the party. Hardest to explain was the nameless odor clinging to all the raiders, a thing which was discussed for weeks. Of the citizen leaders, Captain Whipple and Moses Brown were most severely hurt, and letters of their wives testify the bewilderment which their reticence and close guarding of their bandages produced. Psychologically every participant was aged, sobered, and shaken. It is fortunate that they were all strong men of action and simple, orthodox religionists, for with more subtle introspectiveness and mental complexity they would have fared ill indeed. President Manning was the most disturbed; but even he outgrew the darkest shadow, and smothered memories in prayers. Every man of those leaders had a stirring part to play in later years, and it is perhaps fortunate that this is so. Little more than a twelvemonth afterward Captain Whipple led the mob who burnt the revenue ship *Gaspee*, and in this bold act we may trace one step in the blotting out of unwholesome images.

There was delivered to the window of Joseph Curwen a sealed leaden coffin of curious design, obviously found ready on the spot when needed, in which she was told her husband's body lay. He had, it was explained, been killed in a customs battle about which it was not politic to give details. More than this no tongue ever uttered of Joseph Curwen's end, and Charles Ward had only a single hint wherewith to construct a theory. This hint was the merest thread – a shaky underscoring of a passage in Jedediah Orne's confiscated letter to Curwen, partly copied in Ezra Weeden's handwriting. The copy was found in the possession of Smith's descendants; and we are left to decide whether Weeden gave it to his companion after the end, as a mute clue to the abnormality which had occurred, or whether, as is more probable, Smith had it before, and added the underscoring himself from what he had managed to extract from his friend by shrewd guessing and adroit cross-questioning. The underlined passage is merely this:

I say to you againe, doe not call up Any that you cannot put downe; by the which I meane, Any that can in turn call up somewhat against you, whereby your powerfullest Devices may not be of use Ask of the Lesser, lest the Greater shall not wish to Answer, and shall commande more than you.

In the light of this passage, and reflecting on what lost unmentionable allies a beaten man might try to summon in his direst extremity, Charles Ward may well have wondered whether any citizen of Providence killed Joseph Curwen.

The deliberate effacement of every memory of the dead man from Providence life and annals was vastly aided by the influence of the raiding leaders. They had not at first meant to be so thorough, and had allowed the widow and her father and child to remain in ignorance of the true conditions; but Captain Tillinghast was an astute man, and soon uncovered enough rumors to whet his horror and cause him to demand that his daughter and granddaughter change their name, burn the library and all remaining papers, and chisel the inscription from the slate slab above Joseph Curwen's grave. He knew Captain Whipple well, and probably extracted more hints from that bluff mariner than anyone else ever gained respecting the end of the accursed sorcerer.

From that time on the obliteration of Curwen's memory became increasingly rigid, extending at last by common consent even to the town records and files of the *Gazette*. It can be compared in spirit only to the hush that lay on Oscar Wilde's name for a decade after his disgrace, and in extent only to the fate of that sinful King of Runagur in Lord Dunsany's tale, whom the gods decided must be not only cease to be, but must cease to ever have been.

Mrs Tillinghast, as the widow became known after 1772, sold the house in Olney Court and resided with her father in Power's Lane till her death in 1817. The farm at Pawtuxet, shunned by every living soul, remained to molder through the years; and seemed to decay with unaccountable rapidity. By 1780 only the stone and brickwork were standing, and by 1800 even these had fallen to shapeless heaps. None ventured to pierce the tangled shrubbery on the river-bank behind which the hillside door may have lain, nor did any try to frame a definite image of the scenes amidst which Joseph Curwen departed from the horrors he had wrought.

Only robust old Captain Whipple was heard by alert listeners to mutter once in a while to himself, 'Pox on that——, but he had no business to laugh while he screamed. 'Twas as though the damned——had summat up his sleeve. For half a crown I'd burn his——house.'

CHAPTER THREE

A Search and an Evocation

1

Charles Ward, as we have seen, first learned in 1918 of his descent from Joseph Curwen. That he at once took an intense interest in everything pertaining to the bygone mystery is not to be wondered at; for every vague rumor that he had heard of Curwen now became something vital to himself, in whom flowed Curwen's blood. No. spirited and imaginative genealogist could have done otherwise that begin forthwith an avid and systematic collection of Curwen data.

In his first delvings there was not the slightest attempt at secrecy; so that even Dr Lyman hesitates to date the youth's madness from any period before the close of 1919. He talked freely with his family – though his mother was not particularly pleased to own an ancestor like Curwen – and with the officials of the various museums and libraries he visited. In applying to private families for records though to be in their possession he made no concealment of his object, and shared the somewhat amused skepticism with which the accounts of the old diarists and letter-writers were regarded. He often expressed a keen wonder as to what really had taken place a century and a half before at that Pawtuxet farmhouse whose site he vainly tried to find, and what Joseph Curwen really had been.

When he came across the Smith diary and archives and encountered the letter from Jedediah Orne he decided to visit Salem and look up Curwen's early activities and connections there, which he did during the Easter vacation of 1919. At the Essex Institute, which was well known to him from former sojourns in the glamorous old town of crumbling Puritan gables and clustered gambrel roofs, he was very kindly received, and unearthed there a considerable amount of Curwen data. He found that his ancestor was born in Salem-Village, now Danvers, seven miles from town, on the eighteenth of February (O.S.) 1662–3; and that he had run away to sea at the age of fifteen, not appearing again for nine years, when he returned with the speech, dress, and manners of a native Englishman and settled in Salem proper. At that time he had little to do with his family, but spent most of his hours with the curious books he had brought from Europe, and the strange chemicals which came for him on ships from England, France, and Holland. Certain trips of his into the country were the objects of much local inquisitiveness, and were whisperingly associated with vague rumors of fires on the hills at night.

Curwen's only close friends had been one Edward Hutchinson of Salem-Village and one Simon Orne of Salem. With these men he was often seen in conference about the Common, and visits among them where by no means infrequent. Hutchinson had a house well out toward the woods, and it was not altogether liked by sensitive people because of the sounds heard there at night. He was said to entertain strange visitors, and the lights seen from his windows were not always of the same color. The knowledge he displayed concerning long-dead persons and long-forgotten events was considered distinctly unwholesome, and he disappeared about the time the witchcraft panic began, never to be heard from again. At that time Joseph Curwen also departed, but his settlement in Providence was soon learned of. Simon Orne lived in Salem until 1720, when his failure to grow visibly old began to excite attention. He thereafter disappeared, though thirty years later his precise counterpart and self-styled son turned up to claim his property. The claim was allowed on the strength of documents in Simon Orne's known hand, and Jedediah Orne continued to dwell in Salem till 1771, when certain letters from Providence citizens to the Reverend Thomas Barnard and others brought about his quiet removal to parts unknown.

Certain documents by and about all of these strange matters were available at the Essex Institute, the Court House, and the Registry of Deeds, and included both harmless commonplaces such as land titles and bills of sale, and furtive fragments of a more provocative nature. There were four or five unmistakable allusions to them on the witchcraft trial records; as when one Hepzibah Lawson swore on July tenth, 1692, at the Court of Oyer and Terminen under Judge Hathorne, that 'fortie Witches and the Blacke Man were wont to meet in the Woodes behind Mr Hutchinson's house', and one Amity How declared at a session of August eighth before Judge Gedney that 'Mr C. B. (George Burroughs) on that Nighte putt the Divell his Marke upon Bridgeh S., Jonathan A., *Simon O.*, Deliverance W., *Joseph C.*, Susan P., Mehitable C., and Deborah B.' Then there was a catalog of Hutchinson's uncanny library as found after his disappearance, and an unfinished manuscript in his hand writing, couched in cipher none could read. Ward had a photostatic copy of this manuscript made, and began to work casually on the cipher as soon as it was delivered to him. After the following August his labors on the cipher became intense and feverish, and there is reason to believe from his speech and conduct that he hit upon the key before October or November. He never stated, though, whether or not he had succeeded.

But of greatest immediate interest was the Orne material. It took Ward only a short time to prove from identity of penmanship a thing he had already considered established

197

from the text of the letter to Curwen; namely, that Simon Orne and his supposed son were one and the same person. As Orne had said to his correspondent, it was hardly safe to live too long in Salem, hence he resorted to a thirty-year sojourn aboard, and did not return to claim his lands except as a representative of a new generation. Orne had apparently been careful to destroy most of his correspondence, but the citizens who took action in 1771 found and preserved a few letters and papers which excited their wonder. There were cryptic formulae and diagrams in his and other hands which Ward now either copied with care or had photographed, and one extremely mysterious letter in a chirography that the searcher recognized from items in the Registry of Deeds as positively Joseph Curwen's.

This Curwen letter, though undated as to the year, was evidently not the one in answer to which Orne had written the confiscated missive; and from internal evidence Ward placed it not much later than 1750. It may not be amiss to give the text in full, as a sample of the style of one whose history was so dark and terrible. The recipient is addressed as 'Simon', but a line (whether drawn by Curwen or Orne, Ward could not tell) is run through the word.

Providence, 1 May
Brother:—
My honour'd Antient friende, due Respects and earnest Wishes to Him whom we serve for yr eternall Power. I am just come upon that which you ought to knowe, concern'g the matter of the Laste Extremitie and what to doe regard'yt. I am not dispos'd to followe you in go'g Away on acct. of my yeares, for Providence hath not ye Sharpeness of ye Bay in hunt'g oute uncommon Things and bringinge to Tryall. I am ty'd up in Shippes and Goodes, and cou'd not doe as you did, besides the whiche my farme at Patuxet hath under it That you knowe, that wou'd not waite for my com'g Backe as an Other.

But I am not unreadie for harde fortunes, as I have tolde you, and have long work'd upon ye way of get'g Backe after ye Loste. I

198

laste Nighte strucke on ye Wordes that bringe up YOGGE-SOTHOTHE, and sawe for ye firste Time that face spoke of by Ibn Schacabac in ye——. And IT said, that ye III Psalme in ye Liber-Damnatus holdes ye Clavicle. With Sunne in V House, Saturne in Trine, drawe ye Pentagram of Fire, and saye ye ninth Verse thrice. This Verse repeate eache Roodemas and Hallow's Eve, and ye thing will breede in ye Outside Spheres.

And of ye Seede of Olde shal One be borne who shal looke Backe, tho' know'g not what he seekes.

Yett will this awaite Nothing if there be no Heir, and if the Saltes, or the Way to make the Saltes bee not Readie for his Hands. And here I will owne, I have not taken needed Stepps nor found Much. Ye Process is playing harde to come neare, and it uses up such a Store of Specimens, I am harde putte to it to get Enough, notwithstand'g the Sailors I have from the Indies. Ye People aboute are become curious, but I can stande them off. Ye gentry are worse than the Populace, be'g more Circumstantiall in their Accts. and more believ'd in what they tell. That Parson and Mr Merritt have talk'd some, I am feerfull, but no Thing soe far is Dangerous. Ye Chymical substance are easie of get'g, there be'g II. goode Chymists in Towne, Dr Bowen and San Carew. I am foll'g oute what Borellus saith, and have Helpe in Abdool Al-Hazred his VII. Booke. Whatever I gette, you shal have. And in ye meane while, do not neglect to make use of ye Wordes I have here given. I have them Righte, but if you Desire to see HIM, imploy the Writinge on ye Piece of——, that I am putt'g in this Packet. Saye ye Verses every Roodemas and Hallow's Eve; and if yr Line runn not out, *one shall bee in yeares to come that shal looke backe and use what Saltes or Stuff for Saltes you shal leave him.* Job XIV.XIV.

I rejoice you are again at Salem, and hope I may see you not longe hence. I have a goode Stallion, and am think'g of get'g a Coach, there be'g one (Mr Merritt's) in Providence alreadie, tho', ye Roades are bad. If you are dispos'd to travel, doe not pass me bye. From Boston take ye Poste Rd. thro' Dedham, Wrentham, and Attleborough, goode Taverns be'g at all these Townes. Stop at Mr Bolcom's in Wrentham, where ye Beddes are finer than Mr Hatch's, but eate at ye other House for their cooke is better. Turne into Providence by Patucket falls, and ye Rd. past Mr Sayles's Tavern. My House opp. Mr Epenetus Olney's Tavern off ye Towne Street, Ist on ye N. side of Olney's Court. Distance from Boston Store abt. XLIV miles.

Sir, I am yr olde and true friend and Servt. in Almonsin-Metraton.

Josephus C.

To Mr Simon Orne,
William's-Lane, in Salem.

This letter, oddly enough, was what first gave Ward the exact location of Curwen's Providence home; for none of the records encountered up to that time had been at all specific. The discovery was doubly striking because it indicated as the newer Curwen house, built in 1761 on the site of the old, a dilapidated building still standing in Olney Court and well known to Ward in his antiquarian rambles over Stampers Hill. The place was indeed only a few squares from his own home on the great hill's higher ground, and was now the abode of a Negro family much esteemed for occasional washing, house-cleaning, and furnace-tending services. To find, in distant Salem, such sudden proof of the significance of this familiar rookery in his own family history was a highly impressive thing to Ward; and he resolved to explore the place immediately upon his return. The more mystical phases of the letter, which he took to be some extravagant kind of symbolism, frankly baffled him; though he noted with a thrill of curiosity that the Biblical passage referred to – Job 14, 14 – was the familiar verse, 'If a man die, shall he live again? All the days of my appointed time will I wait, till my change come.'

2

Young Ward came home in a state of pleasant excitement, and spent the following Saturday in a long and exhaustive study of the house of Olney Court. The place, now crumbling with age, had never been a mansion; but was a modest two-and-a-half story wooden town house of the familiar Providence Colonial type, with plain peaked roof, large central chimney and artistically carved doorway with rayed fanlight, triangular pediment, and trim Doric pilasters. It had suffered but little alteration externally, and Ward felt he was gazing on something very close to the sinister matters of his quest.

The present Negro inhabitants were known to him, and he was very courteously shown about the interior by old Asa and his stout wife Hannah. Here there was more change than the outside indicated, and Ward saw with regret that fully half of the fine scroll-and-urn overmantels and shell-carved cupboard linings were gone, whilst much of the fine wainscoting and bolection molding was marked, hacked, and gouged, or covered up altogether with cheap wall-paper. In general, the survey did not yield as much as Ward had somehow expected; but it was at least exciting to stand within the ancestral walls which had housed such a man of horror as Joseph Curwen. He saw with a thrill that a monogram had been very carefully effaced from the ancient brass knocker.

From then until after the close of school Ward spent his time on the photostatic copy of the Hutchinson cipher and the accumulation of local Curwen data. The former still proved unyielding; but of the latter he obtained so much, and so many clues to similar data elsewhere, that he was ready to make a trip to New London and New York to consult old letters whose presence in those places was indicated. This trip was very fruitful, for it brought him the Fenner letters with their terrible description of the Pawtuxet farmhouse raid, and the Nightingale-Talbot letters in which he learned of the portrait painted on a panel of the Curwen Library. This matter of the portrait interested him particularly, since he would have given much to know just what Joseph Curwen looked like; and he decided to make a second search of the house in Olney Court to see if there might not be some trace of the ancient features beneath peeling coats of later paint or layers of moldy wall-paper.

Early in August that search took place, and Ward went carefully over the walls of every room sizeable enough to have been by any possibility of library of the evil builder. He paid especial attention to the large panels of such overmantels as still remained; and was keenly excited after about an hour, when, on a broad area above the fireplace in a spacious ground-floor room, he became certain that the surface brought out by the peeling of several coats of paint was sensibly darker than any ordinary interior paint or the wood beneath it was likely to have been. A few more careful tests with a thin knife, and he knew that he had come upon an oil portrait of great extent. With truly scholarly restraint, the youth did not risk the damage which an immediate attempt to uncover the hidden picture with the knife might have done, but just retired from the scene of his discovery to enlist expert help. In three days he returned with an artist of long experience, Mr Walter Dwight, whose studio is near the foot of College Hill; and that accomplished restorer of paintings set to work at once with proper methods and chemical substances. Old Asa and his wife were duly excited over their strange visitors, and were properly reimbursed for this invasion of their domestic hearth.

As day by day the work of restoration progressed, Charles Ward looked on with growing interest at the lines and shades gradually unveiled after their long oblivion. Dwight had begun at the bottom; hence since the picture was a three-quarter-length one, the face did not come out for some time. It was meanwhile seen that the subject was a spare, well-shaped man with dark-blue coat, embroidered waistcoat, black satin small-clothes, and white silk stockings, seated in a carved chair against the background of a window with wharves and ships beyond. When the head

202

came out it was observed to bear a neat Albemarle wig, and to possess a thin, calm, undistinguished face which seemed somehow familiar to both Ward and the artist. Only at the very last, though, did the restorer and his client begin to gasp with astonishment at the details of that lean, pallid visage, and to recognize with a touch of awe the dramatic trick which heredity had played. For it took the final bath of oil and the final stroke of the delicate scraper to bring out fully the expression which centuries had hidden; and to confront the bewildered Charles Dexter Ward, dweller in the past, with his own living features in the countenance of his horrible great-great-great-grandfather.

Ward brought his parents to see the marvel he had uncovered, and his father at once determined to purchase the picture despite its execution on stationary paneling. The resemblance to the boy, despite an appearance of rather greater age, was marvelous; and it could be seen that through some trick atavism the physical contours of Joseph Curwen had found precise duplication after a century and a half. Mrs Ward's resemblance to her ancestor was not at all marked, though she could recall relatives who had some of the facial characteristics shared by her son and by the bygone Curwen. She did not relish the discovery, and told her husband that he had better burn the picture instead of bringing it home. There was, she averred, something unwholesome about it; not only intrinsically, but in its very resemblance to Charles. Mr Ward, however, was a practical man of power and affairs – a cotton manufacturer with extensive mills at Riverpoint in the Pawtuxet Valley – and not one to listen to feminine scruples. The picture impressed him mightily with its likeness to his son, and he believed the boy deserved it as a present. In this opinion, it is needless to say, Charles most heartily concurred; and a few days later Mr Ward located the owner of the house and a small rodent-featured person with a guttural accent – and obtained the whole mantel and overmantel bearing the picture at a curtly fixed price which cut short the impending torrent of unctuous haggling.

It now remained to take off the panelling and remove it to the Ward home, where provisions were made for its thorough restoration and installation with electric or mock-fireplace in Charles's third-floor study library. To Charles was left the task of superintending this removal, and on the twenty-eighth of August he accompanied two expert workmen from the Crooker decorating firm to the house in Olney Court, where the mantel and portrait-bearing overmantel were detached with great care and precision for transportation in the company's motor truck. There was left a space of exposed brickwork marking the chimney's course, and in this young Ward observed a cubical recess about a foot square, which must have lain directly behind the head of the portrait. Curious as to what such a space might mean or contain, the youth approached and looked within; finding beneath the deep coatings of dust and soot some loose yellowed papers, a crude thick copy-book, and a few moldering textile shreds which may have formed the ribbon binding the rest together. Blowing away the bulk of the dirt and cinders, he took up the book and looked at the bold inscription on its cover. It was in a hand which he had learned to recognize at the Essex Institute, and proclaimed the volume as the '*Journal and Notes of Jos. Curwen, Gent., of Providence-Plantations, Late of Salem.*'

Excited beyond measure by his discovery, Ward showed the book to the two curious workmen beside him. Their testimony is absolute as to the nature and genuineness of the finding, and Dr Willett relies on them to help establish his theory that the youth was not mad when he began his major eccentricities. All the other papers were likewise in Curwen's handwriting, and one of them seemed especially portentous because of its inscription: '*To Him Who Shal Come*

204

After, And How He May Gett Beyonde Time and Ye Spheres.'
Another was in a cipher; the same, Ward hoped, as the
Hutchinson cipher which had hitherto baffled him. A
third, and here the searcher rejoiced, seemed to be a key to
the cipher; whilst the fourth and fifth were addressed
respectively to 'Edw: Hutchinson, Armiger' and 'Jedediah
Orne, Esq.', 'or Their Heir or Heirs, or Those Represent'g
Them'. The sixth and last was inscribed: *'Joseph Curwen his
Life and Travells Bet'n ye yeares 1678 and 1687: of Whither He
Voyag'd, Where He Stay'd, Whom He Sawe, and What He
Learnt.'*

3

We have now reached the point from which the more
academic school of alienists date Charles Ward's madness.
Upon his discovery the youth had looked immediately at a
few of the inner pages of the book and manuscripts, and
had evidently seen something which impressed him
tremendously. Indeed, in showing the titles to the workmen he appeared to guard the text itself with peculiar
care, and to labor under a perturbation for which even
the antiquarian and genealogical significance of the find
could hardly account. Upon returning home he broke the
news with an almost embarrassed air, as if he wished to
convey an idea of its supreme importance without having
to exhibit the evidence itself. He did not even show the
titles to his parents, but simply told them that he had
found some documents in Joseph Curwen's handwriting,
'mostly in cipher', which would have to be studied very
carefully before yielding up their true meaning. It is
unlikely that he would have shown what he did to the
workmen, had it not been for their unconcealed curiosity.

As it was he doubtless wished to avoid any display of peculiar reticence which would increase their discussion of the matter.

That night Charles Ward sat up in his room reading the new-found book and papers, and when day came he did not desist. His meals, on his urgent request when his mother called to see what was amiss, were sent up to him; and in the afternoon he appeared only briefly when the men came to install the Curwen picture and mantelpiece in his study. The next night he slept in snatches in his clothes, meanwhile wrestling feverishly with the unravelling of the cipher manuscript. In the morning his mother saw that he was at work on the photostatic copy of the Hutchinson cipher, which he had frequently showed her before; but in response to her query he said that the Curwen key could not be applied to it. That afternoon he abandoned his work and watched the men fascinatedly as they finished their installation of the picture with its woodwork above a cleverly realistic electric log, settling the mock-fireplace and overmantel a little out from the north wall as if a chimney existed, and boxing in its sides with panelling to match the room's. The front panel holding the picture was sawn and hinged to allow cupboard space behind it. After the workmen went he moved his work into the study and sat down before it with his eyes half on the cipher and half on the portrait which stared back at him like a year-adding, century-recalling mirror. His parents, subsequently recalling his conduct at this period, give interesting details anent the policy of concealment which he practiced. Before servants he seldom hid any paper which he might be studying, since he rightly assumed that Curwen's intricate and archaic chirography would be too much for them. With his parents, however, he was more circumspect; and unless the manuscript in question were a cipher, or a mere mass of cryptic symbols and unknown ideographs (as that entitled

'*To Him Who Shal Come After, etc.*' seemed to be) he would cover it with some convenient paper until his caller had departed. At night he kept the papers under lock and key in an antique cabinet of his, where he also placed them whenever he left the room. He soon resumed fairly regular hours and habits, except that his long walks and other outside interests seemed to cease. The opening of school, where he now began his senior year, seemed a great bore to him; and he frequently asserted his determination never to bother with college. He had, he said, important special investigations to make, which would provide him with more avenues toward knowledge and the humanities thatn any university which the world could boast.

Naturally, only one who had always been more or less studious, eccentric, and solitary could have pursued this course for many days without attracting notice. Ward, however, was constitutionally a scholar and a hermit; hence his parents were less surprised than regretful at the close confinement and secrecy he adopted. At the same time, both his father and mother thought it odd that he would show them no scrap of his treasure-trove, nor give any connected account of such data as he had deciphered. This reticence he explained away as due to a wish to wait until he might announce some connected revelation, but as the weeks passed without further disclosures there began to grow up between the youth and his family a kind of constraint; intensified in his mother's case by her manifest disapproval of all Curwen delvings.

During October Ward began visiting the libraries again, but no longer for the antiquarian matter of his former days. Witchcraft and magic, occultism and demonology, were what he sought now; and when Providence sources proved unfruitful he would take the train for Boston and tap the wealth of the great library in Copley Square, the Widener Library at Harvard, or the Zion Research Library in

Brookline, where certain rare works on Biblical subjects are available. He bought extensively, and fitted up a whole additional set of shelves in his study for newly acquired works on uncanny subjects; while during the Christmas holidays he made a round of out-of-town trips including one to Salem to consult certain records at the Essex Institute.

About the middle of January, 1920, there entered Ward's bearing an element of triumph which he did not explain, and he was no more found at work upon the Hutchinson cipher. Instead, he inauguarated a dual policy of chemical research and record-scanning; fitting up for the one a laboratory in the unused attic of the house, and for the latter haunting all the sources of vital statistics in Providence. Local dealers in drugs and scientific supplies, later questioned, gave astonishingly queer, meaningless catalogs of the substances and instruments he purchased; but clerks at the State-House, the City Hall, and the various libraries agree as to the definite object of his second interest. He was searching intensely and feverishly for the grave of Joseph Curwen, from whose slate slab an older generation had so wisely blotted the name.

Little by little there grew upon the Ward family the conviction that something was wrong. Charles had had freaks and changes of minor interests before, but this growing secrecy and absorption in strange pursuits was unlike even him. His school work was the merest pretense; and although he failed in no test, it could be seen that the old application had all vanished. He had other concernments now; and when not in his new laboratory with a score of obsolete alchemical books, could be found either poring over old burial records down town or glued to his volumes of occult lore in his study, where the startlingly – one almost fancied increasingly–similar features of Joseph Curwen stared blandly at him from the great overmantel on the north wall.

Late in March Ward added to his archive-searching a ghoulish series of rambles about the various ancient cemeteries of the city. The cause appeared later, when it was learned from City Hall clerks that he had probably found an important clue. His quest had suddenly shifted from the grave of Joseph Curwen to that of one Naphthali Field; and his shift was explained when, upon going over the files that he had been over, the investigators actually found a fragmentary record of Curwen's burial which had escaped the general obliteration, and which stated that the curious leaden coffin had been interred '10 ft. S. and 5 Ft. W. of Naphthali Field's grave in y—.' The lack of a specified burying ground in the surviving entry greatly complicated the search, and Naphthali Field's grave seemed as elusive as that of Curwen's; but here no systematic effacement had existed, and one might reasonably be expected to stumble on the stone itself even if its record had perished. Hence the rambles – from which St John's (the former King's) churchyard and the ancient Congregational burying-ground in the midst of Swan Point Cemetery were excluded, since other statistics had shown that the only Naphthali Field (obit. 1729) whose grave could have been meant had been a Baptist.

4

It was toward May when Dr Willett, at the request of the senior Ward, and fortified with all the Curwen data which the family had gleaned from Charles in his non-secretive days, talked with the young man. The interview was of little value or conclusiveness, for Willett felt at every moment that Charles was thoroughly master of himself and in touch with matters of real importance; but it at least forced the secretive youth to offer some rational explanation of his recent demeanor. Of a pallid, impassive type not easily showing embarrassment, Ward seemed quite ready to discuss his pursuits, though not to reveal their object. He stated that the papers of his ancestor had contained some remarkable secrets of early scientfic knowledge, for the most part in cipher, of an apparent scope comparable only to the discoveries of Friar Bacon and perhaps surpassing even those. They were, however, meaningless except when correlated with a body of learning now wholly obsolete; so that their immediate presentation to a world equipped only with modern science would rob them of all impressiveness and dramatic significance. To take their vivid place in the history of human thought they must first be correlated by one familiar with the background out of which they evolved, and to this task of correlation Ward was now devoting himself. He was seeking to acquire as fast as possible those neglected arts of old which a true interpreter of the Curwen data must possess, and hoped in time to make a full announcement and presentation of the utmost interest to mankind and to the world of thought. Not even Einstein, he declared, could more profoundly revolutionize the current conception of things.

As to his graveyard search, whose object he freely admitted, but the details of whose progress he did not relate, he said he had reason to think that Joseph Curwen's mutilated headstone bore certain mystic symbols – carved from directions in his will and ignorantly spared by those who had effaced the name – which were absolutely essential to the final solution of his cryptic system. Curwen, he believed, had wished to guard his secret with care; and had consequently distributed the data in an exceedingly curious fashion. When Dr Willett asked to see the mystic documents, Ward displayed much reluctance and tried to put him off with such things as photostatic copies of the

Hutchinson cipher and Orne formula and diagrams; but finally showed him the exteriors of some of the real Curwen finds – the '*Journal and Notes*', the cipher (title in cipher also) and the formula-filled message '*To Him Who Shal Come After*' – and let him glance inside such as were in obscure characters.

He also opened the diary at a page carefully selected for its innocuousness and gave Willett a glimpse of Curwen's connected handwriting in English. The doctor noted very closely the crabbed and complicated letters, and the general aura of the seventeenth century which clung round both penmanship and style despite the writer's survival into the eighteenth century, and became quickly certain that the document was genuine. The text itself was relatively trivial, and Willett recalled only a fragment:

'Wedn. 16 Octr. 1754. My Sloope the *Wahefal* this day putt in from London with XX newe Men pick'd up in ye Indies, Spaniards from Martineco and Dutch Men from Surinam. Ye Dutch Men are like to Desert from hav'g hearde Somewhat ill of these Ventures, but I will see to ye inducing of them to Staye. For Mr Knight Dexter at ye Bay and Book 120 Pieces Camblets, 100 Pieces Assrtd. Camble-teens, 20 Pieces blue Duffles, 50 Pieces Calamancoco, 300 Pieces each, Shendsoy and Humhums. For Mr Green at ye Elephant, 50 gallon Cyttles, 20 Warm'g Pannes, 15 Bake Cyttles, 10 pr. Smoke'g Tonges. For Mr Perrigo, 1 Sett of Awles. For Mr Nightingale, 50 Reames prime Foolscap. Say'd ye SABAOTH thrice last Nighte but None appear'd. I must heare more from Mr H. In Transylvania, tho' it is Harde reach'g him and exceeding strange he cannot give me the use of what he hath so well us'd these hundred yeares. Simon hath not Writ these V. Weekes, but I expecte soon hear'g from him.'

When upon reaching this point Dr Willett turned the leaf he was quickly checked by Ward, who almost snatched the book from his grasp. All that the doctor had a chance to see on the newly opened page was a brief pair of sentences; but these, strangely enough, lingered tenaciously in his memory. They ran: 'Ye Verse from Liber-Damnatus be'g spoke V Roodmasses and IV Hallow's-Eves, I am Hopeful ye Thing is breed'g Outside ye Spheres. It will drawe One who is to Come if I can make sure he shal bee, and he shall think on Past thinges and looke backe thro' all ye yeares, against ye which I must have ready ye Saltes or That to make 'em with.'

Willett saw no more, but somehow this small glimpse gave a new and vague terror to the painted features of Joseph Curwen which stared blandly down from the over-mantel. Ever after that he entertained the odd fancy – which his medical skill of course assured him was only a fancy – that the eyes of the portrait had a sort of wish, if not an actual tendency, to follow young Charles Ward as he moved about the room. He stopped before leaving to study the picture closely, marveling at its resemblance to Charles and memorizing every minute detail of the cryptical, col-orless face, even down to a slight scar or pit in the smooth brow over the right eye. Cosmo Alexander, he decided, was a painter worthy of the Scotland that produced Raeburn, and a teacher worthy of his illustrious pupil Gilbert Stuart.

Assured by the doctor that Charles's mental health was in no danger, but that on the other hand he was engaged in researches which might prove of real importance, the Wards were more lenient than they might otherwise have been when during the following June the youth made positive his refusal to attend college. He had, he declared, studies of much more vital importance to pursue; and intimated a wish to go abroad the following year in order to avail himself of certain sources of data not existing in America. The senior Ward, while denying this latter wish as absurd for a boy of only eighteen, acquiesced regarding

212

the university; so that after a none too brilliant graduation from the Moses Brown School there ensued for Charles a three-year period of intensive occult study and graveyard searching. He became recognized as an eccentric, and dropped even more completely from the sight of his family's friends than he had been before; keeping close to his work and only occasionally making trips to other cities to consult obscure records. Once he went south to talk with a strange old mulatto who dwelt in a swamp and about whom a newspaper had printed a curious article. Again he sought a small village in the Adirondacks whence reports of certain odd ceremonial practices had come. But still his parents forbade him the trip to the Old World which he desired.

Coming of age in April, 1923, and having previously inherited a small competence from his maternal grand-father, Ward determined at last to take the European trip hitherto denied him. Of his proposed itinerary he would say nothing save that the needs of his studies would carry him to many places but he promised to write his parents fully and faithfully. When they saw he could not be dissuaded, they ceased all opposition and helped as best they could; so that in June the young man sailed for Liverpool with the farewell blessings of his father and mother, who accompanied him to Boston and waved him out of sight from the White Star pier in Charlestown. Letters soon told of his safe arrival, and of his securing good quarters in Great Russell Street, London, where he proposed to stay, shunning all family friends, till he had exhausted the resources of the British Museum in a certain direction. Of his daily life he wrote but little, for there was little to write. Study and experiment concerned all his time, and he mentioned a laboratory which he had established in one of his rooms. That he said nothing of antiquarian rambles in the glamorous old city with its luring skyline of ancient domes and steeples and its tangles of roads and alleys whose mystic convolutions and sudden vistas alternately beckon and surprise, was taken by his parents as a good index of the degree to which his new interests had engrossed his mind.

In June, 1924, a brief note told of his departure for Paris, to which he had before made one or two flying trips for material in the Bibliothèque Nationale. For three months thereafter he sent only post-cards, giving an address in the Rue St Jacques and referring to a special search among rare manuscripts in the library of an unnamed private collector. He avoided acquaintances, and no tourists brought back reports of having seen him. Then came a silence, and in October the Wards received a picture card from Prague, stating that Charles was in that ancient town for the purpose of conferring with a certain very aged man supposed to be the last living possessor of some very curious mediaeval information. He gave an address in the Neustadt, and announced no move till the following January, when he dropped several cards from Vienna telling of his passage through that city on the way toward a more easterly region whither one of his correspondents and fellow-delvers into the occult had invited him.

The next card was from Klausenburg in Transylvania, and told of Ward's progress toward his destination. He was going to visit a Baron Ferenczy, whose estate lay in the mountains east of Rakus; and was to be addressed at Rakus in the care of that nobleman. Another card from Rakus a week later, saying that his host's carriage had met him and that he was leaving the village for the mountains, was his last message for a considerable time; indeed, he did not reply to his parents' frequent letters until May, when he wrote to discourage the plan of his mother for a meeting in London, Paris, or Rome during the summer, when the elder Wards were planning to travel in Europe. His researches, he said, were such that he could not leave his present quarters, while the situation of Baron Ferenczy's castle did not favor visits. It was on a crag in the dark wooded mountains, and the region was so shunned by the country folk that normal people could not help feeling ill at ease. Moreover, the Baron was not a person likely to appeal to correct and conservative New England gentlefolk. His aspect and manners had idiosyncrasies, and his age was so great as to be disquieting. It would be better, Charles said, if his parents would wait for his return to Providence; which could scarcely be far distant.

That return did not, however, take place until May, 1925, when, after a few heralding cards, the young wanderer quietly slipped into New York on the *Homeric* and traversed the long miles to Providence by motor coach, eagerly drinking in the green rolling hills, the fragrant, blossoming orchards, and the white steepled towns of vernal Connecticut; his first taste of ancient New England in nearly four years. When the coach crossed the Pawcatuck and entered Rhode Island amidst the faery goldenness of a late spring afternoon his heart beat with quickened force, and the entry to Providence along Reservoir and Elmwood avenues was a breathless and wonderful thing despite the depths of forbidden lore into which he had delved. At the high square where Broad, Weybosset, and Empire Streets join, he saw before and below him in the fire of sunset the pleasant, remembered houses and domes and steeples of the old town; and his head swam curiously as the vehicle rolled down to the terminal behind the Biltmore, bringing into view the great dome and soft, roof-pierced greenery of the ancient hill across the river, and the tall, colonial spire of the First Baptist Church limned pink in the magic evening light against the fresh springtime verdure of its precipitous background.

Old Providence! It was this place and the mysterious forces of its long, continuous history which had brought him into being, and which had drawn him back toward marvels and secrets whose boundaries no prophet might fix. Here lay the arcana, wondrous or dreadful as the case might be, for which all his years of travel and application had been preparing him. A taxicab whirled him through Post Office Square with its glimpse of the river, the old Market House, and the head of the bay, and up the steep curved slope of Waterman Street to Prospect, where the vast gleaming dome and sunset-flushed Ionic columns of the Christian Science Church beckoned northward. Then eight squares past the fine old estates his childish eyes had known, and the quaint brick sidewalks so often trodden by his youthful feet. And at last the little white overtaken farmhouse on the right, on the left the classic Adam porch and stately bayed façade of the great brick house where he was born. It was twilight, and Charles Dexter Ward had come home.

5

A school of alienists slightly less academic than Dr Lyman's assign to Ward's European trip the beginning of his true madness. Admitting that he was sane when he started, they believe that his conduct upon returning implies a disastrous change. But even to this claim Dr Willett refuses to accede. There was, he insists, something later; and the queernesses of the youth at this stage he attributes to the practice of rituals learned abroad – odd enough things, to be sure, but by no means implying mental aberration on the part of their celebrant. Ward himself, though visibly aged and hardened, was still normal in his general reactions; and in several talks with Willett displayed a balance which no madman – even an incipient one – could feign continuously for long. What elicited the notion of insanity at this period were the *sounds* heard at all hours from Ward's attic laboratory, in which he kept himself most of the time. There were chantings and repetitions, and thunderous declamations in uncanny rhythms; and although these sounds were always in Ward's own voice, there was something in the quality of that voice, and in the accents of the formulae it pronounced, which could not but chill the blood of every hearer. It was noticed that Nig, the venerable and beloved black cat of the household, brisked and arched his back perceptibly when certain of the tones were heard.

The odors occasionally wafted from the laboratory were likewise exceedingly strange. Sometimes they were very noxious, but more often they were aromatic, with a haunting, elusive quality which seemed to have the power of inducing fantastic images. People who smelled them had a tendency to glimpse momentary mirages of enormous vistas, with strange hills or endless avenues of sphinxes and hippogriffs stretching off into infinite distance. Ward did not resume his old-time rambles, but applied himself diligently to the strange books he had brought home, and to equally strange delvings within his quarters; explaining that European sources had greatly enlarged the possibilities of his work, and promised great revelations in the years to come. His older aspect increased to a startling degree his resemblance to the Curwen portrait in his library and Dr Willett would often pause by the latter after a call, marvelling at the virtual identity, and reflecting that only the small pit above the picture's right eye now remained to differentiate the long dead wizard from the living youth. These calls of Willett's, undertaken at the request of the senior Wards, were curious affairs. Ward at no time repulsed the doctor, but the latter saw that he could never reach the young man's inner psychology. Frequently he noted peculiar things about; little wax images of grotesque design on the shelves or tables, and the half-erased remnants of circles, triangles, and pentagrams in chalk or charcoal on the cleared central space of the large room. And always in the night those rhythms and incantations thundered, till it became very difficult to keep servants or suppress furtive talk of Charles's madness.

In January, 1927, a peculiar incident occurred. One night about midnight, as Charles was chanting a ritual whose weird cadence echoed unpleasantly through the house below, there came a sudden gust of chill wind from the bay, and a faint, obscure trembling of the earth which everyone in the neighborhood noted. At the same time the cat exhibited phenomenal traces of fright, while dogs bayed for as much as a mile around. This was the prelude to a sharp thunderstorm, anomalous for the season, which brought with it such a crash that Mr and Mrs Ward believed the house had been struck. They rushed upstairs to see what damage had been done, but Charles met them at the door to the attic; pale, resolute, and portentous, with an almost fearsome combination of triumph and seriousness on his face. He assured them that the house had not really been struck, and that the storm would soon be over. They paused, and looking through a window saw that he was indeed right; for the lightning flashed farther and farther off, whilst the trees ceased to bend in the strange frigid gust from the water. The thunder sank to a sort of dull mumbling chuckle and finally died away. Stars came out, and the stamp of triumph on Charles Ward's face crystallized into a very singular expression.

For two months or more after this incident Ward was less confined than usual to his laboratory. He exhibited a curious interest in the weather, and made odd inquiries about the date of the spring thawing of the ground. One night late in March he left the house after midnight, and did not return till almost morning, when his mother, being wakeful, heard a rumbling motor draw up to the carriage entrance. Muffled oaths could be distinguished, and Mrs

Ward, rising and going to the window, saw four dark figures removing a long, heavy box from a truck at Charles's direction and carrying it within by the side door. She heard laboured breathing and ponderous footfalls on the stairs, and finally a dull thumping in the attic; after which the footfalls descended again, and the four men reappeared outside and drove off in their truck.

The next day Charles resumed his strict attic seclusion, drawing down the dark shades of his laboratory windows and appearing to be working on some metal substance. He would open the door to no one, and steadfastly refused all proffered food. About noon a wrenching sound followed by a terrible cry and a fall were heard, but when Mrs Ward rapped at the door her son at length answered faintly, and told her that nothing had gone amiss. The hideous and indescribable stench now welling out was absolutely harmless and unfortunately necessary. Solitude was the one prime essential, and he would appear later for dinner. That afternoon, after the conclusion of some odd hissing sounds which came from behind the locked portal, he did finally appear, wearing an extremely haggard aspect and forbidding anyone to enter the laboratory upon any pretext. This, indeed, proved the beginning of a new policy of secrecy; for never afterward was any other person permitted to visit either the mysterious garret workroom or the adjacent store-room which he cleaned out, furnished roughly, and added to his inviolably private domain as a sleeping apartment. Here he lived, with books brought up from his library beneath, till the time he purchased the Pawtuxet bungalow and moved to it all his scientific effects.

In the evening Charles secured the paper before the rest of the family and damaged part of it through an apparent accident. Later on Dr Willett, having fixed the date from statements by various members of the household, looked up an intact copy at the *Journal* office and found that in the destroyed section the following small item had occurred;

Nocturnal Diggers Surprised in North Burial Ground

Robert Hart, night watchman at the North Burial Ground, this morning discovered a party of several men with a motor truck in the oldest part of the cemetery, but apparently frightened them off before they had accomplished whatever their object may have been.

The discovery took place at about four o'clock, when Hart's attention was attracted by the sound of a motor outside his shelter. Investigating, he saw a large truck on the main drive several rods away; but could not reach it before the sound of his feet on the gravel had revealed his approach. The men hastily placed a large box in the truck and drove away toward the street before they could be overtaken; and since no known grave was disturbed, Hart believes that this box was an object which they wished to bury.

The diggers must have been at work for a long while before detection, for Hart found an enormous hole dug at a considerable distance back from the roadway in the lot of Amosa Field, where most of the old stones have long ago disappeared. The hole, a place as large and deep as a grave, was empty; and did not coincide with any interment mentioned in the cemetery records.

Sergeant Riley of the Second Station viewed the spot and gave the opinion that the hole was dug by bootleggers rather gruesomely and ingeniously seeking a safe cache for liquor in a place not likely to be disturbed. In reply to questions Hart said he thought the escaping truck had headed up Rochambeau Avenue, though he could not be sure.

During the next few days Charles Ward was seldom seen by his family. Having added sleeping quarters to his attic realm, he kept clearly to himself there, ordering food brought to the door and not taking it in until after the servant had gone away. The droning of monotonous formulae and the chanting of bizarre rhythms recurred at intervals, while at other times occasional listeners could detect the sound of tinkling glass, hissing chemicals, running water, or roaring gas flames. Odors of the most unplaceable quality, wholly unlike any before noted, hung at times around the door; and the air of tension observable in the young recluse whenever he did venture briefly forth was such as to excite the keenest speculation. Once he made a hasty trip to the Athenaeum for a book he required, and again he hired a messenger to fetch him a highly obscure volume from Boston. Suspense was written portentously over the whole situation, and both the family and Dr Willett confessed themselves wholly at a loss what to do or think about it.

<h1 style="text-align:center">6</h1>

Then on the fifteenth of April a strange development occurred. While nothing appeared to grow different in kind, there was certainly a very terrible difference in degree; and Dr Willett somehow attaches great significance to the change. The day was Good Friday, a circumstance of which the servants made much, but which others quite naturally dismiss as an irrelevant coincidence. Late in the afternoon young Ward began repeating a certain formula in a singularly loud voice, at the same time burning some substance so pungent that its fumes escaped over the entire house. The formula was so plainly audible in the hall outside the locked door that Mrs Ward could not help memorizing it as she waited and listened anxiously, and later on she was able to write it down at Dr. Willett's request. It ran as follows, and experts have told Dr Willett that its very close analog can be found in the mystic writings of 'Eliphas Levi', that cryptic soul who crept through a crack in the forbidden door and glimpsed the frightful vistas of the void beyond:

'Per Adonai Eloim, Adonai Jehova,
Adonai Sabaoth, Metraton Ou Agla Methon,
verbum pythonicum, mysterium salamandrae,
cenventus sylvorum, antra gnomorum,
daemonia Coeli God, Almonsin, Gibor,
Jehosua, Evam, Zariathnatmik, Veni, veni, veni.'

This had been going on for two hours without change or intermission when over all the neighbourhood a pandemoniac howling of dogs set in. The extent of this howling can be judged from the space it received in the papers the next day, but to those in the Ward household it was overshadowed by the odor which instantly followed it; a hideous all-pervasive odor which none of them had ever smelt before or have ever smelt since. In the midst of this mephitic flood there came a very perceptible flash like that of lightning, which would have been blinding and impressive but for the daylight around; and then was heard *the voice* that no listener can ever forget because of its thunderous remoteness, its incredible depth, and its eldritch dissimilarity to Charles Ward's voice. It shook the house, and was clearly heard by at least two neighbors above the howling of the dogs. Mrs Ward, who had been listening in despair outside her son's locked laboratory, shivered as she recognized its hellish import; for Charles had told her of its evil fame in dark books, and of the manner in which it had thundered, according to the Fenner letters, above the doomed Pawtuxet farmhouse on the night of Joseph Curwen's annihilation. There was no mistaking that nightmare phrase, for Charles had described it too vividly in the old days when he had talked frankly of his Curwen investigations. And yet it was only this fragment of an archaic and forgotten language: 'DIES MIES JESCHET BOENE DOESEF DOUVEMA ENITEMAUS.'

Close upon this thundering there came a momentary darkening of the daylight, though sunset was still an hour

222

distant, and then a puff of added odor, different from the first but equally unknown and intolerable. Charles was chanting again now and his mother could hear syllables that sounded like 'Yi-nash-Yog-Sothoth-he-lglb-fi-throdag' – ending in a 'Yah!' whose maniacal force mounted in an ear-splitting crescendo. A second later all previous memories were effaced by the wailing scream which burst out with frantic explosiveness and gradually changed form to a paroxysm of diabolic and hysterical laughter. Mrs Ward, with the mingled fear and blind courage of maternity, advanced and knocked affrightedly at the concealing panels, but obtained no sign of recognition. She knocked again, but paused nervelessly as a second shriek arose, this one unmistakably in the familiar voice of her son, *and sounding concurrently with the still-bursting cachinnations of that other voice.* Presently she fainted, although she is still unable to recall the precise and immediate cause. Memory sometimes makes merciful deletions.

Mr Ward returned from the business section at a quarter past six, and, not finding his wife downstairs, was told by the frightened servants that she was probably watching at Charles's door, from which the sounds had been far stranger than ever before. Mounting the stairs at once, he saw Mrs Ward stretched at full length on the floor of the corridor outside the laboratory; and realizing that she had fainted, hastened to fetch a glass of water from a setbowl in a neighboring alcove. Dashing the cold fluid in her face, he was heartened to observe an immediate response on her part, and was watching the bewildered opening of her eyes when a chill shot through him and threatened to reduce him to the very state from which she was emerging. For the seemingly silent laboratory was not as silent as it had appeared to be, but held the murmurs of a tense, muffled conversation in tones too low for comprehension, yet of a quality profoundly disturbing to the soul.

It was not, of course, new for Charles to mutter formulae; but this muttering was definitely different. It was so palpably a dialogue, or imitation of inflections suggesting question and answer, statement and response. One voice was undisguisedly that of Charles, but the other had a depth and hollowness which the youth's best powers of ceremonial mimicry had scarcely approached before. There was something hideous, blasphemous, and abnormal about it, and but for a cry from his recovering wife which cleared his mind by arousing his protective instincts, it is not likely that Theodore Howland Ward could have maintained for nearly a year more his old boast that he had never fainted. As it was, he seized his wife in his arms and bore her quickly downstairs before she could notice the voices which had so horribly disturbed him. Even so, however, he was not quick enough to escape catching something himself which caused him to stagger dangerously with his burden. For Mrs Ward's cry had evidently been heard by others than he and there had come in response to it from behind the locked door the first distinguishable words which that masked and terrible colloquy had yielded. They were merely an excited caution in Charles's own voice, but somehow their implications held a nameless fright for the father who overheard them. The phrase was just this: 'Sshh!—Write!'

Mr and Mrs Ward conferred at some length after dinner, and the former resolved to have a firm and serious talk with Charles that very night. No matter how important the object, such conduct could not longer be permitted; for these latest developments transcended every limit of sanity and formed a menace to the order and nervous well-being of the entire household. The youth must indeed have taken complete leave of his senses, since only downright madness could have prompted the wild screams and imaginary conversations in assumed voices which the present day had brought forth. All this must be stopped, or Mrs Ward would be made ill and the keeping of servants become an impossibility.

Mr Ward rose at the close of the meal and started upstairs for Charles's laboratory. On the third floor, however, he paused at the sounds which he heard proceeding from the now disused library of his son. Books were apparently being flung about and papers wildly rustled, and upon stepping to the door Mr Ward beheld the youth within, excitedly assembling a vast armful of literary matter of every size and shape. Charles's aspect was very drawn and haggard, and he dropped his entire load with a start at the sound of his father's voice. At the elder man's command he sat down, and for some time listened to the admonitions he had so long deserved. There was no scene. At the end of the lecture he agreed that his father was right, and that his voices, mutterings, incantations, and chemical odors were indeed inexcusable nuisances. He agreed to a policy of greater quiet, though insisting on a prolongation of his extreme privacy. Much of his future work, he said, was in any case purely book research; and he could obtain quarters elsewhere for any such vocal rituals as might be necessary at a later stage. For the fright and fainting of his mother he expressed the keenest contrition, and explained that the conversation later heard was part of an elaborate symbolism designed to create a certain mental atmosphere. His use of abstruse chemical terms somewhat bewildered Mr Ward, but the parting impression was one of undeniable sanity and poise, despite a mysterious tension of the utmost gravity. The interview was really quite inconclusive, and as Charles picked up his armful and left the room Mr Ward hardly knew what to make of the entire business. It was as mysterious as the death of poor old Nig, whose stiffening form, with staring eyes and fear-distorted mouth, had been found an hour before in the basement.

Driven by some vague detective instinct, the bewildered

parent now glanced curiously at the vacant shelves to see what his son had taken up to the attic. The youth's library was plainly and rigidly classified, so that one might tell at a glance the books or at least the kind of books which had been withdrawn. On this occasion Mr Ward was astonished to find that nothing of the occult or the antiquarian, beyond what had been previously removed, was missing. These new withdrawals were all modern items; histories, scientific treatises, geographies, manuals of literature, philosophic works, and certain contemporary newspapers and magazines. It was a very curious shift from Charles Ward's recent run of reading, and the father paused in a growing vortex of perplexity and an engulfing sense of strangeness. The strangeness was a very poignant sensation, and almost clawed at his chest as he strove to see just what was wrong around him. Something was indeed wrong, and tangibly as well as spiritually so. Ever since he had been in this room he had known that something was amiss, and at last it dawned upon him what it was.

On the north wall rose still the ancient carved overmantel from the house in Olney Court, but to the cracked and precariously restored oils of the large Curwen portrait disaster had come. Time and unequal heating had done their work at last, and at some time since the rooms's last cleaning the worst had happened. Peeling clear of the wood, curling tighter and tighter, and finally crumbling into small bits with what must have been malignly silent suddenness, the portrait of Joseph Curwen had resigned for ever its staring surveillance of the youth it so strangely resembled, and now lay scattered on the floor as a thin coating of fine bluish-gray dust.

CHAPTER FOUR

A Mutation and a Madness

1

In the week following that memorable Good Friday Charles Ward was seen more often than usual, and was continually carrying books between his library and the attic laboratory. His actions were quiet and rational, but he had a furtive, hunted look which his mother did not like, and developed an incredibly ravenous appetite as gauged by his demands upon the cook.

Dr Willett had been told of those Friday noises and happenings, and on the following Tuesday had a long conversation with the youth in the library where the picture stared no more. The interview was, as always, inconclusive; but Willett is still ready to swear that the youth was sane and himself at the time. He held out promises of an early revelation, and spoke of the need of securing a laboratory elsewhere. At the loss of the portrait he grieved singularly little considering his first enthusiasm over it, but seemed to find something of positive humor in its sudden crumbling.

About the second week Charles began to be absent from the house for long periods, and one day when good old black Hannah came to help with the spring cleaning she mentioned his frequent visits to the old house in Olney Court, where he would come with a large valise and perform curious delvings in the cellar. He was always very liberal to her and to old Asa, but seemed more worried than he used to be, which grieved her very much, since she had watched him grow up from birth.

Another report of his doings came from Pawtuxet, where some friends of the family saw him at a distance a surprising number of times. He seemed to haunt the resort and canoehouse of Rhodes-on-the-Pawtuxet, and subsequent inquiries by Dr Willett at that place brought out the fact that his purpose was always to secure access to the rather hedged-in river-bank, along which he would walk toward the north, usually not reappearing for a very long while.

Later in May came a momentary revival of ritualistic sounds in the attic laboratory which brought a stern reproof from Mr Ward and a somewhat distracted promise of amendment from Charles. It occurred one morning, and seemed to form a resumption of the imaginary conversation noted on that turbulent Good Friday. The youth was arguing or remonstrating hotly with himself, for there suddenly burst forth a perfectly distinguishable series of clashing shouts in differentiated tones like alternate demands and denials, which caused Mrs Ward to run upstairs and listen at the door. She could hear no more than a fragment whose only plain words were 'must have it red for three months', and upon her knocking all sounds ceased at once. When Charles was later questioned by his father he said that there were certain conflicts of spheres of consciousness which only great skill could avoid, but which he would try to transfer to other realms.

About the middle of June a queer nocturnal incident occurred. In the early evening there had been some noise and thumping in the laboratory upstairs, and Mr Ward was on the point of investigating when it suddenly quieted down. That midnight, after the family had retired, the butler was nightlocking the front door when according to his statement Charles appeared somewhat blunderingly and uncertainly at the foot of the stairs with a large suitcase and made signs that he wished egress. The youth spoke no

228

word, but the worthy Yorkshireman caught one sight of his fevered eyes and trembled causelessly. He opened the door and young Ward went out, but in the morning the butler gave in his notice to Mrs Ward. There was, he said, something unholy in the glance Charles had fixed on him. It was no way for a young gentleman to look at an honest person, and he could not possibly stay another night. Mrs Ward allowed the man to depart, but she did not value his statement highly. To fancy Charles in a savage state that night was quite ridiculous, for as long as she had remained awake she had heard faint sounds from the laboratory above; sounds as if of sobbing and pacing, and of a sighing which told only of despair's profoundest depths. Mrs Ward had grown used to listening for sounds in the night, for the mystery of her son was fast driving all else from her mind.

The next evening, much as on another evening nearly three months before, Charles Ward seized the newspaper very early and accidentally lost the main section. This matter was not recalled till later, when Dr Willett began checking up loose ends and searching out missing links here and there. In the *Journal* office he found the section which Charles had lost, and marked two items as of possible significance. They were as follows:

More Cemetery Delving

It was this morning discovered by Robert Hart, night watch-man at the North Burial Ground, that ghouls were again at work in the ancient portion of the cemetery. The grave of Ezra Weeden, who was born in 1740 and died in 1824 according to his uprooted and savagely splintered slate headstone, was found excavated and rifled, the work being evidently done with a spade stolen from an adjacent tool shed.

Whatever the contents may have been after more than a century of burial, all was gone except a few slivers of decayed wood. There were no wheel tracks, but the police have measured a single set of footprints which they found in the vicinity, and which indicate the boots of a man of refinement.

Hart is inclined to link this incident with the digging discovered last March, when a party in a motor truck were frightened away after making a deep excavation; but Sergeant Riley of the Second Station discounts this theory and points to vital differences in the two cases. In March the digging had been in a spot where no grave was known; but this time a well-marked and cared-for grave had been rifled with every evidence of deliberate purpose, and with a conscious malignity expressed in the splintering of the slab which had been intact up to the day before.

Members of the Weeden family, notified of the happening, expressed their astonishment and regret; and were wholly unable to think of any enemy who would care to violate the grave of their ancestor. Hazard Weeden of 598 Angell Street recalls a family legend according to which Ezra Weeden was involved in some very peculiar circumstances, not dishonorable to himself, shortly before the Revolution; but of any modern feud or mystery he is frankly ignorant. Inspector Cunningham has been assigned to the case, and hopes to uncover some valuable clues in the near future.

Dogs Noisy in Pawtuxet

Residents of Pawtuxet were aroused about three A.M. today by a phenomenal baying of dogs which seemed to centre near the river just north of Rhodes-on-the-Pawtuxet. The volume and quality of the howling were unusually odd, according to most who heard it; and Fred Lemdin, night watchman at Rhodes, declares it was mixed with something very like the shrieks of a man in mortal terror and agony. A sharp and very brief thunderstorm, which seemed to strike somewhere near the bank of the river, put an end to the disturbance. Strange and unpleasant odors, probably from the oil tanks along the bay, are popularly linked with this incident; and may have had their share in exciting the dogs.

The aspect of Charles now became very haggard and hunted, and all agreed in retrospect that he may have wished at this period to make some statement or confession from which sheer terror withheld him. The morbid listening of his mother in the night brought out the fact that he made frequent sallies abroad under cover of darkness, and most of the more academic alienists unite at present in charging him with the revolting cases of vampirism which the press so sensationally reported about this time, but which have not yet been definitely traced to any known perpetrator. These cases, too recent and celebrated to need detailed mention, involved victims of every age and type and seemed to cluster around two distinct localities; the residential hill and the North End, near the Ward home, and the suburban districts across the Cranstone line near Pawtuxet. Both late wayfarers and sleepers with open windows were attacked, and those who lived to tell the tale spoke unanimously of a lean, lithe, leaping monster with burning eyes which fastened its teeth in the throat or upper arm and feasted ravenously.

Dr Willett, who refuses to date the madness of Charles Ward as far back as even this, is cautious in attempting to explain these horrors. He has, he declares, certain theories of his own; and limits his positive statements to a peculiar kind of negation. 'I will not,' he says, 'state who or what I believe perpetrated these attacks and murders, but I will declare that Charles Ward was innocent of them. I have reason to be sure he was ignorant of the taste of blood, as indeed his continued anaemic decline and increasing pallor prove better than any verbal argument. Ward meddled with terrible things, but he has paid for it, and he was never a monster or a villain. As for now, I don't like to think. A change came, and I'm content to believe that the old Charles Ward died with it. His soul did, anyhow, for that mad flesh that vanished from Waite's hospital had another.'

Willett speaks with authority, for he was often at the Ward home attending Mrs Ward, whose nerves had begun to snap under the strain. Her nocturnal listening had bred some morbid hallucinations which she confided to the doctor with hesitancy, and which he ridiculed in talking to her, although they made him ponder deeply when alone. These delusions always concerned the faint sounds which she fancied she heard in the attic laboratory and bedroom, and emphasized the occurrences of muffled sighs and sobbings at the most impossible times. Early in July Willett ordered Mrs Ward to Atlantic City for an indefinite recuperative sojourn, and cautioned both Mr Ward and the haggard and elusive Charles to write her only cheering letters. It is probably to this enforced and reluctant escape that she owes her life and continued sanity.

2

Not long after his mother's departure Charles Ward began negotiating for the Pawtuxet bungalow. It was a squalid little wooden edifice with a concrete garage, perched high on the sparsely settled bank of the river slightly above Rhodes, but for some odd reason the youth would have nothing else. He gave the real-estate agencies no peace till one of them secured it for him at an exorbitant price from a somewhat reluctant owner, and as soon as it was vacant he took possession under cover of darkness, transporting in a great closed van the entire contents of his attic laboratory, including the books both weird and modern which he had borrowed from his study. He had this van loaded in the black small hours, and his father recalls only a drowsy realization of stifled oaths and stamping feet on the night the goods were taken away. After that Charles moved back to his own quarters on the third floor, and never haunted the attic again.

To the Pawtuxet bungalow Charles transferred all the

secrecy with which he had surrounded his attic realm, save that he now appeared to have two sharers of his mysteries; a villainous-looking Portuguese half-caste from the South Main Street Waterfront who acted as a servant, and a thin, scholarly stranger with dark glasses and a stubbly full beard of dyed aspect whose status was evidently that of a colleague. Neighbours vainly tried to engage these odd persons in conversation. The mulatto Gomes spoke very little English, and the bearded man who gave his name as Dr Allen voluntarily followed his example. Ward himself tried to be more affable, but succeeded only in provoking curiosity with his rambling accounts of chemical research. Before long queer tales began to circulate regarding the all-night burning of lights; and somewhat later, after this burning had suddenly ceased, there rose still queerer tales of disproportionate orders of meat from the butcher's and of the muffled shouting, declamation, rhythmic chanting, and screaming supposed to come from some very deep cellar below the place. Most distinctly the new and strange household was bitterly disliked by the honest bourgeoisie of the vicinity, and it is not remarkable that dark hints were advanced connecting the Negro establishment with the current epidemic of vampiristic attacks and murders; especially since the radius of that plague seemed now confined wholly to Pawtuxet and the adjacent streets of Edgewood.

Ward spent most of his time at the bungalow, but slept occasionally at home and was still reckoned a dweller beneath his father's roof. Twice he was absent from the city on week-long trips, whose destinations have not yet been discovered. He grew steadily paler and more emaciated even than before, and lacked some of his former assurance when repeating to Dr Willett his old, old story of vital research and future revelations. Willett often waylaid him at his father's house, for the elder Ward was deeply worried and perplexed, and wished his son to get as much sound oversight as could be managed in the case of so secretive and independent an adult. The doctor still insists that the youth was sane even as late as this, and adduces many a conversation to prove his point.

About September the vampirism declined, but in the following January Ward almost became involved in serious trouble. For some time the nocturnal arrival and departure of motor trucks at the Pawtuxet bungalow had been commented upon, and at this juncture an unforeseen hitch exposed the nature of at least one item of their contents. In a lonely spot near Hope Valley had occurred one of the frequent sordid waylaying of trucks by 'hi-jackers' in quest of liquor shipments, but this time the robbers had been destined to receive the greater shock. For the long cases they seized proved upon opening to contain some exceedingly gruesome things; so gruesome, in fact, that the matter could not be kept quiet amongst the denizens of the underworld. The thieves had hastily buried what they discovered, but when the State Police got wind of the matter a careful search was made. A recently arrested vagrant, under promise of immunity from prosecution on any additional charge, at last consented to guide a party of troopers to the spot; and there was found in that hasty cache a very hideous and shameful thing. It would not be well for the national – or even the international – sense of decorum if the public were ever to know what was uncovered by that awestruck party. There was no mistaking it, even by these far from studious officers; and telegrams to Washington ensued with feverish rapidity.

The cases were addressed to Charles Ward at his Pawtuxet bungalow, and State and Federal officials at once paid him a very forceful and serious call. They found him pallid and worried with his two odd companions, and received

234

from him what seemed to be a valid explanation and evidence of innocence. He had needed certain anatomical specimens as part of a programme of research whose depth and genuineness anyone who had known him in the last decade could prove, and had ordered the required kind and number from agencies which he had thought as reasonably legitimate as such things can be. Of the *identity* of the specimens he had known absolutely nothing, and was properly shocked when the inspectors hinted at the monstrous effect on public sentiment and national dignity which a knowledge of the matter would produce. In this statement he was firmly sustained by his bearded colleague Dr Allen, whose oddly hollow voice carried even more conviction than his own nervous tones; so that in the end the officials took no action, but carefully set down the New York name and address which Ward gave them as a basis for a search which came to nothing. It is only fair to add that the specimens were quickly and quietly restored to their proper places, and the general public will never know of their blasphemous disturbance.

On February 9, 1928, Dr Willett received a letter from Charles Ward which he considers of extraordinary importance, and about which he has frequently quarrelled with Dr Lyman. Lyman believes that this note contains positive proof of a well-developed case of *dementia praecox*, but Willett on the other hand regards it as the last perfectly sane utterance of the hapless youth. He calls especial attention to the normal character of the penmanship; which, though showing traces of shattered nerves, is nevertheless distinctly Ward's own. The text in full is as follows:

100 Prospect St.,
Providence, R.I.,
March 8, 1928.

Dear Dr Willett:–

I feel that at last the time has come for me to make the disclosures which I have so long promised you, and for which you have pressed me so often. The patience you have shown in waiting, and the confidence you have shown in my mind and integrity, are things I shall never cease to appreciate.

And now that I am ready to speak, I must own with humiliation that no triumph such as I dreamed of can ever be mine. Instead of triumph I have found terror, and my talk with you will not be a boast of victory but a plea for help and advice in saving both myself and the world from a horror beyond all human conception or calculation. You recall what those Fenner letters said of the old raiding party at Pawtuxet. That must all be done again, and quickly. Upon us depends more than can be put into words – all civilization, all natural law, perhaps even the fate of the solar system and the universe. I have brought to light a monstrous abnormality, but I did it for the sake of knowledge. Now for the sake of all life and nature you must help me thrust it back into the dark again.

I have left that Pawtuxet place forever, and we must extirpate everything existing there, alive or dead. I shall not go there again, and you must not believe it if you ever hear that I am there. I will tell you why I say this when I see you. I have come home for good, and wish you would call on me at the very first moment that you can spare five or six hours continuously to hear what I have to say. It will take that long–and believe me when I tell you that you never had a more genuine professional duty than this. My life and reason are the very least things which hang in the balance.

I dare not tell my father, for he could not grasp the whole thing. But I have told him of my danger, and he has four men from a detective agency watching the house. I don't know how much good they can do, for they have against them forces which even you could scarcely envisage or acknowledge. So come quickly if you wish to see me alive and hear how you may help to save the cosmos from stark hell.

Any time will do–I shall not be out of the house. Don't telephone ahead, for there is no telling who or what may try to intercept you. And let us pray to whatever gods there be that nothing may prevent this meeting.

In utmost gravity and desperation,

Charles Dexter Ward.

P.S. Shoot Dr Allen on sight *and dissolve his body in acid. Don't burn it.*

236

Dr Willett received this note about ten-thirty A.M., and immediately arranged to spare the whole late afternoon and evening for the momentous talk, letting it extend on into the night as long as might be necessary. He planned to arrive about four o'clock, and through all the intervening hours was so engulfed in every sort of wild speculation that most of his tasks were very mechanically performed. Maniacal as the letter would have sounded to a stranger, Willett had seen too much of Charles Ward's oddities to dismiss it as sheer raving. That something very subtle, ancient, and horrible was hovering about he felt quite sure, and the reference to Dr Allen could almost be comprehended in view of what Pawtuxet gossip said of Ward's enigmatical colleague. Willett had never seen the man, but had heard much of his aspect and bearing, and could not but wonder what sort of eyes those much-discussed dark glasses might conceal.

Promptly at four Dr Willett presented himself at the Ward residence, but found to his annoyance that Charles had not adhered to his determination to remain indoors. The guards were there, but said that the young man seemed to have lost part of his timidity. He had that morning done much apparently frightened arguing and protesting over the telephone, one of the detectives said, replying to some unknown voice with phrases such as 'I am very tired and must rest a while', 'I can't receive anyone for some time, you'll have to excuse me', 'Please postpone decisive action till we can arrange some sort of compromise', or 'I am very sorry, but I must take a complete vacation from everything; I'll talk with you later'. Then, apparently gaining boldness through meditation, he had slipped out so quietly that no one had seen him depart or knew that he had gone until he returned about one o'clock and entered the house without a word. He had gone upstairs, where a bit of his fear must have surged back; for he was heard to cry out in a high, terrified fashion upon entering his library, afterward trailing off into a kind of choking gasp. When, however, the butler had gone to inquire what the trouble was, he had appeared at the door with a great show of boldness, and had silently gestured the man away in a manner that terrified him unaccountably. Then he had evidently done some rearranging of his shelves, for a great clattering and thumping and creaking ensued; after which he had reappeared and left at once. Willett inquired whether or not any message had been left, but was told that there was none. The butler seemed queerly disturbed about something in Charles's appearance and manner, and asked solicitously if there was much hope for a cure of his disordered nerves.

For almost two hours Dr Willett waited vainly in Charles Ward's library, watching the dusty shelves with their wide gaps where books had been removed, and smiling grimly at the paneled overmantel on the north wall, whence a year before the suave features of old Joseph Curwen had looked mildly down. After a time the shadows began to gather, and the sunset cheer gave place to a vague growing terror which flew shadow-like before the night. Mr Ward finally arrived, and showed much surprise and anger at his son's absence, after all the pains which had been taken to guard him. He had not known of Charles's appointment, and promised to notify Willett when the youth returned. In bidding the doctor goodnight he expressed his utter perplexity at his son's condition, and urged his caller to do all he could to restore the boy to normal poise. Willett was glad to escape from that library, for something frightful and unholy seemed to haunt it; as if the vanished picture had left behind a legacy of evil. He had never liked that picture; and even now, strong-nerved though he was, there lurked a quality in its vacant panel which made him feel an urgent need to get out into the pure air as soon as possible.

3

The next morning Willett received a message from the senior Ward, saying that Charles was still absent. Mr Ward mentioned that Dr Allen had telephoned him to say that Charles would remain at Pawtuxet for some time, and that he must not be disturbed. This was necessary because Allen himself was suddenly called away for an indefinite period, leaving the researches in need of Charles's constant oversight. Charles sent his best wishes, and regretted any bother his abrupt change of plans might have caused. In listening to this message Mr Ward heard Dr Allen's voice for the first time, and it seemed to excite some vague and elusive memory which could not be actually placed, but which was disturbing to the point of fearfulness.

Faced by these baffling and contradictory reports, Dr Willett was frankly at a loss what to do. The frantic earnestness of Charles's note was not to be denied, yet what could one think of its writer's immediate violation of his own expressed policy? Young Ward had written that his delvings had become blasphemous and menacing, that they and his bearded colleague must be extirpated at any cost, and that he himself would never return to their final scene; yet according to latest advices he had forgotten all this and was back in the thick of the mystery. Common sense bade one leave the youth alone with his freakishness, yet some deeper instinct would not permit the impression of that frenzied letter to subside. Willett read it over again, and could not make its essence sound as empty and insane as both its bombastic verbiage and its lack of fulfilment would seem to imply. Its terror was too profound and real, and, in conjunction with what the doctor already knew, evoked too vivid hints of monstrosities from beyond time and space, to permit of any cynical explanation. There were nameless horrors abroad; and no matter how little one might be able to get at them, one ought to stand prepared for any sort of action at any time.

For over a week, Dr Willett pondered on the dilemma which seemed thrust upon him, and became more and more inclined to pay Charles a call at the Pawtuxet bungalow. No friend of the youth had ever ventured to storm this forbidden retreat, and even his father knew of its interior only from such descriptions as he chose to give; but Willett felt that some direct conversation with his patient was necessary. Mr Ward had been receiving brief and non-committal typed notes from his son, and said that Mrs Ward in her Atlantic City retirement had had no better word. So at length the doctor resolved to act, and despite a curious sensation inspired by old legends of Joseph Curwen, and by more recent revelations and warnings from Charles Ward, set boldly out for the bungalow on the bluff above the river.

Willett had visited the spot before through sheer curiosity, though of course never entering the house or proclaiming his presence, hence knew exactly the route to take. Driving out by Broad Street one early afternoon toward the end of February in his small motor, he thought oddly of the grim party which had taken that self-same road a hundred and fifty-seven years before, on a terrible errand which none might ever comprehend.

The ride through the city's decaying fringe was short, and trim Edgewood and sleepy Pawtuxet presently spread out ahead. Willett turned to the right down Lockwood Street and drove his car as far along that rural road as he could, then alighted and walked north to where the bluff towered above the lovely bends of the river and the sweep of misty downlands beyond. Houses were still few here, and there was no mistaking the isolated bungalow with its concrete garage on a high point of land at his left. Stepping briskly up the neglected gravel walk he rapped at the door with a firm hand, and spoke without a tremor to the evil Portuguese mulatto who opened it to the width of a crack.

He must, he said, see Charles Ward at once on vitally important business. No excuse would be accepted, and a repulse would mean only a full report of the matter to the elder Ward. The mulatto still hesitated, and pushed against the door when Willett attempted to open it; but the doctor merely raised his voice and renewed his demands. Then there came from the dark interior a husky whisper which somehow chilled the hearer through and through, though he did not know why he feared it. 'Let him in, Tony,' it said, 'we may as well talk now as ever.' But disturbing as was the whisper, the greater fear was that which immediately followed. The floor creaked and the speaker hove in sight – and the owner of those strange and resonant tones was seen to be no other than Charles Dexter Ward.

The minuteness with which Dr Willett recalled and recorded his conversation of that afternoon is due to the importance he assigns to this particular period. For at last he concedes a vital change in Charles Dexter Ward's mentality and believes that the youth now spoke from a brain hopelessly alien to the brain whose growth he had watched for six and twenty years. Controversy with Dr Lyman has compelled him to be very specific, and he definitely dated the madness of Charles Ward from the time the typewritten notes began to reach his parents. Those notes are not in Ward's normal style; not even in the style of that last frantic letter to Willett. Instead, they are strange and archaic, as if the snapping of the writer's mind had released a flood of tendencies and impressions picked up unconsciously through boyhood antiquarianism. There is an obvious effort to be modern, but the spirit and occasionally the language are those of the past.

The past, too, was evident in Ward's every tone and gesture as he received the doctor in that shadowy bungalow. He bowed, motioned Willett to a seat, and began to speak abruptly in that strange whisper which he sought to explain at the very outset.

'I am grown phthisical,' he began, 'from this cursed river air. You must excuse my speech. I suppose you are come from my father to see what ails me, and I hope you will say nothing to alarm him.'

Willett was studying these scraping tones with extreme care, but studying even more closely the face of the speaker. Something, he felt, was wrong; and he thought of what the family had told him about the fright of that Yorkshire butler one night. He wished it were not so dark, but did not request that any blind be opened. Instead, he merely asked Ward why he had so belied the frantic note of little more than a week before.

'I was coming to that,' the host replied. 'You must know I am in a very bad state of nerves, and do and say queer things I cannot account for. As I have told you often, I am on the edge of great matters, and the bigness of them has a way of making me light-headed. Any man might well be frightened of what I have found, but I am not to be put off for long. I was a dunce to have that guard and stick at home; for having gone this far, my place is here. I am not well spoke of by my prying neighbors, and perhaps I was led by weakness to believe myself what they say of me.

242

There is no evil to any in what I do, so long as I do it rightly. Have the goodness to wait six months, and I'll show you what will pay your patience well.

'You may as well know I have a way of learning old matters from thing surer than books, and I'll leave you to judge the importance of what I can give to history, philosophy, and the arts by reason of the doors I have access to. My ancestor had all this when those witless peeping Toms came and murdered him. I now have it again, or am coming very imperfectly to have a part of it. This time nothing must happen, and least of all through any idiot fears of my own. Pray forget all I writ you, Sir, and have no fear of this place or any in it. Dr Allen is a man of fine parts, and I owe him an apology for anything ill I have said of him. I wish I had no need to spare him, but there were things he had to do elsewhere. His zeal is equal to mine in all those matters, and I suppose that when I feared the work I feared him too as my greatest helper in it.'

Ward paused, and the doctor hardly knew what to say or think. He felt almost foolish in the face of this calm repudiation of the letter; and yet there clung to him the fact that while the present discourse was strange and alien and indubitably mad, the note itself had been tragic in its naturalness and likeness to the Charles Ward he knew. Willett now tried to turn the talk on early matters, and recall to the youth some past events which would restore a familiar mood; but in this process he obtained only the most grotesque results. It was the same with all the alienists later on. Important sections of Charles Ward's store of mental images, mainly those touching modern times and his own personal life, had been unaccountably expunged; while all the massed antiquarianism of his youth had welled up from some profound subconsciousness to engulf the contemporary and the individual. The youth's ultimate knowledge of

243

older things was abnormal and unholy, and he tried his best to hide it. When Willett would mention some favorite object of his boyhood archaistic studies he often shed by pure accident such a light as no normal mortal could conceivably be expected to possess, and the doctor shuddered as the glib allusion glided by.

It was not wholesome to know so much about the way the fat sheriff's wig fell off as he leaned over at the play in Mr Douglass's Histrionick Academy in King Street on the eleventh of February, 1762, which fell on a Thursday; or about how the actors cut the text of Steele's 'Conscious Lover' so badly that one was almost glad the Baptist-ridden legislature closed the theatre a fortnight later. That Thomas Sabin's Boston coach was 'damn'd uncomfortable' old letters may well have told; but what healthy antiquarian could recall how the creaking of Epenetus Olney's new signboard (the gaudy Crown he set up after he took to calling his tavern the Crown Coffee House) was exactly like the first few notes of the new jazz piece all the radios in Pawtuxet were playing?

Ward, however, would not be quizzed long in this vein. Modern and personal topics he waved aside quite summarily, whilst regarding antique affairs he soon showed the plainest boredom. What he wished clearly enough was only to satisfy his visitor enough to make him depart without the intention of returning. To this end he offered to show Willett the entire house, and at once proceeded to lead the doctor through every room from cellar to attic. Willett looked sharply, but noted that the visible books were far too few and trivial ever to have filled the wide gaps on Ward's shelves at home, and that the meagre so-called 'laboratory' was the flimsiest sort of a blind. Clearly, there were a library and laboratory elsewhere; but just where, it was impossible to say. Essentially defeated in his quest for something he could not name, Willett returned to town before evening and told the senior Ward everything which had occurred. They agreed that the youth must be definitely out of his mind, but decided that nothing drastic need be done just then. Above all, Mrs Ward must be kept in as complete an ignorance as her son's own strange typed notes would permit.

Mr Ward now determined to call in person upon his son, making it wholly a surprise visit. Dr Willett took him in his car one evening, guiding him to within sight of the bungalow and waiting patiently for his return. The session was a long one, and the father emerged in a very saddened and perplexed state. His reception had developed much like Willett's, save that Charles had been an excessively long time in appearing after the visitor had forced his way into the hall and sent the Portuguese away with an imperative demand; and in the bearing of the altered son there was no trace of filial affection. The lights had been dim, yet even so the youth had complained that they dazzled him outrageously. He had not spoken out loud at all, averring that his throat was in very poor condition; but in his hoarse whisper there was a quality so vaguely disturbing that Mr Ward could not banish it from his mind.

Now definitely leagued together to do all they could toward the youth's mental salvation, Mr Ward and Dr Willett set about collecting every scrap of data which the case might afford. Pawtuxet gossip was the first item they studied, and this was relatively easy to glean since both had friends in that region. Dr Willett obtained the most rumors because people talked more frankly to him than to a parent of the central figure, and from all he heard he could tell that young Ward's life had become indeed a strange one. Common tongues would not dissociate his household from the vampirism of the previous summer, while the nocturnal comings and goings of the motor trucks provided their share of dark speculation. Local tradesmen spoke of the queerness of the orders brought them by the evil-looking mulatto, and in particular of the inordinate amounts of meat and fresh blood secured from the two butcher shops in the immediate neighborhood. For a household of only three, these quantities were quite absurd.

Then there was the matter of the sounds beneath the earth. Reports of these things were harder to pin down, but all the vague hints tallied in certain basic essentials. Noises of a ritual nature positively existed, and at times when the bungalow was dark. They might, of course, have come from the known cellar; but rumor insisted that there were deeper and more spreading crypts. Recalling the ancient tales of Joseph Curwen's catacombs, and assuming for granted that the present bungalow had been selected because of its situation on the old Curwen site as revealed in one or another of the documents found behind the picture, Willett and Mr Ward gave this phase of the gossip much attention; and searched many times without success for the door in the river-bank which old manuscripts mentioned. As to popular opinions of the bungalow's various inhabitants, it was soon plain that the Brava Portuguese was loathed, the bearded and spectacled Dr Allen feared, and the pallid young scholar disliked to a profound extent. During the last week or two Ward had obviously changed much, abandoning his attempts at affability and speaking only in hoarse but oddly repellent whispers on the few occasions that he ventured forth.

Such were the shred and fragments gathered here and there; and over these Mr Ward and Dr Willett held many long and serious conferences. They strove to exercise deduction, induction, and constructive imagination to their utmost extent; and to correlate every known fact of Charles's later

246

life, including the frantic letter which the doctor now showed the father, with the meager documentary evidence available concerning old Joseph Curwen. They would have given much for a glimpse of the papers Charles had found, for very clearly the key to the youth's madness lay in what he had learned of the ancient wizard and his doings.

4

And yet, after all, it was from no step of Mr Ward's or Dr Willett's that the next move in this singular case proceeded. The father and the physician, rebuffed and confused by a shadow too shapeless and intangible to combat, had rested uneasily on their oars while the typed notes of young Ward to his parents grew fewer and fewer. Then came the first of the month with its customary financial adjustments, and the clerks at certain banks began a peculiar shaking of heads and telephoning from one to the other. Officials who knew Charles Ward by sight went down to the bungalow to ask why every cheque of his appearing at this juncture was a clumsy forgery, and were reassured less than they ought to have been when the youth hoarsely explained that his hand had lately been so much affected by a nervous shock as to make normal writing impossible. He could, he said, form no written characters at all except with great difficulty; and could prove it by the fact that he had been forced to type all his recent letters, even those to his father and mother, who would bear out the assertion.

What made the investigators pause in confusion was not this circumstance alone, for that was nothing unprecedented or fundamentally suspicious; nor even the Pawtuxet gossip, of which one or two of them had caught echoes. It was the muddled discourse of the young man which nonplussed them, implying as it did a virtually total loss of memory concerning important monetary matters which he had had at his fingertips only a month or two before. Something was wrong, for despite the apparent coherence and rationality of his speech, there could be no normal reason for this ill-concealed blankness on vital points. Moreover, although none of these men knew Ward well, they could not help observing the change in his language and manner. They had heard he was an antiquarian, but even the most hopeless antiquarians do not make use of obsolete phraseology and gestures. Altogether, this combination of hoarseness, palsied hands, bad memory, altered speech and bearing, represented some disturbance or malady of genuine gravity, which, no doubt, formed the basis of the prevailing odd rumors; and after their departure the party of officials decided that a talk with the senior Ward was imperative.

So on the sixth of March, 1928, there was a long and serious conference in Mr Ward's office, after which the utterly bewildered father summoned Dr Willett in a kind of helpless resignation. Willett looked over the strained and awkward signatures of the cheques, and compared them in his mind with the penmanship of that last frantic note. Certainly, the change was radical and profound, and yet there was something damnably familiar about the new writing. It had crabbed and archaic tendencies of a very curious sort, and seemed to result from a type of stroke utterly different from that which the youth had always used. It was strange – but where had he seen it before? On the whole, it was obvious that Charles was insane. Of that there could be no doubt. And since it appeared unlikely that he could handle his property or continue to deal with the outside world much longer, something must quickly be done toward his oversight and possible cure. It was then that the alienists were called in, Drs Peck and Waite of Providence and Dr Lyman of Boston, to whom Mr Ward and Dr Willett gave the most exhaustive possible history of the case, and who conferred at length in the now unused library of their young patient, examining what books and papers of his were left in order to gain some further notion of his habitual mental cast. After scanning this material and examining the youth's note to Willett, they all agreed that Charles Ward's studies had been enough to unseat or at least to warp any ordinary intellect, and wished most heartily that they could see his more intimate volumes and documents; but this latter they knew they could do, if at all, only after a scene at the bungalow itself. Willett now reviewed the whole case with febrile energy; it being at this time that he obtained the statements of the workmen who had seen Charles find the Curwen documents, and that he collated the incidents of the destroyed newspaper items, looking up the latter at the *Journal* office.

On Thursday, the eighth of March, Drs Willett, Peck, Lyman and Waite, accompanied by Mr Ward, paid the youth their momentous call; making no concealment of their object and questioning the now acknowledged patient with extreme minuteness. Charles, though he was inordinately long in answering the summons and was still redolent of strange and noxious laboratory odors when he did finally make his agitated appearance, proved a far from recalcitrant subject; and admitted freely that his memory and balance had suffered somewhat from close application to abstruse studies. He offered no resistance when his removal to other quarters was insisted upon; and seemed, indeed, to display a high degree of intelligence as apart from mere memory. His conduct would have sent his interviewers away in bafflement had not the persistently archaic trend of his speech and unmistakable replacement of modern by ancient ideas in his consciousness marked him out as one definitely removed from the normal. Of his work he would say no more to the group of doctors than he had formerly said to his family and to Dr Willett, and his frantic note of the previous month he dismissed as mere nerves and hysteria. He insisted that this shadowy bungalow possessed no library or laboratory beyond the visible ones, and waxed abstruse in explaining the absence from the house of such odors as now saturated all his clothing. Neighborhood gossip he attributed to nothing more than the cheap inventiveness of baffled curiosity. Of the whereabouts of Dr Allen he said he did not feel at liberty to speak definitely, but assured his visitors that the bearded and spectacled man would return when needed. In paying off the stolid Brava who resisted all questioning by the visitors, and in closing the bungalow which still seemed to hold such nighted secrets, Ward showed no sign of nervousness save a barely noticed tendency to pause as though listening for something very faint. He was apparently animated by a calmly philosophic resignation, as if his removal were the merest transient incident which would cause the least trouble if facilitated and disposed of once and for all. It was clear that he trusted to his obviously unimpaired keenness of absolute mentality to overcome all the embarrassments into which his twisted memory, his lost voice and handwriting, and his secretive and eccentric behavior had led him. His mother, it was agreed, was not to be told of the change; his father supplying typed notes in his name. Ward was taken to the restfully and picturesquely situated private hospital maintained by Dr Waite on Conanicut Island in the bay, and subjected to the closest scrutiny and questioning by all the physicians connected with the case. It was then that the physical oddities were noticed; the slackened metabolism, the altered skin, and the disproportionate neural reactions. Dr Willett was the most perturbed of the various examiners, for he had attended Ward all his life and could appreciate with terrible keenness the extent of his physical disorganization. Even the familiar olive-mark on his hip was gone, while on his chest was a great black mole or cicatrice which had never been there before, and which made Willett wonder whether the youth had ever submitted to any of the 'witch markings' reputed to be inflicted at certain unwholesome nocturnal meetings in wild and lonely places. The doctor could not keep his mind off a certain transcribed witchtrial record from Salem which Charles had shown him in the old non-secretive days, and which read: 'Mr G. B. on that Nighte putt ye Divell his Marke upon Bridget S., Jonathan A., Simon O., Deliverance W., Joseph C., Susan P., Mehitable C., and Deborah B.' Ward's face, too, troubled him horribly, till at length he suddenly discovered why he was horrified. Above the young man's right eye was something which he had never previously noticed—a small scar or pit precisely like that in the crumbled painting of old Joseph Curwen, and perhaps attesting some hideous ritualistic inoculation to which both had submitted at a certain stage of their occult careers.

While Ward himself was puzzling all the doctors at the hospital, a very strict watch was kept on all mail addressed either to him or to Dr Allen, which Mr Ward had ordered delivered at the family home. Willett had predicted that very little would be found, since any communications of a vital nature would probably have been exchanged by messenger; but in the latter part of March there did come a letter from Prague for Dr Allen which gave both the doctor and the father deep thought. It was in a very crabbed and archaic hand; and though clearly not the effort of a foreigner, showed almost as singular a departure from

251

modern English as the speech of young Ward himself. It read:

Kleinstrasse 11,
Altstadt, Prague,
11th Feby. 1928.

Brother in Almousin-Metraton!:–

I this day receiv'd yr mention of what came upp from the Saltes I sent you. It was wrong, and meanes clearly that ye Headstones had been chang'd when Barnabus gott me the Specimen. It is often so, as you must be sensible of from the Thing you gott from ye King's Chapell ground in 1769 and what ye gott from Olde Bury'g Point in 1690, that was like to ende him. I gott such a thing in Aegypt 75 yeares gone, from the which came that Scar ye Boy saw on me here in 1924. As I told you longe ago, do not calle up That which you can not put downe; either from dead Saltes or out of ye Spheres beyond. Have ye Wordes for laying at all times readie, and stopp not to be sure when there is any Doubte of *Whom* you have. Stones are all chang'd now in Nine groundes out of 10. You are never sure till you question. I this day heard from H., who has had Trouble with the Soldiers. He is like to be sorry Transylvania is pass'd from Hungary to Romania, and wou'd change his Seat if the Castel weren't so fulle of What we Knowe. But of this he hath doubtless writ you. In my next Send'g there will be Somewhat from a Hill tomb from ye East that will delight you greatly. Meanwhile forget not I am desirous of B.F. if you can possibly get him for me. You know G. in Philadelphia better than I. Have him up firste if you will, but doe not use him soe hard he will be Difficult, for I must speake to him in ye Ende.

Yogg-Sothoth Neblod Zin
Simon O.

To Mr J.C. in
Providence.

Mr Ward and Dr Willett paused in utter chaos before this apparent bit of unrelieved insanity. Only by degrees did they absorb what it seemed to imply. So the absent Dr. Allen, and not Charles Ward, had come to be the leading spirit at Pawtuxet? That must explain the wild reference and determination in the youth's last frantic letter. And what of this addressing of the bearded and spectacled stranger as 'Mr J. C. '? There was no escaping the inference, but there are limits to possible monstrosity. Who was 'Simon O.'? The old man Ward had visited in Prague four years previously? Perhaps, but in the centuries behind there had been another Simon O.–Simon Orne, alias Jedediah, of Salem, who vanished in 1771, *and whose peculiar handwriting Dr Willett now unmistakably recognized from the photostatic copies of the Orne formulae which Charles had once shown him*. What horrors and mysteries, what contradictions and contraventions of nature, had come back after a century and à half to harass Old Providence with her clustered spires and domes?

The father and the old physician, virtually at a loss what to do or think, went to see Charles at the hospital and questioned him as delicately as they could about Dr Allen, about the Prague visit, and about what he had learned of Simon or Jedediah Orne of Salem. To all these inquiries the youth was politely non-committal, merely barking in his hoarse whisper that he had found Dr Allen to have a remarkable spiritual rapport with certain souls from the past, and that any correspondent the bearded man might have in Prague would probably be similarly gifted. When they left, Mr Ward and Dr Willett realized to their chagrin that they had really been the ones under catechism; and that without imparting anything vital himself, the confined youth had adroitly pumped them of everything the Prague letter had contained.

Drs Peck, Waite, and Lyman were not inclined to attach much importance to the strange correspondence of young Ward's companion; for they knew the tendency of kindred eccentrics and monomaniacs to band together, and believed that Charles or Allen had merely unearthed an expatriated counterpart — perhaps one who had seen Orne's handwriting and copied it in an attempt to pose as the bygone character's reincarnation. Allen himself was perhaps a similar case, and may have persuaded the youth into accepting him as an avatar of the long-dead Curwen. Such things had been known before, and on the same basis the hard-headed doctors disposed of Willett's growing disquiet about Charles Ward's present handwriting, as showed from umpremeditated specimens obtained by various ruses. Willett thought he had placed its odd familiarity at last, and that what it vaguely resembled was the bygone penmanship of old Joseph Curwen himself; but this the other physicians regarded as a phase of imitativeness only to be expected in a mania of this sort, and refused to grant it any importance either favorable or unfavorable. Recognizing this prosaic attitude in his colleagues, Willett advised Mr Ward to keep to himself the letter which arrived for Dr Allen on the second of April from Rakus, Transylvania, in a handwriting so intensely and fundamentally like that of the Hutchinson cipher that both father and physician paused in awe before breaking the seal. This read as follows:

Castle Ferenczy
7 March, 1928.

Dear C.:—

Hadd a Squd of 20 Militia upp to talk about what the Country Folk say. Must digg deeper and have less Hearde. These Romanians plague one damnably, being officious and particular where you cou'd buy a Magyar off ith a Drinke and food. Last Monthe M. gott me the sarcophagus of the Five Sphinxes from ye Acropolis where He whome I call'd up say'd it wou'd be, and I have hadde 3 Talkes *with What was therein inhum'd*. It will go to S.O. in Prague directly, and thence to you. It is stubborn but you know ye Way with Such. You shew Wisdom in having lesse about than Before; for there was no Neede to keep the Guards in Shape and eat'g off their Heades, and it made much to be founde in case of

254

Trouble, as you two welle knowe. You can now move and Worke elsewhere with no Kill'g Trouble if needful, though I hope no Thing will soon force you to so Bothersome a Course. I rejoice that you traffick not so much with *Those Outside*, for there was ever a Mortall Peril in it, and you are sensible what it did when you asked Protection of one not dispos'd to give it. You excel me in gett'g ye formulae so *another* may saye them with Success, but Borellus fancy'd it wou'd be so if just ye right Wordes were hadd. Does ye Boy use 'em often? I regret that he growes squeamish, as I fear'd he wou'd when I hadde him here nigh fifteen Monthes, but am sensible you knowe how to deal with him. You can't saye him down with ye Formulae, for that will Worke only upon such as ye other Formulae hath call'd upp from Saltes; but you still have strong Handes and Knife and Pistol, and Graves are not harde to digg, nor Acids loth to burne. O. sayes you have promis'd him B.F. I must have him after. B. goes to you soone, and may he give you what you wishe of that Darke Thing belowe Memphis. Imploy care in what you calle upp, and beware of ye Boy. It will be ripe in a yeare's time to have upp ye Legions from Underneath, and then there are no Boundes to what shal be oures. Have Confidence in what I saye, for you knowe O. and I have hadd these 150 yeares more than you to consulte these Matters in.

Nephreu – Ka nai Hadoth
Edw: H.

For J. Curwen, Esq.
Providence,

But if Willett and Mr Ward refrained from showing this letter to the alienists, they did not refrain from acting upon it themselves. No amount of learned sophistry could controvert the fact that the strangely bearded and spectacled Dr Allen, of whom Charles's frantic letter had spoken as such a monstrous menace, was in close and sinister correspondence with two inexplicable creatures whom Ward had visited in his travels and who plainly claimed to be survivals or avatars of Curwen's old Salem colleagues. That he was regarding himself as the reincarnation of Joseph Curwen, and that he entertained – or was at least advised to entertain – murderous designs against a 'boy' who could scarcely be other than Charles Ward. There was organized horror afoot, and no matter who had started it, the missing Allen was by this time at the bottom of it. Therefore, thanking Heaven that Charles was now safe in the hospital, Mr Ward lost no time in engaging detectives to learn all they could of the cryptic bearded doctor; findings hence he had come and what Pawtuxet knew of him, and if possible discovering his current whereabouts. Supplying the men with one of the bungalow keys which Charles yielded up, he urged them to explore Allen's vacant room which had been identified when the patient's belongings had been packed; obtaining what clues they could from any effects he might have left about. Mr Ward talked with the detectives in his son's old library, and they felt a marked relief when they left it at last; for there seemed to hover about the place a vague aura of Evil. Perhaps it was what they had heard of the infamous old wizard whose picture had once stared from the paneled overmantel, and perhaps it was something different and irrelevant; but in any case they all half-sensed an intangible miasma which centred in that carven vestige of an older dwelling and which at times almost rose to the intensity of a material emanation.

CHAPTER FIVE

A Nightmare and a Cataclysm

1

And now swiftly followed that hideous experience which has left its indelible mark of fear on the soul of Marinus Bicknell Willett, and has added a decade to the visible age of one whose youth was even then far behind. Dr Willett had conferred at length with Mr Ward, and had come to an agreement with him on several points which both felt the alienists would ridicule. There was, they conceded, a terrible movement alive in the world, whose direct connection with a necromancy even older than the Salem witchcraft could not be doubted. That at least two living men—and one other of whom they dared not think—were in absolute possession of minds or personalities which had functioned as early as 1690 or before was likewise almost unassailably proved even in the face of all known natural laws. What these horrible creatures—and Charles Ward as well—were doing or trying to do seemed fairly clear from their letters and from every bit of light both old and new which had filtered in upon the case. They were robbing the tombs of all the ages, including those of the world's wisest and greatest men, in the hope of recovering from bygone ashes some vestige of the consciousness and lore which had once animated and informed them.

A hideous traffic was going on among these nightmare ghouls, whereby illustrious bones were bartered with the calm calculativeness of schoolboys swapping books; and from what was extorted from this centuried dust there was anticipated a power and a wisdom beyond anything which the cosmos had ever seen concentrated in one man or group. They had found unholy ways to keep their brains alive, either in the same body or different bodies; and had evidently achieved a way of tapping the consciousness of the dead whom they gathered together. There had, it seems, been some truth in chimerical old Borellus when he wrote of preparing from even the most antique remains certain 'Essential Saltes' from which the shade of a long-dead living thing might be raised up. There was a formula for evoking such a shade, and another for putting it down; and it had now been so perfected that it could be taught successfully. One must be careful about evocations, for the markers of old graves are not always accurate.

Willett and Mr Ward shivered as they passed from conclusion to conclusion. Things – presences or voices of some sort – could be drawn down from unknown places as well as from the grave, and in this process also one must be careful. Joseph Curwen had indubitably evoked many forbidden things, and as for Charles – what might one think of him? What forces 'outside the spheres' had reached him from Joseph Curwen's day and turned his mind on forgotten things? He had been led to find certain directions, and he had used them. He had talked with the man of horror in Prague and stayed long with the creature in the mountains of Transylvania. And he must have found the grave of Joseph Curwen at last. That newspaper item and what his mother had heard in the night were too significant to overlook. Then he had summoned something, and it must have come. That mighty voice aloft on Good Friday, and those *different* tones in the locked attic laboratory. What were they like, with their depth and hollowness? Was there not here some awful foreshadowing of the dreaded stranger Dr Allen with his spectral bass? Yes, *that* was what Mr

258

Ward had felt with vague horror in his single talk with the man—if man it were—over the telephone.

What hellish consciousness or voice, what morbid shade of presence, had come to answer Charles Ward's secret rites behind that locked door? Those voices heard in argument – 'must have it red for three months' – Good God! Was not that just before the vampirism broke out? The rifling of Ezra Weeden's ancient grave, and the cries later at Pawtuxet – whose mind had planned the vengeance and rediscovered the shunned seat of elder blasphemies? And then the bungalow and the bearded stranger, and the gossip, and the fear. The final madness of Charles neither father nor doctor could attempt to explain, but they did feel sure that the mind of Joseph Curwen had come to earth again and was following its ancient morbidities. Was demoniac possession in truth a possibility? Allen had something to do with it, and the detectives must find out more about one whose existence menaced the young man's life. In the meantime, since the existence of some vast crypt beneath the bungalow seemed virtually beyond dispute, some effort must be made to find it. Willett and Mr Ward, conscious of the sceptical attitude of the alienists, resolved during their final conference to undertake a joint exploration of unparalleled thoroughness; and agreed to meet at the bungalow on the following morning with valises and with certain tools and accessories suited to architectural search and underground exploration.

The morning of April sixth dawned clear, and both explorers were at the bungalow by ten o'clock. Mr Ward had the key, and an entry and cursory survey were made. From the disordered condition of Dr Allen's room it was obvious that the detectives had been there before, and the later searchers hoped that they had found some clue which might prove of value. Of course the main business lay in the cellar; so thither they descended without much delay, again making the circuit which each had vainly made before in the presence of the mad young owner. For a time everything seemed baffling, each inch of the earthen floor and stone walls having so solid and innocuous an aspect that the thought of a yawning aperture was scarcely to be entertained. Willett reflected that since the original cellar was dug without knowledge of any catacombs beneath, the beginning of the passage would represent the strictly modern delving of young Ward and his associates, where they had probed for the ancient vaults whose rumor could have reached them by no wholesome means.

The doctor tried to put himself in Charles's place to see how a delver would be likely to start, but could not gain much inspiration from this method. Then he decided on elimination as a policy, and went carefully over the whole subterranean surface both vertical and horizontal, trying to account for every inch separately. He was soon substantially narrowed down, and at last had nothing left but the small platform before the washtubs, which he had tried once before in vain. Now experimenting in every way possible, and exerting a double strength, he finally found that the top did indeed turn and slide horizontally on a corner pivot . Beneath it lay a trim concrete surface with an iron manhole, to which Mr Ward at once rushed with excited zeal. The cover was not hard to lift, and the father had quite removed it when Willett noticed the queerness of his aspect. He was swaying and nodding dizzily, and in the gust of noxious air which swept up from the black pit beneath the doctor soon recognized ample cause.

In a moment Dr Willett had his fainting companion on the floor above and was reviving him with cold water. Mr Ward responded feebly, but it could be seen that the mephitic blast from the crypt had in some way gravely sickened him. Wishing to take no changes, Willett hastened out to Broad Street for a taxicab and had soon dispatched the sufferer home despite his weak-voiced protests; after which he produced an electric torch, covered his nostrils with a band of sterile gauze, and descended once more to peer into the new-found depths. The foul air had now slightly abated, and Willett was able to send a beam of light down the Stygian hole. For about ten feet, he saw, it was a sheer cylindrical drop with concrete walls and an iron ladder; after which the hole appeared to strike a flight of old stone steps which must originally have emerged to earth somewhat southward of the present building.

Willett freely admits that for a moment the memory of the old Curwen legends kept him from climbing down alone into that malodorous gulf. He could not help thinking of what Luke Fenner had reported on that last monstrous night. Then duty asserted itself and he made the plunge carrying a great valise for the removal of whatever papers might prove of supreme importance. Slowly, as befitted one of his years, he descended the ladder and reached the slimy steps below. This was ancient masonry, his torch told him; and upon the dripping walls he saw the unwholesome moss of centuries. Down, down, ran the steps; not spirally, but in three abrupt turns; and with such narrowness that two men could have passed only with difficulty. He had counted about thirty when a sound reached him very faintly; and after that he did not feel disposed to count any more.

It was a godless sound; one of those low-keyed, insidious outrages of nature which are not meant to be. To call it a dull wail, a doom-dragged whine or a hopeless howl of chorused anguish and stricken flesh without mind would be to miss its most quintessential loathsomeness and soul-sickening overtones. Was it for this that Ward had seemed to listen on that day he was removed? It was the most

261

shocking thing that Willett had ever heard, and it continued from no determinate point as the doctor reached the bottom of the steps and cast his torchlight around on lofty corridor walls surmounted by Cyclopean vaulting and pierced by numberless black archways. The hall in which he stood was perhaps fourteen feet high to the middle of the vaulting and ten or twelve feet broad. Its pavement was of large chipped flagstones, and its walls and roof were of dressed masonry. Its length he could not imagine, for it stretched ahead indefinitely into the blackness. Of the archways, some had doors of the old six paneled colonial type, whilst others had none.

Overcoming the dread induced by the smell and the howling, Willett began to explore these archways one by one; finding beyond them rooms with groined stone ceilings, each of medium size and apparently of bizarre uses; most of them had fireplaces, the upper courses of whose chimneys would have formed an interesting study in engineering. Never before or since had he seen such instruments or suggestions of instruments which here loomed up on every hand through the burying dust and cobwebs of a century and a half, in many cases evidently shattered as if by the ancient raiders. For many of the chambers seemed wholly untrodden by modern feet, and must have represented the earliest and most obsolete phases of Joseph Curwen's experimentations. Finally there came a room of obvious modernity, or at least of recent occupancy. There were oil meters, bookshelves and tables, chairs and cabinets, and a desk piled high with papers of varying antiquity and contemporaneousness. Candlesticks and oil lamps stood about in several places; and finding a box of matches handy, Willett lighted such as were ready for use.

In the fuller gleam it appeared that this apartment was nothing less than the latest study or library of Charles

Ward. Of the books the doctor had seen many before, and a good part of the furniture had plainly come from the Prospect Street mansion. Here and there was a piece well known to Willett, and the sense of familiarity became so great that he half forgot the noisomeness and the wailing, both of which were plainer here than they had been at the foot of the steps. His first duty, as planned long ahead, was to find and seize any papers which might seem of vital importance; especially those portentous documents found by Charles so long ago behind the picture in Olney Court. As he searched he perceived how stupendous a task the final unravelling would be; for file on file was stuffed with papers in curious hands and bearing curious designs, so that months or even years might be needed for a thorough deciphering and editing. Once he found large packets of letters with Prague and Rakus postmarks, and in writing clearly recognizable as Orne's and Hutchinson's; all of which he took with him as part of the bundle to be removed in his valise.

At last, in a locked mahogany cabinet once gracing the Ward home, Willett found the batch of old Curwen papers; recognizing them from the reluctant glimpse Charles had granted him so many years ago. The youth had evidently kept them together very much as they had been when first he found them, since all the titles recalled by the workmen were present except the papers addressed to Orne and Hutchinson, and the cipher with its key. Willett placed the entire lot in his valise and continued his examination of the files. Since young Ward's immediate condition was the greatest matter at stake, the closest searching was done among the most obviously recent matter; and in this abundance of contemporary manuscript one very baffling oddity was noted. That oddity was the slight amount in Charles's normal writing, which indeed included nothing more recent than two months before. On the other hand, there were literally reams of symbols and formulae, historical notes and philosophical comment, in a crabbed penmanship absolutely identical with the ancient script of Joseph Curwen, though of undeniably modern dating. Plainly, a part of the latter-day programme had been a sedulous imitation of the old wizard's writing, which Charles seemed to have carried to a marvelous state of perfection. Of any third hand which might have been Allen's there was not a trace. If he had indeed come to be the leader, he must have forced young Ward to act as his amanuensis.

In this new material one mystic formula, or rather pair of formulae, recurred so often that Willett had it by heart before he had half finished his quest. It consisted of two parallel columns, the left-hand one surmounted by the archaic symbol called 'Dragon's Tail' or descending node. The appearance of the whole was something like this, and almost unconsciously the doctor realized that the second half was no more than the first written syllabically backward with the exception of

Y'AI 'NG'NGAH,	OGTHROD AI'F
YOG-SOTHOTH	GEB'L – EE'H
H'EE – L'GEB	*YOG-SOTHOTH*
F'AI THRODOG	'NGAH'NG AI'Y
UAAAH	*ZHRO*

the final monosyllables and of the odd name *Yog-Sothoth*, which he had come to recognize under various spellings from other things he had seen in connection with this horrible matter. The formulae were as follows—*exactly so*, as

264

Willett is abundantly able to testify—and the first one struck an odd note of uncomfortable latent memory in his brain, which he recognized later when reviewing the events of that horrible Good Friday of the previous year. So haunting were these formulae, and so frequently did he come upon them, that before the doctor knew it he was repeating them under his breath. Eventually, however, he felt he had secured all the papers he could digest to advantage for the present; hence resolved to examine no more till he could bring the sceptical alienists en masse for an ample and more systematic raid. He had still to find the hidden laboratory, so leaving his valise in the lighted room he emerged again into the black noisome corridor whose vaulting echoed ceaselessly with that dull and hideous whine.

The next few rooms he tried were all abandoned or filled only with crumbling boxes and ominous-looking leaden coffins; but impressed him deeply with the magnitude of Josph Curwen's original operations. He though of the slaves and seamen who had disappeared, of the graves which had been violated in every part of the world, and of what that final raiding party must have seen; and then he decided it was better not to think any more. Once a great stone staircase mounted at his right, and he deduced that this must have reached to one of the Curwen outbuildings —perhaps the famous stone edifice with the high slit-like windows – provided the steps he had descended had led from the steep-roofed farmhouse. Suddenly the walls seemed to fall away ahead, and the stench and the wailing grew stronger. Willett saw that he had come upon a vast open space, so great that his torchlight would not carry across it; and as he advanced he encountered occasional stout pillars supporting the arches of the roof.

After a time he reached a circle of pillars grouped like the monoliths of Stonehenge, with a large carved altar on a base of three steps in the center; and so curious were the carvings on that altar that he approached to study them with his electric light. But when he saw what they were he shrank away shuddering, and did not stop to investigate the dark stains which discolored the upper surface and had spread down the sides in occasional thin lines. Instead, he found the distant wall and traced it as it swept round in a gigantic circle perforated by occasional black doorways and indented by a myriad of shallow cells with iron gratings and wrist and ankle bonds on chains fastened to the stone of the concave rear masonry. These cells were empty, but still the horrible odor and the dismal moaning continued, more insistent now than ever, and seemingly varied at times by a sort of slippery thumping.

2

From that frightful smell and that uncanny noise Willett's attention could no longer be diverted. Both were plainer and more hideous in the great pillared hall than anywhere else, and carried a vague impression of being far below, even in this dark nether world of subterrene mystery. Before trying any of the black archways for steps leading further down, the doctor cast his beam of light about the stone-flagged floor. It was very loosely paved, and at irregular intervals there would occur a slab curiously pierced by small holes in no definite arrangement, while at one point there lay a very long ladder carelessly flung down. To this ladder, singularly enough, appeared to cling a particularly large amount of the frightful odor which encompassed everything. As he walked slowly about it suddenly occurred to Willett that both the noise and the odor seemed strongest directly above the oddly pierced slabs, as if they might be crude trap-doors leading down still deeper to some region of horror. Kneeling by one, he worked at it with his hands, and found that with extreme difficulty he could budge it. At his touch the moaning beneath ascended to a louder key, and only with vast trepidation did he persevere in the lifting of the heavy stone. A stench unnameable now rose up from below, and the doctor's head reeled dizzily as he laid back the slab and turned his torch upon the exposed square yard of gaping blackness.

If he had expected a flight of steps to some wide gulf of ultimate abomination, Willett was destined to be disappointed; for amidst that fetor and cracked whining he discerned only the brick-faced top of a cylindrical well perhaps a yard and a half in diameter and devoid of any ladder or other means of descent. As the light shone down, the wailing changed suddenly to a series of horrible yelps; in conjunction with which there came again that sound of blind, futile scrambling and slippery thumping. The explorer trembled, unwilling even to imagine what noxious thing might be lurking in that abyss; but in a moment he mustered up the courage to peer over the rough-hewn brink, lying at full length and holding the torch downward at arm's length to see what might lie below. For a second he could distinguish nothing but the slimy, moss-grown brick walls sinking illimitably into that half-tangible miasma of murk and foulness and anguished frenzy; and then he saw that something dark was leaping clumsily and frantically up and down at the bottom of the narrow shaft which must have been from twenty to twenty-five feet below the stone floor where he lay. The torch shook in his hand, but he looked again to see what manner of living creature might be immured there in the darkness of that unnatural well; left

267

starving by young Ward through all the long month since the doctors had taken him away, and clearly only one of a vast number prisoned in the kindred wells whose pierced stone covers so thickly studded the floor of the great vaulted cavern. Whatever the things were, they could not lie down in their cramped spaces; but must have crouched and whined and waited and feebly leaped all those hideous weeks since their master had abandoned them unheeded.

But Marinus Bicknell Willett was sorry that he looked again; for surgeon and veteran of the dissecting-room though he was, he has not been the same since. It is hard to explain just how a single sight of a tangible object with measurable dimensions could so shake and change a man; and we may only say that there is about certain outlines and entities a power of symbolism and suggestion which acts frightfully on a sensitive thinker's perspective and whispers terrible hints of obscure cosmic relationships and unname-. able realities behind the protective illusions of common vision. In that second look Willett saw such an outline or entity, for during the next few instants he was undoubtedly as stark mad as any inmate of Dr Waite's private hospital. He dropped the electric torch from a hand drained of muscular power or nervous coordination, nor heeded the sound of crunching teeth which told of its fate at the bottom of the pit. He screamed and screamed and screamed in a voice whose falsetto panic no acquaintance of his would ever have recognized, and though he could not rise to his feet he crawled and rolled desperately away over the damp pavement where dozens of Tartarean wells poured forth their exhausted whining and yelping to answer his own insane cries. He tore his hands on the rough, loose stones, and many times bruised his head against the frequent pillars, but still he kept on. Then at last he slowly came to himself in the utter blackness and stench, and stopped his ears against the droning wail into which the burst of yelping had subsided. He was drenched with perspiration and without means of producing a light; stricken and unnerved in the abysmal blackness and horror, and crushed with a memory he never could efface. Beneath him dozens of those things still lived, and from one of the shafts the cover was removed. He knew that what he had seen could never climb up the slippery walls, yet shuddered at the thought that some obscure foothold might exist.

What the thing was, he would never tell. It was like some of the carvings on the hellish altar, but it was alive. Nature had never made it in this form, for it was too palpably *unfinished*. The deficiencies were of the most surprising sort, and the abnormalities of proportion could not be described. Willett consents only to say that this type of thing must have represented entities which Ward called up from *imperfect salts*, and which he kept for servile or ritualistic purposes. If it had not had a certain significance, its image would not have been carved on that damnable stone. It was not the worst thing depicted on that stone – but Willett never opened the other pits. At the time, the first connected idea in his mind was an idle paragraph from some of the old Curwen data he had digested long before; a phrase used by Simon or Jedediah Orne in that portentous confiscated letter to the bygone sorcerer:

'Certainely, there was Noth'g butt ye liveliest Awfullness in That which H. rais'd upp from What he cou'd gather onlie a Part of.'

Then, horribly supplementing rather than displacing this image, there came a recollection of these ancient lingering rumours anent the burned and twisted thing found in the fields a week after the Curwen raid. Charles Ward had once told the doctor what old Slocum said of

269

that object; that it was neither thoroughly human, nor wholly allied to any animal which Pawtuxet folk had ever seen or read about.

These words hummed in the doctor's mind as he rocked to and fro, squatting on the nitrous stone floor. He tried to drive them out, and repeated the Lord's Prayer to himself; eventually trailing off into a mnemonic hodge-podge like the modernistic 'Waste Land' of Mr T. S. Eliot and finally reverting to the oft-repeated dual formula he had lately found in Ward's underground library: '*Y'ai 'ng'ngah, Yog-Sothoth*', and so on till the final underlined '*Zhro*'. It seemed to soothe him and he staggered to his feet after a time; lamenting bitterly his fright-lost torch and looking wildly about for any gleam of light in the clutching inkiness of the chilling air. Think he would not; but he strained his eyes in every direction for some faint glint or reflection of the bright illumination he had left in the library. After a while he thought he detected a suspicion of a glow infinitely far away, and toward this he crawled in agonized caution on hands and knees amidst the stench and howling, always feeling ahead lest he collide with the numerous great pillars or stumble into the abominable pit he had uncovered.

Once his shaking fingers touched something which he knew must be the steps leading to the hellish altar, and from this spot he recoiled in loathing. At another time he encountered the pierced slab he had removed, and here his caution became almost pitiful. But he did not come upon the dread aperture to detain him. What had been down there made no sound nor stir. Evidently its crunching of the fallen electric torch had not been good for it. Each time Willett's fingers felt a perforated slab he trembled. His passage over it would sometimes increase the groaning below, but generally it would produce no effect at all, since he moved very noiselessly. Several times during his progress the glow ahead diminished perceptibly, and he realized that the various candles and lamps he had left must be expiring one by one. The thought of being lost in utter darkness without matches amidst this underground world of nightmare labyrinths impelled him to rise to his feet and run, which he could safely do now that he had passed the open pit; for he knew that once the light failed his only hope of rescue and survival would lie in whatever relief party Mr Ward might send after missing him for a sufficient period. Presently, however, he emerged from the open space into the narrower corridor and definitely located the glow as coming from a door on his right. In a moment he had reached it and was standing once more in young Ward's secret library, trembling with relief, and watching the sputterings of that last lamp which had brought him to safety.

3

In another moment he was hastily filling the burned-out lamps from an oil supply he had previously noticed, and when the room was bright again he looked about to see if he might find a lantern for further exploration. For racked though he was with horror, his sense of grim purpose was still uppermost, and he was firmly determined to leave no stone unturned in his search for the hideous facts behind Charles Ward's bizarre madness. Failing to find a lantern, he chose the smallest of the lamps to carry; also filling his pockets with candles and matches, and taking with him a gallon can of oil, which he proposed to keep for reserve use in whatever hidden laboratory he might uncover beyond the terrible open space with its unclean altar and nameless covered wells. To traverse that space again would require his utmost fortitude, but he knew it must be done. Fortunately neither the frightful altar nor the opened shaft was near the vast cell-indented wall which bounded the cavern area, and whose black mysterious archways would form the next goals of a logical search.

So Willett went back to that great pillared hall of stench and anguished howling, turned down his lamps to avoid any distant glimpse of the hellish altar, or of the uncovered pit with the pierced stone slab beside it. Most of the doorways led merely to small chambers, some vacant and some evidently used as store-rooms; and in several of the latter he saw some very curious accumulations of various objects. One was packed with rotting and dust-draped bales of spare clothing, and the explorer thrilled when he saw that it was unmistakably the clothing of a century and a half before. In another room he found numerous odds and ends of modern clothing, as if gradual provisions were being made to equip a large body of men. But what he disliked most of all were the huge copper vats which occasionally appeared; these, and the sinister incrustations upon them. He liked them even less than the weirdly figured leaden bowls whose ruins retained such obnoxious deposits and around which clung repellent odors perceptible above even the general noisomeness of the crypt. When he had completed about half the entire circuit of the wall he found another corridor like that from which he had come, and out of which many doors opened.

This he proceeded to investigate; and after entering three rooms of medium size and of no significant contents, he came at last to a large oblong apartment whose businesslike tanks and tables, furnaces and modern instruments, occasional books and endless shelves of jars and bottles proclaimed it indeed the long–sought laboratory of Charles Ward – and no doubt of old Joseph Curwen before him.

After lighting the three lamps which he found filled and ready, Dr Willett examined the place and all its appurtenances with the keenest interest; noting from the relative quantities of various reagents on the shelves that young Ward's dominant concern must have been with some branch of organic chemistry. On the whole, little could be learned from the scientific ensemble, which included a gruesome-looking dissecting table; so that the room was really rather a disappointment. Among the books was a tattered old copy of Borellus in black-letters, and it was weirdly interesting to note that Ward had underlined the same passage whose marking had so perturbed good Mr Merritt at Curwen's farmhouse more than a century and a half before. That older copy, of course, must have perished along with the rest of Curwen's occult library in the final raid. Three archways opened off the laboratory, and these the doctor proceeded to sample in turn. From his cursory survey he saw that two led merely to small store-rooms; but these he canvassed with care, remarking the piles of coffins in various stages of damage and shuddering violently at two or three of the few coffin-plates he could decipher. There was much clothing also stored in these rooms, and several new and tightly-nailed boxes which he did not stop to investigate. Most interesting of all, perhaps, were some odd bits which he judged to be fragments of old Joseph Curwen's laboratory appliances. These had suffered damage at the hands of the raiders, but were still partly recognizable as the chemical paraphernalia of the Georgian period.

The third archway led to a very sizeable chamber entirely lined with shelves and having in the centre a table bearing two lamps. These lamps Willett lighted, and in their brilliant glow studied the endless shelving which surrounded him. Some of the upper levels were wholly vacant, but most of the space was filled with small odd-looking leaden jars of two general types; one tall and without handles like a Grecian lekythos or oil-jug, and the other with a single handle and proportioned like a Phaleron jug. All had metal stoppers, and were covered with peculiar-looking symbols molded in low relief. In a moment the doctor noticed that these jugs were classified with great rigidity; all the lekythoi being one one side of the room with a large wooden sign reading 'Custodes' above them, and all the Phalerons on the other, correspondingly labelled with a sign reading 'Materia'. Each of the jars or jugs, except some on the upper shelves that turned out to be vacant, bore a cardboard tag with a number apparently referring to a catalog; and Willett resolved to look for the latter presently. For the moment, however, he was more interested in the nature of the array as a whole; and experimentally opened several of the lekythoi and Phalerons at random with a view to a rough generalization. The result was invariable. Both types of jar contained a small quantity of a single kind of substance; a fine dusty powder of very light weight and of many shades of dull neutral color. To the colors which formed the only point of variation there was no apparent method of disposal; and no distinction between what occurred in the lekythoi and what occurred in the Phalerons. A bluish-gray powder might be by the side of a pinkish-white one, and any one in a Phaleron might have its exact counterpart in a lekythos. The most individual feature about the powders was their non-adhesiveness. Willett would pour one into his hand, and upon returning it to its jug would find that no residue whatever remained on his palm.

The meaning of the two signs puzzled him, and he wondered why this battery of chemicals was separated so radically from those in glass jars on the shelves of the laboratory proper. 'Custodes', 'Materia'; that was the Latin for 'Guards' and 'Material', respectively – and then there came a flash of memory as to where he had seen that word 'Guards' before in connection with this dreadful mystery. It was, of course, in the recent letter to Dr Allen purporting to be from old Edward Hutchinson; and the phrase had read: 'There was no Neede to keep the Guards in shape and eat'g off their Heades, and it made much to be founde in Case of Trouble, as you too welle Knowe.' What did this signify? But wait – was there not still *another* reference to 'guards' in this matter which he had failed wholly to recall when reading the Hutchinson letter? Back in the old non-secretive days Ward had told him of the Eleazar Smith diary recording the spying of Smith and Weeden on the Curwen farm, and in that dreadful chronicle there had been a mention of conversations overheard before the old wizard betook himself wholly beneath the earth. There had been, Smith and Weeden insisted, terrible colloquies wherein figured Curwen, certain captives of his, *and the guards of those captives*. Those guards, according to Hutchinson or his avatar, had 'eaten their heads off', so that now Dr Allen did not keep them *in shape*. And if not *in shape*, how save as the 'salts' to which it appears this wizard band was engaged in reducing as many human bodies or skeletons as they could?

So *that* was what these lekythoi contained; the monstrous fruit of unhallowed rites and deeds, presumably won or cowed to such submission as to help when called up by some hellish incantation, in the defence of their blasphemous master or the questioning of those who were not so willing? Willett shuddered at the though of what he had been pouring in and out of his hands, and for a moment felt an impulse to flee in panic from that cavern of hideous shelves with their silent and perhaps watching sentinels.

Then he thought of the 'Materia' – in the myriad Phaleron jugs on the other side of the room. Salts too – and if not the salts of 'guards', then the salts of what? God! Could it be possible that here lay the mortal relics of half the titan thinkers of all the ages; snatched by supreme ghouls from crypts where the world thought them safe, and subject to the beck and call of madmen who sought to drain their knowledge for some still wilder end whose ultimate effect would concern, as poor Charles had hinted in his frantic note, 'all civilization, all natural law, perhaps even the fate of the solar system and the universe'? And Marinus Bicknell Willett had sifted their dust through his hands!

Then he noticed a small door at the farther end of the room, and calmed himself enough to approach it and examine the crude sign chiseled above. It was only a symbol, but it filled him with vague spiritual dread; for a morbid, dreaming friend of his had once drawn it on paper and told him a few of the things it means in the dark abyss of sleep. It was the sign of Koth, that dreamers see fixed above the archway of a certain black tower standing alone in twilight – and Willett did not like what his friend Randolph Carter had said of its powers. But a moment later he forgot the sign as he recognized a new acrid odor in the stench-filled air. This was a chemical rather than animal smell, and came clearly from the room beyond the door. And it was, unmistakably, the same odor which had saturated Charles Ward's clothing on the day the doctors had taken him away. So it was here that the youth had been interrupted by the final summons? He was wiser than old Joseph Curwen, for he had not resisted. Willett, boldly determined to penetrate every wonder and nightmare this nether realm might contain, seized the small lamp and crossed the threshold. A wave of nameless fright rolled out to meet him, but he yielded to no whim and deferred to no intuition. There was nothing alive here to harm him, and he would not be stayed in his piercing of the eldritch cloud which engulfed his patient.

The room beyond the door was of medium size, and had no furniture save a table, a single chair, and two groups of curious machines with clamps and wheels which Willett recognized after a moment as mediaeval instruments of torture. On one side of the door stood a rack of savage whips, above which were some shelves bearing empty rows of shallow pedestalled cups of lead shaped like Grecian Kylikes. On the other side was the table; with a powerful Argand lamp, a pad and pencil, and two of the stoppered lekythoi from the shelves outside set down at irregular places as if temporarily or in haste. Willett lighted the lamp and looked carefully at the pad to see what notes young Ward might have been jotting down when interrupted; but found nothing more intelligible than the following disjointed fragments in that crabbed Curwen chirography, which shed no light on the case as a whole:

'B. dy'd not. Escap'd into walls and founde Place below.

'Saw olde V. sage ye Sabaoth and learnt ye Way.'

'Rais'd *Yog-Sothoth* thrice and was ye nexte Day deliver'd.'

'F. soughte to wipe out all know'g howe to raise Those from Outside.'

As the strong Argand blaze lit up the entire chamber, the doctor saw that the wall opposite the door, between the two groups of torturing appliances in the corners, was covered with pegs from which hung a set of shapeless looking robes of a rather dismal yellowish-white. But far more interesting were the two vacant walls, both of which were thickly covered with mystic symbols and formulae roughly chiseled in the smooth dressed stone. The damp floor also bore marks of carving; and with but little difficulty Willett deciphered a huge pentagram in the centre, with a plain circle about three feet wide half way between this and each corner. In one of these four circles, near where a yellowish robe had been flung carelessly down, there stood a shallow Kylix of the sort found on the shelves above the whip-rack; and just outside the periphery was one of the Phaleron jugs from the shelves in the other room, its tag numbered 118. This was unstoppered, and proved upon inspection to be empty; but the explorer saw with a shiver that the Kylix was not. Within its shallow area, and saved from scattering only by the absence of wind in this sequestered cavern, lay a small amount of a dry, dull-greenish efflorescent powder which must have belonged in the jug; and Willett almost reeled at the implications that came sweeping over him as he correlated little by little the several elements and antecedents of the scene. The whips and the instruments of torture, the dust or salts from the jug of 'Materia', the two lekythoi from the 'Custodes' shelf, the robes, the formulae on the walls, the notes on the pad, the hints from letters and legends, and the thousand glimpses, doubts, and suppositions which had come to torment the friends and parents of Charles Ward – all these engulfed the doctor in a trial wave of horror as he looked at that dry greenish powder outspread in the pedestaled leaden Kylix on the floor.

With an effort, however, Willett pulled himself together and began studying the formulae chiseled on the walls. From the stained and incrusted letters it was obvious that they were carved in Joseph Curwen's time, and their text was such as to be vaguely familiar to one who had read much Curwen material or delved extensively into the history of magic. One the doctor clearly recognized as what Mrs Ward heard her son chanting on that noxious Good Friday a year before, and what an authority had told him was a very terrible invocation addressed to secret gods

278

outside the normal spheres. It was not spelled here exactly as Mrs Ward had set it down from memory, nor as yet the authority had shown it to him in the forbidden pages of 'Eliphas Levi'; but its identity was unmistakable, and such words as *Sabaoth, Metraton, Almonsin, and Zariatnatmik* sent a shudder of fright through the searcher who had seen and felt so much of cosmic abomination just around the corner.

This was on the left-hand wall as one entered the room. The right-hand wall was no less thickly inscribed, and Willett felt a start of recognition as he came upon the pair of formulae so frequently occurring in the recent notes in the library. They were, roughly speaking, the same: with the ancient symbols of 'Dragon's Head' and 'Dragon's Tail' heading them as in Ward's scribblings. But the spelling differed quite widely from that of the modern versions, as if old Curwen had had a different way of recording sound, or as if later study had evolved more powerful and perfected variants of the invocations in question. The doctor tried to reconcile the chiseled version with the one which still ran persistently in his head, and found it hard to do. Where the script he had memorized began '*Y'ai'ng'ngah, Yog-Sothoth*', this epigraph started out as '*Aye, cngengah, Yogge-Sothotha*'; which to his mind would seriously interfere with the syllabification of the second word.

Ground as the later text was into his consciousness, the discrepancy disturbed him; and he found himself chanting the first of the formulae aloud in an effort to square the sound he conceived with the letters he found carved. Weird and menacing in that abyss of antique blasphemy rang his voice, its accents keyed to a droning sing-song either through the spell of the past and the unknown, or through the hellish example of that dull, godless wail from the pits whose inhuman coldness rose and fell rhythmically in the distance through the stench and the darkness.

'Y'AI 'NG'NGAH
YOG-SOTHOTH
H'EE – L'GEB
F'AI 'THRODOG
UAAAH!'

But what was this cold wind which had sprung into life at the very outset of the chant? The lamps were sputtering woefully, and the gloom grew so dense that the letters on the wall nearly faded from sight. There was smoke, too, and an acrid odor which quite drowned out the stench from the far-away wells; an odor like that he had smelt before, yet infinitely stronger and more pungent. He turned from the inscriptions to face the room with its bizarre contents, and saw that the Kylix on the floor, in which the ominous efflorescent powder had lain, was giving forth a cloud of thick, greenish-black vapor of surprising volume and opacity. That powder – Great God! it had come from the shelf of 'Materia' – what was it doing now, and what had started it? The formula he had been chanting – the first of the pair – Dragon's Head, *ascending node* – Blessed Saviour, could it be . . .

The doctor reeled, and through his head raced wildly disjointed scraps from all he had seen, heard, and read of the frightful case of Joseph Curwen and Charles Dexter Ward. 'I say to you againe, doe not calle up Any that you cannot putt downe . . . Have ye Wordes for laying at all times readie, and stopp not to be sure when there is any Doubte of *Whom* you have . . . Three Talkes with What was therein inhum'd . . .' *Mercy of Heaven, what is that shape behind the parting smoke?*

280

Marinus Bicknell Willett has no hope that any part of his
tale will be believed except by certain sympathetic friends,
hence he has made no attempt to tell it beyond his most
intimate circle. Only a few outsiders have ever heard it
repeated, and of these the majority laugh and remark that
the doctor surely is getting old. He has been advised to take
a long vacation and to shun future cases dealing with
mental disturbance. But Mr Ward knows that the veteran
physician speaks only a horrible truth. Did not he himself
see the noisome aperture in the bungalow cellar? Did not
Willett send him home overcome and ill at eleven o'clock
that portentous morning? Did he not telephone the doctor
in vain that evening, and again the next day, and had he not
driven to the bungalow itself on that following noon, finding
his friend unconscious but unharmed on one of the beds
upstairs? Willett had been breathing stertorously, and
opened his eyes slowly when Mr Ward gave him some
brandy fetched from the car. Then he shuddered and
screamed, crying out, '*That beard . . . those eyes . . . God, who
are you?*' A very strange thing to say to a trim, blue-eyed,
clean-shaven gentleman whom he had known from the
latter's boyhood.

In the bright noon sunlight the bungalow was unchanged
since the previous morning. Willett's clothing bore no
disarrangement beyond certain smudges and worn places at
the knees, and only faint acrid odor reminded Mr Ward of
what he had smelt on his son that day he was taken to the
hospital. The doctor's flashlight was missing, but his valise
was safely there, as empty as when he had brought it.

Before indulging in any explanations, and obviously with great moral effort, Willett staggered dizzily down to the cellar and tried the fateful platform before the tubs. It was unyielding. Crossing to where he had left his yet unused tool satchel the day before, he obtained a chisel and began to pry up the stubborn planks one by one. Underneath the smooth concrete was still visible, but of any opening or perforation there was no longer a trace. Nothing yawned this time to sicken the mystified father who had followed the doctor downstairs; only the smooth concrete underneath the planks – no noisome well, no world of subterrene horrors, no secret library, no Curwen papers, no nightmare pits of stench and howling, no laboratory or shelves or chiseled formulae, no . . . Dr Willett turned pale, and clutched at the younger man. 'Yesterday,' he asked softly, 'did you see it here . . . and smell it?' And when Mr Ward, himself transfixed with dread and wonder, found strength to nod an affirmative, the physician gave a sound half a sigh and half a gasp, and nodded in turn. 'Then I will tell you,' he said.

So for an hour, in the sunniest room they could find upstairs, the physician whispered his frightful tale to the wondering father. There was nothing to relate beyond the looming up of that form when the greenish-black vapor from the Kylix parted, and Willett was too tired to ask himself what had really occurred. There were futile, bewildered head-shakings from both men, and once Mr Ward ventured a hushed suggestion, 'Do you suppose it would be of any use to dig?' The doctor was silent, for it seemed hardly fitting for any human brain to answer when powers of unknown spheres had so vitally encroached on this side of the Great Abyss. Again Mr Ward asked, 'But where did it go? It brought you here, you know, and it sealed up the hole somehow.' And Willett again let silence answer for him.

But after all, this was not the final phase of the matter.

Reaching for his handkerchief before rising to leave, Dr
Willett's fingers closed upon a piece of paper in his pocket
which had not been there before, and which was com-
panioned by the candles and matches he had seized in the
vanished vault. It was a common sheet, torn obviously from
the cheap pad in that fabulous room of horror somewhere
underground, and the writing upon it was that of an
ordinary lead pencil – doubtless the one which had lain
beside the pad. It was folded very carelessly, and beyond
the faint acrid scent of the cryptic chamber bore no print or
mark of any world but this. But in the text itself it did
indeed reek with wonder; for here was no script of any
wholesome age, but the laboured strokes of mediaeval
darkness, scarcely legible to the laymen who now strained
over it, yet having combinations of symbols which seemed
vaguely familiar.

The briefly scrawled message was this, and its mystery lent
purpose to the shaken pair, who forthwith walked steadily
out to the Ward car and gave orders to be driven first to a
quiet dining place and then to the John Hay Library on the
hill.

At the library it was easy to find good manuals of
palaeography, and over these the two men puzzled till the
lights of evening shone out from the great chandelier. In the
end they found what was needed. The letters were indeed
no fantastic invention, but the normal script of a very dark

283

period. They were the pointed Saxon minuscules of the eighth or ninth century A.D., and brought with them momories of an uncouth time when under a fresh Christian veneer ancient faiths and ancient rites stirred stealthily, and the pale moon of Britain looked sometimes on strange deeds in the Roman ruins of Caerleon and Hexhaus, and by the Towers along Hadrian's crumbling wall. The words were in such Latin as a barbarous age might remember – '*Corwinus necandus est. Cadaver aq(ua) forti dissolvendum, nec aliq(ui)d retinendum. Tace ut potes.*' – which may roughly be translated, 'Curwen must be killed. The body must be dissolved in aqua fortis, nor must anything be retained. Keep silence as best you are able.'

Willett and Mr Ward were mute and baffled. They had met the unknown, and found that they lacked emotions to respond to it as they vaguely believed they ought. With Willett, especially, the capacity for receiving fresh impressions of awe was well-nigh exhausted; and both men sat still and helpless till the closing of the library forced them to leave. Then they drove listlessly to the Ward mansion in Prospect Street, and talked to no purpose into the night. The doctor rested toward morning, but did not go home. And he was still there Sunday noon when a telephone message came from the detectives who had been assigned to look up Dr Allen.

Mr Ward, who was pacing nervously about in a dressing-gown answered the call in person; and told the men to come up early the next day when he heard their report was almost ready. Both Willett and he were glad that this phase of the matter was taking form, for whatever the origin of the strange minuscule message, it seemed certain that the 'Curwen' who must be destroyed could be no other than the bearded and spectacled stranger. Charles had feared this man and had said in the frantic note that he must be killed

284

and dissolved in acid. Allen moreover, had been receiving letters from the strange wizards in Europe under the name of Curwen, and palpably regarded himself as an avatar of the bygone necromancer. And now from a fresh and unknown source had come a message saying that 'Curwen' must be killed and dissolved in acid. The linkage was too unmistakable to be factitious; and besides, was not Allen planning to murder young Ward upon the advice of the creature called Hutchinson? Of course, the letter they had seen had never reached the bearded stranger; but from its text they could see that Allen had already formed plans for dealing with the youth if he grew too 'squeamish'. Without doubt, Allen must be apprehended; and even if the most drastic directions were not carried out, he must be placed where he could inflict no harm upon Charles Ward.

That afternoon, hoping against hope to extract some gleam of information anent the inmost mysteries from the only available one capable of giving it, the father and the doctor went down the bay and called on young Charles at the hospital. Simply and gravely Willett told him all he had found, and noticed how pale he turned as each description made certain the truth of the discovery. The physician employed as much dramatic effect as he could, and watched for a wincing on Charles's part when he approached the matter of the covered pits and the nameless hybrids within. But Ward did not wince. Willett paused, and his voice grew indignant as he spoke of how the things were starving. He taxed the youth with shocking inhumanity, and shivered when only a sardonic laugh came in reply. For Charles, having dropped as useless his pretense that the crypt did not exist, seemed to see some ghastly jest in this affair; and chuckled hoarsely at something which amused him. Then he whispered, in accents doubly terrible because of the cracked voice he used, 'Damn 'em, they *do* eat, but they *don't need to*! That's the rare part! A month, you say, without food? Lud, Sir, you be modest! D'ye know, that was the joke on poor old Whipple with his virtuous bluster! Kill everything off, would he? Why, damme, he was half-deaf with the noise from Outside and never saw or heard aught from the wells. He never dreamed they were there at all! Devil take ye, those cursed *things have been howling down there ever since Curwen was done for a hundred and fifty-seven years gone!*'

But no more than this could Willett get from the youth. Horrified, yet almost convinced against his will, he went on with his tale in the hope that some incident might startle his auditor out of the mad composure he maintained. Looking at the youth's face, the doctor could not but feel a kind of terror at the changes which recent months had wrought. Truly, the boy had drawn down nameless horrors from the skies. When the room with the formulae and the greenish dust was mentioned, Charles showed his first sign of animation. A quizzical look overspread his face as he heard what Willett had read on the pad, and he ventured the mild statement that those notes were old ones, of no possible significance to anyone not deeply initiated in the history of magic. 'But,' he added, 'had you but known the words to bring up that which I had out in the cup, you had not been here to tell me this. 'Twas Number 118, and I conceive you would have shook had you looked it up in my list in t'other room. 'Twas never raised by me, but I meant to have it up that day you came to invite me hither.'

Then Willett told of the formula he had spoken and of the greenish-black smoke which had arisen; and as he did so he saw true fear dawn for the first time on Charles Ward's face. 'It *came*, and you be here alive!' As Ward croaked the words his voice seemed almost to burst free of its trammels and sink to cavernous abysses of uncanny resonance. Willett, gifted with a flash of inspiration, believed he saw the ituation, and wove into his reply a caution from a letter he emembered. 'No.118, you say? But don't forget that *stones re all changed now in nine grounds out of ten. You are never sure till ou question!*' And then, without warning, he drew forth the miniscule message and flashed it before the patient's eyes. He could have wished no stronger result, for Charles Ward ainted forthwith.

All this conversation, of course, had been conducted with he greatest secrecy lest the resident alienists accuse the ather and the physician of encouraging a madman in his lelusions. Unaided, too, Dr Willett and Mr Ward picked up the stricken youth and placed him on the couch. In eviving, the patient mumbled many times of some word vhich he must get to Orne and Hutchinson at once; so vhen his consciousness seemed fully back the doctor told him that of those strange creatures at least one was his bitter enemy, and had given Dr Allen advice for his assassination. This revelation produced no visible effect, and before it was made the visitors could see that their host had already the look of a hunted man. After that he would converse no more, so Willett and the father departed presently; leaving behind a caution against the bearded Allen, to which the youth only replied that this individual vas very safely taken care of, and could do no one any harm even if he wished. This was said with an almost evil chuckle very painful to hear. They did not worry about any communications Charles might write to that monstrous pair in Europe. Since they knew that the hospital authorities seized all outgoing mail for censorship and would pass no wild or outré-looking missive.

There is, however, a curious sequel to the matter of Orne and Hutchinson, if such indeed the exiled wizards were. Moved by some vague presentiment amidst the horrors of hat period, Willett arranged with an international press-cutting bureau for accounts of notable current crimes and accidents in Prague and in eastern Transylvania; and after six months believed that he had found two very significant things amongst the multifarious items he received and had translated. One was the total wrecking of a house by night in the oldest quarter of Prague, and the disappearance of the evil old man called Josef Nadeh, who had dwelt in it alone ever since anyone could remember. The other was a titan explosion in the Transylvanian mountains east of Rak s, and the utter extirpation with all its inmates of the ill-regarded Castle Ferenczy, whose master was so badly spoken of by peasants and soldiery alike that he would shortly have been summoned to Bucharest for serious questioning had not this incident cut off a career already so long as to antedate all common memory. Willett maintains that the hand which wrote those minuscules was able to wield stronger weapons as well; and that while Curwen was left to him to dispose of, the writer felt able to find and deal with Orne and Hutchinson itself. Of what their fate may have been the doctor strives sedulously not to think.

5

The following morning Dr Willett hastened to the Ward home to be present when the detectives arrived. Allen's destruction or imprisonment – or Curwen's, if one might regard the tacit claim to reincarnation as valid – he felt must be accomplished at any cost, and he communicated this conviction to Mr Ward as they sat waiting for the men to come. They were downstairs this time, for the upper parts of the house were beginning to be shunned because of a peculiar nauseousness which hung indefinitely about; a nauseousness which the older servants connected with some curse left by the vanished Curwen portrait.

At nine o'clock the three detectives presented themselves and immediately delivered all that they had to say. They had not, regrettably enough, located the Brava Tony Gomes as they had wished, not had they found the least trace of Dr Allen's source or present whereabouts; but they had managed to unearth a considerable number of local impressions and facts concerning the reticent stranger. Allen had struck Pawtuxet people as a vaguely unnatural being, and there was a universal belief that his thick sandy beard was either dyed or false – a belief conclusively upheld by the finding of such a false beard, together with a pair of dark glasses, in his room at the fateful bungalow. His voice, Mr Ward could here testify from his one telephone conversation, had a depth and hollowness that could not be forgotten; and his glance seemed malign even through his smoked and horn-rimmed glasses. One shopkeeper, in the course of negotiations, had seen a specimen of his handwriting and declared it was very queer and crabbed; this being confirmed by pencilled notes of no clear meaning found in his room and identified by the merchant.

In connection with the vampirism ructions of the preceding summer, a majority of the gossips believed that Allen rather than Ward was the actual vampire. Statements were also obtained from the officials who had visited the bungalow after the unpleasant incident of the motor truck robbery. They had felt less of the sinister in Dr Allen, but had recognized him as the dominant figure in the queer shadowy cottage. The place had been too dark for them to observe him clearly, but they would know him again if they saw him. His beard had looked odd, and they thought he had some slight scar above his dark-spectacled right eye. As for the search of Allen's room, it yielded nothing definite save the beard and glasses, and several penciled notes in a crabbed writing, which Willett at once saw was identical with that shared by the old Curwen manuscripts and by the voluminous recent notes of young Ward found in the vanished catacombs of horror.

Dr Willett and Mr Ward caught something of a profound, subtle, and insidious cosmic fear from these data as they were gradually unfolded, and almost trembled in following up the vague, mad thought which had simultaneously reached their minds. Ths false beard and glasses, the crabbed Curwen penmanship – the old portrait and its tiny scar – *and the altered youth in the hospital with such a scar* – that deep, hollow voice on the telephone – was it not of this that Mr Ward was reminded when his son barked forth those pitiable tones to which he now claimed to be reduced? Who had ever seen Charles and Allen together? Yes, the officials had once, but who later on? Was it not when Allen left that Charles suddenly lost his growing fright and began to live wholly at the bungalow? Curwen – Allen – Ward – in what blasphemous and abominable fusion had two ages and two persons become involved? That damnable resemblance of the picture to Charles – had it not used to stare and stare, and follow the boy around the room with its eyes? Why, too, did both Allen and Charles copy Joseph Curwen's handwriting, even when alone and off guard? And then the frightful work of those people – the lost crypt of horrors that had aged the doctor overnight; the starved monsters in the noisome pits; the awful formula which had yielded such nameless results; the message in minuscules found in Willett's pocket; the papers and the letters and all the talk of graves and 'salts' and discoveries – whither did everything lead? In the end Mr Ward did the most sensible thing. Steeling himself against any realization of why he did it, he gave the detectives an article to be shown to such

Pawtuxet shopkeepers as had seen the portentous Dr Allen. That article was a photograph of his luckless son, on which he now carefully drew in ink the pair of heavy glasses and the black pointed beard, which the men had brought from Allen's room.

For two hours he waited with the doctor in the oppressive house where fear and miasma were slowly gathering as the empty panel in the upstairs library leered and leered and leered. Then the men returned. Yes, *the altered photograph was a very passable likeness of Dr Allen*. Mr Ward turned pale, and Willett wiped a suddenly dampened brow with his hand-kerchief. Allen – Ward – Curwen – it was becoming too hideous for coherent thought. What had the boy called out of the void, and what had it done to him? What really had happened from first to last? Who was this Allen who sought to kill Charles as too 'squeamish', and why had his destined victim said in the postscript to that frantic letter that he must be so completely obliterated in acid? Why, too, had the minuscule message, of whose origin no one dared think, said that 'Curwen' must be likewise obliterated? What was the *change*, and when had the final stage occurred? That day when his frantic note was received – he had been nervous all the morning, then there was an alteration. He had slipped out unseen and swaggered boldly in past the men hired to guard him. That was the time, when he was out. But no – had he not cried out in terror as he entered his study – this very room? What had he found there? Or wait – *what had found him?* That simulacrum which brushed boldly in without having been seen to go – was that an alien shadow and a horror forcing itself upon a trembling figure which had never gone out at all? Had not the butler spoken of queer noises?

Willett rang for the man and asked him some low-toned questions. It had, surely enough, been a bad business.

There had been noises – a cry, a gasp, a choking, and a sort of clattering or creaking or thumping, or all of these. And Mr Charles was not the same when he stalked out without a word. The butler shivered as he spoke, and sniffed at the heavy air that blew down from some open window upstairs. Terror had settled definitely upon the house, and only the businesslike detectives failed to imbibe a full measure of it. Even they were restless, for this case had held vague elements in the background which pleased them not at all. Dr Willett was thinking deeply and rapidly, and his thoughts were terrible ones. Now and then he would almost break into mutterings as he ran over in his head a new, appalling, and increasingly conclusive chain of nightmare happenings.

Then Mr Ward made a sign that the conference was over, and everyone save him and the doctor left the room. It was noon now, but shadows as of coming night seemed to engulf the phantom-haunted mansion. Willett began talking very seriously to his host, and urged that hs leave a great deal of the future investigation to him. There would be, he predicted, certain obnoxious elements which a friend could bear better than a relative. As family physician he must have a free hand, and the first thing he required was a period alone and undisturbed in the abandoned library upstairs, where the ancient overmantel had gathered about itself an aura of noisome horror more intense than when Joseph Curwen's features themselves glanced slyly down from the painted panel.

Mr Ward, dazed by the flood of grotesque morbidities and unthinkably maddening suggestions that poured in upon him from every side, could only acquiesce; and half an hour later the doctor was locked in the shunned room with the paneling from Olney Court. The father, listening outside, heard fumbling sounds of moving and rummaging as the moments passed; and finally a wrench and a creak, as if a tight cupboard door were being opened. Then there was a muffled cry, a kind of snorting choke, and a hasty slamming of whatever had been opened. Almost at once the key rattled and Willett appeared in the hall, haggard and ghastly, and demanding wood for the real fireplace on the south wall of the room. The furnace was not enough, he said; and the electric log had little practical use. Longing yet not daring to ask questions, Mr Ward gave the requisite orders and a man brought some stout pine logs, shuddering as he entered the tainted air of the library to place them in the grate. Willett meanwhile had gone up to the dismantled laboratory and brought down a few odds and ends not included in the moving of the July before. They were in a covered basket, and Mr Ward never saw what they were.

Then the doctor locked himself in the library once more, and by the clouds of smoke which rolled down past the windows from the chimney it was known that he had lighted the fire. Later, after a great rustling of newspapers, that odd wrench and creaking were heard again; followed by a thumping which none of the eavesdroppers liked. Thereafter two suppressed cries of Willett's were heard, and hard upon these came a swishing rustle of indefinable hatefulness. Finally the smoke that the wind beat down from the chimney grew very dark and acrid, and everyone wished that the weather had spared them this choking and venomous inundation of peculiar fumes. Mr Ward's head reeled, and the servants all clustered together in a knot to watch the horrible black smoke swoop down. After an age of waiting the vapors seemed to lighten, and half-formless sounds of scraping, sweeping, and other minor operations were heard behind the bolted door. And at last, after the slamming of some cupboard within, Willett made his appearance, sad, pale and haggard, and bearing the cloth-draped basket he had taken from the upstairs laboratory. He had left the window open, and into that once accursed room was pouring a wealth of pure, wholesome air to mix with a queer new smell of disinfectants. The ancient overmantel still lingered; but it seemed robbed of malignity now, and rose as calm and stately in its white panelling as if it had never borne the picture of Joseph Curwen. Night was coming on, yet this time its shadows held no latent fright, but only a gentle melancholy. Of what he had done the doctor would never speak. To Mr Ward he said, 'I can answer no questions, but I will say that there are different kinds of magic. I have made a great purgation. Those in this house will sleep the better for it.'

6

That Dr Willett's 'purgation' had been an ordeal almost as nerve-racking in its way as his hideous wandering in the vanished crypt is shown by the fact that the elderly physician gave out completely as soon as he reached home that evening. For three days he rested constantly in his room, though servants later muttered something about having heard him after midnight on Wednesday, when the outer door softly opened, and closed with phenomenal softness. Servants' imaginations, fortunately, are limited, else comment might have been excited by an item in Thursday's *Evening Bulletin* which ran as follows:

North End Ghouls Again Active

After a lull of ten months since the dastardly vandalism in the Weeden lot at the North Burial Ground, a nocturnal prowler was glimpsed early this morning in the same cemetery by Robert Hart, the night watchman. Happening to glance for a moment from his shelter at about two A.M., Hart observed a glow of a lantern or pocket torch not far to the northward, and upon opening the door detected the figure of a man with a trowel very plainly silhouetted against a nearby electric light. At once starting in pursuit, he saw the figure dart hurriedly toward the main entrance, gaining the street and losing himself among the shadows before approach or capture was possible.

Like the first of the ghouls active during the past year, this intruder had done no real damage before detection. A vacant part of the Ward lot showed signs of a little superficial digging, but nothing even nearly the size of a grave had been attempted, and no previous grave had been disturbed.

Hart, who cannot describe the prowler except as a small man probably having a full beard, inclines to the view that all three of the digging incidents have a common source; but police from the Second Station think otherwise on account of the savage nature of the second incident, where an ancient coffin was removed and its headstone violently shattered.

The first of the incidents, in which it is thought an attempt to bury something was frustrated, occurred a year ago last March, and has been attributed to bootleggers seeking a cache. It is possible, says Sergeant Riley, that this third affair is of similar nature. Officers at the Second Station are taking especial pains to capture the gang of miscreants responsible for these repeated outrages.

All day Thursday Dr Willett rested as if recuperating from something past or nerving himself for something to come. In the evening he wrote a note to Mr Ward, which was delivered the next morning and which caused the half-dazed parent to ponder long and deeply. Mr Ward had not been able to go down to business since the shock of Monday with its baffling reports and its sinister 'purgation', but he found something calming about the doctor's letter in spite of the despair it seemed to promise and the fresh mysteries it seemed to evoke.

295

April 12, 1928

Dear Theodore:—

I feel that I must say a word to you before doing what I am going to do tomorrow. It will conclude the terrible business we have been going through (for I feel that no spade is ever likely to reach that monstrous place we know of), but I'm afraid it won't set your mind at rest unless I expressly assure you how very conclusive it is.

You have known me ever since you were a small boy, so I think you will not distrust me when I hint that some matters are best left undecided and unexplored. It is better that you attempt no further speculation as to Charles's case, and almost imperative that you tell his mother nothing more than she already suspects. When I call on you tomorrow Charles will have escaped. That is all which need remain in anyone's mind. He was mad, and he escaped. You can tell his mother gently and gradually about the mad part when you stop sending the typed notes in his name. I'd advise you to join her in Atlantic City and take a rest yourself. God knows you need one after this shock, as I do myself. I am going South for a while to calm down and brace up.

So don't ask me any questions when I call. It may be that something will go wrong, but I'll tell you if it does. I don't think it will. There will be nothing more to worry about, for Charles will be very, very safe. He is now — safer than you dream. You need hold no fears about Allen, and who or what he is. He forms as much a part of the past as Joseph Curwen's picture, and when I ring your doorbell you may feel certain that there is no such person. And what wrote that minuscule message will never trouble you or yours.

But you must steel yourself to melancholy, and prepare your wife to do the same. I must tell you frankly that Charles's escape will not mean his restoration to you. He has been afflicted with a peculiar disease, as you must realize from the subtle physical as well as mental changes in him, and you must not hope to see him again. Have only this consolation — that he was never a fiend or even truly a madman, but only an eager, studious, and curious boy whose love of mystery and of the past was his undoing. He stumbled on things no mortal ought ever to know, and reached back through the years as no one ever should reach; and something came out of those years to engulf him.

And now comes the matter in which I must ask you to trust me most of all. For there will be, indeed, no uncertainty about Charles's fate. In about a year, say, you can if you wish devise a suitable account of the end for the boy will be no more. You can put up a stone in your lot at the North Burial Ground exactly ten feet west of your father's and facing the same way, and that will mark the true resting-place of your son. Nor need you fear that it will mark any abnormality or changeling. The ashes in that grave will be those of your own unaltered bone and sinew – of the real Charles Dexter Ward whose mind you watched from infancy – the real Charles with the olive-mark on his hip and without the black witch-mark on his chest or the pit on his forehead. The Charles who never did actual evil, and who will have paid with his life for his 'squeamishness'.

That is all. Charles will have escaped, and a year from now you can put up his stone. Do not question me tomorrow. And believe that the honor of your ancient family remains untainted now, as it has been at all times in the past.

With profoundest sympathy, and exhortations to fortitude, calmness, and resignation, I am ever

Sincerely your friend,
Marinus B. Willett

So on the morning of Friday, April 13, 1928, Marinus Bicknell Willett visited the room of Charles Dexter Ward at Dr Waite's private hospital on Conanicut Island. The youth, though making no attempt to evade his caller, was in a sullen mood; and seemed disinclined to open the conversation which Willett obviously desired. The doctor's discovery of the crypt and his monstrous experience therein had of course created a new source of embarrassment, so that both hesitated perceptibly after the interchange of a few strained formalities. Then a new element of constraint crept in, as Ward seemed to read behind the doctor's masklike face a terrible purpose which had never been there before. The patient quailed, conscious that since the last visit there had been a change whereby the solicitous family physician had given place to the ruthless and implacable avenger.

Ward actually turned pale, and the doctor was the first to speak. 'More,' he said, 'has been found out, and I must warn you fairly that a reckoning is due.'

'Digging again, and coming upon more poor starving pets?' was the ironic reply. It was evident that the youth meant to show bravado to the last.

'No,' Willett slowly rejoined, 'this time I did not have to dig. We have had men looking up Dr Allen, and they found the false beard and spectacles in the bungalow'

'Excellent,' commented the disquieted host in an effort to be wittily insulting, 'and I trust they proved more becoming than the beard and glasses you now have on !'

'They would become you very well,' came the even and studied response, '*as indeed they seem to have done.*'

As Willett said this, it almost seemed as though a cloud passed over the sun; though there was no change in the shadows on the floor. Then Ward ventured:

'And is this what asks so hotly for a reckoning? Suppose a man does find it now and then useful to be twofold?'

'No,' said Willett gravely, 'again you are wrong. It is no business of mine if any man seeks duality; *provided he has any right to exist at all, and provided he does not destroy what called him out of space.*'

Ward now started violently. 'Well, Sir, what *have* ye found, and what d'ye want with me?'

The doctor let a little time elapse before replying, as if choosing his words for an effective answer.

'I have found,' he finally intoned, 'something in a cupboard behind an ancient overmantel where a picture once was, and I have burned it and buried the ashes where the grave of Charles Dexter Ward ought to be.'

The madman choked and sprang from the chair in which he had been sitting:

'Damn ye, who did ye tell – and who'll believe it was he after these full two months, with me alive? What d'ye mean to do?'

Willett, though a small man, actually took on a kind of judicial majesty as he calmed the patient with a gesture.

'I have told no one. This is no common case – it is a madness out of time and a horror from beyond the spheres which no police or lawyers or courts or alienists could ever fathom or grapple with. Thank God some chance has left inside me the spark of imagination, that I might not go astray in thinking out this thing. *You cannot deceive me, Joseph Curwen, for I know that your accursed magic is true!*

'I know how you wove the spell that brooded outside the years and fastened on your double and descendant; I know how you drew him into the past and got him to raise you up from your detestable grave; I know how he kept you hidden in his laboratory while you studied modern things and roved abroad as a vampire by night, and how you later showed yourself in beard and glasses that no one might wonder at your godless likeness to him; I know what you resolved to do when he balked at your monstrous rifling of the world's tombs, *and at what you planned afterward*, and I know how you did it.

'You left off your beard and glasses and fooled the guards around the house. They thought it was he who went in, and they thought it was he who came out when you had strangled and hidden him. But you hadn't reckoned on the different contacts of two minds. You were a fool, Curwen, to fancy that a mere visual identity would be enough. Why didn't you think of the speech and the voice and the handwriting? It hasn't worked, you see, after all. You know better than I who or what wrote that message in minuscules, but I will warn you it was not written in vain. There are abominations and blasphemies which must be stamped out, and I believe that the writer of those words will attend to Orne and Hutchinson. One of those creatures wrote you once, "do not call up any that you cannot put down". You were undone once before, perhaps in that very way, and it may be that your own evil magic will undo you all again. Curwen, a man can't tamper with Nature beyond certain limits, and every horror you have woven will rise up to wipe you out.'

But here the doctor was cut short by a convulsive cry from the creature before him. Hopelessly at bay, weaponless, and knowing that any show of physical violence would bring a score of attendants to the doctor's rescue, Joseph Curwen had recourse to his one ancient ally, and began a series of cabalistic motions with his forefingers as his deep, hollow voice, now unconcealed by feigned hoarseness, bellowed out the opening words of a terrible formula.

'PER ADONAI ELOIM, ADONAI JEHOVA, ADONAI SABAOTH, METRATON . . .'

But Willett was too quick for him. Even as the dogs in the yard outside began to howl, and even as a chill wind sprang suddenly up from the bay, the doctor commenced the solemn and measured intonation of that which he had meant all along to recite. An eye for an eye — magic for magic — let the outcome show how well the lesson of the abyss had been learned! So in a clear voice Marinus Bicknell Willett began the *second* of that pair of formulae whose first had raised the writer of those minuscules — the cryptic invocation whose heading was the Dragon's Tail, sign of the *descending node* —

'OGTHROD AI'F
GEB'L – EE'H

300

YOG-SOTHOTH
'NGAH'NG AI'Y
ZHRO!'

At the very first word from Willett's mouth the previously commenced formula of the patient stopped short. Unable to speak, the monster made wild motions with his arms until they too were arrested. When the awful name of *Yog-Sothoth* was uttered, the hideous change began. It was not merely a *dissolution*, but rather a *transformation* or *recapitulation*; and Willett shut his eyes lest he faint before the rest of the incantation could be pronounced.

Buh he did not faint, and that man of unholy centuries and forbidden secrets never troubled the world again. The madness out of time had subsided, and the case of Charles Dexter Ward was closed. Opening his eyes before staggering out of that room of horror, Dr Willett saw that what he had kept in memory had not been kept amiss. There had, as he had predicted, been no need for acids. For like his accursed picture a year before, Joseph Curwen now lay scattered on the floor as a thin coating of fine bluish-gray dust.